About

Jennifer Hayward began filching her sister's m... Her career in journa... working alongside ... travelling the world, has provided perfect fodder for the fast-paced, sexy stories she likes to write, always with a touch of humour. A native of Canada's East Coast, Jennifer lives in Toronto with her Viking husband and young Viking-in-training.

Maisey Yates is a *New York Times* bestselling author of more than thirty romance novels. She has a coffee habit she has no interest in kicking, and a slight Pinterest addiction. She lives with her husband and children in the Pacific Northwest. When Maisey isn't writing she can be found singing in the grocery store, shopping for shoes online and probably not doing dishes. Check out her website: maiseyyates.com

Maureen Child writes for Mills & Boon Desire line and can't imagine a better job.

A seven-time finalist for a prestigious Romance Writers of America RITA® Award, Maureen is an author of more than one hundred romance novels. Her books regularly appear on bestseller lists and have won several awards, including a Prism Award, a National Readers' Choice Award, a Colorado Romance Writers Award of Excellence and a Golden Quill Award. She is a native Californian but has recently moved to the mountains of Utah.

Billionaires

COLLECTION

January 2019

February 2019

March 2019

April 2019

May 2019

June 2019

Billionaires:
The Hero

JENNIFER HAYWARD

MAISEY YATES

MAUREEN CHILD

MILLS & BOON

First Published in Great Britain 2019
By Mills & Boon, an imprint of HarperCollins *Publishers*
1 London Bridge Street, London, SE1 9GF

BILLIONAIRES: THE HERO © 2019 Harlequin Books S.A.

A Deal for the Di Sione Ring © 2016 Harlequin Books S.A
The Last Di Sione Claims His Prize © 2016 Harlequin Books S.A
The Baby Inheritance © 2016 Maureen Child

Special thanks and acknowledgment are given to Jennifer Hayward and Maisey Yates for their contribution to *The Billionaire's Legacy* series.

ISBN: 978-0-263-27556-8

9-0319

MIX
Paper from
responsible sources
FSC www.fsc.org FSC™ C007454

This book is produced from independently certified FSC™ paper to ensure responsible forest management.

For more information visit: www.harpercollins.co.uk/green

Printed and bound in Spain
by CPI, Barcelona

A DEAL FOR THE DI SIONE RING

JENNIFER HAYWARD

For Melody, who took me into the world
of ultra-luxury hotels and taught me what
a six star property is, what a butler does
and why some day, I must stay in one!
You are one of the special people.

And for my sister, Susan, a brilliant psychologist,
who helps me dig deep into the heads of
my characters. Thank you! Xx

CHAPTER ONE

THE WEALTH AND OPULENCE of Long Island's legendary Gold Coast was like a trip back in time to the old money, scandalous, glamorous tales immortalized in American fiction. High-society dynasties born of the Industrial Revolution had built these lavish mansions and castles one after another along this sweep of the ruggedly beautiful northern coast, with gardens rivaling European grandeur.

They had sought to outdo one another, these American scions, to glitter as the Gold Coast's preeminent jewel. But as with so many other symbols of that lavish time, little of the grandeur of those magnificent estates survived today, with only a few of the massive, character-filled mansions still left standing. Even legendary shipping magnate Giovanni Di Sione's sprawling villa, built in the late eighteen hundreds as a rambling summerhouse to entertain the scion's clients and financiers, had been extensively renovated to stand as a shining symbol of modern architecture.

The ostentatious display of wealth, the almost tangible scent of old money in the air, brought with it familiar irony for Nate Brunswick as he turned his Jaguar down the rolling, winding stretch of road toward the Di Sione estate. He could buy the Gold Coast several times over with the wealth he'd amassed and add it to the vast global property empire he controlled and still never feel like he belonged.

It was a lesson he'd learned the hard way. That all the money in the world couldn't heal old wounds. That new money would always be just that in New York—the spoils of an interloper who didn't really belong. New blood might mix with blue blood, but it would never have the same status in the collective psyche of the elite.

It was a truth he would put right up there with the Ten Commandments: *Thou shalt not aspire to join our realm. It has never been, nor will it ever be, yours.*

He brought the Jag to a halt in front of his grandfather's villa with a defiant squeal of its wheels. The villa's imposing facade gleamed in the late-afternoon sun, the light setting off its graceful arches and multileveled roofline.

He sat for a moment, a heavy weight pressing down on his chest. Always this place inspired a wealth of emotion, all of it complex and decades in the making. But today he felt as if whatever higher power was up there in the sky orchestrating this chess game that was life had reached inside him and yanked out his heart.

His grandfather was dying of leukemia. Nate had been traveling so much of late, overseeing his sprawling, global property empire, he had had little time for his mentor, who had been the only father figure he'd ever known. He'd stood there, shell-shocked, as his half sister Natalia had told him at her art exhibition that his grandfather's leukemia was back, and this time, a bone marrow transplant from Nate would not save him.

Apparently not even the all-powerful Giovanni could cheat death twice.

The swell of emotion he'd been fighting during the drive from Manhattan swept over him, threatened to wipe away the composure he had cultivated as a second skin. He blinked and pushed it away. He would not allow that expression of weakness. Not now and definitely not here.

He swung his long legs out of the car, wincing as his muscles protested the long drive in the low-slung machine. He had barely put his foot on the top step of the sweeping column of stairs that led to the villa's elegant entrance when Alma, the Di Sione family's longtime housekeeper, opened the door.

"Master Nate," Alma greeted him, ushering him in. "Signor Giovanni is enjoying the last rays of the sun on the back veranda. He's been anxiously awaiting your arrival."

A twinge of guilt stirred low in his gut. He should have made more time for his grandfather, but he had fallen into the trap of thinking Giovanni was invincible like everyone else.

A few pleasantries exchanged with Alma, he set off toward the back of the villa, his footsteps echoing on the gleaming marble floors. He'd first visited this house at eighteen, hunted down by his half brother Alex as the only genetic match for a bone marrow transplant that would save his grandfather's life—a man Nate had never met.

A vision of his six half siblings perched on the handmade wrought-iron and stone staircase filled his head. They had sat there, lined up like birds on a telephone wire, big eyes inquisitive as Alex had led Nate past them into the salon to meet an ailing Giovanni for the first time.

Orphaned, they had been taken in by his grandfather after Nate's father, Benito, and his wife, Anna, had been killed in an alcohol-and drug-fueled car crash. A tragedy to be sure but all Nate could remember was the isolation and bitterness his hardened, eighteen-year-old self had felt at the charmed life his half siblings had led while he and his mother had fought to survive.

The family he'd never been privy to as Benito Di Sione's illegitimate child.

Which was ancient history, Nate told himself as he

stepped out onto the veranda with its incomparable views of the sparkling gray-blue sweep of Long Island Sound. He had obliterated that iteration of himself and replaced it with a success story that no one could ignore—not even the aristocrats who loved to snub him.

His grandfather sat in a wooden, high-backed chair, bathed in the dying light of the sun. He turned with that sixth sense of his as Nate approached, a slow smile spreading across his olive-skinned face.

"Nathaniel. I was beginning to think Manhattan had eaten you up whole."

Nate walked around the chair and stood in front of the man who had come to mean so much to him. A lump formed in his throat at how small, how fragile, his once vital grandfather looked, even more wasted away than their last meeting. And now he knew why.

Giovanni stood and drew him into an embrace. The cancer, his treatments, had robbed his olive skin of its robust glow, turning it a sallow hue. His shoulders felt like skin and bone as Nate closed his fingers around them, his throat thickening with emotion. Despite the very mixed, complex feelings he held toward the Di Sione family, Giovanni had been the self-made, ultrasuccessful, honorable man Nate had modeled himself after in the wake of his father's failings. In those formative years, when his life could have gone either way with the anger consuming him, his grandfather had been the difference. Had shown him the man he could be.

He drew back, his gaze moving over his grandfather's ravaged face. "Is there nothing that can be done? Are the doctors sure another transplant won't help?"

Giovanni nodded and squeezed his shoulder. "They only did the transplant the first time because of my name and health, you know that. It's my time, Nathaniel. I've had more of a life than many could ever dream of having. I'm at peace with it."

His grandfather sat down and waved him into a chair. Nate took the one opposite him, declining the offer of refreshments from a maid who appeared in the doorway. "I have plans to review when I get back to Manhattan."

Giovanni told the maid to bring Nate a beer. "You work too much," he admonished. "Life is for the living, Nathaniel. Who is going to keep you company the day you have made so many billions you can't hope to spend it all?"

He had already reached that point. For him work, success, was biological, elemental, spurred by a survival instinct that would never rest as long as there was a deal to be made, another building block to be put into place.

"You know I'm not the type to settle down."

"I wasn't talking about the lack of a permanent woman in your life," his grandfather came back wryly, "although that, too, could use some work. I'm talking about you being a workaholic. About you never getting off that jet of yours long enough to breathe fresh air, to register what *season* it is. You're so caught up in making money you're missing the true meaning of life."

Nate lifted a brow. "Which *is*?"

"Family. Roots." His grandfather frowned. "Your nomadic ways, your inability to put a stake in the ground, it won't fulfill you in the long run. I hope you will realize that before it's too late."

"I'm only thirty-five," Nate pointed out. "And *you* are as much of a workaholic, Giovanni. It's our dominant trait. We don't choose it. It chooses us."

"I seem to be gaining some perspective given my current situation." His grandfather's eyes darkened. "That discipline becomes our vice, Nathaniel, when taken to extreme. I failed your father and, by virtue of that, you, by spending every waking moment building Di Sione Shipping."

Nate scowled. "He failed *himself*. He needed to own his vices but he never could."

"There is truth in that." Giovanni pinned his gaze on him. "I know you have your demons. I have them, too. Ones that have haunted me every day of my life. But for you, it's not too late. You have your whole life ahead of you. You have brothers and sisters who care about you, who want to be closer to you, yet you push them away. You want nothing to do with them."

His jaw hardened. "I flew in for Natalia's art exhibition."

"Because you have a soft spot for her." His grandfather shook his head. "Family should be the rock in your life. What sustains you when the storms of life take over."

The suspicious glitter in his grandfather's eyes, the bittersweet note in his voice, made Nate wonder, not for the first time, about the secrets Giovanni had kept from his grandchildren. Why he had left Italy and come to America with only the clothes on his back, never to have contact with his family again.

"We've had this discussion," he told his grandfather, his response coming out rougher than he'd intended. "I have made my peace with my siblings. That has to be enough."

Giovanni lifted a brow. "Is it?"

Nate expelled a breath. Sank into a silence that said this particular conversation was over.

Giovanni sat back in his chair and rested his gaze on the sun, burning its way into the horizon. "I need you to do me a favor. There is a ring that means a great deal to me I would like you to track down. I sold it to a collector years ago when I first came to America. I have no idea where it is or who possesses it. I only have a description I can give you."

Nate was not surprised by the request. Natalia had mentioned at the gallery all of the Di Sione grandchildren except Alex had been sent on quests around the world to find similar treasures for Giovanni. The trinkets that his grandfather called his Lost Mistresses in the childhood tales he had told his grandchildren were, in fact, real entities his siblings had begun to recover: various pieces of precious jewelry, a Fabergé box and the book of poetry Natalia had found for him in Greece along with a husband in Angelos. What the grandchildren couldn't figure out was the significance of the pieces to their grandfather.

Nate nodded. "Consider it done. What do these pieces mean to you, if you don't mind me asking?"

His grandfather's gaze turned wistful. "I hope someday to be able to tell you that. But first, I need to see them again. The ring is very special to me. I must have it back."

"And you will send Alex on the last task," Nate speculated.

"Yes."

His relationship, or the lack of one, he had with his oldest half brother who ran Di Sione Shipping was volatile and complex. Giovanni had made Alex work his way up the ranks to CEO, starting out at the very bottom loading goods at the shipyards, while in contrast, he had appointed Nate to a desk job straight out of the university education he had provided his grandson—compensation, Nate figured, for his having had so little growing up.

But what ran far deeper than this preferential treatment of Nate at Di Sione Shipping, Nate suspected, was that Alex blamed *him* for his parents' death. The night Nate's mother, his father's mistress, had shown up on Benito Di Sione's doorstep, ten-year-old Nate in tow, begging for financial support, had been the night his father had wrapped his car around a tree and killed himself and his wife. There had been a violent argument between the adults prior to the crash, perhaps the precursor to his father's reckless performance behind the wheel.

"Nathaniel?"

Nate shook his head to clear it of things that could never and would never change. "I'll begin the search right away. Is there anything else I can do?"

"Know your brothers and sisters," his grandfather said. "Then I will die a happy man."

An image of Alex's young face in the window that night Nate and his mother had stood on his father's porch begging for assistance filled his head. The confusion written across his brother's face…

Only Alex had known of Nate's existence in the years that had followed, yet he had never once revealed his secret—not until Giovanni had fallen ill. If Nate wondered why, when surely the revelation would have changed his own life irrevocably, when sometimes the question burned a hole right through the center of him, the two brothers had never discussed it.

And really, he thought, shaking his head and bringing himself back to the present, what was the point? Nothing could ever alter the circumstances of that night. What fate had thrown at all of them… Some things were just better off left alone.

Nate put finding Giovanni's ring at the top of his priority list. He gave the description to the private investigator he used to research the mega-million-dollar deals he made on a daily basis and received a response back within forty-eight hours. The ring had been purchased at auction by a Sicilian family decades ago and was, apparently, not for sale.

A patently incorrect term in Nate's book. *Everything*

and *everyone* on the planet were for sale if the price tag was high enough. He simply had to come up with a number at which the family would find his offer too sweet to resist.

Concluding his business in New York, he had dinner with his mother, who complained per usual that he was never home, neglected to mention he was doing an errand for Giovanni because the Di Siones were always a sore spot for her, then flew to Palermo on Wednesday. Not known for wasting an opportunity, he checked into the six-star Hotel Giarruso he had been eyeing for acquisition and scheduled a meeting with the consortium who owned it for later that day.

His first order of business after he'd been welcomed into the luxury two-level suite with a personal check-in was to make himself human again. He stepped under a bruisingly hot shower in the palatial marble bathroom on the upper level and closed his eyes, letting the punishing spray beat down on him. No matter how luxurious the jet, how smooth the ride, he never slept on planes. His PA, Josephine, liked to call it the control freak in him, but the truth was he always slept with one eye open, a habit he'd developed while living in a series of sketchy Bronx apartments he and his mother had rented where bad things could and did happen on a regular basis.

Installing his mother in a luxury apartment with 24/7 security and ensuring she never had to work again should have provided him with some level of peace. Instead, his wary nature persisted. When you'd run errands for a neighborhood enforcer for a couple of years in your misguided youth before your mother straightened you out, you knew danger lurked everywhere, particularly for someone with his money and reputation. A smart man kept his eyes open.

His humanity suitably revived, he stepped out of the shower, sluiced the water from his face and grabbed a towel to dry off. Intent on answering a few urgent emails before a catnap and his meeting, he headed down to the lounge. His brain busy running the numbers the lawyers had given him for the hotel's value, he didn't notice the chambermaid bent over the cherrywood bar until he'd taken a couple of steps into the room.

His first impression was that she had the sweetest behind he'd ever seen. Round, firm, shapely buttocks stretched the material of her pewter-colored uniform tight across her hips. Spectacular legs completed the picture. His imagination effortlessly supplemented the rest of the tempting scenario: her face and remaining assets would be equally as luscious.

But what the hell was she doing in his suite?

"Would you mind," he requested deliberately, taking the final two steps into the lounge, "telling me what you are doing here when I left explicit instructions with the butler not to be disturbed?"

She straightened and turned, all in one wary slow-motion move. His gaze slid over her. Her waist in the dress, which was stylish for a chambermaid, was tiny, cinched in just above those delectable hips. Her ample cleavage strained the buttons of the modest, short-sleeved style, as if she was too abundant to be contained in it. Her glossy dark brown hair was caught up in a tight ponytail, her cheekbones high and defined under the most stunning pair of espresso-brown eyes he'd ever seen.

He'd been wrong in his estimation. She wasn't just temptingly attractive—she was one of the most beautiful women he'd ever laid eyes on. Exotic in that olive-skinned, perfectly curved Sicilian sense of the word.

His body tightened as biology demanded in the face of

such perfection. He imagined one sultry look from those eyes and most men would be on their knees.

Except right now, he noted, those eyes were aimed at him in a wary perusal, tracing their way down to where the towel was slung around his hips. They widened, darkened into giant espresso orbs. His towel had worked its way lower during his trip down the stairs, sitting now on his hip bones. He was giving her an eyeful. A gentleman would remedy that. But he had never been, nor would he ever be, a gentleman.

This was a six-star hotel he was considering purchasing. He had told his private butler he was not to be disturbed. He wasn't letting it go.

He lifted an eyebrow. "So?"

Dio mio, but he was beautiful. Mina dragged her gaze up to the American's face, her teeth sinking into her bottom lip. He was all defined, perfectly symmetrical muscle, as ideally proportioned as the models in the pictures their teachers had shown them in the anatomy lessons they'd given them in finishing school to prepare the girls to *interact*, as they'd called it, with the opposite sex. As if her classmates hadn't known what the internet was. As if some of them hadn't had their own personal anatomy lesson already...

His dark, brooding gaze slid over her, sending a pulse up her spine. If she had looked up the meaning of *intenso* in the dictionary, his picture would have been right there beside it. Although the glare he wore suggested he had limited patience to go with the definition.

"The butler informed me you were at a meeting." She lifted her chin, pasting a composed look on her face while she searched desperately for the confidence she'd been taught to effortlessly exude. "I knocked before I came in, Signor Brunswick."

"My meeting is this afternoon." His gaze sharpened as it pinned her to the spot. "Isn't that the point of a six-star hotel? To be *six* steps ahead of my schedule, anticipating my every wish?"

Mina's brain went straight to the bedroom on the second level and what this arrogant man would demand of a woman in bed. Her nonexistent experience deferred to her imagination to fill in the blanks. She bet it would be worth every second of her enforced capitulation.

Heat flooded her cheeks. Her fingers tightened around the bar of chocolate she held. His gaze flickered, narrowed, as if he'd read her thoughts down to her final, helpless surrender.

She shifted her weight to both feet, her stomach tying itself in knots. *What was she thinking?* She was *engaged.* And furthermore, she didn't have naughty thoughts like this.

She cleared her throat and held up the chocolate bar. "It *is* my job to anticipate your every need. I was stocking the bar with our fine Sicilian hazelnut chocolate."

The beautiful American strode toward her and took the chocolate out of her hand. A whiff of citrus mixed with spice filled her head. She breathed in deeply as she drank him in. He was even more devastating close up, his thick dark hair spiky and wet from the shower, designer stubble covering the square set of his jaw.

"We make it our policy to know everything about our guests based on past visits," she sputtered nervously. "I brought hazelnut and brazil nut."

He crossed his corded, very fine arms. "Mistake number one… *Lina*," he said, peering at her name tag, which did not use her real name but the name she'd given her manager when she'd taken the job. "I prefer milk chocolate."

"Oh." That threw her for a loop. They were never *wrong* here at Hotel Giarruso. *Ever.* "Well…" she stumbled. "*Sì.* We must have made a mistake. It happens very rarely. I'll fix it."

"What else?" he asked.

"Scusi?"

"What else do you know about me, then?"

Other than the fact that he was known to fraternize with tall, beautiful blondes and that she was not to bat an eye if she came across one in his room who was not registered here, despite their strict security policy?

The heat in her cheeks deepened. His gaze narrowed. She desperately filed through the intelligence she'd been given. "We know that you tend to forget to pack the charger for your laptop. I have brought you a universal one."

He walked over to the coffee table. The towel slipped further, giving her an eyeful of chiseled hip bone. *Maledizione.* She needed to get out of here.

He picked up a cord, a charging pack attached. "Not so much of a perk for me this visit."

Her nails dug into her palms as her even-keeled disposition started to slip. *He was something else.* She nodded toward the bar. "We have stocked your favorite single-malt Scotch."

"Predictable."

Her blood started to boil. Being inquisitioned by an arrogant male in a towel that might fall off at any moment was above and beyond the call of duty. *Way* above her pay grade.

She squared her shoulders. "I understand all of this might not be *revolutionary*, Signor Brunswick, but it's what is expected of us. To surround you with the comforts of home. Although I do agree, we could do better."

Curiosity flashed in those beautiful dark eyes. "Such as?" he purred. "I am all ears."

She took a step back. An amused glitter filled his eyes as he tracked the movement. "I would go beyond cataloging a guest's preferences and start *anticipating* them. For instance, *you* are known to be a morning runner. If it were me arranging things, I would have had a list of suitable routes through some of Palermo's most beautiful neighborhoods sitting on your coffee table for you to follow. Another route to spend much of your run in our most beautiful park. Perhaps one to visit our many famous monuments."

The cynical twist to his mouth smoothed out. "What else?"

"You are a fan of a particular Pinot Noir from the Mount Etna region. I would stock that in your room as we have done so, but I would also include another lesser-known wine from what we Sicilians think is the best vineyard in that region—a wine you cannot purchase in the US."

A gleam of approval fired his eyes. "One more."

She chewed on her lip, her confidence returning. "You are known to appreciate the opera if you are accompanied on a trip with a…*compagno*. I would anticipate an outing for you. Secure tickets at the opera and a gown for the lady, colors suitable for a blonde, of course, as that seems to be your preference."

A smile tugged at his mouth, the dimple that cleaved his cheek transforming him from arrogant to utterly breathtaking. "And you were on such a roll there with your intriguing ideas, Lina. Until you got to the preference for blondes…"

His gaze blazed a deliberate trail over her high ponytail, down over her face to the slightly strained buttons of her dress she'd been cursing since day one of this job. The pure male appreciation in his eyes made her pulse pound.

"It just so happens my last few *compagnos* have been blonde, but in actual fact, I prefer exotic-looking brunettes."

She forgot to breathe, her head spinning from a lack of oxygen. His stark appraisal was most certainly improper. Most definitely had a message attached to it. She knew she should look away, but the heat coursing through her was like nothing she'd ever felt before. It was like her skin was on fire, like he knew exactly what was under her dress and he wanted his hands all over it.

She took a step back and yanked in a deep breath. *Regained her senses.* "Perhaps," she suggested, lifting her gaze to his, "I can have a bottle of the Pinot Noir delivered to your room?"

His long, dark lashes swept down in a heavy-lidded look. "Will you deliver it personally?"

She gasped. Took another step back. "I'm afraid that won't be possible. I'm off duty in an hour. I have a *date* tonight."

He raised an eyebrow. "Undoubtedly."

The towel slipped another inch. She made a garbled sound at the back of her throat, shoved the other two bars of chocolate in her apron on the table and fled, her muttered, *"Buonanotte..."* followed by his low laughter.

"Enjoy your date, Lina. Don't do anything I wouldn't do."

She thought that since this was Signor Brunswick and his improper towel they were talking about, that might give her a great deal of latitude.

Nate watched the chambermaid go, amusement coursing through him. He didn't remember the last time he'd enjoyed himself so much. Yes, it had been a bit cruel to put the delectable Lina through that, but he was meeting with the owners of this hotel in a few hours and a hotel was only as good as its service. He'd wanted to know what kind of people the Giarruso employed, and Lina had potential.

She clearly had brains to go with her beauty. And not just brains, but a keen understanding of the clientele she served and what could enhance their experience. Which had, in the end, made up for the breach in his privacy and his personal butler's mistake.

His chambermaid's ideas had given him food for thought. Certainly society was moving toward personalization in every industry and the products that were being developed reflected that. To offer his clients things they hadn't even asked for but might appreciate complemented some of the ideas he was already working on. It wouldn't work for every client—some would find it an intrusion. But for others it could prove to be that particular experience, that unique value add that developed in them an affinity for the brand.

He had loved Lina's examples. They were doable, creative ideas that would certainly impress.

His butler appeared with a bottle of Marc de Grazia's Guardiola Mount Etna red just before his meeting. Grown at the highest elevation of any red grape varietal in all of Europe, it looked intriguing.

He slid the bottle into the fridge, a smile on his lips. He'd be lying if he said he didn't wish his delectable chambermaid were here to share it with him. That he would have enjoyed sampling it on her fantastic body. He knew the instant attraction he'd experienced toward her had been reciprocated by the flare of awareness he'd seen in her dark eyes. But she was taken, unfortunately, at least for tonight.

And perhaps that was for the best. He was here to retrieve Giovanni's ring. To fulfill his obligation to his grandfather as quickly as possible so that Giovanni could enjoy the sentimental memories associated with the bauble as long as his life allowed. Perhaps pick up a Palermo-based luxury hotel while he was at it.

Seducing an innocent-looking brunette wasn't in the plans, as much as his macho core wouldn't mind demonstrating to Lina how utterly lacking her date would ultimately prove compared to a night with him.

A pity, really.

CHAPTER TWO

"What's the matter, *bella mia*?"

Silvio Marchetti, Mina's fiancé, arched a thick, dark brow at her. "You've been distracted ever since we sat down, and since I know it cannot be my scintillating company that is lacking, you must be worrying about something."

Mina, also known as *Lina* when she was entertaining improper men in towels in luxurious hotel suites, blinked. She'd thought she'd done a good job hiding her distraction from her fiancé, but apparently her expressive face, which had been her downfall in the etiquette classes designed to attract a man just like Silvio, continued to plague her.

"*Mi dispiace.*" She waved a hand in the air. "I've had a busy day."

Silvio's thin lips twisted. "Exhausted ordering your team of wedding planners around? It's a good thing I have a big staff, *cara*. You will have many responsibilities as my wife at Villa Marchetti. You must learn how to multitask."

She was quite adept at multitasking! She'd cleaned a whole floor of hotel suites today in addition to surviving Signor Brunswick's improper inquisition. The latter of which was half of the problem with her distraction tonight. She couldn't get the sizzling connection between her and the beautiful American out of her head.

But Silvio didn't know about any of her extracurricular activities. Her job moonlighting as a chambermaid at the Giarruso to pay off the debt her mother had incurred since her father's death was a secret to everyone but her. It wouldn't do for anyone to know Simona Mastrantino's daughter, engaged to one of Italy's wealthiest men, was cleaning toilets by the hour.

She pinned a smile on her face, the fact that her mother would have a coronary if she knew what her daughter was doing to keep things afloat of secondary importance to her bigger problem—her impending marriage to Silvio, which she could not possibly go through with.

"Maybe I'm having prewedding jitters," she murmured. "It's a big production this wedding. So many people will be there."

Silvio reached for her hand and curled his fingers around it. "All you have to do is look beautiful. The rest will be taken care of."

And then they would consummate their relationship. Her stomach dipped at the terrifying thought. She'd never slept with a man. Hadn't had the opportunity with her mother dragging her from one social event to another husband hunting, advertising her innocence like a detail on a high-end real-estate listing. *Look but don't touch*, her mother's vibe had said. And since Mina had never agreed on any of her mother's choices for a rich husband, her mother had chosen for her.

She studied her fiancé as he poured her more of the terrifically expensive Chianti he'd ordered for them, undoubtedly trying to loosen her up. He was classically, undeniably handsome with his chiseled features and straight Roman nose, but his eyes, which Mina did think were the windows to the soul, were hard and unyielding, dominated by thick dark brows that always seemed to frown. She had never once experienced any chemistry whatsoever when he had touched her, *kissed her*, which was as far as he'd managed with her mother on guard.

And yet this afternoon, she acknowledged with a shiver, all it had taken was one look from the American to send electricity coursing through her from her head to her feet. For her to wonder what it would be like to be taken to bed by him. To *know* it would be as good, as *improper*, as everything else about him.

"Mina?"

"Hmm?"

Silvio narrowed his gaze on her. "I was asking if you would like dessert or some Frangelico and coffee... Keep this up, *cara*, and I *will* start thinking it's my company you are finding tiresome."

The desperation that had been coursing through her veins all day with their wedding looming in just forty-eight hours picked up her pulse, sent her heart hammering in her chest.

"What's bothering me," she blurted out, "is that we hardly know each other, Silvio. Maybe this has all been a bit fast."

That hard edge in his eyes deepened. "Now I *am* thinking you have cold feet, Mina. What more is there to know? I will provide a luxurious life for you to match the one you're accustomed to. You will entertain me in bed and be a good mother to my children. It's very simple."

She pressed a palm to her flushed cheek. She had let the cat out of the bag; she might as well follow through with it.

"When is my birthday?" she asked quietly.

His mouth flattened, a scary, lethal line. "I will, of course, know that when we're married."

"Am I a morning person or a night owl? Can I swim or would I drown if you tossed me over the side of your yacht?"

"I'm considering it," he growled. "*Enough*, Mina."

She sunk her teeth into her bottom lip. "You asked what was wrong. I'm telling you."

Well, not all of it. If she told him the entire truth—that her mother was marrying her off so she inherited the family heirloom, a precious ring her father had bequeathed to her upon her marriage—he might not be so impressed. Of course, she conceded miserably, it changed nothing, really. She was being sold as a possession to bear Silvio Marchetti's *bambinos*, when all she had ever wanted was to go to business school and follow in her father's footsteps.

Silvio threw his napkin on the table. "I think we should get out of here."

Mina's heart collided with the wall of her chest as her fiancé lifted his hand and signaled the waiter. "Perhaps we should have a liqueur," she suggested. *To give this conversation a chance to cool down before they left supervised company.*

He ignored her. Bill secured and paid, he placed a hand at her elbow, brought her to her feet and walked her out of the restaurant with such haste Mina's head swam. She had consumed more than her usual share of wine with dinner with the nerves plaguing her and now it seemed like a particularly bad idea, given she'd gone and voiced thoughts she never should have.

Her mother was going to kill her. Silvio looked like he wanted to kill her.

She was going to face the consequences.

She sat as far away from Silvio as she could in the car that took them home, his usual driver at the helm. Her fiancé sat stone-faced beside her, not uttering a word as they drove through the streets of Palermo to the posh, aristocratic neighborhood of Montepellegrino where she and her mother lived. If it was possible for a man to be utterly furious without showing any outward sign of it, her fiancé had mastered it. His anger emanated from him like a red cloud.

When the car pulled up in front of her mother's house, she breathed a sigh of relief. Silvio got out of the car, came around and opened her door. She took his hand, swung her legs out of the car and straightened. "Silvio—"

"Wait here," her fiancé told his driver in a low tone.

"That isn't necessary," she murmured, panicked because her mother was out at the opera. "I think I'm just tired. I'm sure if I—"

Silvio clamped his fingers hard around hers and propelled her toward the villa. She fumbled in her purse for her keys and found them with shaking fingers. Silvio frowned as she pushed the key into the lock. "Where is the staff?"

"It's Manuel's night off." He had been off for over a year, as in permanently off, but she wasn't about to tell Silvio they had no staff because they were penniless.

Silvio loosened his tie as he walked past her into the salon. "Pour me a drink."

She wanted to refuse, wanted desperately for him to leave, because she didn't like the vibe coming off him, but to reject his suggestion would only add fuel to the fire.

Crossing to the bar, she took a glass from the cabinet and poured him a Cognac, her hands trembling as she put the bottle down. Silvio watched her with a hooded gaze as she turned and carried the glass over to him.

She handed him the tumbler, flinching as his fingers brushed hers. His dark gaze turned incendiary. "We are marrying in front of hundreds of people in two days, Mina. What is behind this sudden display of nerves?"

She didn't love him. She didn't even like him. If the truth be known, she was afraid of him.

Dannazione! If only she could sell the ring her father

had left her without marrying him. But the condition in her father's will had been unbreakable. She had to be married to get her hands on the ring.

"It's like I said." She lifted her gaze to her fiancé's. "It seems very fast and I—I wish I knew you better. I would feel more comfortable."

He took a sip of the Cognac. "You did not go on and on about knowing me when your mother sold you off to the highest bidder. You were happy to snare Palermo's most eligible bachelor. So don't cry foul now, Mina. We will come to know each other."

She lowered her gaze. He was right. It had been as much a business deal as if her mother had forked over an old-fashioned dowry for her except she had nothing and she was being traded for her looks and childbearing ability. Which, she thought hysterically, she didn't even know if she had.

The thud of her fiancé's glass hitting the coffee table brought her head up. "Perhaps you are nervous about *us*," he suggested. "You've been playing the ice queen so long we haven't had a chance to get properly acquainted." His eyes glittered as he wrapped his fingers around her wrist and drew her to him. "Since we are very nearly married, I suggest we take some time to do that now."

Her heart thumped in her chest. "My mother—"

"—is at the opera." He brought his mouth down on hers. "You mentioned that earlier."

He kissed her then, a hard, demanding press of his mouth that was about punishment, not pleasure. Her heart galloped faster at the secure hold he had on her wrist. He was tall and big and she could never get away unless he chose to let her.

He didn't. His mouth continued to punish her, the hand he had on her waist moving down to cup her buttocks through the thin silk of her dress. He pulled her against him in an intimate hold she had never experienced before, his aroused body pressing against hers. It set off alarm bells in her head. "Silvio," she gasped, twisting away from his mouth. "Not like this…"

His face contorted with rage. "It will be *exactly* as I want it, *cara*. *Any* way I want it."

"Silvio—"

He brought the flat of his hand across her cheek so hard her head snapped to the side. Her ears rang with the force of it, her head spinning as a white-hot throb spread across her cheek.

"Refuse me again," he bit out, "and you will discover the depths my anger can sink to. I will not hear one more word of your silly jitters, Mina. Nor will I tolerate you repeating any of them to *anyone*. You are going to be my wife in two days. Our union is the talk of this city. Get yourself together."

The sound of keys in the door brought her head around. Her mother walked in, her gaze flicking from Mina to Silvio, then back again, eyes widening at the mark on Mina's face. "I thought that was your car, Silvio."

Silvio released her and stepped back. Sparing her mother a brief nod, he stalked past her to the door. "My driver will pick you up for the rehearsal dinner at six thirty tomorrow."

The door slammed. Mina's mother unwound her scarf from around her neck and walked slowly toward her, her gaze wary. "What was that?"

The moment she'd found out her fiancé was a violent man. Mina sank down on the sofa and buried her face in her hands.

"I can't marry him."

Her mother sat down beside her. "Let me see your face."

She lifted her head, utterly sure when her mother saw the welt she would agree she couldn't marry Silvio. Her mother sighed, went to the bar for ice, wrapped some in a towel and came back to sit down beside her, pressing it to her cheek. "What Sicilian man doesn't have a temper?"

Mina froze, disbelief plummeting through her, followed by a deep rage that sent blood pumping to every inch of her skin. "Did Father ever hit *you*?"

Her mother's lips pursed. "Your father was a different kind of man."

Yes, he had been. Honorable and loving. He would no more have lifted a hand to his wife or daughter than he would have kicked a dog on a street corner, which, she was sure, Silvio Marchetti would do. She was also sure from what had just happened, her fiancé's behavior would escalate when she was under his roof as his wife.

"I won't do it. We can find someone else."

Her mother shook her head, a resigned look on her face. "You have rejected every choice I've made for over a year now, Mina. You are marrying in front of half of Palermo in two days. Life is not all sunshine and rainbows. Sacrifices must be made and we need your sacrifice now. You know that."

Her mother was okay with sacrificing her to a ruthless, violent man?

Dio mio. She'd always known she was heartless, but *this…* What kind of a monster was she?

Her mother's gaze softened. "I suggest you find some peace with this. Men are men. You happen to be marrying a filthy rich one. Let that be your comfort."

CHAPTER THREE

MINA'S WEDDING DAY dawned sunny and crisp, ushering in the first day of fall in true, glorious Palermo fashion.

Bright rays of sunshine stole through the curtains that swayed in her open bedroom windows, a light breeze kissing her shoulders with a jasmine-scented caress. Temperatures were supposed to skyrocket to an unseasonable warmth as the afternoon went on, making it the perfect day for the lavish outdoor reception she and Silvio would host at Villa Marchetti.

Soon it would be time to slip on the stunning dress hanging in her wardrobe and make her way by horse and carriage to the elegant Palermo cathedral to wed her wealthy, influential groom.

A fairy-tale day it should have been. But inside, Mina was filled with dread. She couldn't seem to function, her every muscle and limb numb as the minutes passed, her stomach barely holding down the light breakfast she'd managed to consume. Today she would marry Silvio, a man she didn't love, who had turned out to be a hot-tempered, violent man. Everything she'd suspected he could be and more. And nothing she had said or done to convince her mother she couldn't do it had worked.

She stared in the mirror as her mother layered thick concealer over the bruise Silvio had left on her cheek, not a hint of emotion on Simona Mastrantino's face to indicate she felt any degree of empathy for her daughter.

"Makeup is a woman's magic." Her mother swept another layer of the thick concealer over her cheek. "No one will see the bruise. But you must remember to tuck this in your purse for touch-ups later with the photographs."

Mina absorbed this latest piece of advice from her mother dazedly, wondering if she could truly be this heartless. There was no question their relationship had always been strained, distant. Simona Mastrantino had made it clear from the very beginning she had no interest in being a mother—she had done it only to keep her husband happy. Off to the nannies Mina had gone while her mother lived a socialite's glamorous life as the wife of the CEO of one of Italy's most successful companies.

Mina had accepted this state of affairs with the innocent obliviousness of a child who knew no different. That Camilla, her nanny, and her beloved *papà* were her source of love and affection, her mother a beautiful, foreign creature who was to be awed from afar, like one of her beautiful dolls, had been her reality.

Her chest throbbed at the memory of her *papà*. He had always come to her first when he'd gotten home, swung her up in his arms and called her his *piccolo tesoro*, his little treasure, as he'd carried her off to bed to read. The bond between father and daughter had been inviolate, her *papà* lavishing upon her the attention her mother had not.

Until the day she'd come home from school to find her *nonna*, Consolata, at the house, and her father dead of a massive heart attack. Mina had clung to her *nonna*, her eight-year-old face a river of tears as she'd begged her to take her to see her father, perhaps instinctively knowing her last grounding force had been taken away. But her *nonna* had refused all of Mina's hysterical demands, telling her a hospital was no place for a child.

The dust had barely settled on her father's grave when her mother had sold the family business and packed a grieving Mina off to boarding then finishing school. Ripped away from everything she knew, without the unconditional love of her father or Camilla, Mina had floundered, filled with confusion and guilt. What was it about her that caused her mother to reject her so completely? It had been her good schoolfriend Celia and her mother, Juliana, who had become a surrogate mother to Mina, who had saved her from the shadows of those miserable years.

Her mother had only recognized Mina's importance when she'd come of age, an attractive bauble to dangle before Palermo's most eligible bachelors to solve their financial problems. Then it had been a relentless pursuit to find her a rich husband to marry, not the bonding Mina had craved.

A lump formed in her throat. "Please don't ask me to do this," she begged her mother through frozen lips, repeating the appeal she'd already made twice today. "We can find someone else, *Mamma*."

Her mother's gaze hardened with impatience. "We've been through this, Mina. You had your chance to pick someone else. You chose no one. I chose Silvio. Stop being so childish and selfish. You are doing your duty to this family. Marry Silvio, sell the ring and all our problems will be solved."

All her mother's problems would be solved. *Hers would just be beginning.* She closed her eyes. This was not how it was supposed to go. Today *was* supposed to be sunshine and rainbows. Her father was supposed to be walking her down that aisle toward a man as besotted with her as her father had been with her mother.

After she'd made a life for herself. After she'd followed in her father's brilliant business footsteps. She may not have Felicia Chocolate left—the family chocolatier her mother had sold—but her time spent in France studying and attaining top grades, learning of the vast and varied world out there, had taught her she could never limit herself to the traditional role of a woman in Sicily. She wanted more, so much more, for herself.

But all of that would be for naught if she married Silvio today. Her fingers curled around the arms of the chair, her knuckles gleaming white. She would spend her days pregnant with his *bambinos*, relegated to an artifact in his beautiful, cold, austere home.

The wedding planner's assistant swept back into the room, Mina's dress draped over her arm, having given mother and daughter a discreet few minutes to cover Silvio's damage. "Are we ready for the dress?"

Her mother straightened and nodded. The wedding planner gave Mina a once-over. "Excellent. You look beautiful."

Mina stood as the wedding planner moved to her side to help her on with the fairy-tale dress, one worthy of Silvio Marchetti's wife. She lifted her arms as the assistant dropped the dress over her head and settled it down around her hips in a whisper of silk and lace. She obediently pulled in a breath as the dress was done up, hugging every curve of her body with its slim, tulip shape. Except she didn't need to expend the effort as the dress did up easily. Too easily. She'd lost weight the last few weeks of fretting.

The wedding planner tutted about this latest wrinkle, producing pins to close the gap below the low, dipping back of the dress. Mina surveyed herself in the mirror, a tumult of emotion swirling through her. She looked impeccable. The dress was perfect, her hair an elegant chignon with tiny, white flowers woven through it, her face a subtle, painted masterpiece.

And it was all wrong. She could not do this. She could not.

Silver stilettos and the diamond choker and drop earrings Silvio had given her as a wedding gift completed her irreproachable appearance. And then it was time to go. She descended the wide circular staircase to the main level of the villa, the wedding planner managing her modest train behind her.

She had not even a bridesmaid to commiserate with. Celia was managing a big product launch in Paris and hadn't been able to make it, which meant the bridesmaids were all Silvio's—strangers to her.

She waited in the salon for the horse and carriage that would transport her to the church. Her mother and the planner would ride on ahead in the limousine Silvio had sent for them to ensure everything was ready for her arrival.

A cloud of perfume preceding her, her mother brushed a kiss against her cheek. "Brighten up, Mina. You will have everything after this."

Except what she really wanted. Her freedom. A man who actually loved her.

The door closed behind her mother in a waft of jasmine and she was alone. Alone in the beautiful dress that flowed around her, the diamond choker growing tighter around her throat with every second that passed.

Her breathing grew shallow, her palms sweaty. She was out of time. Out of options.

The elegant old Mastrantino villa was located in the aristocratic neighborhood of Montepellegrino, with its sweeping views of Palermo, the surrounding mountains and the Tyrrhenian Sea.

As much as Nate appreciated the spectacular view, he was more interested in speaking with the Mastrantinos, acquiring Giovanni's ring and wrapping up his business in Sicily so he could complete stops in Capri, Hong Kong and the Maldives before heading home to hand the ring over to his grandfather.

He had elected not to pursue the Giarruso at this point in time, as it wasn't quite the unique opportunity he'd been searching for to enhance his portfolio—delectable smart chambermaids aside.

The handsome, elegantly stuccoed Mastrantino villa looked as quiet as it had the night before when he'd come seeking the ring only to find no one home. Hoping his luck was better today, Nate asked his driver to wait at the front entrance, strode up the wide set of steps to the front entrance and rang the bell.

When no one answered, he rang again, impatience thrumming through his veins. *Why were there no staff members answering the door?* Were the Mastrantinos out of town? He scowled. That would put a major kink in his plans.

He was about to ring a third time when the door opened and he was faced with a vision in white. A dark-haired vision in white. A wedding dress to be exact, floating around the woman's incredible figure. He lifted his gaze to her beautiful face and shock flooded through him. *Lina. Here?*

"I thought you were my horse and carriage," she breathed, hiking up the train of her dress.

He looked down at her silver, high heel–clad dainty feet, then back at the luxury sedan his driver had parked at the curb, wondering dazedly if he'd been transported into some bizarre real-life Cinderella reenactment. "No," he replied slowly, looking back at Lina, "I most definitely came on four wheels."

She blinked. "Signor Brunswick. What *are* you doing here?"

He noticed then the tears that streaked her perfect makeup, the vulnerable tilt to her chin, the quiver to her mouth, and *damn* if it didn't tear him up inside.

He dragged his gaze back up to hers. "I am looking for the Mastrantinos. Do you live here?"

Her beautiful mouth quivered some more. He ran a hand through his hair. Cursed. Comforting emotional women was not his forte.

She pressed her lips together. "Now is not a very good time."

No kidding. She was apparently getting married today. Not just taken, but marrying someone.

Why was she crying on her wedding day? He was no expert but he had been led to believe it was every woman's dream.

He swallowed. "I am looking for Simona or Mina Mastrantino. They own a ring I would like to purchase. But since this is clearly *not* a good time, as you say, I can come ba—"

"What ring?" Her dark gaze fixed on his.

"The Fountain Ring with the sapphire in it."

Her eyes widened. "How do you know about that ring?"

"My private investigator tracked it down for me. I want to purchase it."

"Why?"

"It has…sentimental value for someone close to me."

A woman walking down the avenue gave them a curious look. Lina stepped back and motioned for him to come in. He stepped in and she shut the door behind him.

"I am… Mina Mastrantino," she said haltingly, digging her teeth into her bottom lip in that trademark nervous tic of hers. "I—I don't use my real name when I work. But you can't—I mean—please keep that between us."

Who was he going to tell? And—*what? Lina was Mina?*
Why in God's name was she working as a chambermaid?

Lina, or rather *Mina*, gestured to a room to the left.
"Please come in. Sit down."

He walked past her into the richly appointed, slightly
outdated salon which had clearly once been the showpiece
of the villa with its hand-carved fireplaces, crystal chan-
deliers and elegant arches. Mina followed and indicated a
chair for Nate while she perched on a sofa. He sat down,
his gaze moving over the distraught bride's face.

Her eyes were full of turmoil as she lifted them to his.
"I would love to sell you the ring, Signor Brunswick, but
unfortunately, I cannot."

"Nate," he corrected. She had seen him in a towel, after
all. "And why not?"

"It's a family heirloom. My father bequeathed it to me
upon my marriage."

He looked pointedly at her expensive wedding dress.
"Which is happening today…"

"Yes." Her lips started to quiver again, a tear escaping
those dark-as-night eyes.

His blood pressure shot through the roof. *Dear Lord,
he didn't need this right now. He really didn't.*

"Mina." He moved across the room to sit beside her on
the sofa, likely not the smartest move given the chemistry
between them, but he couldn't help himself as he lifted a
hand to her delicate jaw to turn her face to him. Her dark
lashes were soaked with tears that ran down her cheek
like sparkling crystals. Her sultry mouth was vulnerable
and bare of color. Undeniably enticing. But it was the dark
shadow on her cheek the sunlight pouring in through the
windows revealed that caught his attention. Turned his
blood to ice.

He knew it was none of his business, knew he should

walk out the door right now and come back tomorrow, but he couldn't seem to move. He was a smart man. He could put two and two together and he did not like what he saw.

"Your fiancé," he said quietly, dangerously, "gave you that bruise on your cheek?"

Her fingers flew up to cover it. "Oh, no, I—"

"Mina…"

She stared at him, dropped her head into her hands and sobbed.

Dammit all. Nate wrapped his arm around her and pulled her onto his lap, cradling her against his chest. She stiffened against him as if ready to bolt, then another sob racked her petite body and she melted into him, her tears soaking his shirt. Shredding his self-possession.

He held her as she cried, ruthlessly commanding his all too aware body that the soft curves that fit so perfectly against him were utterly off-limits. His hand stroked her silky hair, nudging some curly tendrils free from the perfect knot as her sobs dissolved into sniffles, but he didn't care. She was trembling like a leaf.

"Tell me," he ordered, "what is going on here."

She shook her head. "Silvio—my fiancé—he's a very powerful man. He would kill me if I said anything."

He lifted her chin with his fingers. "Funny thing about that, Mina, but I'm a powerful man, too, and I don't hit my women. Silvio *who*?"

She squeezed her eyes shut. "Silvio Marchetti. He owns half of Sicily. You really don't want to get mixed up with him."

He would like to get *very* mixed up with Silvio Marchetti right now. *Violently, aggressively* mixed up with Silvio Marchetti. Unfortunately, he wasn't here for him to inflict the desired punishment.

"Why are you marrying a monster?"

Her dark eyes shone like polished ebony. "He is my mother's choice. It's been…arranged."

He gave her an incredulous look. "That still happens?"

"Here it does."

"Does your mother know he hits you?"

Her chin wobbled.

Hell. "Tell her you won't."

"I have. I—we need this match."

"Why?" She could hardly *need* it.

Mina shook her head. "It doesn't matter. Everyone is at the church already. I am marrying Silvio in front of half of Palermo in—" she looked at her watch "—less than an hour."

"Call it off," he grated. "You can't possibly marry him, Mina. *Look* at you."

She pushed a hand against his chest to get up. He held her firm. "*Why* are you doing this?"

"Because we need the money," she bit out. "I need to marry to get the ring so I can sell it and pay off our debts. My mother and I are *bankrupt*. That's why I was working at the hotel."

So she was going to marry a violent man to make that happen?

He let her go. Watched as she stood and paced the room, the train of her dress following behind her. "Why not marry someone of your own choosing, then?"

"I told you already." She stopped and jammed her hands on her hips. "My mother arranged the match. Silvio was the last of a dozen candidates she put forward. I am out of choices."

"Why did you reject the others?"

"Because I didn't love them."

Oh, boy. She was one of *those*. He hated to burst Ms. Mastrantino's bubble at this particular dire moment in time but… "Love is a myth, Mina." He gave her a hard look. "Find a man you're comfortable with, who treats you right, and marry him."

"It's too late for that." Her gaze swung to the window, a frantic, trapped look in her eyes. "The carriage will be here any minute."

He studied the tension in every muscle of her slim body. The panicked aura that wove itself around her. She was truly terrified. And why not? She was about to marry an abusive man in minutes.

In that moment, he realized he could not leave Mina here to suffer that fate. It was *insane, ludicrous.* He had certainly never pegged himself as anyone's Prince Charming, but he was not walking away and abandoning this vulnerable woman to a violent man. It went against every code of honor his mother had drilled into him.

He stood up and joined her at the window. She turned to look at him, a glazed, resigned expression on her face. "What would you do if you had a choice?" he asked. "If you could marry someone other than Silvio and sell the ring?"

"I would pay off our debts," she said quietly, "walk away and start a new life for myself."

"Silvio will be furious," he said. "To have his bride jilt him at the altar in front of the whole city. You would have to leave town. And quickly."

She stared at him, wide-eyed. "I was merely speaking in 'what ifs.' Of course I would never do it. It's far too late now."

He held her gaze. "Someone I care about very deeply wants that ring back. It was once his—years ago he had to sell it to survive. *You* need to get out of this situation. There is no way you can marry Silvio. So I'm proposing a business solution. Marry me, sell me the ring and I will fly you out of here tonight on my jet. We'll get the marriage annulled immediately after the deal is done. We both get what we need."

She gaped at him. "That is...*crazy.* I—I don't even know you. Silvio will—" she waved a hand at him, the multicarat ring she had not been wearing while cleaning blinding in the light "—lose his mind."

"You had me vetted at the Giarruso," he reminded her. "They do full security checks. And you know this isn't going to get any better. If he's hit you once, he'll hit you again. And again. Until you'll think it's normal to greet the day with bruises. *If* he doesn't send you to the hospital with broken bones."

She stared at him mutely.

"My jet is waiting on standby." He kept his gaze on hers, steady and sure. "I'm offering you a way out of this. The decision is yours. If you choose to marry Silvio, I can come back at a mutually agreed upon time and make you an offer for the ring."

Her cheeks drained of color. She pressed her hands to them and shook her head. "I don't know what to do."

"Make a decision,' he advised, casting a deliberate look toward the window. "And fast. When that carriage arrives, you are out of options."

She paced the length of the room. Back and forth. Finally, she stopped in front of him, her small palms curled into fists by her sides. "You are really willing to do this? What about whatever woman is in your life? How is she going to feel about it?"

His mouth lifted. "There is no current woman, and even if there was, she'd know marriage is never in the cards for me. I'm fine with this, Mina. The question is are you?"

Her chin moved up and down.

"Is that a yes?"

"*Sì.*"

"You're sure?" He held her gaze with his. "You have to be sure. There's no turning back."

"I'm sure." Fear filled her eyes. "What if Silvio comes after us?"

"I will deal with him," he said roughly. *God help the man if he got his hands on him.*

He swung into execution mode. "Get your purse and passport. Everything else can wait."

She turned on her heel and walked out of the room, elaborate dress trailing behind her. Nate raked his hair out of his face. This might be the most unique business deal he'd ever made, but it certainly wasn't the most complex. This one was simple. Marry the girl, get the ring and have their union annulled. As far as marriages went, it was the kind he could wrap his head around.

Mina was in shock. She must be, she decided as she sat in the backseat of the luxury car alongside Nate and attempted to contemplate the enormity of what she was doing. At this very minute, she was standing up Silvio Marchetti, one of Sicily's most powerful figureheads, *at the altar* where her mother and her family and everyone they had known for generations were waiting for her to appear.

An image of her fiancé's hard, unyielding face with its cruel edge flickered through her head. The incredulity of her failure to show up spreading across it until that white-hot rage of his set in. He *would* lose his mind. He would take it out on those around him. Her hands, laced together in her lap upon the fine silk of her dress, went ice-cold.

Would he take it out on her mother as the next best thing to her? Would her mother ever forgive her?

Simona Mastrantino might be an unfeeling, ambitious,

repressed aristocrat willing to trade on her daughter's fate, but she was all the family Mina had.

Would Silvio send his henchmen after her when he discovered what had happened? Did he *have* henchmen?

Her stomach heaved, a determined swallow all that was keeping her breakfast in her stomach. She was giving up *everything* she knew, agreeing to marry a man she hardly knew, to start a life far away from her home. Where would she go? To Paris where Celia was? Where she could use her French? Or was that too close to danger?

Nate continued to make phone call after phone call on his mobile, barking out orders in that deep authoritative tone of his. Phrases and words flew by in rapid succession. Civil ceremony, marriage license, documentation, *prenup*.

Nate flicked her a glance. "Can you have your solicitor give us the ring today? It would be better for us to leave tonight rather than wait around until the open of business tomorrow morning."

Which might give Silvio a chance to track her down in a murderous rage. She shivered. "I will call him and find out."

A quick conversation with Pasquale Tomei determined they were in luck. He had the ring in his home for safe-keeping and could see them late afternoon. Which gave them time to marry first.

They pulled up at the Giarruso minutes later. She kept her head down as Nate put a hand to her back and guided her past curious onlookers through the front doors of the hotel and into the elevators to the penthouse suites. She breathed a sigh of relief as they rode skyward having avoided anyone she knew.

Everything happened in a blur after that. The arrival of the Giarruso butler with the prenuptial agreement Nate's lawyer had sent along with a bouquet of beautiful white flowers for Mina and two simple, elegant gold bands. She kept her back turned as her colleague offered his congratulations to Nate, then left.

The civil registrar who had miraculously been produced to marry them arrived next. It was a testament to the authority of the stranger who was about to become her husband as every detail fell into rapid-fire place, nothing beyond his control.

Then she was standing by Nate's side, her groom-to-be now dressed in a dark, expensive-looking suit rather than the jeans and shirt he'd had on when he'd arrived at her home. *Insanely handsome.*

The registrar began the short, textbook ceremony. Mina recited the words in Italian, Nate in English, words that should have been a sacred affirmation of a love that would last forever conducted in a church with a priest as with the traditions of her own faith.

Nate captured her hand in his as the ceremony came to a close, his dark, fathomless eyes holding hers as he slid the sparkling gold band on her finger. She swallowed hard, took the ring he handed her and slid it onto his elegant, strong hand. A flash of sensual awareness pierced the numbness blanketing her as the heat of his skin bled into hers. Those beautiful hands would be eminently capable of handling a woman.

Devastatingly exciting. Too bad she would never get to find out how exciting.

Her gaze lifted to his, curiosity plastered all over her face. A dark gleam entered his inscrutable gaze, injecting his almost black eyes with a heat that stole her breath.

The registrar indicated Nate could kiss his bride. He lowered his head to hers, his hands resting lightly on her waist to draw her closer. "Just to keep it real," he murmured in her ear.

He pulled back and set his gaze on her lips. Her heart pounded in her chest as he bent his head and claimed her mouth in a whisper-soft kiss, his hard, sensuous lips settling against the pillowy softness of hers with unerring accuracy. For a moment she remained frozen, neither responding nor rejecting. Nate edged her lips further apart with a light pressure that commanded rather than asked. With a helpless sigh, she relaxed against him, sinking into his warmth as his hand came up to cup her jaw, angling her for his consumption.

It was every bit as good as she'd imagined it would be. She grabbed a handful of his shirt to steady herself, knees weak. She'd been kissed before, surely, by a couple of men, but never like this. Never so expertly, so *thoroughly*.

Utterly under his spell, a soft sound escaped her throat. The officiant gave a delicate cough. Nate's hands fell away from her face as he put some distance between them, a flare of something she couldn't read blazing in his eyes. *Disappointment? Desire?*

Her heart, already sorely under duress, beat a jagged rhythm. *What was she doing? Making out with a playboy like Nate Brunswick—her soon-to-be ex-husband?*

Nate turned to thank the registrar, apparently not as gobsmacked by the kiss as she had been. She attempted to gather her composure as he moved with ruthless efficiency to tie up loose ends with the officiant, summoned a bellboy to gather their things and had the car brought around.

When they were ensconced in the back of the sedan again, headed toward the affluent, beachside suburb of Mondello where her solicitor lived, Mina rested her head back against the seat and closed her eyes. Relived that *kiss*. How her knees had literally melted beneath her.

"Are you okay?"

Deep and velvety soft, Nate's sinful voice interrupted her recap.

She opened her eyes. "Why did you do that?"

"Do what?"

"The kiss. That *kiss*."

Amusement darkened his gaze. "That wasn't a kiss, Mina. That was a peck on the mouth to satisfy the registrar's expectations."

She wondered what a real kiss from him would be like. *Unforgettable*, she imagined.

"I will concede," he drawled, his eyes on the hot color flooding her face, "that we have some kind of chemistry, *wife*. Too bad it's a marriage in name only."

She laced her hands together in her lap and glued her eyes to them.

"Surely you've kissed Silvio," he prodded. "Perhaps even bedded him? I looked him up, Mina. He has quite a reputation."

She lifted her chin. "Silvio has always been a gentleman."

His brows lifted.

"Well, until that...*incidente*."

Nate sat back in the seat, arms crossed over his chest after that, watching her with an enigmatic look. Likely glad he was getting rid of her shortly...

They made the reasonably short trip to her solicitor's home quickly in the quiet Sunday traffic.

Pasquale Tomei smiled as he opened the door of his Liberty-style villa. His smile faded as his gaze moved over Mina in her wedding dress and then to Nate. "Where is Silvio?"

"She married me, not him," Nate said matter-of-factly. "True love and all that."

Pasquale's eyes widened. Mina pushed a stray chunk

of hair out of her face and straightened her spine. "We are in a bit of a hurry, Pasquale. If you could give us the ring, we can be on our way."

"I'll need to see the paperwork." The solicitor waved them into the house. "There are terms I need to explain."

Terms? Mina frowned as they followed the lawyer down a hallway and into his office. Sitting down beside Nate on the opposite side of the desk, she handed Pasquale their paperwork. He looked it over and handed it back. "This is quite a change in plans. Your mother was very excited about your and Silvio's union."

The color drained from her face. "Mina is free to marry whom she chooses," Nate interceded, a blunt edge to his voice. "So if we could have the ring…"

Pasquale took a box out of the drawer and handed it to Mina. She opened the navy blue velvet jeweler's box and there it was. The Fountain Ring. A stunning square-cut sapphire of the deepest blue surrounded by diamonds set in a platinum band. A beautiful piece to be sure, but it was its extensive history and the mystery that surrounded the ring's origins that made it so valuable.

She closed the box and looked at Pasquale. "What were the terms you spoke of?"

The lawyer set forth a sheaf of papers that had been sitting on his desk, moving to a page he had marked with a colored tab. "There is one condition I must make you aware of. You must remain married for one year for me to grant you full title of the ring."

If there was any color left in her face, it fled now. Nate's jaw dropped open. *"Why?"*

"Mina's father wanted to see her happily married before the ring was made hers."

Mina shook her head. "That condition was never mentioned to me."

"I'm sorry," the lawyer said. "But as you can see, it's there in black and white."

She turned to absorb the silent tension in the man beside her. His usual even expression was firmly in place, but in his eyes she could read fury. *Barely leashed fury.*

He directed a look at the lawyer. "Mina can keep the ring in her possession during this time?"

"Yes."

"Fine." Nate closed his fingers around her shoulder as he stood up, propelling her with him. "We should go."

They thanked the lawyer. Nate hurried her down the steps and into the waiting car, giving the driver a curt instruction to take them to the airport. *To step on it.*

Her stomach dropped. She waited until the privacy screen had come up between them and the driver before she said quietly, "You are worried he will tip off Silvio."

"Or your mother."

Right. That would be just as bad because her mother would go straight to Silvio and… She took a deep breath and forced herself to remain calm. A tense silence stretched between them. "Nate—" she said haltingly. "I didn't know."

He turned his dark, blazing gaze on her. "It's a pretty big detail to not know about, Mina, given your desire to get your hands on the ring and sell it."

She pressed her lips together. "I was never told about this condition. I *swear*, I did not know."

His gaze raked her face. She squared her shoulders under its hard, cold weight. "What are the terms in the document?"

"What do you mean?"

"I mean, do we have to *live together*? Are there any other stipulations attached to the marriage?"

She shook her head. "That's all the document said."

He lapsed into silence. She curled up in her corner of the seat, blood pounding against her temples. What if he abandoned their agreement? Left her here for Silvio to punish? She had no money, no possessions, *nothing* to get away.

Long moments passed. When she was teetering on the edge of complete and irreversible panic, he turned to her, icy control back in his face. "What was your plan after we left? Where were you intending on having me take you?"

She shook her head, her mouth trembling. "I—I don't have one. I just left my fiancé at the altar, Nate. I—I'm—"

In shock.

"Okay," he said finally after a long moment. "Here's what we're going to do. We're going to get on my jet, we're going to fly to Capri where I have business to attend to, and we will sort this out on the way."

"Capri?"

His mouth tightened. "That's the destination on offer."

She closed her eyes. What choice did she have? Her first course of action had to be to get out of here. Then she could regroup.

The miles flew by and then they were at the airport, an expedited process seeing them quickly through security. The official asked for her passport. Mina handed it to him and smiled when he gave it back. Nate gripped her elbow in a tight hold and started walking her through the doors toward the tarmac. *Fast.*

"Keep your head down," he muttered. "And keep walking."

Her reflexive action, of course, was to turn her head. Two men in dark suits stood arguing with the guards covering the security checkpoint. Her breath caught in her throat. *"Dio mio.* Nate—"

"Put your head down," he barked, "and walk. He isn't going to touch you. I promise."

She kept walking, her knees threatening to give way beneath her. Nate slid his arm around her waist and propelled her forward. Up the steps to the jet they went, the doors closing behind them. Nate told her to sit down and buckle up, then walked into the cockpit to say something to the pilot.

In minutes they were cleared to leave by the control tower. Mina had never felt so light-headed in all her life as they taxied down the runway and took off, lifting sharply as a gust of wind buoyed them higher.

Dread consumed her. "It was Silvio, wasn't it?" She turned to look at Nate as her stomach rose and fell with the ascending aircraft. "Who sent those men?"

CHAPTER FOUR

NATE SURVEYED MINA'S panicked expression, her fear as she curled her hands around the armrests, knuckles white, overriding the fury he felt at his now excessively complicated life. *The fury he felt toward the abusive man who had just tried to come after her.*

"I suspect so," he said grimly. "I will find out for certain. But there's no need to worry. He can't touch you now."

Her eyes flashed. "What if he sends his men after me? Pasquale could give him all our information."

"Then he will know I am not a man to be messed with. That it's fruitless to come after you."

"You're only one man. You saw the men he sent."

"He won't get past my security detail."

"Security detail?"

"I'm a rich man, Mina. It's a prerequisite."

She sat back in her chair, looking so chalk white he feared she might pass out. When the attendant came around to offer them drinks he asked for two glasses of brandy and put one in front of Mina.

"I don't drink liquor."

"Today you do." He nodded toward the glass. "Drink. It'll help your nerves."

She stared dubiously at the amber liquid. Took a little sip and wrinkled her nose. "I don't like it."

"Keep drinking."

He leaned back against the seat, resting his brandy on his thigh. His temporary wife was now his wife for a year, *a year*, a state of being he had never once contemplated entering into nor wanted. That was *if* he chose to go through with the deal he and Mina had made, a *vastly* different one than he had signed on for.

He took in the stunning, innocent creature who was now his wife. Her disheveled hair, streaked makeup and worry lined face. His cynical side suggested she might have known about the year-long clause in the will, perhaps had seen an opportunity for escape in him that had been sweetened by the idea of a rich husband. But his gut told him that wasn't the case. Mina hadn't even blinked when he'd said the word *prenup*. She'd looked as frozen, as in shock, as he'd been when Pasquale Tomei had unveiled that condition. It could not have been manufactured.

With that stipulation, the key to her escape had been stripped from her, the ability to start a life away from her clearly uncaring mother and abusive ex-fiancé. *He* had been the one walking into the middle of things offering solutions. And now he had a much bigger one to find.

What was he going to do with a wife? With Mina? He couldn't just dump her in Capri and tell her to contact him when she could sell him the ring. Marchetti was too likely to get to her there.

She needed his protection. *He* needed that ring to show Giovanni before he died. To give him a chance to reconnect with the past. Which meant his wife was now his responsibility. For a year.

"When you talked about obtaining your freedom," he said, "what did you envision yourself doing?"

"I speak multiple languages. I thought I would follow in my father's footsteps. Become a businesswoman."

"Do you have a business degree?"

"No." She pressed her lips together, her dark gaze dropping away from his. "I went to a finishing school in France."

A *finishing school*. Did those still *exist*? "And your father. What business was he in?"

"He was the CEO of our family chocolate company—Felicia. It was one of the biggest in Europe before my mother sold it to an American conglomerate."

He took a sip of his drink. "Most people who want to get into business today have studied it in school. It's very difficult to find a position without a degree or a diploma."

Her chin rose. "I expect to start out at the bottom. I'd thought maybe I could work as a chambermaid at the Giarruso, then find a higher position."

Admirable if wishful thinking. Unless, of course, a superior was willing to give her a shot in the business as Giovanni had given him.

He thought back to Mina's quick, well-thought-out answers that day at the Giarruso. She had the natural business instincts he himself had once had. A moldable brain. *Was it time for him to pay it forward? To give her the same chance he had been given?*

He had been eighteen, working the night shift at a food warehouse, when Alex had tracked him down to save Giovanni. Eighteen and angry. His mother had managed to straighten him out after his run-in with the dark side in his midteens, begging him to stop running errands for the neighborhood enforcer before he got himself shot or killed. But she hadn't been able to convince him to go back to school. They needed the money and he couldn't just stand by and watch her work herself into her grave while he studied in a useless English lit class.

He'd taken a job at the warehouse where he'd discovered what hell truly felt like. Eight-hour night shifts in the dank, cavernous space, the fluorescent lights beating into his temples as he broke his back hauling flat after flat of produce into place.

He remembered leaving work one morning a few months after he'd started, the faint light of dawn creeping across the sky. Back killing him, lungs tight, he'd stopped and leaned against the building, wondering if this miserable existence was life. Because if this was what it was, he didn't want it. At least when he'd been working the streets he'd had money in his pocket. He'd had his self-respect. He'd *been* somebody.

For the first time in years, he'd allowed his hatred toward his father loose, driving his fist into the concrete facade of the warehouse, leaving him with two broken fingers and no less bitterness. He hadn't wanted a life like his half siblings' lives—but to be the result of his father's slumming? To not even be worthy of acknowledgment? It festered in him like a slow-moving disease.

When Alex had sought him out weeks later, he had been teetering on the edge of darkness and light, his old life a seductive siren's call. Giovanni had made him choose. Embrace the chance you've been offered, he'd said, or forever cling to your anger. There is no in between.

The darkness he'd sensed in his grandfather, the raw acknowledgment he *knew* the dark side because he hadn't been able to pull his own son from it, had touched something inside Nate, perhaps the tiny sliver of hope he had left in him. He had chosen the light.

Blinking, he pulled himself out of the memory to focus on Mina's big dark eyes, the expression in them as adrift, as fear-driven, as his had been. She had no money, nowhere to go. She was as lost a soul as he had been. He couldn't let her fall through the cracks.

By the time they had landed in Capri a short while later, a plan had formed in his head. It would solve all his issues, except, of course, the ring on his finger. That, unfortunately, wasn't going anywhere.

Mina stood on the terrace of the penthouse suite of the Grand Hotel Emelia, the Bay of Marina Piccola sparkling in the distance. She had been to the glamorous island of Capri once with her family when she had been very young, six or seven. She only remembered bits and pieces of the holiday, but it was one of her best memories.

The beautiful beaches and the lovely walks along the coast had been her favorite activities, made extra special by the time she'd gotten to spend with her busy father, who'd taken a real holiday for once. They'd spent hours playing in the sand, digging sand castles and moats while her mother shopped and lunched with the jet-set crowd.

Her father had indulged her mother's every whim on the trip, including generous amounts of both his time and money. Her mother had, in turn, sparkled, and everything had been perfect for once. No arguments between her fiery parents that seemed to come all too frequently at home. Just sunshine and laughter.

She remembered playing with her favorite doll, Eva, on the beach with her father. Ankle-deep in the surf, she'd turned her back on the doll, only to find Eva gone when she turned around seconds later. Her father had spent the better part of an hour trying to retrieve the doll, understanding this was life or death for Mina. When he'd finally found her, laying a soaked, bedraggled Eva in her eager hands, he'd given her one of his stern lectures. "Take care of precious things, Mina. When they're gone, they're gone. I won't always be able to bring them back for you."

Her eyes burned as the glittering water of the bay she'd

misplaced Eva in sparkled in the early-evening sun. How apropos her father's words had been. She'd lost him soon after that—her one grounding force.

Her lashes came down to shield her eyes from the hot glow of the sun, a pang of longing rippling through her. How she wished he was here right now to make sense of everything. If he was, she would never have left her life to venture into the complete unknown. She wouldn't be married to a stranger, *"Bastien Nathaniel Brunswick,"* her marriage certificate had elaborated, who was apparently so wealthy he owned this five-star hotel the glitterati called home. She wouldn't be feeling so wholly, all-encompassingly *lost.*

She wrapped her arms around herself as a chill nipped at her skin, the heavenly scent of bougainvillea and campanula floating on the breeze. She didn't even own the clothes on her back. The expensive dress she was wearing was one Nate had sent down to the boutique for so she could get out of her wedding dress, a good thing because every time she looked at it she thought about Silvio and how furious he must be. How furious her mother must be.

Something Nate was apparently ascertaining as he made a litany of phone calls to *Dio* knew who to find out. Her pulse picked up, her blood thrumming through her veins. What could he possibly say to smooth things over? To fix the mess she'd created? To warn Silvio off?

Was he finishing off his role as hero by ensuring Silvio left her alone before he threw her out and said thank you, but no thank you? *I had only intended a twenty-four-hour marriage and a ring as compensation and this is way, way beyond that…*

A whiff of citrus filled her head just before a delicate silk wrap landed around her shoulders. She jumped as Nate reached around her to tie the silk into a loose knot.

"You're still jumpy." He leaned against the railing beside her, his gaze on her face.

"You caught me off guard." She looked down at the expensive-looking wrap he'd secured around her rather than stare at his smoldering good looks in a white T-shirt and a pair of dark jeans that molded themselves to his muscular thighs and long legs. "Another thing I can't pay you for."

A wry smile crossed his face. "I'm good for it, Mina. That much I know."

What didn't he know? What he was going to do with her? She pressed her lips together as her severely stressed imagination ran away with her. *Get a hold of yourself, Mina.*

"This is a magnificent property." She looked out at the yachts bobbing on the cerulean blue sea as the sun made its descent into the horizon. "You said you named it for your mother?"

He nodded.

"She is special, then?"

His lips curved, a genuine warmth filling his eyes. "Extraordinary."

She tilted her head to one side. "What makes her so extraordinary?"

"She was a single mother. She put me first every day of her life and kept me on the right path."

The bittersweet ache inside of her swelled larger. "You are very lucky to have a mother who cares so much for you."

"Yes."

"And your father?"

"He was never a part of our lives."

She studied the hard set of his jaw. The cold cast that had replaced the warmth in his eyes. Perhaps that was where some of the toughness surrounding this man came from.

She forced herself to ask the question she couldn't avoid. "Was it Silvio who came after us?"

"Yes. But you don't need to worry about him. I've taken care of it."

"How?" She turned to face him, panic clawing at her throat. "He must be beyond furious. To be humiliated like that in front of half the city… He will *want* to punish me."

"He *is* furious."

Her heart leaped into her mouth. "You *talked* to him?"

"Pasquale gave him my name. I stole his bride." He lifted a shoulder. "It was a necessary conversation."

"What did he *say*?"

"Nothing you need to know. Suffice it to say, he won't be bothering you again."

"Nate—"

"Stop." His gaze hardened. "He isn't a nice man, Mina, you knew that. He didn't have nice things to say. All you need to know is that I communicated the point that you are mine. You are safe from him. End of story."

She took a deep breath. Absorbed the deadly glimmer in his eyes. *Who was he* that he could so cavalierly tell Silvio Marchetti to call off the dogs and expect that he would? *Had* she jumped from the frying pan into the fire with him? Or did she trust Nate like she instinctively felt she could?

"What about my mother?" She'd been avoiding her calls to her mobile all day, with no idea what she'd even say if she did pick it up.

"She called me after I spoke with Silvio. Was *worried* about you, wanted to reassure herself you were okay." His smile was grim. "I told her you'd like a few days of privacy to enjoy our honeymoon and then you would call her."

Her mouth dropped open. "What else did you say?"

"That we are in love. That today was a mad, passionate impulse on our part." He lifted a broad shoulder. "It seemed as good a story as any to get Silvio off your back. I mentioned your cold feet were a product of our short but *intense* courtship."

Oh, mio Dio. She pressed her hands to her face. "You did not."

"I needed to give him a good reason to leave you alone, Mina. Now he has one. A man like Silvio would consider you used goods."

Used goods? She shook her head at the insanity of it all and paced to the end of the terrace. Now Silvio and her mother thought she had been intimate with Nate while she'd been engaged to Silvio. *Maledizione.* She didn't even want to think of how her mother had reacted. Or the harsh words that were undoubtedly on her voice mail.

"What did Silvio say to all this?"

"He said he was done with you. I said, *Good*. Because I'd take him apart if he came anywhere near you. So put your mind at ease, Mina. It's going to be fine."

Easier said than done. Her head spun as he disappeared inside and returned with a bottle of champagne and two glasses. She watched him warily as he uncorked the bottle. "I think the brandy was quite enough."

"You're wound tight as a bow." He worked the cork out of the bottle, a loud pop cutting through the air. "A glass of wine will help. And," he added, flicking her a glance from beneath dark lashes, "I have a proposition for you."

His request to deliver the Marc de Grazia Guardiola personally to his hotel room filled her head. He didn't mean—

"No, I don't mean that." His mouth twisted as he read her thoughts. "As much as I think *that* would loosen you up, what I have in mind involves another business proposition for you and I. Because like it or not, Mina, we are stuck together."

They were? Hope flared inside of her. "You're proposing we stay married?"

"I see no other option." He poured the champagne in the glasses. "As certain as I am that I got the message across to Silvio today that you are untouchable, I'm not about to set you loose on the streets of Capri like…an orphan searching for a home."

She frowned.

He waved a hand at her. "The point is I need that ring to show my grandfather. You need to be protected. So we stay together for the year and, like our original plan, we both get what we need."

Relief flooded through her. "I don't want to be a burden. I could work for one of your hotels. Pay my way. I'm a very good chambermaid."

"You're smarter than that." He handed her a glass of champagne. "You proved to me what an innovative thinker you are that day at the Giarruso. You have great ideas, Mina. I'm offering to take you on as my protégée for the year."

"Protégée?" Her fingers tightened around the stem of the glass.

He nodded. "I own a chain of luxury hotels from one side of the globe to the other. The best of the best. If you want to learn about business I can teach you everything you need to know."

She frowned. "Why would you do that? I mean, I know you said I had good ideas, but surely you must be too busy for something like that?"

He leaned back against the railing, champagne glass in hand. "I got my start in business from someone who took a chance on me. I believe in paying it forward."

She thought about what few options she had—as in none without a cent to her name, without a home to go back to.

She'd made a decision when she'd left with Nate: to stand on her own two feet; to not allow herself to be controlled by anyone anymore; to make her own way in the world. The only path left was forward.

Nate was offering her a chance to fulfill her dream—to follow in her father's footsteps. A once-in-a-lifetime opportunity to work with the best because he thought she was smart and had potential. Because he thought she was more than the pretty face her mother had always pegged her as.

A warm feeling spread through her, heat infusing her cheeks at the validation she had craved. To say the thought of becoming Nate's protégée was intimidating vastly understated the apprehension snaking through her insides. The combined terror and exhilaration the thought inspired. And yet she trusted him. Had instinctively trusted him this entire, crazy day. He hadn't blinked once at coming to her aid despite what she'd thrown at him. Yes, he wanted the ring, but there was more to it than that. He *cared* despite his tough exterior.

"I don't know what to say," she said finally. "You're an honorable man, Nate Brunswick. *Grazie.*"

"Not so honorable, Mina." A dark glitter entered his eyes. "You called me improper not so long ago. I can be that and more. I am a hard, ruthless businessman who does what it takes to make money. I will turn a hotel over in the flash of an eye if I don't see the flesh on the bones I envisioned when I bought it. I will enjoy a woman one night and send her packing the next when I get bored of her company. Know what you're getting into with me if you accept this. You will learn the dog-eat-dog approach to life, *not* the civilized one."

Why did something that was intended to be a warning send a curious shudder through her? Mina drew the wrap closer around her shoulders, her gaze tangling with Nate's.

The glitter in his eyes stoked to a hot, velvet shimmer as he took a step forward and ran a finger along the line of her jaw. "Rule number one of this new arrangement, should you so choose to accept it, is to not look at me like that, *wife*. If we do this, we keep things strictly business so both of us walk away after the year with exactly what we want."

Her gaze fell away from his, her blood hot and thick in her veins. "You're misinterpreting me."

"No, I'm not." He brought his mouth to her ear, his warm breath caressing her cheek. "I have a hell of a lot more experience than you do, Mina. I can recognize the signs. They were loud and clear in my hotel room that day and they're loud and clear now."

She took a deep, shuddering breath. To protest further would be futile when her skin felt like it was on fire, her knees like jelly. He watched her like a cat played with a mouse, all powerful and utterly sure of himself. "The only thing that would be more of a disaster than this day's already been," he drawled finally, apparently ready to have mercy on her, "would be for us to end up in bed together. So a partnership it is, Mina." He lifted his glass. "What do you say?"

She seized hold of her senses. "So we have a marriage in name only and a business partnership. How are we positioning the marriage to others?"

"As if it's a real marriage." He shrugged. "I see no harm in that and there is the Silvio factor."

"And what about—" A wave of heat sped to her cheeks. "I mean, if we're not sleeping together, how will you— you know…?"

A wicked smile curved his mouth. "*Relieve myself?* There are ways. And if I choose to indulge, I'll do it discreetly."

Right. She dug her teeth into her bottom lip. Seized

the moment. "Yes," she said, lifting her glass. "*Grazie*, Nate. I accept."

Her dark and apparently not so honorable husband pointed his glass at her. "Then tomorrow we begin. Get some good sleep tonight, Mina. You're going to need it for the ride I'm going to take you on."

CHAPTER FIVE

MINA DIDN'T SLEEP WELL. For hours she'd lain awake, terrified that despite Nate's assurances she was safe, Silvio would come after her. That perhaps his declaration it was over between them had just been to lull Nate into a false sense of complacency before he came after her to seek revenge.

"Refuse me again and you'll discover the depths to which my anger can sink. I will not tolerate you repeating any of your silly jitters to anyone, Mina."

She had trumped that. She had married another man!

She had little time to nurse her coffee over breakfast with Nate, however, her brain barely awake when he hit her with his Business Rule Number One. "You only get one chance to make a first impression. *Looking* the part is the first step to realizing the role."

She couldn't disagree with that, because clad in a silver-gray suit with an ice-blue tie, handmade Italian shoes gleaming on his feet, Nate looked every bit the power broker that he was. So off she went with Susana, the manager of the hotel's boutique, to outfit herself with a casual and business wardrobe.

Susana had opened the boutique early just for them. She installed Mina in a chair in the fitting area with a tablet and coffee while she and an assistant gathered clothes. Mina used the time to research her enigmatic husband, hoping for some clues as to what made him tick.

It turned out to be a rather useless activity, because none of the business profiles she pulled up on Nate delved into anything more personal than she already knew. The grandson of legendary shipping tycoon Giovanni Di Sione, he had worked his way up the ranks of Di Sione Shipping, eventually running various overseas branches of the company before leaving to start Brunswick Developments, his multibillion-dollar real-estate development firm.

> *A self-made man who has used his uncanny business acumen, aggressive street smarts and brutal negotiating tactics to land marquee deals that put him on the* Forbes *billionaires list at age thirty-four.*

Giving in to an urge she couldn't suppress, she typed in her husband's name plus the word *woman*. A slew of photos came up. True to his word, the majority of his dates at the high-society events he frequented were brunettes, with a few blondes of late. All stunning. All vastly more sophisticated than her.

"Ready?" Susana bustled into the changing area with another armful of clothes. Mina put the tablet down and got to her feet to take half the pile.

"Can I give you some advice?" the other woman said, glancing down at the tablet. "Don't do that. A man like Nate is going to have a past. You'll only torture yourself."

Heat scored her cheeks. "I will say congratulations on doing the impossible," continued Susana as she hung up the suits. "Mingmei will undoubtedly be wondering how you did it."

"Mingmei?"

"The manager of our Hong Kong hotel. Better you

know about *that* one before you come face-to-face with her. Mingmei and Nate had an affair before she came to work for him."

"How long ago was that?"

"Three years ago. Clearly it ended well because he hired her, but Mingmei—"

"—still desires Nate."

"Perhaps." Susana handed her a cream-colored suit. "How did you and Nate meet?"

Mina's brain worked furiously. "We met at the hotel in Sicily where I worked. In the bar. It was…love at first sight."

Susana smiled. "*That* I would have liked to have seen. It would have been entertaining to watch the Ice Man fall."

Mina diverted the conversation to clothes after that before she stumbled over another answer. Three hours of endless fittings later, she walked out of the boutique the owner of a stylish, power-based wardrobe with some pretty things for the evening. "You'll need it," Susana had advised. "Nate's social calendar is daunting."

Her phone rang as she walked back across the courtyard. She glanced at the screen, her stomach doing a slow churn. *Her mother.* Maybe it was better to get it out of the way.

She sat on a bench and took the call. "*Ciao*, Mamma."

There was silence on the other end of the line. Then, *"Che pensi che stai facendo,* Mina*?"* *What do you think you're doing?*

Her cheeks fired, her fingers trembling around the phone. "I couldn't marry Silvio, Mamma. I told you that but you wouldn't listen."

"So you disgraced your fiancé, this *family,* in front of the entire city?"

She bit her lip. "He hit me. I can't live with a man like that."

"And you expect your American tycoon to be any different? Men are all the same. They want a beautiful wife on their arm who obeys them, Mina. Who *uncomplicates* their life. Start disagreeing with your American after the rosy glow is over and see how he acts."

"Nate would never hit me."

A pause. "Where are you now?"

She chewed hard on her lip.

Her mother made a strangled sound. "What will you do? Go live with him in America? You will surely have to now, because your reputation is in tatters. This *family's* reputation is in tatters."

A lump formed in her throat. She didn't even know where Nate lived. Only that it was in New York.

"Mi dispiace," she murmured huskily. "You left me no choice, Mamma."

"You disappoint me, Mina."

What was new about that? She had always disappointed her mother. Had never understood why when she'd done everything asked of her. Had attained top grades at school, had dated her endless contingent of bachelors, and still been found lacking.

"What about our plan? To sell the ring?"

Her heart sank. There it was. What her mother truly cared about. "It hasn't changed. I will sell the ring and pay off our debts. But as I'm sure Pasquale told you, I can't do that for a year."

"Perhaps," her mother said deliberately, "your husband could help."

She closed her eyes. "I won't ask that of him, Mamma."

There was silence on the other end of the line. There would be no inquiry as to how she was. Whether she was happy. None of that mattered to her mother. Had never. "I have to go," she said thickly.

"Mina—"

She ended the call. A deep, all-encompassing throb moved through her. Made it hard to breathe. She'd gotten past her naïveté about her mother a long time ago. It was the depth to which she didn't care that shocked her now.

She was alone in this world. Utterly alone. Her life would have to be shaped by her and her alone.

Nate had just finished reviewing the financials for the Emelia when Mina walked through the door in a charcoal-gray suit, her traffic-stopping legs clad in a pair of finely made Italian heels.

If he'd thought a suit would help dull his attraction to her he had been entirely wrong. The suit was conservative, covered all the requisite parts adequately; it was what was under it that was unavoidable. The fitted jacket highlighted her tiny waist and taut high breasts, the knee-length pencil skirt skimmed generous hips.

A power suit to be sure, but on his wife it swayed all the power in favor of her innate sensuality.

He brought his gaze back up to her face. Studied the pallor that blanched her honey-colored skin. "What's wrong? Did Silvio contact you?"

She set down the bag she was holding and slid off her shoes. "No—it's—I'm fine."

"You were having nightmares about it last night. You're not fine."

A flush filled her cheeks. "I woke you?"

"I was still working. Mina, I promised to protect you and I will. You don't need to worry about him."

"I know. I do. It's just—sometimes my imagination gets the better of me." She raked her hair out of her face.

"That's not why I'm upset. My mother called. She was furious. Not that I hadn't expected that. My reputation is in tatters. Also not surprising."

"Then why the lost look? What did she say to you?"

She shook her head. "You are my boss now. I should keep this professional."

He gave her a wry look. "We are also married. I think we have a rather unique relationship. What did she say?"

She exhaled. "She wasn't worried about me. She didn't ask if I was okay. She didn't care if I was happy with you. She said I'd disappointed her."

He lifted a brow. "For running away from a monster to marry a man who professes to love you and will keep you safe? For delivering the exact same result in the sale of the ring? What kind of a mother is she?"

She shook her head. "She never wanted children. My father did. I was always with my nanny, Camilla. As soon as my father died, she sent me off to boarding school in France, as if she couldn't wait to get rid of me. I always came home with good grades, top of my class, but it seemed inconsequential to her. She just didn't care."

"How old were you when your father died?"

"Eight."

The image of a tiny Mina being sent off to school at such a young age pulled at his heartstrings. "You've never talked to her about it? Asked her why?"

She lifted a shoulder. "My *mamma*—she is cold. It's her way. I told myself to let it go. To not wish for the impossible. But sometimes I do. I wish I knew what she finds so...*lacking* in me so I can fix it."

He knew how that felt. To always wonder what it was about you that was so defective your own father wanted nothing to do with you. That he could turn his back on his own flesh and blood and slam a door in your face when you had come to beg for assistance. To deny you even existed. But he knew it was a fruitless pursuit. A soul-destroying pursuit.

"It's better not to wonder," he told Mina roughly, "to look for that flaw in yourself you think they see in you. Because it's not you, it's her. She should have been a proper mother to you and she wasn't. That's her cross to bear, not yours. Don't waste your life trying to figure out something you'll likely never get an answer to."

She blinked. "Are you talking about your father?"

He ignored that. "Learn how to stand on your own two feet. How to exist without her approval. It will be the most empowering thing you can ever do."

She nodded, but hurt still throbbed in her eyes.

He sighed. "What?"

"She's all I have."

His heart squeezed. "You're better off without her. That's not how a true parent acts."

Her mouth compressed. Turning on her heel, she walked into her bedroom, came back and handed him the massive diamond solitaire Silvio had given her. "I need to give this back."

He took the small fortune out of her hands. "I'll have it sent to him. Speaking of which, we'll need to get you a rock for show."

"It's not necessary."

"You're my wife, Mina, it is. People will be looking."

She sat down on the sofa and poured herself a cup of coffee. "Susana asked me how we met. I was unprepared for the question. I told her we met in the bar at the Giarruso. It was the first response that came to me."

His mouth curved. "That I picked you, extraordinarily innocent Mina, up in a hotel bar after work?" He sat down on the sofa opposite her. "Seems a stretch but we'll go with it."

"I should know a few pertinent details about you if we're to carry this off. It was awkward with Susana."

He lifted a brow. "Such as?"

"Where do you live in New York?"

"I have a penthouse off Central Park in the heart of Manhattan. It's not as beautiful as Sicily, but I think you'll enjoy the energy of the city."

"You said we're not going back to New York right away?"

"We have week-long stops in Hong Kong and the Maldives after Capri, then we head home."

She blinked at the blindingly fast pace of her new life. "Brothers or sisters?"

"I have seven half siblings from my father's marriage."

"Are you close to them?"

What to say? That he and his brothers and sisters were perhaps the most dysfunctional clan on the planet? That there was not only a deep wedge between himself and Alex, but a distance he kept with all of them because every single one of them was a bit broken from their past and it was easier not to open up old wounds?

"I'm not sure I'd characterize it as close," he said finally, "but we do interact from time to time."

"I know you run and like the opera, but do you have any other hobbies? Other leisure activities I should know of that are a passion?"

His mouth twisted. "Work is my passion. I work fourteen-…fifteen-hour days, Mina. Not much time for anything else. Which," he suggested, "is what we should focus on now. Unless you have more questions?"

She shook her head. "That will do for now."

He picked up the report on the Emelia's financials and

handed it to her. "Review this. We'll talk it over after you've had a chance to read it, but first I want to go over the ground rules of how we'll work together."

She crossed her legs primly and sat back to listen.

"First of all," he said, "you are here to learn. So learn. The most valuable thing you can do over the next year is to sit back and listen, soak up everything that's being said, conduct your own analysis, and afterward, when it's just the two of us, you can ask any questions you may have.

"Secondly, I want you to watch the people in this meeting or any meeting we're in. Watch their body language, look for their nonverbal cues, because they are often more telling than what is coming out of their mouth. Always look for an angle, because *everyone* has an angle in business, an agenda they're walking into the room with. Understanding these goals and different agendas is a crucial skill in any negotiation—antagonistic or friendly."

"I've been told my father was brilliant with people." A proud light entered Mina's eyes. "He once solved a strike that had been going on for weeks at one of our plants by walking into the picket lines and hashing out a deal with the workers."

"Which translates into my third rule," said Nate. "I want you to be a problem solver. Come to me with a solution, not an issue."

She nodded. *"Bene."*

"That's it for now." He nodded toward the report. "Profits have been sagging over the past year at the Emelia. We need to light a fire under things. See what you think."

The meeting with Giorgio and the Emelia management team went worse than Nate had expected. Complacency had set in at the hotel and it seemed his general manager had no plan how to lift sagging profits because he didn't think he *had* a problem.

"The market is down, Nate," Giorgio soothed in that smooth-as-silk voice of his. "We're doing everything we can to entice new customers to the hotel, but we can't *manufacture* them."

Nate directed a look at Mina. "Was the Giarruso's occupancy rate down this year?"

She frowned. "Not much. I think the manager said five percent."

"And you are down fifteen percent," Nate said to Giorgio.

Giorgio put his hand on Mina's arm as if she were a child in need of correction. "It must have been more than five percent. Perhaps you have the numbers wrong."

"No," said Mina. "It was nowhere near fifteen percent."

Giorgio sat back and crossed his arms over his chest. "What do you propose I do? Alter the economies of the western world? Manipulate the markets? We've upped the sales and marketing budgets. The effort is there, Nate."

"The effort is *ineffective*."

Giorgio's face reddened. Silence fell at the table.

"What about repeat guests?" Mina interjected. "Your number is way down. What if you—"

Nate shot her a withering look. She sat back in her chair and closed her mouth.

"What is your plan of attack for them?" Nate asked Giorgio.

"We've done a whole discounted rate campaign. It isn't moving rooms."

"Then it isn't compelling enough."

Giorgio looked at Mina. "What were you going to suggest?"

Nate nodded tightly at her to go ahead.

"I was thinking of a 'remember the memories' type campaign," Mina said. "I was here in Capri on holidays with my family years ago. When we arrived it brought back such great memories. So perhaps something more emotion based than financial."

Giorgio steepled his hands together. "I like it."

Nate liked it, too, but wished the idea had come from his manager and not his protégée. He continued to grill his top man until the end of the three-hour meeting, then mercifully ended it, ushering Mina up to their suite in tight-lipped silence.

"I know," Mina said in a preemptive strike, the minute the door closed behind them, "I wasn't supposed to talk. It's just it was getting *painful* and I had an idea."

"Painful is *good*. Discomfort shakes people up and pushes them outside of their comfort zone. Which, quite frankly, Giorgio needs desperately right now or he will be out of a job."

Her eyes widened, color washing her cheeks. "I thought by offering up an idea, Giorgio might build on it."

"And by doing so you *undermined* my attempt to teach him a lesson. After I told you not to talk." Nate pinned his gaze on her. "When I put someone in the hot seat I'm doing it for a reason, Mina. So keep your mouth *shut*."

She took a step back. "*Mi dispiace.* I—I didn't realize that's what you were doing. It won't happen again."

"No, it won't," he agreed, his voice sharp as a knife. "Because you will stick to my rules or you won't play at all."

She nodded rapidly, pupils as big as saucers, hands clenched by her sides. He did a double take. *She was afraid of him?*

Then he remembered what she'd just gone through... How intimidating he must look to her at twice her size towering over her. Furious. Mina wasn't one of his toughened, worldly employees used to his rants. She was a baby chick who'd just taken fledgling steps out of the nest.

He shoved his hands in his pockets and blew out a breath. "Business isn't the glorified interaction of a tea party, where everyone plays nice and leaves with a smile on their face. It's a ferociously competitive playground where only the strongest survive. I could leave you in a back office, give you research work and not let you experience what it's really like, but that's no way to learn. So find yourself a thick skin, Mina. Learn to be a gladiator, because people's feelings don't matter in this game."

A determined glint entered her eyes as the fear faded from her face. "I can and I will, Nate. I apologize again. I did not mean to undermine your authority."

"Fine." He nodded. "Go get changed for the party."

She started toward her room.

"Mina?"

She turned around. "I thought your idea about the repeat guests was right on the money. Emotional affinity is the reason people will spend money in a downturn. I'm going to direct Giorgio to investigate with his marketing team."

Her face brightened. It was like the sun had come out. "*Grazie*, Nate."

His lips curved. "We'll see if you're still saying that after a month with me."

CHAPTER SIX

"WILL THIS DO?"

Nate shifted his gaze from the smartphone he'd been perusing to the spectacular set of legs in front of him. Moved up past rounded hips outlined in a shimmering midnight blue fabric to a modestly covered but spectacularly presented cleavage. The term *less is more* came to mind. With Mina less was always more. A man could be forgiven for concluding she was best left entirely unclothed for his undeniable pleasure.

And yet Mina, it seemed, had no idea of just how stunning she was, a fact that only increased her appeal. Lip caught between her teeth, a finger twirling a curl around it, her gaze on his for approval, it amused him to think of what her response would have been had he suggested what would have been on his mind had she been his wife in more than name.

Her eyes on his in the ornate mirror on the wall, her palms flat on the antique table in front of it, her dress around her waist as he put that *just taken* glow in her cheeks that marked her his.

Mina's eyes widened. Her lashes came down to fan her cheeks.

"You look stunning," he said, before he shocked her from here to New York. "The color suits you."

"Grazie." She smoothed the dress over her hips. "So tell me the goal for the evening."

She was learning. "The Grand Hotel chain," he said, tucking his smartphone into the pocket of his jacket, "has partnered with Hollywood legends Antonio Davis and Franco Messini on a series of nightclubs located in select properties around the world—London, LA, Capri and New York. Curious—the nightclub brand—reflects the exclusive, adventurous cross section of clientele who frequent it and the unique experiences the nightclub offers."

"I know Antonio Davis," Mina said, her eyes shining. "He's a legend. I love his movies."

"He's also a shrewd businessman. Brilliant at extending his brand to other realms. Tonight," he said, buttoning his jacket, "is the opening night for Curious in Capri. Antonio and Franco have flown their entourages in for the event, the goal to stir up excitement for the launch."

"And what will be the unique experience tonight, then?"

"It's an Arabian Nights theme. Exotic, sensual. All the usual decor. But there will also be a tattoo artist who is doing henna tattoos. It's a unique branding opportunity guests will show off after the event, keeping the buzz going."

"Henna tattoos are all the rage in the magazines."

"I think they look very sexy on a woman." He arched a brow at her. "Have you tried?"

"I don't think it's really me."

"You never know until you try." The wicked note to his voice brought a pretty pink flush to her cheeks. "Antonio's entourage is fine to mingle with, by the way. Franco's can be questionable. Steer clear of them."

She nodded, a flicker of something he couldn't read in her eyes.

"What?"

"You think I'm hopelessly naive."

His mouth tipped up at one corner. "Aren't you?"

She stared at him for a long moment, the flush in her cheeks increasing, then bent to retrieve her wrap from a chair. "Who am I supposed to be this evening? Your protégée or your pretend wife?"

"My jaw-droppingly beautiful wife." He swiped the wrap from her and draped it around her shoulders, his fingertips brushing against her enticing golden skin. "The big bad wolves are coming out to play tonight, Mina. Thus the warning."

She lifted her chin. "I've attended more society parties than I'd care to count. I'll be fine."

"Not like this one."

Her gaze lowered to his hands, still resting on her bare shoulders, as if she wondered why they were still there. He wondered, too. Wondered why every excuse to touch her was irresistible.

Perhaps the wolves were inside, too…

His hands slid from her shoulders. "Tonight will be a good dry run for you for New York. The news that we're married will filter back to the press. They'll be all over us for a bit, I expect."

An apprehensive look entered her beautiful brown eyes. He pressed his palm to her back and propelled her to the door. "You're a gladiator, remember? This is a piece of cake."

The Curious party, held in the Emelia's sleek outdoor lounge that overlooked the bay, was in full swing when they arrived. To the outward eye it looked as if it had been flawlessly executed by Giorgio's staff. Arabian Nights–style tents in vibrant jeweled colors blanketed the furniture-strewn space, varying in size and complexity. Gauzy green and purple curtains, both drawn and open, hinted at two degrees of interaction, both social and seductively intimate.

The interior of the tents was over-the-top fantasy, those same jeweled tones reflected in the pillows and throws that covered the low-slung divans and rich tapestries. Copious amounts of candles, ornate lamps, bejeweled belly dancers giving partygoers seductive performances and the tattoo artists completed the ambience. It was as if you'd just made your way through the desert and stumbled upon an oasis filled with the most beautiful people on earth.

Jewels were abundant, paid escorts, too, accompanying the rich men who required a beautiful woman by their side.

"Paid escorts?" Mina didn't seem to get the concept. "You mean *prostitutes*?"

"I doubt they would appreciate that terminology," he drawled. "I expect some will provide recreational activity and some are here for appearances only."

"Oh." She shut up after that as he networked his way through the space with ruthless efficiency. He wasn't a natural-born socializer. It was a means to an end, a necessary requirement of the job. His wife, on the other hand, was in her element, circulating with an effortless poise, murmuring polite phrases in that sexy Italian lilt of hers, adjusting to the interests and personality of everyone that she met on the fly to put them perfectly at ease. He found himself captivated by her charm, by the chameleon that she was, his attention focused on her with an unwavering fascination that was a new experience for him.

Antonio Davis separated himself from the crowd when he saw them, drawing his longtime Hollywood starlet of a girlfriend, Evangelina, toward them. Antonio wrapped an arm around Nate and gave him a slap on the back. "Heard you were here. Also heard you were *married* to this stunning creature. What gives? No invitation?"

"We married rather…impulsively yesterday or you most certainly would have been invited." Nate nodded at Mina. "Mina meet Antonio Davis and his other half, Evangelina Cabriera."

Antonio gave Mina a kiss on both cheeks as did Evangelina. Mina gave the actor a shy look. "I love your films. I learned to speak English with your movies."

The aging Hollywood heartthrob, whose outward cool masked the intensely ambitious, genuinely likeable guy he was inside, smiled. "So one of your first phrases was, 'Shoot 'em up, Charlie'?"

"I think it was actually, 'I'm no hero, kid. I'm just a man with a good horse and impeccable timing.'"

Antonio threw back his head, a deep booming laugh escaping him. The cowboy lingo delivered in Mina's sexy Italian accent didn't quite have the same ring to it. "Liked Carson, did you?"

"Loved him. It was so fun watching him discover Charlie was a girl."

"Fun role to play." Antonio lifted a brow at Nate. "Seen Franco?"

"Not yet."

Antonio grimaced. "He's been *otherwise occupied*."

Nate didn't want to know what that might be. Hollywood's resident bad boy didn't seem to recognize he was far past the age where he should be doing all-nighters with copious amounts of illegal drugs. He dealt with Antonio and left Franco out of it and they ran a squeaky clean business together.

"Any interest in joining Evangelina for a tattoo?" Antonio asked Mina. "She's dying to have one and I have a bit of business I wanted to discuss with Nate."

Mina looked to Nate for confirmation. He gave her

a challenging glance that said, *Expand your horizons.* Mina's chin lifted. "I'd love to."

Antonio filled him in on the new business idea he had for a stand-alone series of nightclubs. Nate liked it immediately. Liked even more that Franco was not involved. "Send the proposal over."

"You got it." The actor smiled and waved at someone. "Hey, there's a financier here you should meet."

He scanned the crowd for Mina. She and Evangelina were in the middle of Franco's crowd. His gaze narrowed on Franco in a flashy white suit, his megawatt predatory smile fixed firmly on Mina.

"She's a big girl," Antonio said, sliding an arm around his shoulders. "She'll be fine."

Mina was trying to relax and enjoy herself, she really was. But this party was like nothing she'd ever experienced before. Evangelina was throwing back drinks twice as fast as she was and introducing her around to famous actors, actresses and producers at such a pace her head spun. She was afraid she was going to insult somebody by not remembering them and the men seemed inordinately *friendly*, their admiring eyes seeming to linger just a bit too long.

The buzzing atmosphere only heightened the chaotic feeling inside of her the last twenty-four hours had induced. Walking away from her home, that awful phone call with her mother this afternoon, Nate's anger at her for overstepping her bounds in that meeting. She would have preferred to be curled up in their suite watching one of Antonio's Westerns.

"Hey, beautiful." Franco Messini took advantage of a break in Evangelina's watch over her to grab her hand and lead her to the bar.

"I don't really need another glass of wine."

"Can't leave my lovely guest empty-handed," Franco purred, raising his hand to signal the bartender. Securing them two glasses of champagne, he directed her away from the crowd at the bar. "I heard you say you were a fan of Sybil Atkinson. I just saw her. Let me introduce you to her."

Mina thought that was a fine idea. The less interaction she had with Franco alone, the better.

He led her through the crowd toward one of the tents. She followed him inside the small, intimate space with its seductive dim lighting. It was empty.

"I guess she moved on," she said lightly. "I really should get back to my husband. He's likely looking for me."

"He should be keeping closer tabs on you." Franco moved closer, his bulky body blocking out the light. The suspicious shimmer in his blue eyes sent a frisson of unease through her. She wondered if he'd been indulging in more than just alcohol. "You're the most beautiful woman at this party, Mina."

She licked dry lips as he continued to move closer. "That's very nice of you to say. But I really think I should get back to Nate."

"In a minute." Franco ran a finger down the bare skin of her upper arm. "It isn't a crime to look at another man's wife, is it?"

But he was *touching* her. She took a step backward, the unsettled feeling inside of her unraveling into alarm. Her palms sweaty, pulse racing in her throat, she swallowed hard. "I'd like to get back to the others."

"Don't look so threatened." Franco's confident, aggressive gaze mocked her as he closed the space between them again. "You haven't given me the time of day since we met.

I just want to get to know you better. You are my business partner's wife, after all."

"I don't think that's a good idea. My husband—he—he's the jealous sort."

The actor lifted a hand and ran a finger down her cheek. "Maybe he should learn to share… Nate's always been a smug bastard. Too much so for my taste."

Her pulse pounded harder, her palms growing ice cold now. She darted a glance at the exit, blocked by Franco's big body. Told herself to stay calm. But an image of Silvio manacling her wrist, kissing her, the crack of his hand snapping her head sideways, sent her heart slamming against her chest.

Franco was so much bigger than her.

The air in the tent seemed to dissolve. Her breath came faster, tighter, intensifying the cloudy feeling in her head.

"Please—" she murmured in a broken tone.

Franco dragged his thumb across the edge of her jaw. "Please what?"

Please let me go.

"You'd best be taking your hands off my wife."

Nate's voice, low and tight, cut through the air. Franco turned, revealing her husband silhouetted in the light, standing just inside the entrance to the tent. His gaze was trained on the actor, a quiet, white-hot fury on his face.

Franco eyed Nate. He was equally as tall as the actor, but less bulky, with more lean-packed muscle. Ferociously intimidating in the way he carried it. Franco registered it, too, apparently, for he stepped back, hands raised. "Easy, Brunswick. We were just talking."

"Which explains why my wife looks petrified." Nate walked to Mina and slid an arm around her. She leaned into him, her knees going weak.

"You try my patience, Franco." Nate fixed his gaze on

the actor. "Clean up your act or I will end this partnership, no matter how much I like Antonio."

Franco scowled. "You have far too much invested to do that."

"*Watch me.* Get lost, Messini. You ever come within ten feet of my wife again and I will take you apart."

Franco's belligerent gaze tangled with Nate's. For a heart-stopping minute she wasn't sure which way it was going to go. Then Franco turned on his heel and left.

Mina sagged with relief. Nate turned her around, keeping his arm banded around her waist. "What happened?"

She shook her head. "Nothing—he—I should never have allowed him to bring me here. He said he was going to introduce me to Sybil Atkinson, but when we arrived, there was no one here."

His mouth flattened. "I told you not to mess with Franco or his crowd."

"I wasn't. I was avoiding him. Then Evangelina went off to talk to someone and he just swooped in."

"What did he say to you?"

She frowned. "Something just seemed *off* in the way he was looking at me. I told him I wanted to go, but he wouldn't let me… He started touching me. He said it wasn't a crime to look at another man's wife. That—" her chin dipped "—you were a smug bastard who should learn to share."

Black heat shimmered in his eyes. "He said *that*?"

"*Sì.*" Her stomach clenched at the sudden stillness in his tall, lean body. "I'm sure it was all, what do you Americans call it? *Bravado?*" she said hurriedly. "That I was overreacting. I—I saw Silvio in my head. I went back to the night he hit me and I froze. I told myself to walk away, to come find you, but my legs wouldn't work."

The aggression in his gaze softened. "It's common for

a person put into a threatening situation to freeze. To shut down." He shook his head. "It's my fault. I should never have left you alone with this crowd."

He wrapped his fingers around hers. "Let's go."

She followed him out of the tent. Balked when he headed toward the exit. "I don't want to ruin your evening. I've already caused enough problems between you and Franco."

"Franco and I already had issues. And *you* did not cause that scene. Franco did." He put a hand to her back and propelled her through the crowd. "I was coming to find you to leave."

The lights of Capri glimmered around them as they rode the glass elevator up to their penthouse suite. She started to feel silly as she studied Nate's grim face. She had totally overreacted. Franco hadn't really been a threat. He'd been trying to push Nate's buttons. *Hers.* And she had let him.

Nate was probably wondering what in *Dio*'s name he'd signed on for with her.

"You okay?"

She sighed. "I feel like you're always rescuing me. You must think I'm some kind of damsel in distress who can't take care of herself."

He shook his head. "This was my fault tonight, Mina."

"No. It's just—" She bit her lip. "I'm not normally like this."

"What are you normally like?"

She lifted a shoulder. "Self-sufficient. Strong. I was eight when I was sent to that boarding school in France. I didn't speak the language. I was brutally lonely. I learned to be a survivor."

"You are," he pointed out. "You could have allowed yourself to be a victim with Silvio. You could have married him and suffered a lifetime of abuse. But you didn't. That took guts."

She nodded. It's just that she hated that person she'd been tonight. Hated *everything* being so out of her control. That she couldn't seem to trust her instincts anymore.

"You've had your life turned upside down over the past forty-eight hours, Mina." Nate rested his gaze on her face. "Cut yourself some slack. You need to honor your fear as well as put it behind you when you're ready."

He was right. She knew that.

"Have you ever considered taking martial arts?"

She frowned. "I'm not sure it's my thing."

"You should consider it. It's very empowering for a woman to learn how to defend herself."

"Do you do it?"

He nodded. "Karate."

"How good are you?"

"A black belt. But you don't have to be skilled to defend yourself. You just need to know the basics."

"That's very impressive," she told him as he guided her off the elevator and into the penthouse. *Also sexy.*

He undid his jacket and shrugged it off. "I grew up in a rough neighborhood. I needed to protect myself. There were two ways to do that—with weapons or as your own personal weapon. I eventually chose karate."

"Eventually?"

His dark lashes fanned down over his cheeks. "I had a few iffy years before I made that choice."

She absorbed that piece of new information. She'd imagined being a Di Sione or half of one would have meant being brought up in luxury. The fact that he hadn't had an entitled upbringing seemed to better reflect the man. The uncivilized edge beneath the veneer Franco had taken one look at tonight and walked away from.

He threw her a glance as he loosened his tie and undid

the top couple of buttons of his shirt. "So? I could sign you up for some classes at my gym in New York."

"I don't know," she said dubiously. "I'm not a very physical person."

"You're a gladiator, remember?"

Not much of one tonight.

"I can show you how you would have gotten out of that situation with Silvio if that would make you feel better."

Her brow creased. "How? He's far bigger than me."

"If you knew self-defense, you could have. Show me what happened that night. I'll teach you a couple of simple self-defense techniques."

"Now?"

He gave her an amused look. "Now."

She chewed on her lip. The desire to take back control, to wipe the fear from her head, was too strong to resist. "*Sì.* Please show me."

He nodded. "Tell me what happened that night."

"We were in my mother's salon. I had just poured Silvio a drink. He was angry with me for telling him I had cold feet about the marriage. He—he grabbed my wrist and pulled me toward him and started kissing me. I was... surprised. He hadn't been aggressive with me before. The kiss—it started to get...*intimo.*" Her gaze dropped away from his. "I didn't like it so I tried to push him away, but he wouldn't let me go. Then he hit me across the face."

Nate stepped toward her. "Show me how close you were to him."

She stared at him. "What?"

"I need to know how far apart you were. How much room you had to maneuver. That determines what self-defense techniques you use."

"Oh." She thought back. "We were very close."

"Like this?" He took her wrist and pulled her to him.

The brush of his tall strong body against hers sent heat rushing to her cheeks. Every nerve ending in her body flickered to life, making her so utterly aware of him she could hardly look at him.

"Maybe this isn't such a good idea," she murmured.

"*Show me*, Mina."

"We were closer than this."

"How close?"

She stepped into him until every centimeter of their bodies were touching from chest to knee. Her breasts brushed against his chest, her hips rested in the cradle of his, and *Dio mio*, this was not good. He was too overwhelmingly male. And she was having the opposite reaction to him than she'd had to Silvio.

"Where were his arms?"

"One was on my waist—well lower," she corrected hesitantly. "The other, I don't remember."

Nate slid his arm around her waist. "We'll go with this. This about right the way we're standing?"

"*Sì.*"

He lowered his head and brought his mouth to within a centimeter of hers.

Her heart stuttered. "What are you doing?"

"Push me away."

Right. Dannazione, Mina—focus. She lifted her hand and pushed hard against his shoulder. It was like trying to move a brick wall.

"When you are this close," he told her, "you lose power. You have no room to maneuver. You either have to make space so you can attack him, which you aren't going to be able to do in this situation, or go for the vulnerable points."

"Vulnerable points?"

"My groin," he said pointedly. "Try bringing your knee up hard and fast."

"*No.*"

"You're a gladiator."

She gritted her teeth and tried to lift her leg. She got exactly nowhere.

"Not enough room, right?"

She shook her head.

"What are my other vulnerable points?"

"Your face?"

"Be more specific."

"Your eyes?"

"And what else?"

"Your nose?"

"Yes, but the throat is better. A quick, hard strike against the throat—the Adam's apple of a man in particular—is perfect. It shocks me enough to let you go. Gouging at the eyes is also good. Your goal is to stun me long enough to get away."

She nodded.

"Let's try it from the beginning."

"The beginning?"

"You need to put yourself back in the scenario. Imagine it's happening, remember the sequence and go for one of my vulnerable points. I won't know which way you're going to go, which gives you the element of surprise that you would have in that situation."

She pressed her lips together. "Okay."

He slid an arm around her waist and tugged her close. "Ready?"

"*Sì.*"

He brought his mouth down to hers, and this time he kissed her. Unlike the first kiss he'd given her in front of the registrar, this one was unavoidable, *dominant*, meant to simulate the one Silvio had given her. She trusted Nate. She did. Her heart pounded, anyway, at how helpless she felt. How much stronger he was. When he took the kiss deeper, made a claim on her she wasn't willing to submit to, she stiffened, gathered her strength and slammed her right hand hard in his throat.

Nate released her, his hands lifting to his throat. "Nice job," he rasped, half coughing, half speaking. "I expected you to go for the eyes."

Mina stared at him, hands clenched by her sides, adrenaline racing through her. "Are you okay?"

"Fine." His gaze narrowed. "The kiss was necessary, Mina. It had to be real. To evoke the violent reaction it did in you so you could use your power."

She nodded.

"And what did you do?"

"I got away."

"What would you have done next?"

"Run."

"Where?"

"Out the front door. The house was empty."

"Exactly," he said. "Move toward people. Help."

She unclenched her fists. Took a deep breath as she attempted to calm her body down.

"You've just taken back your power, Mina." Nate stepped toward her. "I *knew* the blow was coming and you still incapacitated me long enough for you to get away."

She nodded. Instructed her pounding heart to relax because this was Nate in front of her, not Silvio.

"If you have that power," he said, "you can choose who you trust. You can choose what situations you put yourself in. Not all men are violent. Some would only want to kiss you for pleasure—yours and their own."

She knew that. But the way she'd felt when Nate had just kissed her...

"What?"

She put a hand to her heart. "This *panic*. I know I can trust you and still I felt terrified."

"Like I said. Give yourself some time."

She forced a smile. "You're right. I just hate giving him that power over me."

He was silent for a long moment. "Then don't."

She blinked. *"Scusi?"*

"You trust me?"

She nodded.

"Then get back on the wagon." He took another step toward her, stopping just short of her personal space. "We're attracted to each other, Mina. Intensely attracted to each other. But I am not Silvio. I can kiss a woman and walk away, no matter how hot and bothered I am, regardless of where my emotions lie, because I am in control of them. I would never hurt a woman. So," he said deliberately, "kiss me right now. Replace that image of what happened with Silvio with a positive experience."

She gaped at him. "We can't do that. We made a rule."

"So we break it for one kiss. The longer you let this eat away at you, the harder it's going to be to leave behind."

She had a feeling that was true. She didn't want to carry this victim mentality with her. Didn't want to give it a chance to take hold. Because this Mina Mastrantino she'd been tonight was not the real Mina. The Mina who had chased away her childish ghosts in boarding school because there'd been no one else to do it for her. The Mina who'd learned to survive without love when it seemed like everyone around her had it but her, by telling herself someday she would have it, too. The Mina who was stronger than this.

"Sì," she said. "Let's do it."

"Come here."

For a brief, heart-stopping moment, Mina thought she

might actually be insane. Because this man was dangerous. Beautifully, undeniably, self-admittedly dangerous.
Yet, she conceded, she trusted him implicitly.

He was letting her take control. He wouldn't make the
first move.

She took a step forward, then another, until she was almost touching him. There she stopped, her innate shyness
kicking in. Nate's gaze caught hers, pulled her in. She took
the last step forward, sucking in a breath as he reached
out, curved a hand around her waist and brought her to
him in a loose hold that continued to give her every option.

She thought he would lean down and kiss her then. Instead, he focused on her lips, as if they were the most fascinating thing in the world. As if he had all the *time* in the
world. Her breathing quickened, anticipation firing her
blood. He brought his mouth down to hers without touching. Their breath mingled first, then the lush surfaces of
their mouths. *Oh, mio Dio.* She was practically panting by
the time he angled his head and took her mouth.

He brought his fingers up to capture her jaw, lightly, as
if she might bolt at any minute. Explored the surface of
her mouth with an exquisite thoroughness that just about
brought her to her knees. Long and mesmerizing, the kiss
went on and on, until she was boneless beneath his fingers,
her blood moving through her veins in a hot, restless purr.

He moved his hands to her hips and brought her closer.
About as close as their practice kiss. Except this time she
didn't feel any fear. She just wanted *more*.

His tongue traced her bottom lip, laving it. Then he
nipped gently, taking the sensation to a whole other level.
The moan that came from her throat was low, instinctive.
He satisfied her demand, dipping his tongue inside her
mouth and turning the kiss into a hot, uninhibited exploration.

Her insides contracted. She'd never been kissed like this before. Like he wanted to devour her. *Possess* her. The kisses she'd received from the men she'd dated on her quest to find a husband had been tame. *This was far from tame. It was toe-curlingly sensual, like an overture to an opera, slowly building to the main act.*

She met the bold strokes of his tongue with tentative forays of her own. It was a poor attempt but Nate seemed to like it, stroking her, urging her on with a low husky voice. She grabbed a fistful of his shirt for balance, arching instinctively into him as her body caught fire. His hands shaped her against him, molded her to the hard contours of his powerful body as if he'd been expecting it, waiting for it. She tilted her head back to his demand as he consumed her more deeply.

The thick, powerful evidence of his arousal burned an imprint into her, shocking her, heating the blood in her veins to a whole new level. Her hands curled tighter in his shirt, but she didn't let go. Not when his kiss, when *he*, felt this intoxicatingly good.

Lost in a universe that was all Nate, all about the feel of his hard, hot body against hers, it was a full second or two before she registered the fact that all that heat was gone. That Nate had set her away from him with firm hands that remained on her hips to steady her as her heart pounded near through her chest. As if he knew how completely *unbalanced* she was.

"One kiss," he rasped, his eyes on her face. "And now I'm walking away, Mina. Just like I said I would."

She stared at him. "I—that was—"

"What I hope will erase that other kiss from your memory." His mouth twisted. "Never to happen again."

She nodded. *"Esattamente,"* she agreed shakily. Exactly. Never to be *experienced* again, either, she was fairly sure.

He picked his jacket up off the chair. *"Buonanotte."*

She watched him walk away, as if he regularly brought women to their knees...metaphorically. *Now* she knew why she hadn't accepted any of the suitors her mother had tried to foist on her. Because none of them, not one of the eligible and some of them very good-looking bachelors that had been presented to her, had ever made her feel even one-tenth of what Nate had just done.

Pulling in a deep breath, she kicked off her shoes, picked them up and headed for her bedroom. That might have done the job and knocked everything else clean out of her head. Proved to her she could trust her instincts. The issue, she predicted, was going to be finding a way to think of anything *but* what had just happened.

CHAPTER SEVEN

MINA HAD BEEN RIGHT on her wedding day. A real kiss from Nate *was* unforgettable. She'd spent a sleepless night in her big, soft bed tossing and turning, *imagining* what it would be like to be in his arms. *Wondering* about all the things he would teach her.

Which would stay right there in her imagination, she told herself as she sat in on a marketing meeting with Giorgio and his team to discuss the repeat guests campaign. What Nate had given her was priceless—a chance to prove she was more than just a pretty face whose only opportunities lay in trading on her looks. A chance to prove she was capable of more than providing a graceful introduction at an afternoon tea or cleaning toilets at the Giarruso.

Nate had also given her something perhaps even more important. He'd reminded her last night that despite how overwhelmed she felt in her current situation, she was not simply a creature of God's universe, being batted to and fro by the whims and mercies of the world around her. She was a woman who'd chosen her destiny, who was finally standing on her own two feet.

It was something Celia's mother had taught her on the school holidays she'd spent with the Bettencourts in Nice while her mother jet-setted around the world. When the gaping hole inside of her at never belonging to anything, at being so lonely it ached, had gotten a bit much to take, the certainty she must somehow be defective to never warrant her mother's attention overwhelming the fragile vision of herself she'd built.

"You are special," Juliana Bettencourt had told her. *"You are a bright light, Mina, inside and out. Never forget that. Choose a future for yourself that brings you everything you deserve."*

She was determined to do just that as the marketers around her in the meeting threw about foreign terms like *CRM*—customer relationship management—data and click-through rates. She couldn't blow this opportunity over a kiss, no matter how incredible it had been. Not even if it had made her feel truly alive for the first time in her adult life. Not even if the magnetic, combustible attraction she and Nate shared seemed like the once-in-a-lifetime type.

Over the next few days, she sat in on meetings with Nate about the expansion of the Grand's conventions and meetings program and on a conference call with the global marketing team. On Thursday, they met with the local public relations agency Giorgio and his team used to execute their marketing campaigns. She took the brainstorming ideas they'd generated back to Nate, who added his thoughts, told her they were solid and gave her feedback to take to Giorgio. Having her own project to own and manage put a glow in her cheeks and a spring in her step.

By the time she and Nate stepped on the jet to fly to Hong Kong on Saturday, she was settling nicely into her new role and had lost a bit of her deer-in-the-headlights aura, as Nate liked to describe her as having.

If it hurt that her mother hadn't bothered to call again, the fact that Silvio had also left her alone compensated for it. Apparently he really was done with her.

That worry behind her, all signs pointed straight ahead, no looking back. That's where she was going.

Nate was getting good at this game. He'd spent the last week steadfastly ignoring the explosive chemistry between him and his wife. Putting his protégée through a ruthless schedule of work designed to wipe that kiss from her head.

For the most part, his strategy had worked. Mina had taken everything he'd thrown at her and dedicated herself to producing a thorough, well-thought-out result. The keen insight she'd shown in his suite that day at the Giarruso had proven his instincts about her right. It wouldn't be long before she was an asset to his business.

Where his strategy wasn't so effective, where he and Mina got into trouble, was in the in-between moments, such as this long flight from Capri to Hong Kong via London. Left alone together long enough, the attraction between them began to simmer, find its way through the cracks in their interaction until one of them had to consciously turn it off.

Mina would shoot him one of the sideways glances she'd been directing his way ever since that admittedly hot kiss, her curiosity about what it would be like between them utterly transparent. He, in turn, would deflect those looks with the ruthless efficiency of a man who knew trouble when he saw it.

He'd flicked a switch in his innocent wife's head that night. Awakened her to what true chemistry looked like with a kiss that had gotten a lot more intense than he'd intended. And although he couldn't deny he was curious, too, wouldn't be human if he didn't wonder what peeling back his beautiful wife's layers would reveal, it wasn't going to happen.

Theirs was a marriage of convenience. A business transaction, albeit a slightly more complex one than usual. If that wasn't enough of a deterrent not to take her to bed, the fact that she was a virgin was. He would lay odds of a million to one that his wife was untouched. As such, she was off-limits to him. Virgins were, as a matter of policy, not to be played with.

As Franco had done the night of the Curious party.

A grimace twisted his mouth at the unfinished business he and the actor had. Franco had been like a big cat that night, swiping at Nate's possession with a paw to rile him. The depths to which he had wanted to take him apart for scaring Mina so badly shocked him. It was another reason to stay away from his wife—this intense sense of protectiveness he had toward her. Had had from the beginning.

Mina was too unsullied to exist in his world where relationships were transactional. Where the women in his bed were those who knew their tenure there was temporary. *Exceedingly* temporary. A hot weekend in Rio…a night out at a five-hundred-dollar-a-plate dinner in Manhattan in the name of a good deed…a chance for their name to end up in the society column… It was symbiotic at best. No false expectations; merely the pursuit of mutual pleasure.

Mina was a whole other story. A female of the most dangerous variety, whose innocence and vulnerability demanded everything from a man or nothing at all. He fell into the latter category because creating ties wasn't in his DNA.

He wasn't even willing to invest in his own family. In his half sister Natalia, whose intense vulnerability after she'd been kidnapped and held for ransom while on a gap year in South America had, until recently, kept her housebound. In Dario and Dante, his twin brothers, whose feud had torn the Di Sione family apart. In Matteo, his youngest brother, who had built his wildly successful hedge fund on calculated risks.

Investing in other people simply wasn't part of his portfolio. It came with too much fine print.

Mina, curled up in the seat beside him asleep, stirred, her tousled dark hair and voluptuous curves drawing his eye. It was not a stretch to imagine what she'd look like in his bed as he lavished attention on her from the top of her beautiful head to her equally perfect feet with a long stop in between to idolize the sensational curve of her behind.

The predatory male in him liked the idea of being the first to touch all of that forbidden beauty. The realist knew he could never satisfy the clauses that came with it.

Mina opened her eyes, brown orbs fully alert, as if she'd just been catnapping. He wiped his face clean of his wayward thoughts, but wasn't fast enough. A deep red stain spread across her sleep-flushed cheeks. "What time is it?"

He cursed himself inwardly at the slip. "We have another hour and a half left. I'll brief you on the agenda when you've had a chance to freshen up."

She nodded, rolled to her feet and headed for the bathroom with the haste of a woman who knew what was good for her.

Dio mio. Mina splashed water on her face in the tiny washroom, attempting to wake up her sluggish brain, which seemed to be caught in a time zone somewhere between here and Capri.

She had to stop fantasizing about what it would be like to *be* with her husband. It was never going to happen. Nate had made that clear. But then he went and did something like *that*. Looked at her like he wanted to inhale her, and all their rules went up in flames.

Grabbing a towel, she dried her face and applied a coat

of lip gloss to her mouth, her only concession to makeup while traveling. Telling herself sternly to focus, she made her way back into the cabin, pulled a notepad and pen out of her bag and sat down beside Nate.

"We have two goals in Hong Kong." he began. "The first is to meet with a Michelin-starred chef named Sheng Zhu about a potential in-house restaurant he's proposing for the Grand. It would be a huge coup for the hotel to have him. Mingmei, my manager at the Grand, has been handling the negotiations, but wanted me in attendance to sign the final deal."

Mingmei, his former lover. She ignored the twinge of jealousy that stirred. He had only kissed her to demonstrate a point, for heaven's sake. Nothing more. "Didn't he win one of those top chef shows?"

He nodded. "Unfortunately, he also has a big personality to go with the name. The question is—is he worth the risk? Mingmei thinks he is."

"And the second goal?"

"We'll meet with Mingmei and her team for some general updates on the business this afternoon. Present the global marketing and business plans to the executive team. I'm going to have lunch with a key investor who lives locally to discuss a project. I'll have you take Mingmei through the marketing plan since you know it while I'm tied up. That'll save some time."

By the time Nate finished briefing her and walking her through Sheng Zhu's proposal, they had landed at Hong Kong International Airport. The car Mingmei had sent for them was waiting at the exit, Mingmei herself standing on the sidewalk when the limousine pulled up in front of the red awning of the gold-accented Grand Hotel.

Tall and slim as a wand, the impossibly beautiful Mingmei Gao, as Nate's manager introduced herself, pressed a warm kiss to both Nate's cheeks. Her long, straight jet-black hair, her dark eyes with pencil-thin brows and perfectly shaped red-lipped mouth conspired to make Mina feel a bit lacking in comparison.

The thorough, unabashed appraisal Mingmei gave her cataloged her assets from head to foot. "Welcome to the Grand Hotel Hong Kong," she murmured in impeccable, lightly accented English. "Congratulations on your and Nate's marriage. I hope you'll both be very happy."

If Nate's former lover felt any emotion at all toward her husband, as Susana had hinted was the case, she hid it behind her perfectly composed facade.

"Thank you," Mina replied. "It's been a bit of a… *whirlwind*."

"So much of a whirlwind you haven't taken the time to organize a honeymoon, according to Josephine." Mingmei directed the chiding comment at Nate. "I took the liberty of planning something special for you the night before you leave."

"Special?"

Mingmei's mouth curved. "I have the honeymoon suite for you, of course. The occupants were more than happy to move to the presidential suite."

"That really wasn't necessary."

"Of course it is. Let me show you up."

Another glass elevator, a signature of the Grand, sent them swishing up to the fifty-second floor. Mingmei ushered them into the large, opulent suite, its muted, ambient lighting setting off the luxurious interior done in rich jewel tones. The view of Hong Kong through the floor-to-ceiling windows was breathtaking. But Mina's gaze was fixed on the massive, king-size bed that dominated the adjoining room, rose petals strewn across its ruby-red silk coverlet.

There was only one bed.

Nate turned to Mingmei, a wry look on his face. "You've outdone yourself. Really you didn't need to do this. We can have a regular suite."

Mingmei gave him a pointed look. "You may not be a romantic, but I'm sure Mina appreciates the room."

Mina forced a smile to her frozen face. "*Sì.* It's…amazing. *Mille grazie.*"

Mingmei smiled. "I'll leave you to freshen up. I'll meet you in the executive offices at noon, Mina. We can have some lunch and go over the marketing plan."

Mina nodded. Stood staring at the giant, rose petal–covered bed as Nate walked Mingmei to the door.

He had taken a soul-searing possession of her with his kiss that night in Capri. She'd relinquished all common sense, all rational thought. Nate had been the one to call it off. *What was going to happen when they shared a bed together?*

The side of her she was desperately trying to avoid, the newly discovered part of her that clamored to feel more of that sensory overload Nate had evoked in her, knew it for a bad idea. But the desire to experience that kind of passion again—but this time more, *all of it*—was shockingly strong.

"We can't share that bed," she blurted out as Nate walked back into the room.

An amused smile twisted his lips as he came to stand in front of her. "I'm afraid we have no choice."

She glanced around in desperation. "I'll sleep on the floor."

His smile deepened. "No one is sleeping on the floor, Mina. But just for the record, is your adamant proclamation we can't share that bed because you think *you* can't restrain yourself? Because *I* have proven I can be a good boy."

Her jaw dropped. "Do women actually find this...this *arrogance* appealing?"

"Yes," he murmured, bending to bring his mouth to her ear. "You're doing an admirable job of trying to hide your curiosity, Mina, but not quite good enough."

Her heart leaped into her mouth. She stepped back, *away* from all that testosterone. "This is *not* solving our problem."

He nodded toward the bed. "*That* problem I will solve by wearing boxers just for your benefit. Our other problem? We go with avoidance. It's been marginally effective so far."

That Nate ordinarily slept in the nude was disturbing enough to her senses. What he would *look* like in boxers more so.

"You've seen me in a towel," he reminded her. "Same thing. Out of curiosity," he ventured, tilting his head to the side, "what would you have done if the towel had fallen off?"

"Sued you for indecent exposure." Spinning on her heel, she headed for the bathroom. Nate's laughter followed her.

"I wouldn't have been much good as your knight in shining armor sitting in jail now, would I?"

You couldn't think of beds and boxer shorts when you were presenting the global marketing plan to your husband's ex-lover. A respite it would have been if Mina hadn't felt so intimidated in the other woman's presence. Mingmei was as brilliant as she was exquisitely beautiful, asking probing, thoughtful questions about the marketing plan that never would have occurred to Mina. By the time they finished, she felt like a rank amateur.

Her mouth tightening, she clicked out of the presentation and sat back in her chair. "Any further questions?"

Mingmei crossed her arms over her chest. "None of my questions were a criticism, Mina. I wouldn't have expected you to know the answers. They were discussion points to take back to the global team for further thought."

Her chin dipped. She really needed to master that tightly schooled expression her social behavior coaches had failed to conjure up in her.

When Nate texted to say he was running late with his investor lunch, Mingmei's executives had already started to show up for their scheduled meeting. "Why don't you present the marketing plan?" Mingmei suggested. "Nate can do the rest when he comes."

A wave of panic enveloped her. She knew the presentation. But to present it to a team of executives after being on the job for a week? Nate had made it clear she was to stay within her role.

"You want my advice?" Mingmei directed a pointed look at her. "Seize every opportunity you get. If you don't feel comfortable doing something, do it, anyway. Fake the confidence until you have it."

Mina swallowed past the tension climbing her throat. She knew the presentation inside out.

"Sì," she said. "I'll do it."

Her knees knocked together as she stood at the front of the conference room, Mingmei introducing her to the half dozen executives who ran the sales, customer service and marketing teams. Her mouth like sawdust, her hands clammy, she clicked the remote to start the presentation. A *gladiator*, she told herself. She was a gladiator.

Her voice tight, her delivery far too rapid, she began. It was a friendly room, thank goodness, with the executives stopping her to ask a question when they wanted to explore a point further. She felt her shoulders and voice loosening as the session turned interactive. By the time

Nate walked into the room fifteen minutes later, she was midway through the presentation and firmly in her groove.

His gaze widened, moved from Mina to the table of executives and then back again. She thought he might interrupt and take over. Instead, he pulled up the chair closest to the door and sat down.

Mina kept going, thinking he didn't look angry like he had in the meeting with Giorgio, so maybe she'd made the right choice. Nate watched her from the head of the table, his dark gaze inscrutable as he joined in wherever he was needed, but let her take the reins with the rest.

When she'd finished the presentation, she sat down, her legs like jelly. Her heart was pounding, her head buzzing, an extreme high enveloping her. She hadn't let fear rule her, the fear she wasn't good enough, as it had so many times in her life, and it felt good. *Molto bene.* As if she'd begun to slay her demons.

Nate said nothing until their meetings concluded and they rode the glass elevator skyward to their suite.

"Whose idea was it for you to present?"

"Mingmei suggested I do it." She threw him a sideways look. "Is it okay that I did?"

He nodded. "You did a great job."

She exhaled. "I was worried you'd be angry."

"If you'd gone up there and presented the financial results for the year I would have been, yes. But you presented material you knew." He rested an appraising gaze on her. "I'm thinking of offering you a dual role when we get back to New York. Part of the time as my protégée and part of the time on the global marketing team. *If* you want to go in that direction."

"Sì." She gave a sharp nod of her head. "I do. *Mille grazie.* That means so much to me, Nate."

His mouth quirked. "See what you think when you meet

my director of marketing. She's a fire-breathing dragon. But the best in the business."

They joined Mingmei for dinner in the rooftop restaurant with its spectacular view of the city. Watching Nate's former lover more closely, she determined Susana had been right. Mingmei's repartee with Nate was utterly professional, but every once in a while Mina caught a glimpse of something in the other woman's eyes. *A wistfulness?* An admiration that extended to the man beneath the title.

"Mingmei is lovely," she said as they walked into their suite.

Nate flicked a glance at her. "You should know we were once lovers. In case you hear talk."

She shrugged off her wrap. "Susana told me. I think she thought it was better I knew."

"It was three years ago, before she came to work for me. There is nothing between us now."

On his part. She pressed her lips shut, her gaze dropping away from his. "You don't have to explain your personal life to me."

With that, she took her irrational jealousy off to the bathroom to wash up before bed. Nate was still working when she wished him good-night, offering an absent-minded one in return. Determined to be asleep by the time he joined her, she quickly swept the rose petals out of the bed and into the trash can and curled up with a book to put herself to sleep. An hour and a half after she'd gone to bed, she was still awake, staring at the ceiling, when Nate came in.

She averted her gaze as he stripped, hung up his suit and got into bed.

"Can't sleep?"

"No."

"Want me to tell you a bedtime story?"

"No."

Laughter rumbled from his throat. "Likely a good thing. The only ones I can think of would be strictly X-rated."

"Nate!"

"Go to sleep, Mina."

She squeezed her eyes shut. He turned on his side and all was quiet. The clocked ticked loudly on the mantelpiece over the fireplace. *Dannazione*, but she was restless. Rolling on her side she hugged her pillow. It was too soft—she *hated* soft pillows. Reaching for the other pillow she'd dropped on the floor, she tried that one out. It was too hard.

A sigh left her throat.

"Good God." Nate reached over and flicked on the light. Which put his amazing, sculpted chest on display. She'd never *seen* anything like it, muscle and sinew converging in a mouthwatering work of art.

His gaze raked over her face. Dropped lower to the lace nightie Susana had insisted she buy for her honeymoon. The look on his face sent all the blood in her body rushing to her twin heated cheeks.

"I don't sleep much," he said grimly, returning his gaze to her face, "but I do need a few hours. So let me assure you I am not crossing the center line tonight. Despite that enticing scrap of lace you're wearing. Despite the fact that it has *Take me* written all over it and it's not helping by adding to my list of fantasies."

Her gaze tangled with his. His eyes were so dark she could walk right into them and lose herself completely. It was tempting, so tempting, to do so. To throw common sense out the window.

"Susana made me buy it," she whispered. "Not my idea."

His laser-like stare said that fact was inconsequential.

She turned her back on him, clutching the hard pillow to her, her heart slamming in her chest. She wanted so badly to know what those fantasies were. Wanted his beautiful hands on her as he acted them out. Wanted to feel as alive as he'd made her feel that night in his arms in Capri. To know for once in her lonely life what it was like to be the center of someone's orbit—a man like Nate's orbit. To experience that heady, inescapable passion…

But she wasn't going to be the one to cross the line, either. She had far too much at stake.

CHAPTER EIGHT

THE WEEK IN Hong Kong flew by at a blindingly fast pace. They had an initial meeting with Sheng Zhu the following day in which the celebrity chef outlined his vision for a new avant-garde restaurant at the Grand that, he promised, would be the talk of the city.

Mina got a chance to see the razor-sharp, ruthless side of her new boss as Nate systematically picked Sheng Zhu's proposal apart and pressed for additional exclusivity. She had no doubt he'd walk away from the partnership if it wasn't tailored to his liking, and apparently neither did Sheng Zhu, who promised to return the morning they were to fly out with an updated proposal.

She spent the rest of the week learning the operations of the hotel alongside Nate and Mingmei. By the end of the week her head was so crammed full of information she had almost been able to forget about her and Nate's sleeping arrangements.

Almost. Not that Nate slept. He worked more than any human being she'd ever encountered, coming to bed long after she'd fallen asleep and rising before she did. She had no idea how he functioned with such little rest, but it did the trick, minimizing the contact between them.

Tonight, however, their last night in Hong Kong, was going to be a challenge. Mingmei had prepared a special honeymoon dinner for them in their suite. Unless they wanted to look ungrateful they were going to have to go through the motions.

She eyed the suite warily as she and Nate returned from their meetings. The dining table near the windows with the spectacular view of the harbor had been set for two, tall, tapered candles flickering in the center of it, champagne cooling in an ice bucket. The lighting had been muted, a classic piece by Ella Fitzgerald playing in the background, a tray of oysters at the ready.

Her mouth went dry. Ignoring her attraction to Nate was one thing in a room full of people. Another entirely in the middle of a seduction scene.

A sparkle caught her eye. Moving further into the salon she found an evening gown draped over a chair, a delicate pair of glittering stiletto heels beside it and a card that said *"Wear me"* propped up beside the dress.

Nate strolled over to pick up the embossed envelope that sat beside it.

Sliding the card out, he read its contents. "'A 2002 Piper-Heidsieck is on its way. Enjoy the music and some dancing before your six-course dinner featuring some of Hong Kong's great delicacies.'"

Nate raised an eyebrow at Mina's expression.

"Afraid I'll step on your toes? I happen to be a very good dancer."

He knew exactly what it was she was afraid of and it wasn't the dancing! She tossed her hair over her shoulder in what she hoped was a nonchalant gesture. "I am sure you are very smooth. Part of your lady-killer image."

An openly amused look crossed his face. *"Lady-killer? Where did you get that from? An old movie?"*

She ignored him and picked up the dress. The Asian-inspired design was done in a deep buttercream color with the most exquisite beadwork and embroidery she'd ever seen.

"Go put it on before the champagne comes," said Nate.

She did, if only to distract herself. The dress might have encompassed plenty of material, but it was snug, molded to her body in a perfect fit that emphasized all her curves. The only nod toward daring was the low back that left much of her skin bare.

That Mingmei clearly had a perfect eye for style didn't surprise her in the least. Slipping on the sparkly stilettos, which fit perfectly, she returned to the salon. Nate had taken his jacket off, elegant and minimalistic in a silver-gray shirt and black trousers that molded his muscular body to perfection. His inescapable virility in the suddenly very small space rolled over her in a heady wave of awareness.

His gaze ate her up in a frank appraisal that made her lungs tight. "I should have left my jacket and tie on. In the face of such perfection…"

The breath whished from her lungs. "You're far more relaxed when you're not in a suit and tie."

"I'm not sure relaxed is the state of mind I should be aiming for right now."

Her stomach plummeted. "This…*talk*," she pointed out weakly, "is not helping the situation."

His mouth curved. "I think being self-aware is not a bad thing at the moment."

A discreet cough alerted her to the fact that they were not alone. Turning, she found a black-coated waiter at her elbow, holding a white cloth–wrapped champagne bottle and glasses. Apparently they had their own personal waiter for the evening, a fact that eased her nerves considerably. A chaperone was exactly what she and Nate needed.

The waiter filled their glasses, returned the bottle to the

ice bucket and stepped back to stand unobtrusively by the door. Nate set a hand to the small of her back and guided her out onto the terrace with its spectacular views of Victoria Harbor, Hong Kong Island and Kowloon. The press of his strong fingers against the bare skin of her back sent a tremor reverberating through her.

Dannazione. She needed to get a handle on herself.

She focused on the view in front of her. Found herself transfixed by the light exploding over the city. Laser beams and searchlights in a rainbow of hues shot off the tops of the buildings, casting rays of light into the inky sky and harbor. Fireworks dazzled the eye, timed to music she could just make out from this distance. It was a choreographed spectacle the likes of which she'd never seen.

"Fantastico," she breathed. "What's the occasion?"

"It's called the Symphony of Lights. It happens every night. It's meant to celebrate the energy and diversity of Hong Kong."

Mina watched, transfixed. Thought about how spectacular, how *foreign*, it was. She might have been a whole planet away from her home rather than just on another continent.

It struck her then how much her life had changed in two weeks. How exhilarating, terrifying and irrevocable those changes were.

"That's a contemplative look." Nate rested his elbows on the railing and looked over at her.

"This," she said, waving her hand at the view, "feels bittersweet. I wanted it so badly—my freedom. The chance to make my mark. But I also feel...*torn*. Homesick." She sighed. "How silly is that? For a mother who barely tolerates me...a life that made me miserable."

"It's what you know," he said quietly. "Walking into the unknown, even though you know it's the right path, is scary. Sometimes you want to retreat. To stay with the known even though it makes you unhappy."

"Did you feel like that once?"

"More than once." His mouth curved. "I've taken a lot of risks in my life. You don't achieve success without them. But that doesn't mean I've never been afraid—afraid of making the wrong call, afraid the magic will disappear someday just like it appeared. It's human to be afraid. It's what you do with the fear that defines a person."

She found that thought vastly comforting. That Nate, as successful as he was, had once not been so completely sure of himself.

She took a sip of her champagne. Watched another round of fireworks light up the sky. "I used to lie in bed at school at night after my father died, so scared of the future, of what would happen to me. I'd wonder why God had taken him and not my mother. I used to secretly wish that he *had*, then be terrified he'd punish me for thinking such awful thoughts."

"I would say that's understandable thinking coming from an eight-year-old."

"Perhaps." She lifted a shoulder. "To me they seemed wicked and irredeemable thoughts. So I made up a pretend family instead to keep me company. I had five brothers and sisters so I'd never be lonely, a dog named Gigi, who slept on the end of my bed, and parents who came to get me for every holiday."

He frowned. "Your mother left you alone for some of them?"

"Often. After I met my friend Celia, I would spend the holidays with her family."

He was silent for a long moment. "You'll have a family of your own someday," he said finally.

Would she? Did she crave the fantasy more than the reality? She had so much she wanted to accomplish before then, most of all finding out *who* she really was. *What* she wanted.

"Who was your mentor?" she asked Nate. "The one you spoke of?"

"My grandfather, Giovanni. He put me through university, took me in to work at Di Sione Shipping with him."

"Is this the same grandfather who wants the ring?"

"Yes."

"You said before your father wasn't a part of your life. How did you come to know your grandfather?"

"My father died in a car accident when I was ten. My relationship with Giovanni began in my late teens when he developed leukemia and needed a bone marrow transplant. None of my half siblings were a match, so my eldest brother, Alex, sought me out to see if I was. I was a match and I did the transplant. Our relationship developed from there."

Wow. "That must have been an incredibly emotional introduction to each other."

"It was…intense."

"You said you weren't close to your brothers and sisters?"

He took a sip of his champagne. Rested his glass on the railing, a distant look in his eyes. "There is too much history between us to make that possible."

"How so?"

"A lot of complicated relationships with many layers. Sometimes it's simply easier to leave the past in the past. To not reopen old wounds."

She recalled the lack of a personal background in his media profiles. It had not been an accident. He was protecting a past he had distanced himself from.

What had driven his father to abandon him? What had

happened to keep him and his siblings from becoming close after his father's death when one would think it would have been the ultimate bonding experience to give his grandfather his life back?

It was an incredibly enticing train of thought to want to pursue, but she left it at that because the walls around him as he stared out into the night said that particular conversation was over.

"Giovanni is very lucky to have had you."

The lazy, seductive bars of a Duke Ellington tune filled the silence that followed. "I think it's the other way around," he said finally. "But I won't have him for much longer. His leukemia is back and this time it will kill him."

Her stomach dropped. That was why his grandfather wanted the ring. To reclaim a piece of his past before it was all lost to him.

"Nate—" She put a hand on his arm. "*Mi dispiace.* I'm so sorry."

His expression hardened. "It's fine. I'm lucky to have had him as long as I have."

Except it wasn't fine. She could see just how *un*fine it was in the glitter of emotion that darkened his eyes. In the clench of his jaw. The way his gaze refused to meet hers. He was suffering but you would never have known it. Taking a precious memory back to his mentor, who had perhaps been the father figure he'd never known, only to watch him die.

"It's okay," she said quietly, "for it not to be fine."

He spared her a glance. "What else can it be? He's dying and there's nothing I nor anyone can do to prevent it."

"Talking about it might help."

"I've come to terms with it." Storm clouds gathered in his eyes. "Leave it alone, Mina."

She did. The pieces of her enigmatic husband starting

to fall into place, she finished her champagne in silence. So much loss, so much pain, and no way to express it because he considered himself the ultimate gladiator. He would never show weakness.

A Frank Sinatra tune she loved drifted out to them on the night air. Nate put his glass down and held out his hand. "So we can say we danced at least one song after all the trouble Mingmei went through."

She thought maybe that was a bad idea. The champagne was starting to hit her bloodstream, infusing her with that languorous, dangerous desire to play with fire. Not a good idea when keeping things on a business level between her and Nate seemed so very important.

He pulled her close. Close enough that she felt his hard thighs brushing against hers, the intoxicating, spicy smell of him filling her senses. His big hand was laced through hers, while the other rested lightly on her waist as he guided her expertly through the steps.

He hadn't been lying about being a good dancer. He was rather dreamy, in fact. She'd danced with a great deal of men at all the social events she'd endured, but somehow dancing under the stars with Nate with only Sinatra to accompany them was an experience of an entirely different realm.

He was so strong, so heart-poundingly virile, it was impossible not to think how easily he could command her if he wanted to. To do all sorts of *unthinkable* things. Her thoughts should have put her guard up. Instead, she was afraid of what he might *never* do to her. What might never happen between them.

"She's in love with you, you know."

"Who?"

"Mingmei. She didn't say it, but I can see it."

An impassive expression claimed his face. "We ended things on good terms. Mingmei knew the deal with me."

The question that had been burning a hole in her head all week tumbled from her lips. "Why? Why break things off with her? Mingmei is stunning, intelligent, extroverted, *entertaining*... How could she possibly be lacking in any department?"

"It isn't about how amazing a woman is or isn't. I'm not interested in a permanent relationship with anyone."

"Don't you ever get lonely?"

His lips curved in a cynical twist. "I don't mean sex," she qualified, blushing. "I mean for true companionship."

"And how would you define true companionship sweet, innocent Mina?" He swung her into a tight circle, his gaze holding hers. "Having *sleepovers* with the women I date so I can spill my deepest, darkest secrets to them? Telling her how I *feel* over breakfast so I can start the day a *whole* man?"

Her chin lifted. "I mean someone who's there at the end of the day to confide in, whether you've had the best day or the worst. Someone who *cares* what your day is like. Who nurtures the emotional side of you."

"I don't *have* an emotional side."

Not one he would admit. Pretending he didn't care was his self-defense mechanism as much as hers had been withdrawing into herself for so many years. Because she had *seen* him care. Everything he had done for her had been about caring for her welfare. It was more than just paying it forward.

"Everyone needs human connection, Nate. I told myself I didn't need it. I spent my whole life without it, but nothing can replace what the unconditional love of someone gives us. We *need* emotional connection to survive."

"Some of us do. And some of us exist better as solitary beings." His mouth curled. "Get married and have your white picket family, Mina. All the power to you. But that's not me."

"Who says I want to settle down now? I want my free-dom now that I have it. The rest can come later."

"You *think* you want your freedom. Soon you'll want more. All women have the nesting gene."

His condescending attitude irked her. "I guess that's right if you say so."

His gaze sharpened. "Picking a fight, Mina? That's a new one."

"Maybe I'm tired of being told what I want. There's a whole world out there for me to experience, Nate. Not just business. I plan on doing so."

His steps slowed as another, lazier, Sinatra tune fol-lowed the last. "I'm all for seizing the moment," he murmured idly. But the gaze he had trained on her was anything but. "So what will you do when our year is up, then? Take a series of lovers to satisfy your need for *human connection*? Keep your affairs short and sweet so no one gets too attached?"

"You're playing with me now."

"I'm *curious*. You forget I know you're an innocent, Mina. How does that factor into all this? Do you plan to simply give your virginity away to the first man who *does* it for you?"

Her lashes lowered. *If that were the case, she'd be giv-ing it to him.*

"My virginity is a matter of circumstance. A bargain-ing tool my mother used to *sell* me. I refuse to treat it as such. When I decide to give it to a man it will be because I made a conscious decision to do so without overcompli-cating things."

"I *see*." He nodded thoughtfully. "That's quite a thing

to lay at a man's doorstep. What happens if he falls for you? You simply kick him out the door and say you're not ready?"

She frowned. "Who says it would be me kicking him out?"

"Because you are devastatingly, undeniably desirable, Mina. With just the right air of vulnerability to have men falling over themselves to claim you if you offer them your innocence. They won't stand a chance."

Her gaze locked with his for a long, heated moment. It seemed ridiculous to be speaking of other lovers when the only man's hands she wanted on her were Nate's. When that's all she'd wanted ever since he'd unleashed that devastating kiss on her.

"Not happening, Mina." His husky drawl slid over her sensitized flesh like a slow, potent caress. "*We* have a very functional partnership going on here."

She knew it. He knew it. But she couldn't seem to tear her gaze away from his. "I know," she agreed. "I know it's insanity, but I—I can't seem to stop thinking about what happened between us. About how alive…how *lost* I felt."

"Try harder," he bit out. "*This, we,* cannot happen. I don't mix business with pleasure."

"You're the one who said we hardly have a straightforward business relationship. I believe you called it… *unique.*"

"Unique enough," he growled. The storm in his eyes intensified. "You are vulnerable, Mina. You are looking at me like I'm some knight who's come to your rescue when I am anything but. You have no idea what you are throwing out there right now."

She swallowed hard. "I *am* vulnerable right now but I *want* to feel vulnerable. I *want* to want what I want. I want to figure out who I am. And I am under no illusions as to what this would be between us. I've just said I'm not looking for a commitment. Not now. Not for a long while."

He was silent, so heart-stoppingly silent she could hear her heart pounding in her ears. "Just to be clear," he rasped finally, "you're telling me you want us to go to bed together. And to hell with the consequences?"

She bit the inside of her mouth. *Hard.* "You keep baiting me, Nate. You won't leave it alone, either. What do *you* want?"

She had a point, Nate thought blackly. *What did he want?* Because he couldn't seem to leave this thing with Mina alone. Not when she felt this good in his arms. When the floral, delicate smell of her, the soft curves that tempted him beyond reason, were his for the taking.

He had gone on the offensive to try and distract her when she'd started prying into the pieces of his life he would never expose. In doing so, he'd started something he couldn't finish. *Definitely couldn't finish.* Proving that seemed to be the way to go.

He let go of her hand. Reached up to trace a line down the silky-soft skin of her cheek to her mouth, his thumb dragging across the plump skin of her lower lip. "What you should be afraid of," he drawled, "is me taking you up on your offer, Mina, because even I have my limits and I'm fast approaching them, common sense be damned."

Her eyes widened. But she drifted closer, not further away as he explored her lips with the rough pad of his fingertip.

"Mina," he growled. "You should walk away. I'm not your human connection project. I promise you that."

She stayed where she was, her gaze fixed on his. He sank his thumb into the warmth of her mouth. Watched the heat in her beautiful dark eyes catch fire. And lost his mind just that much more.

His hands dropped to her hips, tugging her forward until her delectable curves were pressed against him. Mina's long, silky lashes arced over her cheeks as he angled his head and brought his mouth down on hers.

Urgently, deliberately, he drank her sweetness in, tasted her endlessly until there was not one millimeter of her lips he hadn't explored. When her hand curled around the back of his neck and urged him closer, he teased her mouth further apart and invaded with his tongue. She had learned from the last time they'd kissed, found her rhythm quickly now, her tongue sliding delicately against his. His body hardened in an instant visceral response that should have stopped him. Instead, it spurred him on.

The bare skin exposed by the back of her dress was an irresistible temptation. He swept his palm from her shoulder blades to the base of her spine, urging her closer. Her shocked gasp as she came into contact with his aroused, pulsing body heated his blood.

"There's still time to run," he murmured, dragging his mouth across her cheek and up to her earlobe.

She did the opposite, arching into him, fitting herself to him so perfectly it tore a groan from his throat. Holding her with the fingers he had pressed against the small of her back, he held himself completely still. "You make me crazy," he muttered, wrapping his lips around the tender flesh of her lobe and nipping at it. "Move, Mina. *Now.*"

She tipped her head back and gave him more room to explore. He took her lobe deeper into the heat of his mouth and scraped his teeth across it.

"Nate…" she breathed in that way of hers that made it sound more like *Neet.*

Crazy sexy.

He worked his way down the column of her throat to the place where her pulse raged at the base of her neck. Pressed hot, openmouthed kisses against the delicate flesh he found there. Mina shuddered. Wrapped her fingers in his hair.

He brought his mouth back up to hers and took her lips in a hard, hot kiss. Unable to resist, he cupped one of her perfect, uptilted breasts in his palm. She stiffened as he ran his thumb over its delicate, half-erect peak. Over and over again until she moaned and melted into him.

"You like that?" he murmured against her lips, transferring his attention to her other rounded globe.

"Sì," she whispered. "I feel like I'm on fire, Nate."

His head exploded. Dissolved into urgent flames that obliterated any last vestiges of common sense. Rasping his thumb across her nipple, he teased it into a hard, urgent pebble that matched its twin.

Mina moved insistently, urgently, against him now. He cupped her derriere, that part of her he'd been wild for from the beginning, and adjusted the fit so she had him between the V of her thighs. Taut and perfectly shaped, she fit the palms of his hands so well he knew that would be how he'd take her. *If* he took her, which of course he wouldn't.

Their first course was coming any minute. Time was running out.

Mina moved against the solid column of his flesh, rubbed against him like a cat scratching an itch. "*Sì*, just like that. Nate—*per favore*—"

Mother of God. She was so far gone.

He backed her up against the wall. Sliding his hands up the backs of her legs, he brought her dress up with them. Relief was all he was giving her. Then he was ending this insanity.

Her gasp as he cupped the warmth between her thighs was so intoxicating he almost lost it right there. Tightening his fingers, he moved them against her in a slow rock that had her hips thrusting against his hand. *Dear Lord, but she was responsive.*

Moving his hand back up the flat plane of her stomach, he sank his fingers beneath the waistband of her panties and found her hot, velvet warmth. She felt like heaven. *So aroused, wet for him.* It made the blood in his head pound against his temples.

"Spread your legs, baby," he whispered in her ear. "I need room."

She moved her thighs apart for him, her legs trembling so much he had to hold her up with one hand while he brought the thumb of his other to the tight bundle of nerves at the heart of her. Slowly, languorously, he rotated his thumb against her. Italian words tumbled out of Mina's mouth, husky, unbearably sexy. Her hands gripped the concrete behind her, her eyes closed.

He bent and took her mouth with his own, swallowing every cry, every moan, as he stroked her wet heat. She writhed as he moved his thumb against her clitoris in an erratic movement that prolonged her pleasure, kept her orgasm just out of reach. Mina arched her back and sunk her teeth into that delectable bottom lip. Her breathing grew fractured, desperate. "*Per favore.* More."

He gave it to her, sinking two of his long fingers inside her tight, wet heat. Slowly at first, he entered her, giving her a chance to get used to him. Then he picked the rhythm up, plunging deep inside of her.

Her cries came fast and urgent against his mouth. "Nate…"

Neet.

Gritting his teeth against the surge of lust that knocked him sideways, he found her core with his thumb and made her come in a deliberate series of movements that pushed her over the edge. Long and hard, the orgasm shook her petite frame. He caught her against him as her knees gave way and held her through every last shudder of it.

Never had a woman's release turned him on more. Never had it made him shake with the need to have her.

It brought him hurtling back to vivid, mind-altering reality. *To what he had done.*

He told himself he hadn't taken her. That he could still bring this back under control…

It was a lie he couldn't force himself to swallow. *Hadn't crossed a line? He'd just crossed the Great Divide.* He had wanted to touch Mina. He had goaded himself and her into it, to the point of no return, and then he'd walked across the line.

The sound of dishes rattling came from inside the suite. *Their first course.*

He set Mina away from him with unsteady hands, his head too full of emotion for the first time in his life to make sense of what had just happened. To process any of it. He could no more eat dinner right now than he could look at the stripped-down, dazed look on his wife's face. *His wife's face. Dear Lord.*

"I need to go."

"What?" Mina pushed her dress down around her hips. "Dinner is here."

He raked a hand through his hair. "Eat without me."

Her face crumpled. "Nate—"

He turned on his heel and left.

CHAPTER NINE

"SHOULD WE MOVE ON to the timeline?" Sheng Zhu prompted.

Nate nodded. He'd heard enough during the first ten minutes of the celebrity chef's presentation to know it was a partnership the Grand would sign on to. Sheng Zhu was offering the five-year exclusivity he'd demanded, the numbers looked sound and it was clear the chef was a smart businessman first, hotheaded personality second. He'd given them everything they'd wanted.

Unfortunately, the significant part of a bottle of his favorite single-malt Scotch, consumed in a swank watering hole called the American Bar last night, hadn't solved his other problem. All it had done was give him a throbbing headache and no answers about what to do with his sexy, irresistible wife.

He sat back in his chair and brought his steaming cup of coffee with him, wincing as his head protested the movement. Mingmei threw him one of those curious glances she'd been sending his way, as if her spies had told her he'd walked out on his and Mina's dinner. Or maybe it was just because he'd tuned out half an hour ago.

He'd been a fool to think he could ever control this thing between him and Mina. Their chemistry was too strong, the opportunities to exploit it too plentiful. He'd like to say he could turn back the clock and wipe out that brief moment of insanity last night, but it wasn't going to happen. Not when the awareness between him and Mina pulsed across the table like a living, breathing entity. Not when he'd put his hands on her in the most intimate way possible and made her cry out his name with the lights of Hong Kong blazing around them.

Mina gave him a veiled look from beneath her lashes. *Confusion, hurt, apprehension.* He hadn't come back to their suite until well past midnight last night, the six-course dinner long cleared away. Had gone to the gym early this morning to keep some distance between them.

He cared about her. Genuinely cared about her, which was a first for a woman. But he could never offer Mina what she would eventually want—that white picket fence and a family to banish the loneliness she'd carried with her for so long.

She claimed she could handle an affair between them, but could she really? Would it turn their working relationship into an awkward, untenable partnership that worked for neither of them when it was over? Could she give him her virginity in the uncomplicated transaction she'd spoken of and walk away after this year without emotional ties?

If he didn't take her up on the offer, then someone else would. He closed his eyes as the image of a man like Franco becoming Mina's first lover made his head throb.

He took a long sip of his coffee. He could shut it down between them. Fall back on his excuse he never mixed business with pleasure, but Mina was right. Their relationship had already blurred so many lines, there was no going back. The only question was how to move forward.

Mina stood and forced a smile to her face as they concluded their meeting with Sheng Zhu, exchanging bows all around. It had been easy to keep to her role of active listener today. Her brain was running in circles, like a dog chasing its tail, humiliation and confusion taking turns preserving the momentum.

Why had Nate walked out on her like that? What had she done wrong? Why had he looked so angry?

She didn't regret one second of what had happened between them. Learning to go after what she wanted in life, enjoying these heady initial successes, had stoked her craving to experience everything life had to offer. But, she acknowledged miserably, if it was going to ruin everything she and Nate had started to build together, then it had been a big mistake.

Which it might just have been. She had fallen asleep at midnight with Nate still not back, the sumptuous dinner Mingmei had arranged for them sent back virtually untouched. Then woken up to his stone-cold, unapproachable face this morning when he'd come back from the gym.

Had she pushed him too far? He had been pushing, too. Challenging her. Tempting her. It had not been a one-way street.

Swallowing the lump in her throat, she headed for the coffee machine before their next meeting. Nearly jumped out of her skin when a shadow fell over her.

"A word, please."

Nate's sophisticated cologne filled her head in a tantalizing reminder of last night. She risked a look up at him. He still looked distinctly *agitated*.

He jerked his head toward the hallway. She followed him, the snap of the door as it shut behind them making her flinch.

He turned and rested a hand against the wall. "We need to talk."

Sì. They did. Before she crawled right out of her skin.

"I think it should wait until we get to the Maldives," he

said tersely. "I have a pile of work to do on the flight. And this particular conversation needs to be done in private."

She couldn't read anything from his expression. *Nothing*.

"I agree."

But it wasn't so easy to endure an entire morning of meetings before they boarded the jet for the Maldives. Nor the several-hour flight in a strained silence between them. By the time they set down on the short, single runway in the tiny island republic in the middle of the Indian Ocean, she *had* crawled out of her skin.

A car took them to the harbor, where a boat transported them the rest of the way to the exclusive resort Nate was about to buy, situated on its own private island. Mina's breath caught as the boat pulled up alongside a dock with a private villa attached to it. Perched in the middle of the ocean with only a narrow walkway connecting it to the island and resort, it was a floating paradise.

Lights glittered inside the grass-roofed villa as sunset approached, illuminating its luxurious interior. A private plunge pool, Jacuzzi and lounge area completed the idyllic picture. But all Mina could look at was the endless vista of blue all around them, as if they were alone in the middle of the ocean.

This was where they were staying? It seemed far too intimate, far too inescapable, no matter which way their conversation went.

A white-shirted butler emerged from the villa, introduced himself and spirited their luggage inside. Nate went with him. Mina stayed outside drinking in the view. They had beautiful beaches in Sicily, but they were crowded and busy and this...this was like nothing she'd ever experienced before.

Nate appeared beside her, his jacket and tie gone, the

top buttons of his shirt undone. "I thought we could have a drink and enjoy the sunset before dinner."

Her pulse kicked up, her palms growing damp. She nodded and swallowed back her nerves. "I'd like to change first."

He inclined his head toward the villa. "I'll see what there is to choose from."

She found her luggage in the airy, dark-paneled bedroom with its king-size bed, perfectly positioned to enjoy the sunset and sunrise from through the tall, sliding glass doors that fronted the villa.

One bed. Was it an indication of where Nate's thoughts lay? Or what had been appointed to them? Rather than cater to the nerves consuming her, she exchanged her pants and shirt for a white floral printed dress and rejoined Nate on the terrace.

He was standing, his gaze on the horizon as the sun sank below it, a fiery ball of flame on a canvas of turquoise blue. She padded across the warm wood in her bare feet to his side.

"It's almost unreal, isn't it?"

He nodded. "Perhaps unfair only a select few ever get to experience it."

"The deal is almost done, you said?"

"We should finalize it this week if all the requested enhancements have been made to the property."

And then they would head home to New York. *Her* home now. The thought of being immersed in Nate's world, taking her place as his wife with so much tension between them, made her stomach tighten.

He plucked a bottle of wine from the ice bucket and poured them both a glass of the rosé. She eyed the glass he handed her warily, a flush filling her cheeks. "I'm not sure I should have any of that."

His gaze rested on her with disturbing precision. "The way you responded to me last night was beautifully uninhibited, Mina. A massive turn-on for a man. It's not something to be ashamed of."

Then why had he walked away?

He set a palm to the small of her back and directed her toward the lounge area. She sat down on the sofa beside him, curling her bare legs beneath her as a breeze sent a delicious waft of air over her heated skin.

Nate took a sip of his wine, then cradled the glass against his chest, his gaze resting on her. "I needed to give us both time to think last night. To slow things down so we use our heads and not our hormones to decide if us having an intimate relationship is a good idea."

Her breath snagged in her throat. *So he was considering it.* She set her wine on the coffee table. "You think I didn't mean what I said. That because I have no experience, I can't handle a relationship with you."

"Can you? Can we layer the complexity of a sexual relationship onto what we already have and expect it to be manageable for both of us? Because if we can't, if we don't walk into this with the same expectations, we need to shut this down. *Now.* My primary concern is ensuring you flourish, Mina, so you build a career for yourself and you can stand on your own two feet when this is over. You've gone through too much for me not to do that."

She nodded. "You've set me on that course. You know how much I appreciate it. But nothing is going to distract me from it. It means too much to me."

He gave her a long look, his dark gaze contemplative. "I'm not sure you can separate your vision of me as hero with the reality of who I am. *What* I am."

That may be true, but she wasn't sure that was possible in any aspect of their relationship. What they were was unique because of the way it had started. That was never going to change. But what happened next was about them both making adult decisions fully conscious of what they were doing. And she knew what she was doing.

She took a sip of wine to bolster her courage. "I want you to be my first lover, Nate. I want to experience that with you. I want it to be as memorable as I know it can be. I don't expect anything more of you and I won't let it affect our working relationship."

His gaze widened imperceptibly. "I'm not sure you can make that assurance."

"I can and I will."

He turned his gaze to the horizon. Silence fell between them, the cry of the birds flying overhead the only sound to break it. "Maybe I should ask the same of you," she ventured quietly. "What do you want of me, Nate?"

He looked back at her, the glitter in his eyes sending her heart into a free fall. "I want what I've wanted from the beginning. You in my bed, Mina. To explore every perfect inch of you with my mouth and my hands and everything else at my disposal."

She sucked in a breath. They were surrounded by hazy, purple sky, but it didn't seem to be supplying enough oxygen to her brain to fix her spinning head.

Wine seemed to be the answer. The sparkling rosé was delicious: tart and refreshing. It slid down easily as the sun sank into the sea, leaving behind it a stunning dusky-pink-stained sky. By the time she'd finished it, she'd almost convinced herself it was doing the trick—relaxing her taut limbs and clearing her head. Then Nate set his hand over hers, laced their fingers together and her pulse flatlined.

She looked down at his strong, elegant hand. Thought about what he'd done to her with it last night and her stomach did a slow roll.

"You want dinner?" he asked quietly.

She lifted her gaze to his and shook her head.

A purposeful heat blazed to life in his eyes. He took the empty glass from her hand and set it on the coffee table. His hands settled around her waist to lift her up and bring her down on his lap so her knees straddled his thighs.

Her breath caught in her throat. *Dio mio.* He was all hard muscle beneath her, the intensity of his dark gaze fixed on hers. She might have been tempted to run if the want in his eyes hadn't drawn her in and kept her right where she was.

"You are so very beautiful," he said huskily. "You do something to me, Mina. I forget my common sense. I forget everything but having you."

She wasn't sure if that was a compliment or a criticism. She didn't much care when he lowered his head and took her mouth in one of those teasing, devastating kisses that rendered her brain useless. Her hands settled on his jaw, her mouth seeking his. Back and forth they exchanged the initiative, kissing and being kissed. Exploring and being explored. Slow, lazy kisses that seemed to match the night darkening around them, pulling them further and further under each other's spell.

Lips, tongue, sexy little nibbles. They did it all, for ages, until she wondered if Nate would do anything *else*.

She gave his lip a frustrated tug with her teeth. Nate pulled back, an amused glint in his eyes. "What was that for?"

"Aren't you going to—I mean—*you know…*?"

He reclined back against the seat, his mouth curving. "I'm right here, Mina. Yours for the taking."

Her insides twisted at the invitation. But his mouth was soft from their kisses, his eyes a molten dark brown. He was letting her take the lead, making sure she was comfortable. Putting her first as he always did. She swallowed, her chest tight.

Pulling her gaze from his hot, watchful study, she worked the top button of his shirt free, then painstakingly worked her way down the row. Her throat went dry as she exposed more and more of his beautiful torso. Flat, hard and defined, he was incredible. His swift intake of air when her fingers brushed against his lower abs was headily empowering.

The last button undone, she found her next move surprisingly intuitive. Splaying her palms across his hot, hard skin, she bent her head and pressed her lips to the sinewy solid muscle, absorbing his earthy, salty flavor. Nate made a sound of approval low in his throat, his hands falling to the sofa to give her better access.

Pulling back, she moved her fingertips down over his pectoral muscles to the hard points that were so much alike, yet so very different from hers. Nate sucked in a breath. "Careful. Men are very sensitive there."

She traced him gently. Moved her thumbs back and forth over him. He let her play for a few moments, then grabbed her hands and dragged them down to her sides. "Enough of that."

She wondered where to go next, but she needn't have worried. Nate took control, pressing a hot kiss to the sensitive skin at the base of her neck as he swept the straps of her dress off her shoulders. His mouth followed his hands as he eased the material away from her skin, his lips finding the soft flesh of her upper breasts, the hollow in between. She held her breath as he pushed the material lower and bared her breasts to his gaze. The lust in his eyes as he palmed her flesh made her stomach curl. "So beautiful."

She closed her eyes. The brush of his thumbs across her nipples in a slow sweep made her gasp. The sensation of his touch on her bare skin was even better than last night. So much more intense…

A wet heat enveloped one of the peaks. Her eyes flew open. Nate's dark head was bent to her, his mouth closed around her aching flesh. She squeezed her eyes shut as he laved her with his tongue, scraped at her with his teeth, sucked on her. A low moan escaped her throat.

"You like that?" he asked. Mina's head tipped up and down. He lavished the same treatment on its twin until her fingers were in his hair holding on for dear life and her whole body felt tense and on edge.

"Nate," she begged. "It's too much."

He lifted his head. Settled her further back on his thighs. The sweep of his hot palms up her inner thighs, squeezing her flesh as he went, was tantalizing, blindingly intimate. "You don't need less," he murmured. "You need different."

She remembered *different* from last night. She wanted more of it. Except it was too intimate, him watching her face as he moved closer to the heat between her legs. Her eyes drifted closed. *Waiting, anticipating.*

His hands stilled. "Open your eyes. I want to see what I do to you."

Her breath left her in a whoosh. *"No."*

"Yes."

She opened her eyes. He swept the filmy material of her panties aside and slid his fingers against her hot, wet flesh. Her lashes fluttered closed as a bolt of heat went through her. *She couldn't do it.*

His wicked fingers played over her, slid inside her. She arched against them, urged him on. Nate's breath was hot at her ear, telling her how much he loved how she responded to him, how sexy she was. As wicked as his hands were, his raspy voice was sexier, unearthing a heated flush all over her body. *Hot*, she was far too hot to breathe.

"Nate," she gasped.

His ebony gaze scorched hers. "Baby, the way you say my name…it makes me crazy."

His hands slid away from her. She started to protest, her body screaming for relief. He lifted her off him and set her on the sofa, dropping to his knees in front of her.

"Nate—"

"Relax," he murmured. "I'm not finished."

She gaped at him. "What are you—Nate, you can't do that."

He nudged her legs apart and moved between them. "You'll like it, I promise."

"Yes, but—"

He slid the hem of her dress unerringly up her thighs. "But what?"

"It's *shocking*."

"Shocking," he agreed, sliding his hands under her buttocks to pull her to the edge of the sofa.

Oh, mio Dio. Her head fell back against the cushions as his hands swept the lacy underwear off her and tossed them to the side. Her eyes closed, her heart slamming in her chest as his palms pushed her thighs apart and his fingers parted her most intimate flesh. A long, slow lap of his tongue brought her hips off the sofa. "Nate—" she breathed. He set a hand to her stomach to ground her, held her in place while he consumed her, every stroke against her hot, moist flesh taking her past her initial sensitivity into a deeper, headier pleasure.

Again and again he stroked her until she was begging, saying his name in a broken tone. Voicing his husky approval, he brought his fingers back into play, easing them inside of her. The penetration along with his hot, amazing mouth on her drove her higher, past where she'd been last night. Until she could take it no more.

"*Per favore.* Please—"

He closed his mouth over her clitoris and sent her tumbling into another universe.

She was still coming down from her orgasm when Nate scooped her up and carried her into the dark, silent bedroom. She stood, knees shaking, legs ready to give way, as he flicked on a light and cast the room in a soft glow.

The lust on his face as he wrapped a hand around her waist and drew her back to him made her even weaker. "Okay?"

She nodded.

A smile tipped his lips. "That wasn't too improper?"

"*Sì*, it was. But I liked it."

The fire in his eyes made her insides dissolve into a throbbing pool of heat. He tipped her chin up with his finger and pressed a lingering kiss against her mouth. She stood on tiptoe, wound her arms around his neck and kissed him back. Pressed against him in search of closer contact. Froze as she felt his rock-hard erection throb against her belly.

Goodness, but he was big. *Was that normal?* How would she handle him?

She stepped back. Pulled in a deep breath. Nate frowned, looking more than a little hot and bothered. "What?"

"*That.*" Her gaze dropped to the bulge in his pants. "I—should I be doing something about that for you now? The girls in school said—"

"Said what?"

"That a woman could—you know—take the edge off for a man."

His mouth twitched. She had the awful feeling he was laughing at her. "It's true," he said solemnly. "Men do enjoy that. I'd prefer to take the edge off *with* you, however."

Her insides did a slow twist. "*Sì*. That's fine, then."

Nate turned her around. Set his lips to her nape. "It will be more than fine."

She quivered under his kiss as he slid the zipper of her dress down to her waist. He pushed it off her shoulders and let it slide to the floor. Air wafted across her shoulders in a delicate caress. He pressed a kiss to her shoulder blades, sank to his knees and continued his kisses, lingering at the indentation at the small of her back. Then his mouth was on the curve of her bottom.

She pulled in a breath. "Nate. What *are* you doing?"

"Indulging myself," he said huskily, his mouth against her skin. "I've had fantasies about this particular part of your anatomy."

Oh. Hands on her hips, he turned her around. His dark gaze was hot on her body. Far too intense to take. "Stunning," he said quietly. "You are every man's dream."

She stared at him, unable to look away. She didn't care if she was anyone else's dream. She only wanted to be his.

His hands tightened around her hips, drawing her to him. Mina watched as his eyes zeroed in on the dark curls between her legs. "No," she said, grabbing a handful of his hair. "Nate—no—"

He put his mouth to her. Stirred her back to life with every reverent kiss. Her body tightened. Thought ceased. By the time he rose to his feet, lifted her into his arms and deposited her on the bed, she was panting for him.

He stripped off his shirt, then the rest of his clothing. Mina's eyes grew wide. *How was this going to work? It couldn't work.*

He came down on the bed beside her. Brought his mouth to hers. "You were made to take me," he murmured against her lips. "I promise you, Mina. Trust me."

She did. Her mouth softened beneath his, her body slackening under his caresses. His hands left her to roll a condom on, his jerky, quick movements telling her how much he wanted her. Then he was between her legs, sliding her knees further apart and moving his hand beneath her bottom to cup her buttock. Palming himself, he lifted her and brought his huge shaft to her core. Mina closed her eyes and waited for the pain. Nate played with her instead, getting her used to the feel and pressure of him.

When she could take it no longer, she arched her hips. "Nate. *Per favore.*"

His ebony eyes flashed in the dim light. "You want me, baby?"

"*Sì.*"

He sank into her just enough to stretch her body. Waited while she accommodated him. When she raised her hips for more, he gave it to her, watching her face the entire time, making it such an intensely erotic experience she forgot her fear.

She arched her hips again, took more of him in until she felt a pressure, a resistance. "A little bit of pain and then lots of pleasure," he promised huskily. She nodded and grabbed a handful of sheet as he surged forward and broke through the barrier. A searing pain lanced through her. She breathed through it, Nate holding himself completely still. Then the pain was fading and she felt only full, stretched by his virility. *Possessed.*

"Okay?" His dark eyes were glazed with the effort it was taking him to hold back.

She nodded. Forced her limbs to relax as he started to move, ever so slowly as her body softened around him. Discomfort turned to pleasure as he stroked every nerve ending inside of her, filling her, then withdrawing. Her hips started to move, demanding more. Nate's gaze burned into hers. "Good?"

"*Sì.* So good, Nate. I had no idea it could be so…*good.*"

"I told you," he said, taking both her buttocks in his hands now as he brought his mouth down on hers, "your beautiful body was made for me."

His words did something to her insides. Dissolved her into a pool of lust as he stroked deeper. But it was more than that. He might not see the connection between them but she did. It was special. *Powerful.*

She arched her hips and took him deeper. Begged for more against his mouth. He made her say his name as she begged, filling her deeper, harder. Again and again until she was burning up. His hand at her buttock angled her, then as he moved even deeper, touched a place inside of her that promised pleasure like none before. She bit into his lip to urge him on. Nate growled and surged harder inside of her. "I need you with me, baby. Can you feel that?"

"*Sì.* Oh, Nate."

He drove into her then, the animalistic, desperate pace he set stirring her blood to a fever pitch. She matched him stroke for stroke until he hit that spot inside of her and tore her apart, her orgasm so intense she buried her fingernails in his thighs.

His big body tensed, then shuddered against her, his hands clamping hard around her buttocks. When he was finally still, he rolled over on his back and brought her down on his chest. Slowly her world righted itself.

She kept her eyes shut. Wanted to memorize every detail, every minute of what had just happened, it had been so perfect.

Too restless to sleep after that mind-bending experience taking his wife's innocence, Nate left Mina sleeping and ordered them a light meal in case she woke up hungry. Then he took his laptop back out to the terrace to work.

Resting his head against the back of the sofa, he watched

the play of the light on the water. It flickered like flames lapping the blue-black canvas that surrounded him. If he'd anticipated bedding Mina would be more about him ensuring her first time was good for her, he had clearly underestimated his wife's effect on him. How every inch of her inflamed his senses. How every innocent, passionate response to his lovemaking had pulled him deeper and deeper into the web she'd so effortlessly spun around him. Into the incandescent spirit that was Mina.

To go through what she had and emerge with such strength, such belief in the world around her, was remarkable to him. The survivor in her was just as sexy to him as the delectable packaging.

The distant roar of a jet taking off brought his head up. Pierced the almost eerie stillness around him, forcing his brain to admit the truth along with it. He couldn't call what they'd just done sex. Even a man hell-bent on deluding himself would be a fool to make that claim.

He felt something for Mina, something he'd never felt for a woman before. It went beyond the protectiveness he'd initially felt for her to a place deep inside his chest. A place he'd long ago marked forbidden for him.

He knew what it was like to allow yourself to feel, to want things you couldn't have. Because contrary to what his grandfather thought, what Mina had accused him of, he had made an effort to connect with his brother Alex. He had sought him out, made tentative overtures when he'd begun his tenure at Di Sione Shipping, thinking they had been similar animals—wounded beasts who had made themselves into warriors. Perhaps to attempt to put his and his brother's dark past to rest. Only to have Alex shut him down cold. As if he wasn't good enough to breathe the same air as him.

His fingers tightened around the steel casing of his laptop—the tool he used to command an empire built brick by brick by his need to prove none of it mattered to him. That he could shine the brightest.

Some days he managed to convince himself it was true. On others, his past ate away at his insides, slowly but surely corroding his soul. The price he paid for choosing the life he had.

The smoky trail of the departing jet dissolved into the sky, a wisp of gray against black. Mina's dark, dark eyes as he'd taken her filled his head. The *wonder* in them at what they created together. He was playing a dangerous game with her. He knew it. As inevitable as it seemed, the rules he'd insisted on seemed more important than ever.

He had nothing to offer Mina except what his tutelage and position could provide in the way of a successful transition into a business career when their year was up. Some other man would give Mina the happily-ever-after she craved, the *unconditional love*.

Confining himself to the mutual satisfaction they'd promised each other was the only way forward. Or he would break her heart. Not an option when his wife's heart had already been shattered one too many times.

CHAPTER TEN

EVERYTHING FELT DIFFERENT after Mina's earth-shattering night with Nate. The world seemed to come into a bright, intense focus as they toured the island with the resort manager and viewed the enhancements that had been recently made, all of it so much more vividly real to her than it had been before. As if Nate had awoken part of her sensory being she'd never tapped into before. Hadn't even known existed.

The extent to which she *hadn't* been living was thrown into stark relief. Anger at herself for allowing it to happen, for allowing her mother to rule her life, became a thankfulness that she had finally taken control of her destiny. It made her determined to seize every moment and relish it.

Another disconcerting reality came to light during those heady two days in the Maldives. She was falling for Nate. *Hard.* Something she'd said she wouldn't do. She tried to tell herself it *must* be part of the knight in shining armor fantasy she'd built around him. For what he'd given her—the precious freedom to pursue her life on her own initiative. But she worried it was much, much more than that.

And how unwise was that? she thought as they flew across the world to New York—her new home. To allow herself to fall for a man who had no interest in a permanent relationship with anyone. Who would run in the opposite direction if he knew her feelings.

She stole a glance at her husband as he frowned over a report in the seat beside her. She wasn't even sure how it had happened. Perhaps it had been when he'd claimed her innocence with such achingly tender care. When she'd seen in his dark eyes an equally emotional response to what she'd been feeling. As if what they shared was as rare and monumental as it seemed.

And perhaps that was just in her imagination.

She gave her head a shake and picked up her steaming mug of what you could barely call coffee. To try and convince herself Nate had feelings for her would be making an even bigger mistake than she'd already made. Better to bury whatever infatuation she'd developed deep and use her mental energy to fortify herself for her introduction to New York.

Already the tabloids had caught wind of her and Nate's nuptials. It seemed one of the employees at the Grand Hong Kong had given a reporter a scoop on the real-estate magnate's new marital status. The reporter had dug a bit into Mina's aborted vows in Palermo and had dubbed her *"Nate's stunning runaway Sicilian bride."*

Her stomach rolled. She had the social skills to assume the role of Nate's high-society wife, but she had a feeling her level of sophistication would prove woefully inadequate when it came to the circles he traveled in. And then there was the coming challenge of proving herself in her new marketing role...

She gave an inward shiver. She'd never been to America. Had never visited the intimidating city of New York she knew only from movies. It seemed full of slickly dressed businesspeople who talked fast and had extremely dry senses of humor.

What would they make of her?

"Stop fretting," Nate murmured. "Or I will be forced to find a way to divert you."

The glitter in his heavy-lidded gaze brought every cell in her body to instant attention. "I'm not fretting." His brow lifted. "*Ebbene*, I am," she conceded. "What if my coworkers don't like me? What if your friends, the press, don't like me?"

His gaze softened. "They will love you because you have an innate charm that will win everyone over, Mina. And you are talented. Be yourself and you'll be fine."

She held that close to her heart as they landed at a small private airfield in New Jersey and climbed into the car that was waiting for them. Nate made a phone call to his grandfather to see if they could drop by and show him the ring before the workweek started. When he ended the call, his face was dark.

"He hasn't been well this week."

Her heart squeezed. "Should we go another time?"

"A short visit is fine. He's anxious to see the ring."

Traffic was thick on the highway, slowing to almost a crawl. Mina took the ring out of her purse and studied the beautiful, priceless sapphire.

"You said the Fountain Ring was once Giovanni's? Why did he have to sell it?"

"He came to America from Italy following the Second World War with only the clothes on his back. He needed to sell it to make his start here."

She turned the ring over. "It has an inscription on the inside. I saw it in Pasquale's office. '*Mistress of my heart—BA.*'"

He frowned and took it from her. "Those aren't Giovanni's initials."

She thought about it. "Perhaps they aren't initials. Perhaps it's some sort of a message to a lover?"

* * *

Nate thought about that as they made the rest of the slow trip to Long Island. *Had Giovanni had a lover he'd left behind in Italy?* It fit to some extent with the items his siblings had recovered, all of them precious mementos you might give to a lover.

Or perhaps they had nothing to do with an old love affair and were all distinct, separate memories his grandfather had for different times and places of his life?

Giovanni had been married to his wife, Maria, for almost twenty-five years, happy enough from what he'd discerned. But his grandfather was a mystery. Had always been. He had a feeling there was a lot more to know about the legendary shipping tycoon than what he'd revealed.

The clue to his grandfather's past rattled around his brain until they arrived at the Di Sione villa. The doctor was just leaving.

"Keep it brief," he said. "He needs the rest."

A tightness seized Nate's chest. "Is there a revised timeline?"

The doctor shook his head. "He has good weeks and bad. This one was tough. The drugs are helping with the pain but they're also sedating him."

Nate led Mina up the ornate, finely carved staircase to Giovanni's suite of rooms. He held up a hand for her to wait at the door, then ventured inside. His grandfather was lying in the massive mahogany bed, looking heart-droppingly small. Propped up by a mound of pillows, his eyes were half-closed. "Nathaniel," he said, his voice low and raspy. "Did you bring your new wife?"

The tabloids. Nate nodded and beckoned to Mina. "I'd like you to meet my grandfather Giovanni. Giovanni, it was Mina's family who owned the ring."

Giovanni sat up straighter. Gestured for Mina to come

closer, then pressed a kiss against her cheek. "I thought I must be hallucinating when I read the newspaper story. Although I knew Nate would fall hard when he met the right one."

Mina smiled. "It all happened rather quickly."

"Did you really leave your fiancé at the altar?"

"*Sì*. Nate and I...it was love at first sight."

"As it should be," said Giovanni, a distant look in his eyes. "It's the way of great love."

Mina's smile faltered. His grandfather didn't notice, his eyes trained on the box she held. "May I see the ring?"

She handed it to him. Giovanni removed the spectacular sapphire from the box. "Exactly as I remembered," he murmured, setting it on his palm and staring at it. "Funny how something precious can be lost to you through the passage of time, but a stone like this? It will be with us always."

Nate wanted desperately to ask his grandfather what the ring meant to him. But Giovanni had already made it clear he wasn't willing to share that information.

"Can I keep it for a few days?" his grandfather asked.

Mina nodded. "I cannot sell it to you until a year is up, as I'm sure Nate has told you. It was a condition my father made when he bequeathed it to me."

His grandfather nodded, shut the box and blinked rapidly. Nate stared hard at him as a tear rolled down Giovanni's weathered face. A fist reached in and clenched his heart. He had never seen Giovanni cry. Not once.

"I am very tired," said his grandfather. "I hope you will forgive me if I keep our visit short today?"

Nate nodded, his throat tight. "Of course."

His grandfather clasped his hand around his wrist and drew him close. "She's lovely. Be happy, Nate."

He opened his mouth to tell him he would visit again

during the week, but the emotion clogging his throat made it impossible.

He rested his forehead against his grandfather's. "I love you," he whispered.

Giovanni's fingers tightened around his. Something ripped loose in Nate's chest, casting him adrift in a stormy sea that threatened to swallow him whole. He turned and walked out of the room before it did.

Nate delivered Mina to his penthouse on the fifty-fifth floor of the Grand New York, a marquee space with sweeping vistas of the city. "Let Rosa know if you need anything," he said, showing her the suite he'd allocated for her.

They were the first words he'd issued since he'd walked out of his grandfather's house, his emotions too big for his heart to hold.

Leaving her to unpack, he went into his study and stood staring out the window at a gray Manhattan. The rage that rose inside of him was so swift and all-encompassing it blurred his vision. Blinded him to anything but the need to strike back. To escape the pain tearing his insides apart.

A sweep of his hand across his desk sent papers flying: contracts, letters of intent, reports on how much money he was worth. When that wasn't satisfying enough he picked up his CEO of the Year award and hurled it at the wall. A hand-carved glass paperweight followed it.

Chest heaving, he rested his palms on his desk, hung his head and cursed himself for taking everything for granted. For assuming this charmed life of his, which was in fact a hollow, poor excuse for an existence, could make up for wanting things that had never been his. For keeping his grandfather at a distance when Giovanni had offered him everything his pride would not allow him to take.

The love his father had refused to give him. The chance

to *belong* to something bigger than the lonely existence he had led.

Except even the all-powerful Giovanni could not wipe away the wounds a tragedy had left behind. The dysfunction his father and Anna's volatile relationship had wreaked. He and his Di Sione siblings were proof of that.

"Nate."

He levered himself away from the desk to find Mina standing in the doorway, eyes wide, hands clenched at her sides.

"Leave me alone."

"Nate—"

"Leave me the hell alone."

Her face paled. She turned on her heel and left.

Mina finished unpacking in the suite Nate had appointed her, eyes burning, heart thumping. The verbal slap he'd administered stung. He was hurting. Hadn't said two words since they'd left Long Island. Then that *display* just now... the loss of his supreme control. The animallike pain in his eyes.

She wanted to help him, to comfort him. But Nate was a solitary animal. He didn't want her in his head. He didn't want her sharing his pain. He wanted to bury it until he went off like a time bomb.

The last of her suits hung up, she scooped her lacy underwear into a drawer. He'd made that part of their arrangement clear. *Don't expect intimacy from me.* It was just sex.

But she couldn't deny it hurt. Couldn't deny it stung after three nights of sleeping in his arms. Of sensing an emotional connection between them that was, perhaps, only in her own head.

Leaning against the exquisite hand-carved cherrywood dresser, she raked a hand through her hair. Breathed past the painful squeeze of her chest. *What was she doing?* Allowing herself to get pulled in even deeper with feelings for a man she couldn't have. Shouldn't want to have.

An affair was all it was supposed to have been. To experience everything she'd missed with a worldly, exciting man who made her toes curl. Allowing herself to develop feelings for Nate when he would walk away from her when his attention span waned was setting herself up for a fall. To have something she so desperately wanted and to once again be left alone was too much of a threat to the fragile sense of worth she'd acquired.

It would prove she was not lovable enough to keep. *Not good enough.* And she was never going there again. Ever.

Pushing away from the dresser, she walked past Nate's study. It was empty, the penthouse silent. He must have gone out, his usual pattern of walking when his emotions grew too great to bear.

Finding her way back to the gleaming stainless steel showpiece of a kitchen, she poured herself a glass of water and took it out to the terrace. The vast concrete and steel metropolis that spread out in front of her was gray and forbidding. A hazy layer of smog sat over the buildings like an embrace; the air felt gritty, harsh in her lungs; and beeping horns, whistles and sirens blended together in a chaotic symphony that would surely keep her up all night.

A wave of longing descended over her. For the vibrant blue sea and sky. The taste of salt air on her lips...

"Not a very good introduction." Strong hands slid around her waist and drew her back against Nate's hard body. "But it can be very beautiful and alive. Give it a day and it will pass."

Her spine remained rigid. He drew her closer, his lips nuzzling her nape. "I shouldn't have taken my anger out on you. I'm sorry."

She softened. "You were hurting."

"Yes. I thought I had dealt with my emotions, but clearly I hadn't."

"You love him. This isn't going to be easy for you."

Silence stretched. "I hadn't told him I loved him until today. It hit me that I could have lost him and he would never have known."

She twisted around in his arms. "He knows. You only have to see you two together to know that."

His mouth flattened, pain darkening his eyes. "I've wasted so much time."

"Then make the most of what you have left. Forge a deeper connection with your siblings."

"We've been through this," he said abruptly. "There is too much baggage there. Too much history to make that happen."

"Says who? Who doesn't want a relationship? You or them?"

His body stiffened. She thought she might have pushed it too far, her muscles tensing for an explosion. A long, silent moment passed. Then he expelled a breath and raked a hand through his hair.

"My mother was my father's secretary. She had an affair with him during a rough patch in his marriage, thinking he loved her, that he would leave his family for her. But that was the way of my father and his wife Anna's relationship. They were big partyers, volatile personalities. They repaired their marriage and my father ended things with my mother. She is a very proud woman. She left her job with Benito and found another. Then she discovered she was pregnant. She couldn't keep the job she'd taken—it was too demanding. She found another but it didn't pay much. My father had made it clear he wanted nothing to do with her. She waited until we were nearly broke before she went to his house one night with me to ask for financial assistance. He shut the door in our faces."

Her breath caught in her throat.

"My father and Anna argued after my mother and I left. They were supposed to attend a party that night, one of those drug-infused affairs of the day where the wealthy blew all their money playing far too hard. My father was notorious for his love of illicit drugs and drink. After their argument, he wrapped their car around a tree and killed himself and Anna."

Oh, mio Dio. "What happened to your siblings?"

"Giovanni took them in."

"But he didn't find out about you until later," she said, remembering. "When Alex found you. How did *he* know about you?"

"He was watching from the window that night. He put two and two together."

She tilted her head to one side and asked the question that had been on her mind since Hong Kong. "Why didn't you bond with your siblings then? That must have been an incredibly emotional experience giving your grandfather his life back."

"Because I didn't want a relationship with them," he said roughly. "I wanted nothing to do with the Di Siones. I couldn't refuse Giovanni's offer to put me through school, to give me a start in business, but that didn't mean I wanted anything to do with a family who'd never acknowledged my existence. Who didn't think I was good enough to be a part of it."

"That wasn't your siblings' fault. It was your father's."

"I made overtures. Overtures which were rebuffed. I knew where I stood."

"Perhaps your siblings have gained a different perspective now." She bit her lip, then plunged into the deep end.

"You will regret it if you don't make another attempt. Do you know how much I wish I had brothers and sisters? Yes, maybe they would have come with baggage, but at least they would have been there for me. I would have had *somebody* to lean on."

"This is different." His eyes flashed a warning. "There is no point rehashing a past that can't be changed. Leave it alone, Mina."

She shook her head. "You can't run from your emotions, Nate. Throw away something so valuable. Or what happened today will happen again. Only worse. And then maybe it *will* be too late."

"Mina," he growled, snaking an arm around her waist and dragging her to him. "I said *no more.*"

Fury pulsed in his gaze like a living, breathing entity. The hands that held her were full of leashed aggression. Intensity surrounded him like a black cloud. He was seconds away from another explosion.

"Bene," she breathed. *"Bene."*

Her heart tattooed itself against her chest as he slid an arm underneath her knees and picked her up.

"What are you doing?"

"Shutting you up."

Nate carried his wife into his bedroom, a maelstrom of emotion coursing through him. Big emotions, intense emotions Mina managed to pull out of him with that caring, empathetic side of her that never judged, only validated, making him want things he'd long ago decided were impossible.

It was like walking in a minefield, allowing his feelings to surface. To acknowledge just how much his grandfather meant to him. Just how angry he was at himself. Too viciously painful to venture any further into, so he retreated by turning his intensity on the woman he couldn't seem to get enough of. The woman who blanked his brain of anything but her when he came within a five-foot radius of her.

He set Mina down on the floor. "Take off your clothes."

She gave him one of those wide-eyed looks as he started to strip. He thought she might refuse given the mood he was in. Then heat took hold in her beautiful eyes, the attraction she couldn't fight. The trust she reserved for him no matter what he asked of her.

Her hands moved to the top button of her blouse. She undid the buttons slowly, clumsily, until the last was undone. He watched her the whole time, holding her gaze with his. She unzipped her skirt, pushing it off her hips with a wriggle that turned him hard as stone. Clad in her lacy underwear, her eyes drank him in. Fell to the last piece of clothing he wore. His boxers did nothing to disguise his arousal.

"Come here."

She blinked. Hesitated. Then walked toward him, stopping a couple of inches away. She was so beautiful standing there, so perfectly formed, so highly desirable, his throat went dry.

He nodded his head toward his boxers. "Take them off."

She swallowed convulsively. A silence followed, then she stepped forward, slid her fingers beneath the elastic of his underwear and pushed them down so his pulsing arousal sprang free.

He stepped out of them and kicked them to the side. Gave in to the fantasy that had been raging in his head ever since she'd offered it to him that night in the Maldives. "I have an edge that needs to be taken off," he drawled in a gravelly voice full of need. "If you are so inclined."

A flush spread across her cheeks. His heart pounded painfully in his chest. When she sank to her knees, her dark eyes liquid with desire, the blood roared in his head.

"Sì," she murmured. "I am. But you need to tell me if I'm doing it all wrong."

He would have told her that every time she touched him was *right* if his brain had been working. But it had ceased functioning when she'd dropped to her knees.

She took him in her hands and closed her fingers around his shaft. Her tentative, exploratory movements as she worked her way up and down the length of him fired his blood like no practiced touch had ever done. The pleasure that wrote itself across her face as he thickened, lengthened, for her inflamed him. And that was before she took him into the heat of her mouth and just about destroyed him.

He buried his hands in her hair and told her how good it felt. How he wanted it. Where he wanted it. Mina indulged him, seemingly as intoxicated as he was. And then he was there, too fast.

He manacled his fingers around her wrist. "You take more of an edge off," he muttered roughly, in response to the dismayed look on her face, "and it'll be all over."

He bent, picked her up and carried her to the bed. She watched as he rolled on a condom, so much bolder than she'd been that first night. Everything was on display in that face of hers, her open lust for him almost pushing him over the edge.

The mattress depressed as he joined her on the bed. Sinking his palms into her waist he lifted her atop him, his aroused body brushing against her in the most potent of caresses. Mina closed her eyes, allowing him to control the contact. "Nate," she breathed.

Her slick arousal admitted him easily. He brought her down on him, slowly, so she felt every bit of him fill her. Her low moan sent his blood pressure skyrocketing. He wanted, needed, her too much. Needed her to anesthetize his brain as he knew she could.

He flexed his hips and filled her completely. Her gasp split the air. "Okay?" he gritted.

"Sì." Her eyes were glued to his, glazed with pleasure. "It's so *good* like this."

A muttered oath escaped him. He lifted her up and brought her down on him again. Again and again, driving deeper into her slick, tight body with every thrust.

"Nate," Mina cried, her body tightening around his, *"Dio mio,* Nate…"

He wrapped his fingers around her nape and brought her forward until he could see the pleasure exploding in her eyes. "That's it, beautiful," he murmured. "Come for me."

Her eyes went a molten espresso as she contracted around him. The sensation sent him into a mind-blowing climax that made the room rock.

It was long moments before his brain returned to earth, his hands sliding over Mina's ample curves. She arched like a kitten into his touch, her eyes heavy-lidded. "Do you want me to go to my own room?"

His heart lurched at the question. He should take her there. Establish some boundaries from the start so they both had their space. But he'd gotten used to having her in his arms. And since when had resisting Mina gotten him anywhere?

"Stay," he murmured, brushing his lips against her temple. "I'm going to turn out the lights and I'll be back."

She curled into his warmth when he returned, already drifting into unconsciousness as he wrapped himself around her. He tuned out the fact he'd never let another female stay the night in this bed along with the premonition this dangerous game he was playing with his wife was on a course for disaster.

The time for turning back had long passed.

CHAPTER ELEVEN

IF MINA HAD THOUGHT her first few weeks working for Nate had been tough, her first couple at the Brunswick Developments head office were an exercise in survival. Nate's marketing director came exactly as advertised. A tough, native New Yorker, she had little time to pander to the CEO's wife. Not that Mina wanted her to—she wanted exactly the opposite, to stand on her own two feet.

And stand on her own two feet she did, as Carole put her to work immediately with a get-busy-ask-questions-as-you-need-to approach.

After floundering through one project, afraid to appeal to her intimidating new boss for help, Mina started asking questions. She tapped her boss when she needed to and winged it when she could, learning more in those two weeks than she was sure she would have in a year at school.

When Carole capped off her second week with praise for her first complete marketing plan, she thought she'd died and gone to heaven. It was almost enough to banish her nerves as she and Nate drove uptown to his mother's penthouse for the cocktail party she was throwing in their honor.

Nate had put his mother off as long as he could manage to give Mina time to adjust to the city and her new job, but he could stall no longer, so tonight was the night she was to be introduced to the toast of New York society.

The nerve-racking drive with Nate weaving in and out of traffic, combined with her nerves, started to make her feel nauseous. Odd when she didn't ever remember getting carsick, but this was Manhattan they were talking about.

Nate studied her face as they rode the elevator to his mother's apartment. "You okay? You look a little green."

She forced a smile. "Nerves, combined with your driving, I expect."

He put a hand to the wall beside her. "You don't get carsick."

"Not usually."

"Don't be nervous." He cupped the back of her head. "You're stunningly beautiful, Mrs. Brunswick. You'll charm them all."

She wanted to tell him to stop calling her that. That every time he did, every time he kissed her, she fell harder for him. But his lips were on hers then, driving everything from her head. Even the fear she was in love with him.

He lifted his head as the elevator pinged their arrival, his breath mingling with hers. "Now you look the part," he murmured, jabbing a button to keep the doors closed. "Fix your lipstick."

Her makeup repaired, they joined the party. Emily Brunswick, a dynamic, attractive woman in her late fifties Mina had liked from the moment she'd met her, made it her mission to introduce Mina to everyone in the room. Her nausea abated, Mina actually enjoyed herself with Emily easing the way.

She was in the middle of a conversation with her mother-in-law and the director of an art gallery when the strong smell of an hors d'oeuvre turned her stomach. Her nausea resurfaced with a vengeance, a wave of perspiration blanketing her. She had barely enough time to excuse herself and make it to the powder room before her stomach announced its intentions to vacate itself.

When she'd decided the heaving had stopped for good, she got to her feet, splashed water on her face and attempted to repair her makeup.

"Mina?" Nate's voice pierced the wooden door.

She opened it to find him standing there, a frown on his face. "You were sick?"

"No," she denied, "I'm fine."

"You're a terrible liar," he said flatly. "We're leaving."

"But your mother went to all this trouble..."

It was no use. He was already pulling her toward Emily to say good-night. Mina assured Nate's mother she was fine, likely just exhausted, and apologized for cutting the evening short. In the car, she sat through a lecture from Nate about how she shouldn't let things like this get to her.

"I don't think it was the party." She pressed her head back against the seat. "I was fine after the first few minutes. Your mother is lovely."

He glanced over at her. "A bug, maybe?"

"Probably."

Except she never got stomach sick from bugs. Maybe once in her life. And she never got carsick. The more she thought about it, the colder she got, mixing with the perspiration to make her feel distinctly clammy. *There was no way she could be...*

Her heart seized. She'd gone to a doctor to get birth control pills as soon as she'd arrived in New York to be doubly sure there was no chance she could get pregnant. Because getting pregnant would be a disaster.

Maledizione. She wiped a palm over her brow. She was making herself ill just thinking about it.

Nate put her to bed when they got home and went off to do some email, promising he'd check on her in a few minutes. She rested her head against the pillows and stared blankly out at the spectacular view of New York. She could not be pregnant. It was impossible. Nate wore condoms; she was on the pill, *newly* on the pill but...

She got out of bed. Pulled on yoga pants, a T-shirt and running shoes, grabbed her purse and took the long way around the penthouse to the door to avoid Nate's study. Riding the elevator to ground level, she headed toward the drugstore in the lobby. Surprisingly, enough people must wonder if they're pregnant while on vacation or business trips because the shelves were liberally stocked. Heart pounding, she snatched up two and got into line to pay.

The lineup was five people deep. She tapped her foot impatiently as she waited. Finally, she got to the front of the line, paid and hightailed it back up to the penthouse. Pressing her thumb on the biometric scan, she walked into a solid wall of... *Nate.*

Lurching backward, she shoved the bag behind her. "*Dannazione.* You scared me."

Nate eyed her darkly. "What were you doing roaming the streets while you're sick? Roaming the streets at night, *period*?"

She pulled in a breath. "I needed a...a book. And I wasn't roaming the streets. I went to the store in the building."

"Really?" He nodded toward the hand she had behind her back. "What kind of books are you buying?"

"Not ones you need to see." She went to walk past him. Nate caught her wrist in a firm grip.

"What's in the bag, Mina?"

She cocked her head to one side. "Honestly, can a girl not have a little privacy?"

"Not tonight she can't. Not when you were upending

the contents of your stomach into the toilet an hour ago and that's a drugstore bag behind your back."

Her brain worked furiously. "It's an old-fashioned remedy we Sicilians use."

"Fascinating. Show it to me."

"Nate—"

He reached around her with catlike swiftness and plucked the bag out of her hand. Mina pressed her palms to her eyes.

The longest silence of her life followed. She dropped her hands. Nate was *gray*. "It's just a precaution," she said, talking fast. "It can't possibly be that. My imagination was running away with me and—"

"I used a condom every time. You're on the pill."

"Sì," she said, nodding quickly. "Like I said, it's just a precaution. I only did it because I didn't feel well yesterday, either, and I thought why… Nate," she said, frowning as he turned even grayer, "maybe you should sit down."

He ran his palm over the stubble on his chin. "I think you," he said slowly, handing her the bag, "should go do the tests. One—two—whatever works."

She closed her fingers around the bag. Decided there was nothing else *to* do. She walked with a pounding heart toward the powder room, closed the door and leaned against it. *You can do this.*

Two positive tests later, she was sitting on the decorative love seat in the powder room composing herself when Nate flung the door open. "Out."

She handed the tests to him, walked past him and collapsed on the sofa in the salon. The door to the garbage can thumped shut, a long silence followed and then Nate walked into the salon, headed straight to the bar and poured himself a drink. *Not fair.*

"Mi dispiace," she said quietly.

He gave her a grim look. "Why are you apologizing? It takes two to make a baby."

"Because this is a disaster."

He didn't refute the statement. Instead, he sat down beside her and downed a healthy gulp of the amber liquid in the glass.

"I would never—"

"Stop," he said harshly. "I would never suggest that."

The funny expression on his face caught her off guard. Then she realized what she'd said. Nate had been the result of an unexpected pregnancy...

"I didn't mean—"

"I know you didn't."

The seconds rolled by, the ticking of the clock on the wall excruciatingly loud to Mina's sensitized nerve endings. With every second that passed, with every moment that frozen, dismayed look continued to sit on Nate's face, her heart slipped deeper into despair. He didn't want a relationship, let alone a baby. He was horrified.

She had just attained her freedom, had begun a job she loved. It couldn't be worse timing.

Her head throbbed, blood hammered against her temples. She wanted to feel joy, because surely a baby was a wonderful thing. Instead, she dropped her head in her hands and prayed for this to be a dream she'd wake up from soon.

"Stop panicking," Nate rasped. "We will figure this out."

"How?" She lifted her head. "You can't even be in a relationship, Nate. How are you going to handle being a father?"

"Day by day, step by step. And I think we are already doing a pretty good approximation of a relationship."

"Because you know you can walk away the minute you

feel claustrophobic. The minute your attachment antenna picks up too strong a signal, we're done."

He rested his dark, fathomless gaze on her. "If that were true I would have already cut things off."

So he knew. Knew that she was in love with him. Hot color climbed into her face. "Why haven't you? Why break your rules for me, Nate? Because of that knight in shining armor complex you have for me you deny but is so patently obvious? Because you think I'm so vulnerable I'll break if you do?"

His gaze dropped away from hers. "I don't know."

"Well, I do." Humiliation and pain brought everything spilling out. "You have feelings for me. You won't allow yourself to explore them because you're afraid they'll bring this house of cards you have built tumbling down."

Heat blazed in his eyes. "I have let you in, Mina. I have shared things I've never shared with anyone before."

"Because there's no risk! I'm out the door in a year. You have a built-in out." She waved her arms around her. "None of this is threatening because we're just playing our roles. You're the honorable knight, I'm the damsel in distress. It justifies everything."

He slapped the glass down on the table and glared at her. "What do you want from me? I care about you. You know that. I have opened up my life to you, tried to give you everything you need."

"And I will never be able to repay you for that." She met the frustration burning in his eyes with a lifted chin. "What you have given to me, Nate, is a gift. You walked into my life and not only saved me from Silvio, you saved me from *myself.* From sacrificing my life out of some misguided sense of loyalty to my mother. You have *empowered* me to be the person I knew I could be but was too afraid to realize. But this," she said, pointing at her stomach, "is real. It's our wake-up call. We can't play this game anymore."

He stared at her silently. She sucked in a deep breath, forcing herself to do what he wouldn't. "If you don't see our relationship ever moving past the status quo—that's fine. Honestly, Nate, it's fine. I told you in the beginning I could handle this and I can. I—" she broke off, raking a hand through her hair "—I just need to know."

Ice crackled as he picked up his glass, put it to his mouth and took another long sip. His face was impassive. "We have a good thing, Mina. The way I see it, we don't have much choice in the matter. We make this marriage permanent and do what's right by this child."

Her chest tightened. *Not because he loved her. Not because he wanted her in his life.* "Because you won't see this child abandoned by its father like you were?"

"Because it's the right thing to do." The edge to his voice sliced across her skin in sharp rebuke. "This child deserves the presence of both its parents in its life."

She closed her eyes against the pain in her temples. She'd been afraid to admit she loved him because of this. Because she'd feared her feelings wouldn't be returned. And now she had her answer.

A vision of the soul-destroying kind of a relationship she and Nate would share filled her head. How she would always be secretly hoping he'd learn to love her just as she had done her entire life with her mother, only to have it never be returned.

She wrapped her arms around herself, bile rising in her throat. She couldn't go back to being that lonely, desperate for affection version of herself she'd hated. Not ever again.

"Mina." Nate curled his fingers around her arm. "We are good together. You're flourishing at Brunswick Developments. It makes sense."

She opened her eyes, the affection she saw in his dark gaze driving her misery even deeper. "A loveless marriage isn't an option for me. No matter how practical."

An emotion she couldn't read flickered in his eyes. "This isn't one of those Hollywood movies you love. Being good together can go a long way."

She shook her head. "It wouldn't work. You'd come to resent me. Me and the baby. You said it yourself, a white picket fence existence isn't for you. You're a solitary creature, Nate. You need your space. My feelings for you would sit between us like this awkward thing we both won't address until you'd wished you'd ended it now."

The ensuing silence broke the rest of her heart. "You're not well," he said finally. "Not thinking rationally. We'll talk about this tomorrow."

It wouldn't change anything, she speculated miserably as he put her to bed and left her to no doubt ruminate about what a big mess they'd created. It had been her fault letting herself fall in love with him. Convincing herself he could change when he never would.

CHAPTER TWELVE

MINA WOULD COME AROUND.

It wasn't the first time Nate had told himself that on a dull, gray Manhattan afternoon, days after his and Mina's fruitless discussion about their future had ended in stalemate.

It had taken him that long to emerge from the numbness that had invaded his brain, the complete sense of unreality that had taken over his life. *He was going to be a father.* The one challenge he'd been sure he'd never take on. Had never wanted to take on.

Restless as he waited for a call from the West Coast that was now five minutes behind schedule, he pushed his chair back from his desk, got up and walked to the elegantly cased, floor-to-ceiling windows designed to provide maximum light to his sleek, darkly furnished office space. Gray New York in the dog days of winter didn't help his mood.

Further contemplation hadn't crystallized his and Mina's situation. The only thing he'd been able to coherently articulate to his wife in the strained conversations they'd had was his sense of responsibility when it came to their child. He would never allow his son or daughter to grow up without a father. He would stand by Mina and this child, he would give up the freedom he cherished so greatly and he would do his best by both of them.

That had to be enough.

As for the gray areas? His feelings for Mina. Her demand he address them. His confusion on all of the above. Avoidance had been his strategy. When Mina saw reason, that they were good together, that they were better off raising this child together, it would all sort itself out. Pushing himself into saying things he'd regret, making promises he couldn't keep, was not how he was going to play this.

Walking to his desk, he buzzed through to Josephine. "Can you find out why the West Coast call is late?"

"Will do. Oh, Nate?"

"Mmm?"

"Mina left early. Said she'd see you at home."

He frowned. "Was she not feeling well?"

"She seemed fine. A little pale, maybe. She's been working long hours."

He sat down at his desk after Jo went to chase his call. Mina always waited for him. She always had more than enough work to do. Was she not feeling well?

This morning she'd been unusually silent in the car as they'd driven in. She'd been off, in her own head since the revelation she was pregnant, but this morning had been different. She'd been completely distant.

An uneasy feeling working its way through him, he got to his feet, collected his jacket, grabbed his briefcase and stopped by Jo's desk. "I'll take the call in the car."

His sense that something was wrong grew as he sat in gridlocked traffic. By the time he walked into the penthouse he was cranky and worried. Stalking through the salon he found his wife in her bedroom. Absorbed the neatly packed suitcase on the floor.

"What is *that*?"

Mina folded the sweater she'd been holding and dropped

it into the case. Her hands clenched by her sides as she absorbed his aggressive stance. "I'm leaving."

He stepped closer, a buzzing sound filling his head. "*Where* exactly are you going?"

"Paris. I'm going to stay with Celia for a bit."

A seething anger, a fury he couldn't explain, spread through him. "Is this what you do? Run from everything?"

Her eyes darkened. "*That* is not fair."

He jammed his hands on his hips. "We can make this work, Mina. If you'd stop living in that fairy-tale world of yours and accept the fact that love is this mythological concept you women create that lasts exactly as long as the pheromones do."

She lifted her chin. "My *mamma* told me the night before my wedding, the night Silvio hit me, that life is not all sunshine and rainbows. Well, I disagree. I want that. I'd rather have a few years of wonderful than never knowing love at all."

Dear God. He expelled a breath. "So you're just going to give up the opportunity of a lifetime at Brunswick Developments, jet off to Paris and then what?"

"I was hoping you would help me with a job at the Grand in Paris."

A heavy feeling weighted his stomach. *She was serious.*

"I live here. When am I going to see my child?"

She gave him an even look. "You live on your jet. Even if I was in New York you'd rarely be home. You can come to Paris just as easily."

He pushed a hand through his hair. He didn't like the idea of her being an ocean away, and it didn't all have to do with the baby. "You don't have to work, regardless of what we do."

"I want to." Her gaze held his. "All of this, *everything* you've given me, has shown me how much I want this.

To stand on my own two feet. To go after my dreams and make my father proud. It won't be easy with this baby, but I'll make it work."

Reluctant admiration cooled his ire. "Why don't you just stay?" he said softly. "Don't throw away the life you've started to build. We'll find you your own place."

"Because you're here." Her mouth quivered with the admission. "Because I love you. You know I do. It would kill me to see you with other women because I know how it feels to have something so perfect now. To know I can have that with you. And I can't settle for anything less."

His heart stopped in his chest. He inhaled, tried to pull a breath in. "Mina—"

"Let me go," she said softly. "Let me be the gladiator you taught me to be."

He wished in that moment he had never taught her that damn analogy. That she didn't have the strength to walk away, because he didn't have the guts to stop her. Not when the price was opening himself up to all the pain the world had to offer. To the disillusionment in Mina's eyes when she discovered how empty he really was inside.

"Okay," he said. "I'll have the Grand contact you. When is your flight?"

The shattered look in her eyes almost unmanned him. "It's a red-eye tonight. I was going to take a cab. There's no need for you to drive me."

Tonight? A sharp stab of pain lanced through him. "I'll drive you," he said roughly. "Tell me when you're ready."

Traffic was surprisingly light for a weekday evening. They got to the airport in record time. Nate pulled the car up in front of the busy departures entrance and got out to help a pale Mina with her luggage.

"Are you sure you're fit to travel?"

"I have the medicine the doctor gave me in my purse."

Mina reached up to press a kiss against his cheek, looking so small and vulnerable it was all he could do not to haul her against him and forbid her to go. "I'll text you when I get to Celia's."

Don't let her go. A voice inside his head said it would be the biggest mistake he ever made. But the survival instinct in him was stronger. He opened his mouth to say something, *anything*, but she was already turning on her heel and walking away.

She did not look back.

He got into the car and watched her disappear into the terminal. Thought about that day she'd opened up the door to him in Palermo, a vision in white in her beautiful wedding dress. His for the taking. How he wasn't man enough to claim the gift that she was.

Nate finished his second Scotch in the quiet, oppressive confines of the penthouse and considered a third. Splayed out in his favorite chair, his eyes on the New York skyline, he tried to block out the delicate scent of Mina's perfume still lingering in the air. How her presence seemed to be everywhere. In his head. In his heart.

When the valet had asked after her tonight upon his return, he'd just looked at him dumbly as if the young college student had asked him why the moon was yellow.

He was in love with her. Had been for weeks. *He* who didn't even believe in the concept of the word. Or perhaps, more accurately, rejected it for what it had come to symbolize. *Pain, rejection, heartache.*

The emptiness he felt now was different from the constant, recurring version of it that had characterized his life. The knowledge that perhaps he could be whole if he had Mina made it particularly acute. Because he had been happy with her for the first time in his life.

He'd embarked on this three-act play of a marriage with her with the caveat it wasn't real. It was all about the end goal—a ring for his grandfather to make him happy in his dying days, and a new life for Mina. When, in fact, everything about them had been real.

Instead of facing the truth—instead of facing his feelings for Mina head-on—he'd decided to allow the story to run to its inevitable conclusion. Hoping he'd never have to make a conscious decision, an admission about how he felt about his wife.

Except Mina had called his bluff. He might have taught her how to be a warrior, but *she* had taught him survivors like them had to fight their inner battles, too. Disarm the defenses they'd constructed to have a chance at a future that transcended their past. In that, she was way ahead of him.

She had given him precious months with Giovanni, had taught him to acknowledge his feelings would not destroy him—they would free him. And yet he had let her walk away. As if he could exist without her now. *Hell.* He scowled and reached for the bottle.

He had the cap off before he stopped, screwed it back on and picked up the phone.

"Nate." Surprise edged Alex's voice. "What's up?"

"Can we meet for a drink?"

"Now?"

"Now. Tomorrow. Whatever works."

A pause. "Sure. You want to meet at that new place in the Ritz?"

Thirty minutes later, he was sliding into a chair opposite his elder brother in the upscale bar that overlooked Central Park.

"Nate." Alex nodded at him in that measured way of his.

"Alex."

As dark-featured as he was, with the same designer stubble and hard edge, the resemblance between the two of them was unmistakable. But it went deeper than the cosmetics—right down to their personalities, which tended toward the moodier side of the spectrum.

Alex moved his gaze over Nate's rumpled shirt and hair. "You look like you could use a drink."

"Might as well continue my momentum."

His brother flagged a waiter and asked for a bottle of Scotch. A wary silence followed.

"Thank you for coming," Nate said at last. "How did your mission for Giovanni go?"

"I have the painting. And a princess."

"A *princess*?"

"A long story. The painting—the portrait—Giovanni sent me to retrieve is of Lucia, the exiled queen of Isola D'Oro. A very *intimate* painting of her." Alex shook his head. "But why Giovanni wanted it…it makes me wonder, might he have a whole past we know nothing about?"

Nate frowned. "While I was in Sicily I had a PI do a search for the Di Sione family. There is no trace of Giovanni. Not only in Livorno, *nowhere* in Italy."

Alex nodded. "Maybe we'll find out the truth now that Giovanni has all the pieces of the puzzle back. You managed to retrieve yours?"

"Yes, the ring. Mina noticed an inscription on the ring. *'Mistress of my heart—BA.'*"

The waiter arrived with the Scotch. Alex paused, taking this in before he poured them both a hefty portion.

Alex frowned. "Who is BA?"

"I have no idea."

"I have a feeling," Alex said, tipping his glass against Nate's, "you asked me here to talk about more than Giovanni."

Nate took a long swallow of Scotch, set the glass down and lifted his gaze to his brother's. "Mina's pregnant."

Alex's eyes widened. "Congratulations... I *think*."

"I want to know about Benito," Nate said abruptly. "What kind of a father was he? What kind of a man was he?"

"Deeply flawed." His brother sat back in his chair and brought his Scotch with him. "He and Giovanni had issues we were never privy to. My father refused to work with him at Di Sione Shipping. He started business after failed business Giovanni kept funding but nothing ever stuck."

"His partying and drug habits didn't help, I'm sure."

Alex nodded. "My mother cleaned herself up. Exchanged her drug and alcohol habit for a shopping addiction. But we were never a *family*. Neither of them had any interest in being parents. The nannies raised us."

All the pieces started to lock into place in Nate's head. Why all his siblings had struggled so much.

"You're afraid you won't be a good father," Alex speculated, his gaze narrowing on his. "Because you never had one. Because my father was the man he was."

"Isn't that the way it goes?" Nate rasped, lifting his glass to his lips. "Lead by example..."

"Except you have a mother who loves you, something we Di Siones never had. Someone who inspired you to reach for your dreams, who shaped you into the man that you are. Your name is the key to entry to any boardroom on this planet, Nate, and yet I think the big chip you carry around on your shoulder affects your self-perception." He pointed his glass at Nate. "I should know, I carry one myself."

Nate blinked. Absorbed his brother's words. "When I reached out to you when I started at Di Sione, I thought we had a lot in common, you and I. But you blew me off. Acted as if I wasn't fit to breathe the same air as you."

"It was difficult for me," he conceded. "You were a reminder of that night…the night my parents died. Of my own failure. To you. Keeping you a secret might have been easier for me but I'm sure it was hell on you. Seeing you there…watching my grandfather attempting to atone for my sins was difficult."

Nate shook his head. "I was never comfortable with that. I think his vaulting me ahead in the company was Giovanni's way of making up for the past. But I never wanted it."

"I know. But I couldn't handle it then. I was young and anger was a lot easier to feel than guilt. Hell, it still is."

Nate was silent for a long moment. "I'm sorry," he said finally, "that it worked out that way."

Alex shook his head. "It's me who should be apologizing. You reached out to me when you needed an ally and I wasn't there for you. I regret that now. I regret a lot of things."

Nate sat back and absorbed the epiphany that had just transpired. How everything you thought you knew was, in fact, not so clear-cut. That life had layers you had to burrow through to find the truth. How his self-perception was indeed flawed.

"Life is complex," he said. "*Relationships* are complex."

Alex lifted his glass in a toast, a cynical smile curving his lips. "Welcome to the Di Siones. The most dysfunctional clan on the planet."

Something shifted inside of Nate as he touched his glass to his brother's. A hope, perhaps, that the future could be different.

"When do I get to meet Mina?"

"I'm not sure that's going to happen." He set his glass down and flicked his brother a glance. "She's on a plane to Paris as we speak."

"You want to talk about it?"

"You got all night?"

His brother nodded toward the Scotch. "Why do you think I got a bottle?"

CHAPTER THIRTEEN

MINA FIGURED GLADIATORS were allowed to cry if they had a really, really good reason for it.

Walking away from the man you loved while he stood there and watched you do it seemed worthy enough, particularly when the end of your affair had driven home how very deluded you were. How the emotions you'd been so convinced the man in question felt for you had been nothing more than a display of honor on his part, the very same honor he'd been demonstrating from the beginning. And weren't you stupid to have thought it was more than that?

She had done the right thing, she told herself on the long flight from New York to Paris on which she'd miraculously been upgraded, her husband's influence no doubt. She had tried to see the practicality of remaining married to Nate that last week with him, putting her head down at work and burying herself in her assignments. But watching Nate struggle to pretend he was happy about becoming a father and permanent husband when it was so clearly anathema to him had been too painful to stand.

She would get over Nate in time. But if she'd stayed, he would have claimed more and more of her soul every day, until he'd had all of her. Until it would have been impossible for her to leave. Both of them would have begun to hate each other for what they wanted and could never have.

She thought she'd pretty much gotten herself together by the time Celia picked her up at the airport and drove her home to her beautiful, old apartment in the heart of Paris. But after her best friend had demanded a full recap, the tears had started anew.

"Don't waste any more time on him," Celia had stated in that blunt, very French way of hers. "Men are like seasons. They come and they go. I have my book club this week. Read the book, enjoy some good gossip and it will be all better."

Mina read the book, lounged on Celia's sofa and ate copious amounts of cheese and crackers to keep the nausea at bay. By the time the book club was assembled in Celia's tiny salon on Monday, crowded into every remaining space, she was doing a better job at hiding her heartbreak.

Brigitte, the last remaining member of the group, was arriving late from a work event. When the buzzer went off at seven, Celia opened the door, still talking, her words dying on her lips when she saw who it was. The blood drained from Mina's face.

"This is a book club," Celia said to Nate, recovering faster than Mina did. "No men allowed."

Nate blinked. "What book are you reading?"

"The Age of Innocence."

"Can't help you there." He pointed the bouquet of fresh flowers he held at Mina. "I was hoping I could take you for dinner."

Dinner? He had somehow materialized in Paris and wanted her to go to dinner with him? She stared at the man she'd cried too many tears over, dark and dangerous in jeans and a leather jacket.

Swallowing hard, she found her voice. "I'm afraid I'm not in the market for a knight in shining armor."

His gaze speared hers. "How about a man who deeply

regrets watching the best thing that's ever happened to him walk out of his life? Who wants to replay this from the beginning, this time for real? No one saving anyone, Mina, no Hollywood reenactments, just the raw, unadulterated truth."

Her breath caught in her throat. The girl beside her set her paperback down. "This is better than the book."

"You don't want him," the beautiful blonde on her other side murmured, "I'll take him."

That brought Mina to her feet. She collected her wrap from the sofa and crossed the room to Nate on legs that felt like spaghetti. He'd missed a button on his shirt, heavy dark stubble covered his jaw and the slightly askew, spiky hairstyle he wore looked a bit...*undone*.

Her heart squeezed. Nate handed the flowers to Celia with his most charming smile. "Would you?"

"Oui," she said curtly, giving him a long look. "You hurt her. I hurt you."

Nate captured Mina's hand in his in the car that sat waiting for them at the entrance. *Guard your heart*, she told herself. *You haven't heard what he has to say yet.* But the tense, hard line of her husband's jaw kept her palm in his. She had never seen Nate nervous. Ever.

They pulled up in front of the Grand Paris a short time later. A trademark glass elevator sent them swishing to Nate's rooftop penthouse. Nate guided her out onto the terrace where a table was set for two, a sparkling view of Paris as a backdrop.

Mina sank down on one of the sofas in the lounge area, her gaze on her husband's tense face. "What did you mean by us 'replaying this from the beginning'?"

He sat down beside her. "You forgot 'the raw, unadulterated truth.'"

"Nate..."

He expelled a breath. "When I was five I asked my mother why I didn't have a father like all the other kids I knew. She told me mine had another family—that he loved me very much, but he couldn't take care of us both. I accepted that with the innocence of a five-year-old, but I kept asking when he was going to come visit. Eventually I stopped when he never came.

"The night my mother took me to my father's house was the first time I'd met him. I was wary, *excited*, curious—every emotion in the book. I had this picture of him in my head. Then he opened the door, took one look at my mother and me and told us to get off his property."

She laced her fingers through his and squeezed.

"My mother begged him to listen, to help us. He told her to stop lying. That she was a slut who wanted to take his money with a child that wasn't his."

Her jaw dropped open. "How could he do that?"

"He wasn't in his right mind. Anna came to the door, all hell broke loose. My mother was scared. We left and went home. I remember thinking, was he lying, had my mother lied to me? She put me to bed. I could hear her crying. It hurt so much I willed myself to sleep. I woke up in the middle of the night, my bed covered in vomit."

She tightened her fingers around his, her heart breaking for him.

"I'm not telling you this for your pity. I'm telling you this because I watched my mother, the strongest person I know, die that night. She worked two jobs to put food on the table. She kept our family in one piece, but she was never the same person after that. She still *loved him*."

"And you decided you would never make yourself that vulnerable to a woman."

"To anyone. I quit school, I worked the streets with a gang. I was headed for a bad place when Alex came and found me. I had a choice to choose the right or wrong path then and luckily I had Giovanni to guide me. I channeled my obsession with proving my father wrong about me into my career. I would become so successful *no one* could ignore me. But my first year at Di Sione Shipping wasn't easy. I felt out of my depth. Adrift in a foreign world.

"Alex and I—we seemed cut from the same cloth. Not the worlds we lived in, of course, but we were both struggling with our pasts—wounded beasts trying to make ourselves into warriors. I approached him one night and asked him out for a beer. He looked at me as if I were nothing."

Her heart throbbed. He had been rejected not once, but twice, by the Di Siones.

He shook his head. "It wasn't Alex's fault. Giovanni had put us in an awkward position, vaulting me forward in the company and leaving Alex to climb the ranks. Alex felt guilty for keeping my existence a secret. There were a lot of layers to our relationship."

"But I should not have pushed you when I didn't know the whole story."

"You were *right* to push me. I called Alex. We had a drink. It's far from perfect, but it's a start."

A wet heat stung the backs of her eyes. Nate brushed his thumb across her cheek, his eyes softening. "I have been running away from this thing between us because you made me want what I had told myself was impossible—you, a relationship with my siblings, everything I'd accepted I could never have. You were willing to be a gladiator—to fight for what you wanted—but I was not."

A tear slipped down her face. "You're the one who gave me that."

"No," he said, wiping the tear away with his thumb. "The strength you have comes from inside you. You are a survivor. You have chosen to rise above your past. All I did was show you how to use it. Whereas I," he said, his mouth twisting, "used my past as an excuse to withdraw. I refused to believe in the concept of love because to me loving, making yourself vulnerable, has only meant pain in my life.

"I convinced myself what I felt for you was all about the protective instincts I had," he continued, "because admitting I cared for you, admitting I loved you, meant letting you in. Allowing you to see the broken, empty part of me I have never shown to anyone. The part," he said, his eyes on hers, "I was afraid you would reject."

Her vision blurred, tears running down her cheeks in a steady stream now. "We're all broken, Nate. Every single one of us. It's what we do once we acknowledge it that matters."

He nodded. "I went to talk to Alex because I'm scared to death of being a father. I had no example set for me. Had no idea even what kind of a father my own was. Which didn't help matters, because he was, apparently, no kind of a father. But what I do know," he said, a determined glitter in his eyes, "is that I want to be a father to our baby. To do the best job I can."

She swallowed hard, thinking how badly she'd misinterpreted his fear. "You don't think I'm frightened? That I don't wonder the same thing with a mother like mine?"

He reached for her and gathered her onto his lap. "You will be a great mother *because* of your past, not in spite of it. You've used the challenges in your life to make you stronger, not weaker. And you will give that strength of spirit to our child."

She traced the hard line of his jaw with her fingers. "What about your need for freedom? What if you end up resenting me and the baby and want your life back?"

His gaze darkened. "It won't happen. I haven't slept this

week. Haven't eaten. Because you weren't there. I *need* you in my life, Mina."

She ran her finger down the front of his shirt. "I noticed you missed a button. You're looking a little disheveled."

He ignored the tease, lifting her chin with his finger. "So," he said roughly, "you have the unvarnished truth now. Your human connection project is complete. Tell me if you still want me, Mina, because if you say yes now, it's forever."

"Do you have to ask?" she said softly. "Your human side only makes you more attractive, Nate Brunswick. And I was already falling over myself for you the first time I met you."

The tension in his face eased. "You were ridiculously sexy in your maid outfit."

"And you were *very, very* improper."

He brought his mouth down to hers. "You loved every minute of it."

"*Sì.* I did."

He kissed her then, a long, slow kiss that cemented the promises they'd made to each other under a clear, star-strewn Paris sky. That they would rise above their pasts and grasp this chance at happiness with both hands. Two survivors who'd learned that destiny was not a foregone conclusion—it was all in the choices they made.

She hadn't been wrong, Mina thought, wrapping her arms around her husband's neck and kissing him back. She had been so very, very right.

She was a gladiator, after all. Faith was a prerequisite.

EPILOGUE

New York—nine months later

THE HISTORIC THIRTEENTH-CENTURY Gothic cathedral on Manhattan's west side glimmered with an almost ethereal light as the late-afternoon sun pressed against its elaborate, showstopping stained glass windows.

It was almost enough to match the incandescent glow filling Mina as Nate slid a diamond-studded eternity band on her finger to join the ring he'd placed there a year ago on that tumultuous, emotion-filled day in Palermo which had changed their lives.

This time as she stepped toward him and lifted her face for his kiss, the reconfirming of their vows complete, there were no nerves involved, no questions about her future, only the butterflies in her stomach that came with a kiss from her husband, butterflies she suspected would never go away.

"Enough sunshine and rainbows for you?" Nate murmured against her lips.

"Sì," she returned huskily, curving her fingers around his jaw and lifting up on tiptoe for his kiss.

The priest coughed as the expression of affection went on a fraction too long. Laughter danced in Nate's eyes as he lifted his head. "Have to up my game."

Mina stepped back, the glow inside of her almost too much to contain. The ceremony concluded, she collected two-month-old Giovanni Vincenzo Brunswick from Natalia to make their walk down the aisle.

The Di Sione clan looked on approvingly on their left, a miraculous feat to have them all in one place. Mina's mother, her *nonna*, a handful of her cousins and Celia sat on the right, the intimate, private ceremony to cement their vows what she and Nate had both wanted.

A reception followed at the Brunswicks' Westchester estate, which did not feature a white picket fence, but did include lavish gardens little Giovanni could someday play in, and a koi pond Mina loved. Much wine was consumed and a great deal of laughter filled the fairy-tale gardens as the Di Siones and Mastrantinos mixed, her mother thankfully on her best behavior.

It warmed Mina's heart to watch her husband with his half siblings. He was gradually letting his guard down— forging deeper relationships with all of them, particularly Alex, who did seem so much in character like Nate. The party lasted into the wee hours, until finally, her husband gave the guests some pointed glances, everyone headed for their cars and they went inside to relieve the nanny from her duties.

Giovanni, so very tiny Mina had been terrified to touch him at first, was sound asleep, his fist shoved in his mouth. Nate ran a finger down the baby's cheek, the glitter in his eyes saying everything he found it hard to verbalize. He had fallen instantly in love with their son, would sometimes stand there fascinated, watching him until Mina had to call him to bed.

But not tonight. "I thought they were never going to leave," he growled, switching off the light and propelling her from the room.

"They were having fun."

She toed off her shoes in their room, her heartbeat kicking up at the look of primal hunger on her husband's face. Stepping toward him, she presented him with her back so he could unzip her dress.

His fingers dispensed with the zipper, his mouth consuming a mouthful of her bare shoulder. "Are you exhausted?"

Usually she was. She'd wanted to be a hands-on mother despite the permanent position she'd taken in the Brunswick Developments marketing department, which had meant collapsing into bed at night for the last few weeks since she'd been back to work—weeks in which the doctor had finally cleared her and Nate to be intimate again. Not ideal when Nate's primary strength wasn't patience.

She turned around and met her husband's hungry gaze. "No."

"Good," he said roughly as he pushed the dress off her shoulders to pool in a puddle of silk at her feet. "Because I am definitely *on edge.*"

A fire lit her belly. "Is that a request?"

"Not this time." He brought his palm between her thighs, seeking out her most intimate flesh. Mina threw back her head as he caressed her in that way that made her crazy.

"It's been too long," she moaned.

"An understatement." He swung her up in his arms, carried her to the bed and brought her down to straddle his thighs. His eyes on hers, he captured her hand and brought it to the zipper that covered the hard bulge beneath his pants, his directive clear.

"Nate—" she breathed, absorbing the pulsing, urgent power of him.

"Shocking—I know," he murmured in her ear. "Do it, anyway."

She did, releasing him and taking him deep inside of her, her fingers curling in his shirt as she rode him to completion, her husband still fully clothed.

"I love you," he murmured against her lips when they finally came up for air. "Even more than I did before."

Her heart dissolved. "Well, that's good," she returned huskily. "Because you promised me forever."

He caught her hand in his, pressing the back of her knuckles to his mouth. "I always follow through on my promises, Signora Brunswick."

So he did. She curled her arms around his neck. "Take me to bed, Signor Brunswick. Before your son wakes me up at some ungodly hour."

He did. Not that he had sleep on his mind.

* * * * *

THE LAST
DI SIONE CLAIMS
HIS PRIZE

MAISEY YATES

To the authors that have brought me
countless hours of reading pleasure.
You inspire me

CHAPTER ONE

IT WAS RUMORED that Alessandro Di Sione had once fired an employee for bringing his coffee back two minutes later than commanded and five degrees cooler than ordered. It was rumored that he had once released a long-term mistress with a wave of his hand and an order to collect a parting gift from his assistant in the following weeks.

There were also rumors that he breathed fire, slept in a dungeon and derived sustenance from the souls of the damned.

So, when his shiny new temporary assistant scurried into the room, with red cheeks and an apologetic expression, on the heels of his grandfather—who appeared neither red-cheeked nor sorry for anything—it was no surprise that she looked as though she was headed for the gallows.

Of course, no one denied Giovanni Di Sione entry to any place he wished to inhabit. No personal assistant, no matter how formidable, would have been able to keep his grandfather out. Age and severely reduced health notwithstanding.

But as his typical assistant was on maternity leave and her replacement had only been here for a couple of weeks, she didn't know that. She was, of course, afraid that Giovanni was an intruder and that she would be punished for the breach of security.

He saw no point in disabusing her of that notion. It was entirely possible she would spend the rest of the day deconstructing the meaning to his every glance in her direction. Likely, in the retelling, she would talk about the blackness of his eyes being a reflection of his soul, or some other such nonsense. And so, his reputation would darken even more, without him lifting a finger.

"I'm very sorry, Mr. Di Sione," she said, clearly out of breath, one palm pressed tightly over her rather unimpressive breasts.

He made a low, disapproving sound and raised one dark brow.

She was trembling now. Like a very small dog. "Should I go back to work, sir?" she asked, nervous eyes darting toward the door.

He waved his hand and she scurried back out much the same as she had scurried in.

"I see you're up and moving around," Alex said, not descending into sentimentality because his relationship with Giovanni didn't allow for that. With each returned Lost Mistress, Giovanni's health had recovered bit by bit.

"It's been a while since my last treatment, so I'm feeling better."

"Good to hear it."

"The way you acted toward your assistant was not overly kind, Alessandro," his grandfather said, taking the seat in front of Alex's desk somewhat shakily.

"You say that as though you believe I have a concern about being perceived as kind. We both know I do not."

"Yes, but I also know you're not as terrible as you pretend to be." Giovanni leaned back in his chair, both hands planted on his knees. He was getting on in years and, after seventeen years in remission, his leukemia had returned. At ninety-eight, Giovanni likely didn't have many years left on the earth regardless of his health, but it had certainly added a bit of urgency to the timeline.

The goal being to recover each and every one of Giovanni's Lost Mistresses. Stories of these treasures were woven into Alex's consciousness. His grandfather had been spinning tales about them from the time Alessandro was a boy. And now, he had tasked each of his grandchildren with finding one of those lost treasures.

Except for Alex.

He had been expecting this. Waiting for quite some time to hear about what part he might play in this quest.

"Maybe not," Alex said, leaning back in his chair, unconsciously mimicking his grandfather's position.

"At least you do not dare to behave terribly in my presence."

"What can I say, *Nonno*? You are perhaps the only man on earth more formidable than I."

Giovanni waved his hand as if dismissing Alex's words. "Flattery is not the way with me, Alessandro, as you well know."

He did know. His grandfather was a man of business. A man who had built a life out of nothing upon his arrival to America, a man who understood commerce. He had instilled that in Alex. It was how they connected. Where their minds met.

"Don't tell me you're feeling bored and you wanted to get your hands back into the shipping business?"

"Not at all. But I do have a job for you."

Alex nodded slowly. "Is it my time to take a mistress?"

"I have saved the last one for you, Alessandro. The painting."

"Painting?" Alex lifted a paperweight from his desk and moved it, tapping the glass with his index finger. "Don't tell me you were a great collector of clowns on velvet or some such."

Giovanni chuckled. "No. Nothing of the kind. I'm looking for *The Lost Love*."

Alex frowned. "My art history is a little bit faint at my advanced age, but the name does sound familiar."

"It should. What do you know about the disgraced royal family of Isolo D'Oro?"

"Had I known there would be a test, I would have studied before your arrival."

"You were given a very expensive education at a very high-end boarding school. I would hate to think my money was wasted."

Alex shifted, his hands still curled around the paperweight. "A school filled with teenage boys halfway across the world from their parents and very near a school filled entirely with teenage girls in the same situation. What is it you think we were studying?"

"This subject would have been *related* to your particular field of study. *The Lost Love* is a very scandalous piece of royal history. Though it was only a rumor. No one has ever seen it."

"Except for you, I take it."

"I am one of the few who can confirm its existence."

"You are ever a man of unfathomable depths."

Giovanni chuckled, inclining his head. "I am, it's true. But then, that should be a perk of living a life as long as mine. You ought to have depths and secret scandalous paintings in your past, don't you think?"

"I wouldn't know. My life primarily consists of long hours in the office."

"A waste of youth and virility in my opinion."

It was Alex's turn to laugh. "Right. Because you did not spend your thirties deeply entrenched in building your fortune."

"It is a privilege of the elderly to see things in hindsight no one can see in the present, and attempt to educate the young with that hindsight."

"I imagine it's the privilege of the young to ignore that advice?"

"Perhaps. But in this, you will listen to me. I want that painting. It is my last Lost Mistress. *My* lost love."

Alex looked at the old man, the only father figure he'd ever truly possessed. Giovanni had been the one to instill in Alex a true sense of work ethic. Of pride. Giovanni had raised him and his siblings differently than their parents had. After their deaths he had taken them in, had given them so much more than a life of instability and neglect. He had taught them to take pride in their family name, to take nothing for granted.

His son might have been a useless, debauched partyer, but Giovanni had more than made up for mistakes he made with him when he had assumed the job of raising his grandchildren.

"And you intend to send me after it?"

"Yes. I do. You spend too much time at work. Think of it as a boy's adventure. A quest to retrieve a lost treasure."

Alex picked up the paperweight again. It hovered an inch or so off the desk before he set it back down with an indelicate click. "I should think of it as what it is. A business transaction. You have been very good to me. Without your influence in my life I would likely be completely derelict. Or worse, some sort of social climber working his way through champagne and sunless tanner in South Beach."

"Dear God, what a nightmarish prospect."

"Especially as, by extension, I would be doing it with your money."

"Your point is made. I am a steadying and magnificent influence." The ghost of a smile that played across his grandfather's ancient features pleased him. "I need you to retrieve the painting for me. It took all of my strength to put my socks on and come down here today. I can hardly track across the Mediterranean to Aceena to retrieve the painting myself."

"Aceena?" Alex asked, thinking of what little he knew about the small island. With its white sand beaches and jewel-bright water, it was famous the world over.

"Yes, boy. Honestly, now I want a refund from that boarding school."

"I know where and what Aceena is, *Nonno*. But as far as I'm aware their primary attraction is alcohol and their chief import is university students on spring break."

"Yes. A hazardous side effect of beachfront property, I suppose. But also, it is where the D'Oro family has spent their banishment."

"On spring break?"

"In an estate, I'm told. Though I fear Queen Lucia's children have been on perpetual spring break ever since carving a swath of scandal through Europe. The queen lives there with her granddaughter. She was the rumored subject of the painting—" his grandfather paused "—and the last person to have it. So I've heard."

Alex wasn't a fool, and he didn't appreciate that the old man was playing him for one. Giovanni wouldn't send him off to Aceena because of half-heard rumors. And he would know full well who the subject of that painting was, had it been in his possession.

Leave it to Giovanni to have a portrait of a disgraced queen in his collection of lost treasures.

"You seem to know a great deal about the royal family," Alex said.

"I have some ties to Isolo D'Oro. I…visited for a time. There are…fond memories for me there and I carry the history with me."

"Fascinating."

"You don't have to be fascinated, Alessandro, you have to do my bidding."

Of course, if Giovanni asked, Alex had to comply. He *owed* him. Giovanni had raised Alex after the death of his parents. Had given him a job, instilled in him the work ethic that had made him so successful.

Without Giovanni, Alex was nothing.

And if his grandfather's dream was to see his Lost Mistresses reunited, then Alex would be damned if he was the weak link in the chain.

Enough suffering in his family was tied to his pigheadedness. He would not add this to the list.

"As you wish," Alex said.

"You're turning this into a clichéd movie, Alessandro."

"A quest for a hidden painting secreted away on an island by disgraced royals? I think we were already there."

CHAPTER TWO

"THERE IS A man at the door, here to see Queen Lucia."

Princess Gabriella looked up from the book she was reading and frowned. She was in the library, perched on a velvet chair that she privately thought of as a tuffet, because it was overstuffed, with little buttons spaced evenly over the cushion, and it just *looked* like the word sounded.

She hadn't expected an interruption. Most of the household staff knew to leave her be when she was in the library.

She pulled her glasses off and rubbed her eyes, untucking her legs out from underneath her bottom and stretching them out in front of her. "I see. And why exactly does this man think he can show up unannounced and gain an audience with the queen?"

She slipped her glasses back onto her face and planted her feet firmly on the ground, her hands resting on her knees as she waited for a response.

"He is Alessandro Di Sione. An American businessman. And he says he is here to see about…to see about *The Lost Love*."

Gabriella shot to her feet, all of the blood rushing to her head. She pitched sideways, then steadied herself, waiting for the room to stop spinning.

"Are you all right, ma'am?" asked the servant, Lani.

"Fine," Gabriella said, waving her hand. "*The Lost Love?* He's looking for the painting?"

"I don't know anything about a painting, Princess."

"I do," Gabriella said, wishing she had her journal on hand so she could leaf through it. "I know plenty about it. Except for whether or not it actually exists."

She had never outright asked her grandmother about it. The older woman was loving, but reserved, and the rumors about the painting were anything but. She could hardly imagine her grandmother engaging in the scandalous behavior required for *The Lost Love* to exist…and yet. And yet she had always wondered.

"Forgive me, but it seems as though knowing whether or not something exists would be the most essential piece of information to have on it."

"Not in my world."

When it came to researching genealogical mysteries, Gabriella knew that the possibility of something was extremely important. It was the starting point. Sometimes, collecting information through legend was the key to discovering whether or not something was real. And often times, confirming the existence of something was the *final* step in the process, not the first.

When it came to establishing the facts of her family's banishment from Isolo D'Oro, legend, folktales and rumor were usually the beginning of every major breakthrough. In fact, her experience with such things was leading her to odd conclusions regarding yetis and the Loch Ness monster. After all, if multiple cultures had rumors about similar beasts, it was logical to conclude that such a thing must have a grain of truth.

But until she was able to sift through the facts and fictions of her familial heritage, she would leave cryptozo-oology for other people.

"What should I do with our visitor, ma'am?"

Gabriella tapped her chin. She was inclined to have their visitor told that she and her grandmother were Not at Home, in the Regency England sense of the phrase. But he knew about *The Lost Love*. She was curious what exactly he knew about it. Though she didn't want to confirm the existence of it to a total stranger. Particularly when she hadn't established the existence of it in all certainty to herself.

She had to figure out what his game was. If this was just a scammer of some sort determined to make a profit off an elderly woman—and that was likely the case— then Gabriella would have to make sure he was never given entry.

"I will speak to him. There is no sense in bothering the queen. She is taking tea in the morning room and I don't wish to disturb her."

Gabriella brushed past the servant, and headed out of the library, down the richly carpeted hall, her feet sinking into the lush, burgundy pile. She realized then that going to greet a total stranger with bare feet was not the most princess-like act. She did quite well playing her part in public. A lifetime of training made a few hours of serene smiling and waving second nature. But when she was home, here in the wonderful, isolated estate in Aceena, she shut her manners, along with her designer gowns, away. Then unwound her hair from the tight coil she wore it in when she was allowing herself to be trotted out in front of the public, and truly let herself simply be *Gabriella*.

She touched her face, her glasses. She also didn't go out in public in those.

Oh, well. She didn't want to impress this stranger; she wanted to interrogate him, and then send him on his way.

She padded through the grand entryway, not bothering with straightening her hair or preening in any way at all.

He had already been admitted entry, of course. It wouldn't do to have a man like him standing outside on the step. And she could see what kind of man he was immediately as he came into her view.

He was...striking. It reminded her of an experience she'd once had in a museum. Moving through wall after wall of spectacular art before entering a small room off to the side. In it, one painting, with all of the light focused on it. It was the centerpiece. The only piece that mattered. Everything that had come before it paled in comparison.

The journey had been lovely, but this man was the destination.

He was like a van Gogh. His face a study in slashing lines and sharp angles. Sharp cheekbones, an angular jaw roughened with dark stubble. There was a soft curve to his lips that spoke of an artist with a deft hand. Who knew that after so much hardened and fearful symmetry there needed to be something different to draw the eye. There was a slight imperfection in his features, as well, one peak of his top lip not quite rising as high as the other. It gave a human quality to Alessandro that was missing from the rest of him. Those broad shoulders, muscular chest and slim waist covered by his severely tailored suit. Long, strong legs, feet covered by handmade shoes.

Yes, everything about him was formidable perfection.

Except for that mouth. The mouth that promised potential softening. That hinted at the fact that he was a man, rather than simply a work of art.

She blinked, shaking her head. That was a lengthy flight of romantic fantasy. Even for her.

"Hello?" She took a step deeper into the entry. "Can I help you?"

His dark eyes flickered over her, his expression one of disinterest. "I wish to speak to Queen Lucia about *The Lost Love*."

"Yes. So I was told. However, I'm afraid the queen is unavailable to visitors at the moment." She resisted the urge to push her glasses up her nose, and instead crossed her arms, trying to look slightly regal, though she was wearing black leggings and an oversize sweatshirt.

"So she sent…I give up. What are you exactly? The resident disaffected teenager? Ready to head out to a mall or some such?"

Gabriella sniffed. "Actually, I am Princess Gabriella D'Oro. So when I say that my grandmother is not available to see you, I speak from a place of authority. This is my home, and I regret to inform you that we have no space for you in it."

"Strange. It seems quite spacious to me."

"Well, things are organized just so. Quite a few too many American businessmen have been by of late. We would have to store you in the attic, and you would just collect dust up there."

"Is that so?"

"I fear you would atrophy completely."

"Well, we can't have that. This is a new suit, and I don't particularly want to atrophy in it."

"Then perhaps you should be on your way."

"I came a great distance to speak to your grandmother. This may surprise you, but I did not come to Aceena to engage in frivolity. But rather to speak to her about a painting."

"Yes, so you said. I regret to inform you there is no such painting. I'm not entirely certain what you heard about it…"

"My grandfather. He is…the collector. I came to see about purchasing the painting on his behalf. I'm willing to offer a generous sum. I imagine disgraced royals might not be in a position to turn such an offer down."

"Oh, we do just fine, thank you for your concern.

Should you like to make a donation to someone in actual need of your charity, I would be happy to provide you with a list."

"No, thank you. The charity was only a side effect. I want that painting. I'm willing to pay whatever the cost might be."

Her mouth was dry. It made it difficult to speak, and yet she found she also couldn't stop the flow of words. "Well, I'm afraid to disappoint you. While we do have paintings, we do not have that painting. That painting, if you weren't aware, might not even exist."

"Oh, I'm well aware that it's what your family would like the public to think. However, I think you know more than you're letting on."

"No," she said, and this time she did push her glasses up her nose. "I'm just a teenager headed out to the mall. What could I possibly know that you," she said, sweeping her hand up and down, "in all your infinite and aged wisdom, do not?"

"The appeal of Justin Bieber?"

"I'm not entirely certain who that is."

"I'm surprised by that. Girls your age love him."

"In that case, can I offer you a hard candy? I hear men your age love those."

She was not sure how this had happened. How she had wound up standing in the hallowed entry of her family estate trading insults with a stranger.

"I'll accept the hard candy if it means you intend to give me a tour while I finish it."

"No. Sorry. You would be finishing it on the lawn."

He rubbed his hand over his chin and she shivered, an involuntary response to the soft noise made by the scrape of his hand over his whiskers. She was a sensualist. It was one of her weaknesses. She enjoyed art, and soft cushions, desserts and lush fabrics. The smell of old books and the feel of textured pages beneath her fingertips.

And she noticed fine details. Like the sound skin made when scraping over stubble.

"I'm not entirely certain this is the tactic you want to use. Because if you send me away, then I will only circumvent you. Either by contacting your grandmother directly, or by figuring out who manages the affairs of the royal family. I am certain that I can find someone who might be tempted by what I offer."

He probably wasn't wrong. If he managed to find her parents, and offer them a bit of money—or better yet, an illegal substance—for some information on an old painting, they would be more than happy to help him. Fortunately, they probably had no idea what the painting was, much less knew any more about its existence than she did.

But they were wretched. And they were greedy. So there was very little that she would put past them.

Still, she was not going to allow him to harass her grandmother. Tempting as it was to keep him here, to question him. She'd been studying her family history for as long as she'd known how to read. Rumors about this painting had played a large part in it.

Part of her desperately wanted him to stay. Another part needed him gone as quickly as possible. Because of her grandmother. And partly because of the dry mouth and sweaty palms and strange, off-kilter feeling that had arrived along with him.

Those things defeated curiosity. He had to go.

"I'll chance it. Do feel free to meander about the grounds before you go. The gardens are beautiful. Please consider limitless viewing time on the topiaries a conciliatory gesture on my end."

The corner of his mouth worked upward. "I assure you, I have no interest in your…topiaries."

Something about the way he said it made her scalp prickle, made her skin feel hot. She didn't like it.

"Well, my topiaries are all you're going to get. Good day to you, sir."

"And good day to you," he said, inclining his head.

He sounded perfectly calm, but a dark note wound its way around his words, through his voice, and she had a feeling that somewhere within it was also woven a threat.

However, she didn't allow him to see that she had picked up on it. Instead, she turned on her heel—ignoring the slight squeak her bare skin made on the marble tile—and walked out of the entry without a backward glance, leaving him there. She fully expected a servant would show him out. Either that or she would have to have him installed in the attic. The idea of collecting a man like him and putting him in the attic like one might do to an old, rusted suit of armor amused her.

She let that little smile linger on her lips as she made her way down the hall, toward the morning room where her grandmother was having her breakfast.

"There was a man here, Gabriella. Who was he?" The queen's voice, wispy, as thin as a cobweb, greeted Gabriella as soon as she walked into the ornate room.

There was no sense asking how her grandmother knew about the visitor. She was never ignorant about the goings-on in her own household.

"An American businessman," Gabriella said, walking deeper into the room, feeling somewhat sheepish, yet again, about her bare feet.

Her grandmother was, as ever, impeccably dressed. The older woman made no distinction between her public and private persona. As always, her crystal white hair was pulled back into a neat bun, her makeup expertly done. Her fingernails were painted the same pale coral as the skirt she was wearing, her low, sensible heels the same cream as her blouse.

"I see," the queen said, setting her teacup down on the table in front of her. "And what did he want?"

"This is not something we've ever discussed before, I know, but he was…he was inquiring about a painting. *The Lost Love.*"

Her grandmother continued to sit there, poised, her hands folded in her lap. Were it not for the subtle paling of her complexion, Gabriella would have thought she had merely been commenting on the weather. There was no mistaking her grandmother's response to what she had just said.

"But of course," Gabriella continued, "I told him that it has never been confirmed that there is any such painting. I told him it was nothing more than salacious rumor. And I sent him on his way. Though he may be meandering around the gardens."

Her grandmother turned her head to the window and Gabriella did the same. Just in time to see a figure in a dark suit pass by quickly before disappearing down the path.

Something in Lucia's expression shifted. "Call him back."

"I can't. I just… I just sent him away. That would be… Well, it would seem fickle. Plus, it's rather silly."

"You must call him back, Gabriella." When Lucia used that tone there really was no point in arguing. Still, Gabriella thought she might try.

"I don't trust him. I didn't want him to upset you."

"I need to know who he is. I need to know why he is asking about the painting. It's important." There was a thread of steel woven into her voice now, a command that Gabriella could not deny.

"Of course, Grandmother. I will go after him right away."

"For heaven's sake, girl, put some shoes on."

Gabriella nodded, turning and scampering out of the room, heading down the corridor toward her bedroom. She found a pair of easy slip-on canvas shoes, then continued to head out to the front door. It was firmly closed, the visitor nowhere to be seen.

She opened the door, heading down the paved walk, toward one of the gardens. He didn't exactly seem like the kind of person who would take her up on the offer of a garden tour, but she had to make sure. He might still be here.

Her grandmother had commanded an audience with him, and she would be darned if she would disappoint the older woman.

Her grandmother meant the world to her. Her parents had preferred a life of partying to that of raising children. Her brothers were so much older than her so she could scarcely remember a time when they had lived in the same household. As soon as Gabriella had been old enough to have a say in her own situation, she had asked to go to Aceena to live with Queen Lucia. The older woman had been more of a mother to her than her own had ever been, and she could deny her nothing.

She looked around, and she didn't see him. Of course he was gone. And she hadn't gotten any of his contact information, because she hadn't wanted it. She was annoyed. At him, at herself. But mostly at him.

She walked farther down the manicured lane, turned left at the first hedge, ran squarely into a broad back covered in very high-quality black fabric. She could tell the fabric was high quality, not just because of how it looked, but because of the way it felt squished up against her face.

She stumbled backward just as he turned to face her. He was even more arresting, even more off-putting, up close. He exuded… Well, he just exuded.

"Well, I see you were making use of my offer to tour the gardens."

He straightened his tie, the action drawing her eyes to his hands. They were very large. Naturally, as he was quite a large man. So really, they were nothing quite so spectacular. They were proportional. Useful. In possession of the typical number of fingers.

"No. I was skulking. I thought I might hang around long enough that I can try my hand at getting an audience with your grandmother later."

"That's quite sneaky."

"Sneaky is not typically a word I associate with myself, but I'll take it. Determined, I think sums it up."

"I don't see why you can't be called both."

"Whatever makes you happy. Why exactly are you looking for me?"

"It turns out…my grandmother wants to speak to you."

"Oh," he said, a slow smile spreading over his arrogant face. "I take it you're not the voice of authority when it came to your grandmother's desires, then?"

"I was trying to protect her. Surely, you can't fault me for that."

"Sure I can. I can fault you for anything I like."

She looked hard at him. It was impossible to tell if he was teasing. Impossible to tell if he had the capacity to tease or if he was deadly serious down to his bones. "Which, in a nutshell is exactly why I couldn't allow you to see her. You're a strange man. A stranger, I mean. You also don't seem very…sensitive."

"Do I not?"

She narrowed her eyes. "No."

"Well, I shall endeavor to work on that during the walk from the garden to where your grandmother is waiting for me."

Her lips twitched, but she wouldn't allow them to

stretch into a smile. "If you would be so kind as to do just that, it would be greatly appreciated."

"I live to serve."

She had no doubt he did *not*.

She led the way from the palace gardens back through to the estate; as they walked through the halls she kept her eyes on his face, trying to suss out exactly what he was thinking. His expression was neutral, and he wasn't nearly as impressed as she felt like he should be. The halls of the Aceena estate were filled with beautiful, classic art. Paintings, vases, sculpture. Really, he should be quite impressed.

She supposed that was the hazard with very rich men. It was hard to show them anything they hadn't seen before.

She had grown up in this luxury and she never took any of it for granted. There was always new beauty in the world to discover. It was why she loved art. Why she loved history. There were centuries of beauty stretching back as far as humanity had been in existence. And the future stretched before them, too. Limitless. Infinite in its possibilities. There was hardly a chance to get bored with anything.

Gabriella didn't see the point in jaded cynicism, though she knew some people found it a sign of intellectual superiority.

She just found it sad.

He was probably like her parents. Sensory seekers who were never satisfied with what was around them. Things had to be grand, loud, crowded. Otherwise, they could scarcely feel, could scarcely see.

Gabriella on the other hand needed very little to be entertained. A nicely appointed room, a good book. A lovely piece of art.

She appreciated small things. Quiet things.

She felt very sorry for those who didn't.

"She's in here," Gabriella said, pausing at the doorway.

He arched his brows. "Is she? What are you waiting for? Are you going to go in and announce me?"

"Well, very likely I *should*. I'm very sorry, I know you gave your name to the staff member who greeted you, but I seem to have forgotten it."

She was lying. Alessandro was his name, she remembered. But she didn't want him to think that he was so important he had taken up any space in her brain.

"Alex," he said.

"No last name?" she pressed.

"Di Sione."

"Should that name mean anything to my grandmother?"

He shrugged. "Unless she follows gossip about American businessmen, I don't know why it would. My grandfather made quite a name for himself both in the States and abroad, and I haven't done badly myself, neither have my various and sundry brothers and sisters. But I'm not certain why our names would matter to royalty."

"What is his interest in the painting?" Gabriella asked.

A brief pause. "He is a collector."

She didn't believe him.

Gabriella let out an exasperated breath. "Be cryptic if you must. But I'm sure there's more to the story than that."

Alex chuckled. "Oh, I'm certain there is, too, but you make a mistake if you think I know more than I'm letting on. I think you and I might occupy very similar positions in the lives of our grandparents."

"How do you mean?"

"We are subject to their dictates."

Shocked laughter threatened to bubble to the surface and she held it in check. She was *not* going to allow him to amuse her. "Well, regardless. Come with me."

She pushed the door open and stepped inside. Her grandmother was sitting in the same seat she had been in when Gabriella had left her. But she seemed different somehow. Not quite so tall. Slightly diminished.

"Grandmother, may I present Mr. Alex Di Sione. He is here to talk to you about *The Lost Love*."

"Yes," her grandmother said, gesturing for them to come deeper into the room. She turned her laser sharp focus onto Alex. "My granddaughter tells me you're interested in the painting."

"Yes," he said, not waiting to be invited to sit. He took his position in a chair opposite her grandmother, his long legs sprawled out in front of him, his forearms resting on the arms of the chair. He looked exceedingly unconcerned with the entire situation. Almost bored. Her grandmother, on the other hand, was tense.

"What is your interest in it?" she asked.

"I am acting on behalf of my grandfather." Alex looked out one of the floor-to-ceiling windows, at the garden beyond. "He claims the painting has some sentimental value to him."

"The painting has never been confirmed to exist," Queen Lucia said.

"I'm well aware. But my grandfather seems to be very confident in its existence. In fact, he claims he once owned it." His dark focus zeroed in on the queen. "He would like very much to have it back now."

Silence settled between them. Thick and telling. A fourth presence in the room. Gabriella noticed her grandmother studying Alex's face. She looked… She looked stricken. As though she was seeing a ghost.

"Your grandfather, you say?" she asked.

"Yes. He is getting on in years and with age has come sentimentality, I'm afraid. He is willing to pay a great deal for this painting."

"I'm afraid I can't help you with that," the queen said.

"And why is that?" he asked, a dangerous note in his voice.

"I don't have it. I haven't possessed it for…years."

"But the painting exists?" Gabriella asked, her heart thundering in her ears.

This was… Under any other circumstances, this would have been incredibly exciting. But Alex Di Sione was here and that just made it feel fraught.

"Yes," her grandmother said, her voice thinner, more fragile all of a sudden. "It is very real."

"Why have you never mentioned that before?"

"Because some things are best left buried in the past. Where they can no longer hurt you," the queen said.

"Do you have any idea where the painting might be now?" Alex asked, obviously unconcerned with her grandmother's pain.

"Yes, I know exactly where it is. Unfortunately, it's on Isolo D'Oro. One of the many reasons I have never been able to reclaim it."

"Where on the island is it?" he asked, his tone uncompromising.

"You wait outside for a moment, young man," the queen said, her tone regal, leaving no doubt at all that she had ruled a nation for a great many years and expected her each command to be obeyed without question.

And Alex didn't question it. Strange, since she imagined he wasn't a man who bowed to many. But at her grandmother's request, he stood, brushing the creases from his dress pants and nodded his head before he made his way out the door.

"You must go with him to find the painting," her grandmother said the moment he was out of earshot.

"Why?" Gabriella asked, her heart pounding in her ears.

"I…I should like to see it again. One last time. And because…because just in case, I shouldn't like for this man to be in possession of it if he is a fraud."

"I don't understand," Gabriella said, trying to process all of the information being given to her. "If he's a fraud in *what* way?"

"It isn't important."

"I think it must be quite important. We've never discussed the painting, but I've long suspected that it was real. I know…I know it was controversial. I know that it concerns you."

"Yes," her grandmother said. "At the time it was quite controversial. Evidence that…that the princess had a lover."

Her grandmother had been the princess then. Young. Unmarried. And it had been a very different time.

It was difficult to imagine her grandmother taking a lover. Difficult to imagine her doing anything quite so passionate or impetuous. She was the incomparable matriarch of the family. The figurehead so established, so steady, she might very well already be carved of marble, as she would now no doubt be in the future.

But if the painting existed, then she was the subject. And if that were the case, then of course it had been commissioned by a lover.

"I see," Gabriella said. "And…*did* you?"

Her grandmother let out a long, slow breath, raising her eyes to meet hers. In them, Gabriella could see so much. A wealth of sadness. Deep heartbreak.

Things Gabriella had read about, but never experienced.

"It is very easy when you are young, Gabriella, to lead with your heart instead of your head. You have seen this, time and again, with your parents. And they no longer carry youth as an excuse. This is why I have always told you that you must be in possession of your wits. It does not do well for a woman to lose her mind over passion. It doesn't end well. Not for us. Men can carry on as they see fit, but it isn't like that for women."

Gabriella nodded slowly. "Yes, I know." She thought of her brothers, who most certainly carried on exactly as they pleased. Of her father, who seemed to escape the most scathing comments. The worst of it was always reserved for her mother. She was a renowned trollop whose every choice, from her wardrobe to which man she chose to make conversation with at a social event, was analyzed, was taken as evidence of her poor character.

Gabriella knew this was true. It was just one of the many reasons that she had chosen to embrace her more bookish nature and keep herself separate from all of that carrying-on.

"Our hearts are not proper guides," her grandmother continued. "They are fickle, and they are easily led. Mine certainly was. But I learned from my mistakes."

"Of course," Gabriella agreed, because she didn't know what else to say.

"Go with him," Queen Lucia said, her tone stronger now. Decisive. "Fetch the painting. But remember this conversation. Remember what I have told you."

"I don't think there's any danger of my heart getting involved on a quest of this nature."

"He is a handsome man, Gabriella."

Gabriella laughed. "He's a stranger! And old enough to be… Not my father, *certainly* not. But perhaps a young uncle."

The queen shook her head. "Men like that have their ways."

"And I have my way of scaring them off. Please, tell me when a man last danced with me more than once at a social function?"

"If you didn't speak so much of books…"

"And weevils." She had talked incessantly about weevils and the havoc they played in early English kitchens to her last dance partner. Because they had been the subject of the last book she'd read and she hadn't been able to think of anything else.

"Certainly don't speak of that."

"Suffice it to say I don't think you have to worry about me tumbling into a romance. The only problem is… Why would he take me with him? Now that he knows the painting exists, and that it is on Isolo D'Oro, he'll no doubt have an easy enough time figuring out *where* it is. And I'm sure he'll have no trouble finding someone to impart what information they might have about it, for the right price."

"No," her grandmother said, "he won't."

"Why is that?"

"Because. Because *you* have the key. You're the only one who has the key."

Gabriella frowned. "I don't have a key."

"Yes, you do. The painting is hidden away in one of the old country estates that used to belong to the royal family. It is in a secret room, behind a false wall, and no one would have found it. So long as the building stands, and I have never heard rumors to the contrary, the painting would have remained there."

"And the key?"

Her grandmother reached out, her shaking hands touching the necklace that Gabriella wore. "Close to your heart. Always."

Gabriella looked down at the simple flower pendant that hung from the gold chain she wore around her neck. "My necklace?"

It had been a gift to her when she was a baby. A piece of the family's crown jewels that her mother had considered beneath her. So simple, but lovely, a piece of art to Gabriella's mind.

"Yes, your necklace. Did you ever wonder why the bottom of it had such an odd shape? Once you get into this room, you fit this into a slot on the picture frame on the back wall. It swings open and, behind it, you will find *The Lost Love*."

CHAPTER THREE

TRULY, HIS GRANDFATHER had a lot to answer for. Alex was not the kind of man accustomed to doing the bidding of anyone but himself. And yet, here he was, cooling his heels in the antechamber of a second-rate country estate inhabited by disgraced royals.

If he were being perfectly honest—and he always was—one royal in particular who looked more like a small, indignant owl than she did a princess.

With her thick framed glasses and rather spiky demeanor it did not seem to him that Princess Gabriella was suited to much in the way of royal functions. Not that he was a very good barometer of exceptional social behavior.

Alex was many things, *acceptable* was the least among them.

Normally, he would not have excused himself from the room quite so quickly. Normally, he would have sat there and demanded that all the information be disseminated in his presence. Certainly, Queen Lucia was a queen. But in his estimation it was difficult to be at one's full strength when one did not have a country to rule. In truth, the D'Oro family had not inhabited a throne in any real sense in more years than Princess Gabriella had been alive.

So while the family certainly still had money, and a modicum of power, while they retained their titles, he did not imagine he would bring the wrath of an army down on his head for refusing a direct order.

However, he had sensed then that it was an opportune moment to test the theory of catching more flies with honey than vinegar.

He did so hate having to employ charm.

He had better end up in possession of the painting. And it had better truly be his grandfather's dying wish. Otherwise, he would be perturbed.

The door behind him clicked shut and he turned just in time to see Princess Gabriella, in her fitted sweatshirt and tight black leggings, headed toward him. She was holding her hands up beneath her breasts like a small, frightened animal, her eyes large behind her glasses.

That was what had put him in the mind of her being an owl earlier. He did not feel the need to revise that opinion. She was fascinating much in the way a small creature might be.

He felt compelled to watch her every movement, her every pause. As he would any foreign entity. So, there was nothing truly remarkable about it.

"Well, my princess," he said. "What have you learned?"

"I know where the painting is," she said, tucking a silken strand of dark hair behind her ear before returning her hands back to their previous, nervous position.

"Excellent. Draw me a map on a napkin and I'll be on my way."

"Oh. There will be no direction giving. No napkin drawing."

"Is that so?"

She tossed her hair and for a moment he saw a glimmer of royalty beneath her rather dowdy exterior. And that was all the more fascinating. "No. I'm not giving you directions, because *I* have the directions. You are taking me with you."

He laughed at the imperious, ridiculous demand. "I most certainly am not."

She crossed her arms, the sweater bunching beneath them. "Yes, you are. You don't know how to get there."

"Gabriella, I am an expert at getting the information I want. Be it with money or seduction, it makes no difference to me, but I will certainly get what I need."

Her cheeks turned a rather fetching shade of pink. He imagined it was the mention of seduction, not bribery, that did it.

"But *I* have the key," she insisted. "Or rather, I know where it is. And trust me when I tell you it is not something you'll be able to acquire on your own."

"A key?" He didn't believe her.

"And the…the instructions on how to use it."

He studied her hard. She was a bookish creature. Not terribly beautiful, in his estimation. Not terribly brave, either. Intensely clever, though. Still, the lack of bravery made it unlikely that she was lying to him. The cleverness, on the other hand, was a very large question mark.

It made her unpredictable.

This was why he preferred women who were not so clever.

Life was complicated enough. When it came to interactions with the female sex he rather liked it simple, physical and brief.

He had a feeling his association with Gabriella would be none of those things and that only set his teeth on edge all the more.

"I do not believe that you have the key, or rather, have access to it that I cannot gain."

"Okay, then. Enjoy the journey to Isolo D'Oro without me. I'm sure when you get there and find that you hold nothing in your hand but your own—"

"Well, now, there's no need to get crass."

She blinked. "I wasn't going to be crass. I was going to say you hold nothing in your hand but your own arrogance."

He chuckled. "Well, I was imagining you saying something completely different."

"What can I have possibly—?" She blinked again. "Oh."

He arched a brow. "Indeed."

She gritted her teeth, her expression growing more fierce. "Crassness and all other manner of innuendo aside, you are not gaining access to the painting without me."

"Right. So, you know where it is, and you clearly possess the key. Why not go without me?"

"Well, it isn't that simple. I am a member of the D'Oro family. And while technically I can return to the island because I am only of the bloodline, and I never ruled, gaining access could still be a problem."

"I see. So, how do we play this? Wealthy American businessman on a vacation takes a beautiful…" He paused for a moment, allowing his eyes to sweep over her, not hiding how underwhelmed he was by the sight. "A beautiful princess as his lover?"

"Absolutely not!" She turned a very intense shade of pink, and he found himself captivated by the slow bleed of color beneath her skin.

"You have a better suggestion?"

"I want to prevent scandal. I want to bring the painting back here with as little fanfare as possible. I don't want you making a big production of things."

"And I assure you I will not. This is for a private collection and has nothing to do with causing embarrassment to the royal family."

She worried her lip between her teeth. "I don't trust you."

"Excellent. I wouldn't trust me, either."

"Excellent. No trust." Her cheeks were getting redder.

This time, he figured it was from frustration. "I want to go with you. But I don't want to cause a scene. I can't cause a scene. You have no doubt seen the kind of scandal my parents create in the headlines with their drug use, affairs, separations, reconciliations… The press would love to smell blood in the water around me and I just can't chance it."

An evil thought occurred to him and it made him smile. "Well, if you don't wish to go as my lover—"

"I don't!"

"Then I'm afraid you'll have to come as my assistant."

"No one will believe that I'm your assistant. I'm a princess." She lifted her little nose in the air, dark hair cascading over her back like spilled ink. Now she did indeed look every inch insulted royalty.

"What do you typically look like when you go out and about? I imagine it isn't like this," he said, indicating her rather drab trappings.

"I don't go out frequently. But when I do I have a stylist."

"Your glasses?"

"I normally wear contacts."

He nodded slowly. "Princess Gabriella D'Oro. I *have* seen pictures of you—it's only that I would never have recognized you in your current state. The difference is remarkable."

He had an immediate picture in his mind of a glossier, more tamed version of the woman in front of him. Sleek and, actually, quite beautiful. Though not remotely as interesting as the version of Gabriella that stood before him.

She waved a hand. "Between professionally fitted dresses, undergarments to hold in all undesirable lumps and bumps, makeup to cover every flaw, false eyelashes, red lips…I'm scarcely the same person."

"A good thing for our current situation." He regarded her for a longer period of time. "Yes, that will do nicely.

You will come as my assistant. With your hair just like this. With your glasses. And with some horrible pantsuit. No one will ever believe you are Princess Gabriella. No one will look twice at you. Certainly not close enough to identify you. That eases any and all problems we might have with the press, with the local government and with scandal."

He could see that she was fuming, *radiating* with indignity. He quite liked it. He didn't have a lot of time. He certainly didn't have *extra* time to stand around negotiating about keys and directions with a silly girl.

So she would come. It was no difference to him either way.

"That is a ridiculous idea," she said. "Anyway, I've never traveled. I mainly stay here in the estate."

"Curled up on a cushion reading a book?"

She blinked. "What else would one do on a cushion?"

"Oh, I can think of several things."

"Drinking tea?"

"No. Not drinking tea."

Her expression was a study in confusion. It was almost cute. Except that he had no interest in bookish virgins.

She was…naive. Young. For a moment he was concerned about how young. "How old are you?"

She sniffed. "I'm twenty-three. You can stop looking at me like I'm some sort of schoolgirl."

"*Cara mia*, you are a schoolgirl to me."

"How old are *you*?"

"That is none of your business."

"Am I to respect my elders?"

He laughed, he couldn't help it. Rare was the person who poked back at him. He rather enjoyed having fun at other people's expense, but they didn't dare have it at his.

His secret was that he found it rather entertaining just how afraid everyone seemed to be in his presence. His formidable reputation afforded him a great deal of enjoyment. Though the fact that he took pleasure in making people quake in his presence was likely why he had so few friends. Not that he minded.

He had sycophants, he had business associates and he had mistresses. He had no room in his life for anything else. Nor had he the desire for them.

Unfortunately, he also had family, and with them came obligations. Family was, after all, how he found himself here now.

"Then it is decided. You will be my personal assistant, a college student, doing a work experience program. Traveling with me to Isolo D'Oro to take in some of the local culture and scenery while I negotiate a business deal."

"I'm supposed to be your…intern?" She was positively incandescent with irritation now.

"Yes. Of course, Gabriella is a little bit posh for that. How about Gabby? It has a very nice ring to it. Don't you think, *Gabby*?"

"I hate being called Gabby."

"But I'll wager you hate scandal even more. So, Gabby my assistant you will be, and we will not create any of it."

She frowned, her dark brows lowering, disappearing behind the thick frame of her glasses. "If you're going to be this exasperating for the entire journey I can see it's going to be a problem."

"I don't plan on being this exasperating for the entire journey." She breathed out a sigh of relief. "I plan on being at least twice as exasperating."

Her eyes flew wide. "And why is that?"

"Oftentimes I find life short on entertainment. I do my best to make my own fun."

"Yes, well, I live in an estate with an old woman in her nineties. I make a lot of my own fun, too. But typically that involves complicated genealogy projects and a little bit of tatting."

"Tatting?"

"You can never have too many doilies. Not in a house this size."

He arched a brow, studying her face to see if she was being sincere. He couldn't get a read on her. "I will have to take your word for that."

"Don't you have doilies?"

He lifted his shoulder. "I might in one of my residences. I can't say that I ever noticed."

"I could make you some. No one should have a doily deficiency."

"God forbid." He turned and began to walk away from her. "Aren't you going to show me to my room?"

"Excuse me?" she asked.

"Aren't you going to show me to my room?" he repeated. "We will leave early tomorrow morning for Isolo D'Oro. I don't see any point in my staying elsewhere. You have a great many rooms in the estate. And they are replete with doilies, I hear. Which means you should be able to accommodate me."

He turned his most charming and feral smile in her direction. Usually women shrank back from them. Or swooned.

She did neither.

"I did not invite you to stay. And it's particularly impolite of you to invite yourself."

"It wasn't particularly hospitable of *you* to not invite me. I will put aside my pique for the sake of convenience, and a more companionable journey tomorrow. Now," he said, his tone uncompromising. He excelled at being uncompromising. "Be a good girl and show me to my room."

CHAPTER FOUR

"WHAT IS THIS?"

Gabriella came out of the bedroom positioned toward the back of his private jet. She was wearing her glasses, as instructed, her dark hair pulled back into a ponytail. She was also newly dressed in the outfit he had gone to great lengths to procure for her before his plane had departed this morning for Isolo D'Oro. Well, one of the palace servants had gone to great lengths to procure it. He had taken a rather leisurely breakfast during which he had checked his stocks and made sure that things were running smoothly back at his office in Manhattan.

"Your costume, Gabby," he said.

Had she been an owl he was certain that at the moment her feathers would have been ruffled. "It isn't very flattering."

"Well, neither was the sweatshirt you were wearing when we met yesterday. But that did not seem to stop you from wearing it."

"I was having a day at home. I had been sitting in the library reading."

"Naturally."

She frowned. "What does that mean?"

"You look like the type. That's all."

She shifted slightly, her frown deepening. "Yes, I sup-

pose so. But I'm not entirely lacking in vanity. This…"
She indicated the black dress pants, tapered closely to
her skin—much more closely than he had anticipated—
and the white blouse she was wearing, complete with a
large pin that should have looked more at home on her
grandmother than on her, but managed to look quite stylish. "This is not the kind of thing I'm used to wearing in
public."

She didn't look like a princess—that much was true.
But the outfit was not actually unflattering. The outfit
was very nearly fashionable, albeit in a much lower-rent
way than she was no doubt used to looking.

"What exactly is the problem with it?"

"The pants are very tight."

"Their most redeeming feature in my opinion."

He was rewarded with another of her blushes. "I do not
like to draw attention to my body."

"Believe me when I tell you this, Gabriella. You do not
have to do anything to draw attention to your body. The
very fact that it exists does draw attention to it." He found
it was true even as he spoke the words. He had not readily
noticed her charms upon his arrival at the estate yesterday, but she was certainly not lacking in them. Her figure
was not what was considered attractive these days. There
was no careful definition of muscles earned through long
hours in a gym. No gap between her thighs.

She was lush. Soft. Average-size breasts that were remarkable if only because breasts always were, a slender
waist and generously rounded hips. Hips that were currently
being flaunted by the pants she was complaining about.

"Oh. Well. That is… Was that a compliment?"

"Yes. It was a good compliment."

"Sorry. I'm not used to receiving compliments from
men."

He found that hard to believe. She was a princess.

Moreover, she wasn't unattractive. Usually one or the other was enough. "Do you ever leave the estate?"

"In truth, not that often."

"That must be your problem. Otherwise, I imagine you would be inundated with compliments. Sincere and otherwise."

"Why is that?"

"Because. You have quite a few things men would find desirable."

"Money."

"That is certainly one of the things. Though right now you could easily pass for a personal assistant. Which is exactly what we are going for." He took a seat in one of the plush armchairs and picked up the mug of coffee he had poured himself earlier.

"What are the other things?"

"Your body. And its various charms. I thought I made that clear."

She frowned. He expected her to...well, to get angry. Or shrink up against the wall like all bookish virgins should do. Instead, she walked through the plane and took the seat opposite from him, crossing her legs at the ankles and folding her hands in her lap. "You're very blunt."

"Yes. I find it frightens people. Which I very much enjoy."

"I'm not certain if I'm blunt in quite the same way you are. But I do tend to say whatever pops into my mind. Often it's about something unrelated to the situation. That also seems to frighten people. Men specifically."

"The reason you don't receive many compliments?"

"My mother always told me to keep conversation to the topic of the weather. But we live on an island. Unless a hurricane or tsunami is threatening, the weather isn't all that interesting."

"That's the point. A great many men prefer their women to be dull on the inside and shiny on the outside."

"You among them?"

He chuckled. "Oh, I am *chief* among them."

She tilted her head to the side, a rather bemused and curious expression on her face. "Why is that?"

"Why is what, *cara mia*?"

"Why do so many men prefer their women to be quite the opposite of what one should prefer in a person?"

"Because. Those sorts of men, myself included, don't want women for sparkling conversation. They want them for one thing, and one thing only."

She sighed, a rather heavy, irritated sound. "I imagine you mean sex."

He was momentarily surprised by her directness. Not that directness shocked him in any manner; it was simply that this kind of directness coming from *her* was shocking.

"Yes," he said, not seeing why he shouldn't be equally direct in return.

"Predictable. I suppose that's why my mother is able to skip through life behaving so simply. She's a prime example of what you're talking about. Someone who is all sparkle and shine. My father no longer even possesses any shine. But I imagine in his case it's the promise of money and an eventual payoff that bring women into his bed."

"That sounds quite familiar to me."

She studied him, a confused expression crossing her face. "But—and I'm speaking in a continued metaphor— you seem to be *quite* shiny."

He laughed. No one had ever characterized him as shiny before. "I wasn't thinking of myself. It's true, I have my own set of charms that bring females into my bed. Money. Looks, so they tell me. But in this case I was thinking of my parents."

"Oh?"

"Yes. It sounds very much like they would have been friends with yours."

"Do your parents enjoy drugs, wild affairs and questionable fashion sense?"

He laughed, but this time the sound was bitter. "They liked nothing more. In fact, they loved it so much it killed them."

She seemed to shrink in her seat, the regret on her face pronounced. "Oh. I'm sorry. I should not have made light of it. Not without knowing your background."

He picked up his clear mug of coffee and turned it until the light coming from outside the plane window caught hold of the amber liquid, setting it ablaze. "One *must* make light of these things. Otherwise, it's all darkness, isn't it?"

"Some things are only dark, I fear."

He shrugged, taking another drink. "They don't have to be."

"How did your parents die?"

The question struck him. She genuinely didn't know. But then, it stood to reason. She'd had no idea who he was when they had first met. Rare was the person who didn't know his entire family history before introducing themselves to him. She was an odd creature. And her cleverness was *still* off-putting. But he found small pieces of her to be a breath of fresh air he hadn't realized he'd been craving.

"They died in a car accident," he said. "They were having one of their legendary fights. Fueled by alcohol, drugs and a sexual affair. Basically, all of their favorite things combined into one great fiery ball of doom."

"Oh. That's awful."

"Yes. I suppose it is. But I was very young. And not much a part of their lives." He did his best to keep the memories of that night from crowding in. Snowy. The roads filled with ice. His parents shrieking obscenities. And a small boy standing out in the cold, looking lost and lonely. "I find them a tragedy. A cautionary tale. I might be a bit jaded, but I'm not a total libertine. I suppose I have their tragedy to thank for that."

She nodded, as though she completely understood what he was talking about. He had no doubt she had little experience of libertines outside the pages of a book.

"If it weren't for my parents," she said, her words coming slowly, "who knows how I would be? It is their example that has kept me so firmly planted in the estate in Aceena. It's their example that has caused me to crave a quieter existence."

That surprised him. It seemed she *did* understand. At least a little bit better than he had guessed she might. A little bit better than most.

All of his siblings had started life with the same parents he had, and yet he had been the only one affected in quite this way.

His twin brothers were hellions. They were playboys who lived their lives entirely as they saw fit. At least, they *had* been before their respective *true loves* had come into their lives.

But always, they had lived with much more passion than Alex ever had. Even now that they had settled down, they continued to live with more passion and emotion than Alex would ever consider.

"Everything makes much more sense if you see life as a business," he said, speaking the thought before he had decided he would.

"Do you think so?"

He nodded. "Yes. Business is sensible. Everyone is in it to make money. That's the bottom line. Because of that, everyone's motives are transparent from the beginning. They're going to serve themselves. Sometimes favors are traded. Contracts are drawn up, terms are met."

"A bit more clear-cut than people," she said.

"I've always found it slightly strange that divorce is much easier than breaking a business contract. If people took marriage as seriously as they took business deals, the world would be a different place." He leaned back in his chair. "Of course, you could go about metaphorically hopping into bed with other partners after taking on exclusive deals with another. But you would quickly lose your credibility, and your business with it. It wouldn't serve your bottom line. Personal relationships are much more murky. There is no common bottom line. I find that disturbing."

"I see what you're saying," she said. "I hadn't thought about it that way. But then, I suppose it's because I don't have a head for business."

"What is it you have a head for, Gabby?"

She bristled at the nickname. "Books, I suppose."

"What sorts of books?"

"All sorts."

His eyes narrowed. "You said you liked genealogy."

"Yes. I do. I'm very interested in my family history. I find it completely fascinating. I believe that history contains truths. I mean, history goes beyond what's been published in the media. What the press reports…that isn't real history."

"I suppose the granddaughter of some of the world's most infamous disgraced royals would feel that way."

She lifted her shoulder, an unconscious gesture she seemed to do a lot. She had a very delicate frame; whether in glasses or ill-fitting clothing, that couldn't be denied. She was like a strange, old-fashioned doll.

He was rather disturbed by the part of him that felt compelled to lean in and pull her from the shelf, so to speak.

"I suppose I would," she said. "But that isn't why I'm doing this. I quite like the idea of uncovering the truth, in an unbiased fashion."

"And so you study your family history."

"Yes."

Her eyes had grown brighter when the subject was introduced. Strangely, he found he quite liked it. It was very interesting to make conversation with a woman about something other than shallow topics. And in this instance, it had been quite easy. Was she truly so different?

It made him wonder if the women he conversed with were actually as shallow as he imagined or if they thought *him* to be shallow. Strange that it should matter to him at all. It shouldn't. Not when he purposefully kept those interactions as meaningless as possible.

He kept a wall between himself and others, using all manner of methods, and limited conversation with his lovers was one of those methods.

It didn't matter what he thought of them. It didn't matter what they thought of him. It only mattered how it felt when they were in bed.

"You will find this trip back to your homeland fascinating, then."

He wanted to try out a bit more of that excitement. He wondered what it must be like, to possess that level of enthusiasm. God knew he no longer had the ability. He had seen what happened with passion. Had seen it firsthand when his parents were killed, lost forever in a storm of twisted steel and broken glass. He had no desire to be a part of anything like that. He led with his mind. He had relationships that were mutually beneficial for both parties involved.

They never ended in screams and accusations of infidelity. No. He always gave his women a gift, made sure he complimented their beauty, lied about how diverting he found their company and promised to cherish their time together always and to remember them fondly.

He never did.

The moment they walked out of his bedroom he forgot their names. He simply didn't possess the capacity to care about people with any real depth. At least, people outside of his family.

He couldn't see the value in it. He could only see the cost.

"I expect it will be wonderful. My grandmother has told me stories about the old family estates. About the palaces. But I've never been to see them myself. All I've ever seen are old, faded pictures."

"Why exactly was the royal family expelled from the country?"

"Oh, there are a great many rumors of unfair taxation. Of my great-grandfather being a tyrant. Greedy. But I'm not entirely convinced. And certainly, that isn't my grandmother's take on the situation. Regardless, there was an uprising and the family had to escape in the dead of night. They're lucky to have escaped with their lives. Most royal families don't make out quite so well during violent depositions."

"You speak the truth there."

"I think I'll be the first in my family to set foot on Isolo D'Oro since then. It's probably a good thing that I'll be incognito."

"Probably."

She smiled, her whole face brightening. It was like watching light shift over the ocean. The color moving from slate gray to a brilliant blue. "This is all a bit like a good adventure story, don't you think?"

It reminded him of something his grandfather had said. About the whole thing being like a boy's adventure. Why were people eternally attempting to excite him about something that felt like little more than a menial task?

"I consider it an errand," he said, lifting his glass to his lips again. "One that I intend to do and do well, because as

I said, I believe in business. In fairness. I owe my grandfather and I am determined to repay him. But that's it."

His dry response doused her smile and he cursed himself. "Well, I think anything can be considered an errand with the incorrect mind-set. And anything can be a game if you purpose for it to be."

"All I need is a spoonful of sugar?"

She smiled. "It couldn't hurt."

"No, I suppose it couldn't." The plane began to descend, and Alex could see the scenery below growing larger. Could begin to make out the whitecaps of the waves on the bright water. "You had better buckle yourself, Princess. We are about to arrive in Isolo D'Oro. And that is the last time you will be called *Princess* for the foreseeable future."

CHAPTER FIVE

GABRIELLA WAS STUNNED by the view spread before her. Her grandmother had told her how beautiful her homeland was, but she hadn't been prepared for the true splendor of it.

The city that she and Alex were staying in was filled with ornate, old-world architecture, the Mediterranean Sea spread out before it like a gem. It was a glorious mixture of old and new. High-rises being built in a new section of the city, dedicated to bringing much needed commerce to the nation. While the old historic districts remained unchanged.

She wanted to go out and explore. She did *not* want to cool her heels in the grand hotel suite that Alex had installed them in. But Alex had insisted that he had some work to do, and it would not do to have her wandering around the country by herself.

She supposed that she could defy him on the matter, but she honestly had such limited travel experience that she didn't feel terribly inclined to do that. She was much more likely to stick close to the large American businessman acting as her escort, as she had a feeling he would be a little bit more accomplished at guarding her physical safety than she would.

Not that anything about Isolo D'Oro seemed menacing, but stories of how her family had escaped under threat echoed in her mind. It wasn't something she could simply forget.

"How are your impressions so far?"

Alex chose that moment to come out of his bedroom. He had discarded his suit jacket, his white shirt unbuttoned at the collar, revealing a wedge of tan skin covered with just the right amount of dark chest hair.

She questioned that thought the moment it entered her mind. What on earth was the appropriate amount of chest hair, and how was she so certain that he was in possession of it? It wasn't as though she was an expert on men's chests or the quantity of hair on them.

How strange that she was putting so much thought into his.

"It's lovely," she said, turning her focus back to the view, and resolutely away from his chest.

"I'm glad you think so."

She studied him closely. "Are you?"

He smiled and the impact of it felt like a punch in the chest. He was an irritatingly large presence. His every movement set the hairs on her arms on end, his shifting expressions creating a seismic reaction in her internal organs.

"No," he said. "I don't actually care what you think. It just seemed a polite thing to say."

She looked at him, unable to get a genuine read on him. "I can't decide whether or not I'm amused by you," she said.

"I believe the general consensus of me is that I'm *horrifying*."

"Hmm. Really?"

"My reputation precedes me in all corners of the earth. I'm known to be quite hard. Demanding. A perfectionist in areas of business. Sometimes scarcely human. Some say that if you cut me, I would, in fact, not bleed."

"Well, that is ridiculous. Because everybody bleeds," she said.

"For such a clever creature, you are alarmingly literal."

"It is ridiculous," she insisted. "All of it. Obviously you're human."

His smile only grew broader. "*Is* it obvious? I feel it isn't to many. But then, I find that amusing and don't do much to dispel the idea that I might be some kind of monster."

"Why?"

He walked across the small living area, heading back toward the bedroom he had just come out of and pushing the door open. "Coming?" he asked.

Her heart slammed against her rib cage. "What?"

"You asked a question. I thought you might want to hear the answer. But I have to go into my room to get my jacket and retrieve my tie."

She scrambled after him, feeling a little bit silly that she had somehow read something *else* into those words. Of course he wasn't asking her to come into the bedroom for…well, anything that might be done in the bedroom.

She wasn't the kind of woman who invited seduction. And she was genuinely fine with that. Someday, she would find a man. A suitable man who would make a suitable match. Possibly a minor role. Or someone who moved in high European society but who also liked books and dusty libraries. Yes, that. Most likely. Definitely not an American businessman who took joy in tormenting others with his dry sense of humor and seemed to regard her love of reading and research with the kind of curiosity one usually reserved for a bug under a microscope.

"You want to know why I enjoy keeping others at a distance?"

"I am curious, I admit," she said.

She was also surprised that he was even pretending he

was going to give her an answer. After all, if he truly enjoyed keeping people at a distance, why would he disclose any information that might bring the two of them closer together? It didn't make sense.

"I like the freedom it affords me," he said. He opened up the closet and pulled out a jacket and a tie. Both black, exactly like the ones he'd worn earlier. Though she had a feeling they were a different set than before. "When people fear you they tend to defer to you. That ensures I get my way most of the time."

"What are they afraid you'll do?"

"I don't know." He began to button his shirt collar. "That's the most amusing part. For all the rumors of my misdeeds, I have yet to actually throw anyone in a dungeon. Neither have I ever sucked anyone's blood. However, my legend looms large, and who am I to argue with that?"

"I don't think I have a legend. Well, obviously I don't, as you had never heard of me when you arrived at the estate."

He lifted a shoulder as he looped the tie around his neck. "But then, you had never heard of me, either, *cara*."

"True enough. But I'm rather cloistered there at the estate. There are a great many things I haven't heard of."

He arched a dark brow. "Does your grandmother not have Wi-Fi?"

"Yes, we have the internet. It's just that I don't often make use of it."

"And why is that?"

"It's very disconcerting to know you could log into a news website at any time and your family is the headline. I just…" Her stomach twisted just thinking about it. "I prefer to avoid it. My brothers… Well, they're as rich as you are. Just as ruthless. Libertines, as you put it earlier. My parents are worse. At least my brothers have some good qualities to redeem them. They are amusing. When they want to be. And they're quite nice actually. To me. Their ex-mistresses would tell you a different story. But even if they've earned it…even if parts of it are true…I don't really enjoy seeing what the media has to say about my family."

"No," he said, his voice softer all of a sudden. "You prefer to gather facts."

"Yes. Exactly that."

"You like to control the story."

She shook her head. "No, it isn't about me controlling a story. I want to know the truth."

"That's a lie, Gabby. You like to control the story. You like to hear it first. You like to decide what is done with it. You want to make sure that you are able to collect the information at the speed in which you can process it. You like to ensure that you are the one who gets to form the first opinion. There isn't anything wrong with it. But it is the truth."

She felt as though he'd run her through with a scabbard. It hurt terribly and made her feel exposed. As though he'd seen down deep into parts of her she'd never even examined before.

And the only reason it felt that way was because…it was true.

"Why is it you seem to think you know me so well?" she asked.

His dark eyes leveled with hers. "I recognized something of myself in you. On that same topic, I'm never entirely certain whether or not you amuse me."

She looked down, clasping her hands together and picking at her thumbnail. "Not very many people find me amusing. I think they find me boring."

"Now that, I can't imagine. You are the farthest thing from boring. In fact, I find that to be one of your foremost negative qualities."

She frowned. "Why would being entertaining be a negative quality?"

"Because I *like* boring women. Boring women are easy to sleep with and forget about. Boring women are the best kind."

A rash of heat broke out over her skin, color flooding her face. "I'm not going to sleep with you so my...*interestingness* shouldn't be a problem for you."

He chuckled. "I wasn't making an offer."

Shame washed over her. Of course he wasn't. Of course he hadn't meant that. But she was still talking and she couldn't stop herself. "When I do make room in my life for that sort of relationship, I will most definitely be pursuing a man closer to my own age who has interests in common with my own."

"Oh, right. I forgot. We have quite the generational gap between us."

"It's prohibitive. We won't even like the same music."

He chuckled softly. "But you don't like popular music. You like classical music."

This statement infuriated her, because it was true, too. Just like the last one. Was she somehow telegraphing her private thoughts via her eyeballs?

"And what sort of music do you like?" she asked.

"Classic rock." He smiled. "You're right, it isn't to be. We're too different."

"Ah, well, just allow me to get the broom and dustpan so I can sweep up the pieces of my broken heart."

"I would, but we haven't the time for such carrying-on. We have a meeting."

She blinked rapidly. "We do?"

"Yes. We have a meeting with the prime minister of Isolo D'Oro."

"But... When?"

He raised his hand and looked down at his wrist, at the

watch he wore that no doubt cost more than some people's yearly salary. "In about ten minutes."

She took in his perfectly pressed appearance. The sharp white shirt, and the rest, all an inky black to match his hair and eyes. He was like a dark angel come to life in Armani. And she was…well, she was wearing polyester pants.

"Wait a second! That isn't fair. You had a chance to change your clothes. I'm still wearing the same thing that I was wearing on the plane."

"Which is perfect. Because you are my assistant, not a lover. Not a princess." He reached back into the closet and pulled out a garment bag. "So, in the next ten minutes, I would like you to make sure that you put this out for the hotel staff. The jacket I was wearing earlier. It needs to be cleaned."

She sputtered. "I'm going to meet the prime minister of Isolo D'Oro in these ridiculous skinny…pants…whatever they are. And now I have to do your menial chores?"

"Well, Gabby, had we decided to go with the story that you were my current mistress I would have draped you in silks. As it is, I'm going to have to drape you in my dry cleaning."

She sniffed. "You don't have to enjoy this so much."

He chuckled, a darkly amused sound. "Oh, yes, I absolutely do have to enjoy this. As I told you before, I'm accustomed to making my own fun. And I'm finding this quite unexpectedly fun."

CHAPTER SIX

THE TROUBLE WITH meeting politicians was that they always came with an unreasonable amount of security detail and other various hangers-on. Of course, there were a few paparazzi, as well. But Alex knew that the prime minister was the quickest way to gaining access to the various historic sites they would *need* access to in order to find *The Lost Love*.

Most of the dining room had been cleared in preparation for his arrival, and it was almost entirely empty except for the three of them, seated at a table in the far corner.

When the man had finally arrived at the hotel restaurant a good fifteen minutes after he had said he would, he had spent an age pouring over the wine list and finding things disappointing.

Immediately, Alex found him insufferable. A pale man with a weak chin who clearly thought his time was precious, but had thought nothing of keeping Alex and Gabriella waiting. Or of insulting the hotel staff with comments about the wine, while not bothering to make a formal introduction.

Alex made it a point not to telegraph any of his irritation to the other man. As soon as the wine had been selected, Alex turned his focus to the business at hand.

"Alessandro Di Sione," he said, extending his hand. "It's good to meet you, Prime Minister Colletti. This is my assistant, Gabby. A university student doing a bit of work experience. She's come with me to help me on my mission."

"And what exactly is that?" asked the prime minister, leaning back in his chair, his arms behind his head.

"I've become somewhat of an avid art collector of late. I heard that the collection here on Isolo D'Oro is beyond price. I'm interested in acquiring some pieces. Particularly those that belonged to the former royal family because of the...significance of the time period."

"A historian *and* an art enthusiast?"

"Absolutely," Alex said.

The other man smiled. "Which sorts of art are you most interested in?"

Alex hesitated. His grandfather was right. He probably *was* owed a refund on that expensive boarding school education.

"Portraiture primarily," Gabriella interjected. "Oils on canvas, mostly. Though I know that there are some excellent marble busts. And also some paintings that depict the scenery. Some wonderful depictions of farms? I have heard tell—I mean, Alessandro has told me. He is quite enthusiastic about the painting of the geese."

The prime minister laughed. "Yes. One of my favorites. I don't think I could part with it."

"Everything has a price," Alex said.

"Some things."

"Either way, we would be very interested in seeing the collection," Alex continued.

"And I am happy to show it. The palace is home to the art collections of the royal family, so you'll find whatever you like there. But I'm curious. You're currently in charge of a vast shipping company, is that correct?"

Now, the other man was speaking Alex's language. Alex leaned forward, suddenly feeling much more interested in the interaction. "Yes, I am."

"I might have need of your services. The entire country might. It would be interesting to see if we can come to some sort of agreement."

"Yes, that *would* be interesting," Alex said.

It was suddenly clear why Prime Minister Colletti had been so eager to meet with them. Money. Alex's very favorite language.

"Well, but we're here to study art," Gabriella protested.

"A good businessperson learns to multitask early on, as you will learn when you discover more about the world," he responded.

She said nothing to that, but he could tell she wanted to kick him under the table.

"Wonderful," the prime minister said. "It just so happens that I'm having an open house party at the palace. Celebrating fifty years of independence for Isolo D'Oro."

He could feel Gabriella quivering with rage, and for once, not all of it was directed at him. He reached beneath the table and quickly squeezed her hand. A warning.

What he hadn't anticipated was how soft her skin would be. How smooth.

He withdrew his touch quickly, keeping his focus trained on the prime minister.

"I would very much like to have you attend the party," the other man was saying. "Your assistant is welcome also. That way, you can see some of the art, a bit of the architecture and we can also discuss the possibility of a business partnership."

"That sounds perfect," Alex said, thinking it sounded anything but. A house party. Out in the country. It sounded like an awful costume drama. All they'd need was for the butler to murder somebody and for an elderly lady detective to show up and try to solve the crime.

"Excellent. We will discuss business over the next week. And until then we will just enjoy the dinner."

CHAPTER SEVEN

STANDING IN A hotel room and looking down at the magnificent views of Isolo D'Oro had been a magical moment for Gabriella. But it hadn't truly hit her until the limousine sent by Prime Minister Colletti rolled up to the grand estate that this was her *home*.

At least, in heritage. These magnificent, sprawling grounds should have belonged to her family. The beautifully appointed house with the magnificent stonework around the windows, the grand pillars and the arched doorway had been property of the royal family once. Until they had been driven out, banished from the nation that was in their blood.

For centuries, her ancestors had ruled. For centuries, they had inhabited these walls, walked through the gardens. Now, her grandmother couldn't even return to fetch a painting that held value to her that went far beyond money. Far beyond the attached history.

That was what struck her so hard, so deeply, as she walked through the front door, as they were led through the halls to the quarters in which they would be staying. This wasn't just history in the broad sense of the word. This was *her* history. Her family history. The blood of her ancestors might as well be in the stonework. Babies had been born here, the elderly had died here. Her people. Her ancestors.

It felt very personal. Almost painful.

And yet, at the same time, her heart felt swollen. She felt so connected to this place around her that it emboldened her. Filled her with a sense of confidence. Of belonging.

She had never felt so right before. As if this place was woven through her, a part of her she hadn't known she'd been missing.

All of that lasted for a spare few moments before they were shown to a magnificent suite with a small room off to the left. The tiny quarters belonged to her, the proximity of her room to Alex's of course intended to allow him easy access to her when he might need her to...assist him with whatever she was meant to be assisting him with.

Once the staff who had ushered them in was gone, Alex smiled. "It is comforting to know that if I have need of your services, you will be nearby," he said, looming large in the small doorway of her humble living quarters.

Her cheeks flamed. She knew that he didn't mean it in any kind of lecherous way, but for some reason her body insisted on interpreting it that way.

"After all," he continued, "you are my assistant. And I may well be in need of some *assistance* in the middle of the night."

She gritted her teeth, well aware that her cheeks were glowing an incandescent pink. He could not be in denial about her thoughts. And she had a feeling that now he was just trying to wind her up.

"In case you need a glass of milk?"

"Yes." A wicked smile curved his lips. "I do often enjoy a glass of *warm milk* in the middle of the night. I find it helps me sleep."

"I'll be sure to give it to you early. The middle of the night for someone your age is what…eight o'clock?" She almost regretted taking that cheap shot. *Almost.* If only because it revealed the fact that she found him very disconcerting.

"Yes," he said, arching a brow. "Do bring it to me along with my vitamins."

Drat him. He wasn't even perturbed by that.

"I will do so, as you have requested, sir."

"I like that," he said, his voice a low rumble that rolled through her like thunder.

He had the ability to touch her, all through her body, without ever getting near her, and she couldn't quite understand how he managed it.

She wrenched her focus from him and looked around the modest room. Really, it wasn't bad. Everything was clean, and elegant. The walls were a mint green with white molding adding texture to them. There was no art in this room, but there was a lovely view of the gardens. And that, in her estimation, counted as art.

Alex moved away from the door and she followed him through, not quite sure why. She only knew that he seemed to draw her to him, like he was pulling her on a string.

She was too fascinated by it to fight it.

In contrast to her room, Alex's was sumptuously appointed. The walls had dark wood paneling and a great deal of classical art. There were floor-to-ceiling windows, but she couldn't tell what the view might be because the rich, velvet drapes were drawn over them. Then, in the back corner, there was a large bed with lots of fabric hanging from the ceiling, promising to seclude the sleeper from any unwanted light or noise.

"I don't think they've redecorated since the turn of the century. Last century," Alex said.

"Yes, I suppose this is all original. But that's part of the charm."

"Do you think? I find your perspective on things quite fascinating. You are a romantic."

She frowned. She had never thought of herself as a romantic before. She didn't think he was right. "I'm rather more invested in fact than fancy."

"So you say. But you are always delighted by the beauty around you. There is nothing terribly practical about beauty. And it isn't absolute. One person can find something beautiful when someone else finds it wholly unremarkable. Similarly," he said, speaking slowly, his dark eyes lingering on her in a manner that left her feeling hot, that left her feeling like he had touched her, "one can look at something every day for quite some time and never notice the beauty of it. Then suddenly, one day it might become beautiful to them. Beauty is strange that way. It hides in plain sight."

She swallowed hard, not quite sure why she felt like she was on fire. "I suppose the reverse is also true. Beauty can be obvious. And as it proves itself to be nothing more than pale vanity it can lessen."

"Speaking of your mother and father?" he asked, the question bold and insensitive.

She supposed he was entitled, as she had been rather bold and insensitive herself when they had discussed his parents. "Yes. Does it remind you of yours, as well?"

"Very much."

"All right, I will concede then that maybe you're correct about me. I do like art. I do like frivolous things. Just not…the same kinds of frivolous things as some in my family."

"There is nothing wrong with enjoying the frivolous. I'm not even sure I would call it frivolous. Many people would argue that it is the beauty around us that makes life rich, don't you think?"

She nodded slowly. "I do agree. My life is very quiet compared to most people in my family. Really, it's very quiet compared to most people in my age group, I know. I live with an old woman and I suppose my habits are more reflective of hers than the average twenty-three-year-old. But I like it. I like to read. I like to listen to the sound of the rain on the roof. I like to watch the drops roll down the windowpane. I enjoy the quiet. I enjoy art for all that it doesn't tell us. For the fact that it makes us think and draw our own conclusions. I suppose I enjoy genealogy for the same reasons. We have to extract our own meaning from what we see before us and, from there, guess what the truth might be."

"A very interesting way of looking at it," he said, his tone different now.

"Is that how you see things?"

He shook his head. "I do not have much time for art. Or for books. Or for sitting and listening to the rain."

Her heart sank. "Oh. I thought… By the way you were talking…"

"I've lost the ability to appreciate beauty in the way you seem to. But it doesn't mean I don't appreciate your perspective."

"I suppose you are too jaded."

"Yes," he said, his tone taking on a rather black quality. "I suppose I am a bit too jaded. But then, living the sort of life I have, opulence all around me, my every whim, my every desire, so easily serviced, I don't know how I could be anything but."

"I've had a similar experience, don't forget."

"Yes, you seem to have practiced the art of self-denial a bit more successfully than I have."

"I don't consider it denial."

"Another of your virtues, I'm certain."

She frowned, walking slowly past him, pacing the length of the room, the marble floor clicking beneath her low-heeled shoes. She studied the paintings on the walls, depictions of the scenery around them. During another time. During other seasons. "My parents have indulged in everything imaginable, and yet, they still live life with a fair amount of excitement and passion. I want nothing to do with it. It looks exhausting. Dangerous. Selfish. But…for all their sins they aren't jaded. I feel they enjoy their excess, or they wouldn't continue in it. For you… You seem very bored. And I wonder why that might be."

"I think perhaps the problem with my life, Princess, is that I have seen where the road ends. There is desperate poverty in this world. Tragedies. And I know that there are those who believe that if they simply had one more *thing*, a little bit more money, they would find happiness. But my parents had everything. They had wealth. They had family. They had beauty. Sex, drugs and alcohol in every combination. They had everything. And they were never satisfied. They never stopped searching. They were hungry, always. When they should have been full. It was that continued searching that took everything beautiful they had in their lives and twisted it beyond reason. They had marriage. They had children. And yet, they went out and had affairs. My father made a child with another woman. A child that he never acknowledged. A child whose existence only hurt everyone involved. When you have so much, and yet you have no satisfaction. When you have so much and yet you must continue going until you destroy it all, I can only conclude that there was no happiness to be found in any of it. Not really. And so, I suppose having seen the end my parents came to I have trouble putting much hope in any of the things around me."

"You think it's pointless."

"I don't think it's pointless or I would have thrown myself off a building by now. I think there are aspects of life to enjoy. There is music I like. I enjoy my work. I certainly enjoy my money. I quite enjoy sex. But I'm not certain the satisfaction is to be found. I'm not certain that happiness is a thing that truly exists."

"That all sounds quite…hopeless."

"Maybe it is. Or maybe that's why I choose to take things in life with a healthy dose of cynicism. There are worse things, I should think."

"I think that there's happiness. I don't think that life is quite so meaningless as all that."

He lifted a broad shoulder and she was drawn to the way he moved. He was like a big cat, a predator. Lying in wait for his prey to make the wrong move. The one that would trigger the attack.

She had to wonder if she was the prey in this scenario.

"We all have our coping mechanisms," he said. "You have chosen to try and find satisfaction in the opposite things. While I have decided that I won't find whatever magic cure my parents were looking for within life's various debaucheries."

She paused in her pacing, turned to face him. "Do you think you'll find it anywhere?"

"I have my doubts."

"Do you believe in anything? Do you believe in love?"

He only looked at her, his dark eyes a bottomless well. "No."

"But you're here for your grandfather. Surely—?"

"I believe in fairness. I believe in faithfulness. I believe in keeping my word. As I told you before, I am a man who believes in business."

"Follow your head and not your heart, in other words."

"My head is the only thing I trust."

She let out a heavy sigh, looking back toward her bedroom. It was going to be strange, sharing such a close space with him. Last night in the hotel suite had been strange enough, but there had been a living area between their two bedrooms. This felt…rather more intimate. She should think nothing of it. It should be…nothing. That he was a man and she was a woman shouldn't matter because they wouldn't be engaging in any…man/woman things.

But it still felt strange.

"Then maybe you could use that very large head of yours to figure out how we'll find the painting in this enormous palace?" Her uncertainty, the fluttering in her stomach, made her feel cross.

"I could, I suppose." He tapped his chin as though he were thinking very hard. "The easiest thing to do would be to take a tour. It's likely the hiding place would be revealed to us during it."

"Sure. If only we could arrange that."

"Well, there will be tours. The biggest thing is that we can't turn the pockets of the place out, then leave with a valuable work of art. We have to appear to have come for reasons of business and pleasure. We have to stay. Anyway, I sincerely intend to work up some sort of trade agreement, so we will stay until the last evening party."

"There are parties?"

"Every night. He emailed me a PDF of the itinerary. Very helpful," he said, his tone dry. "But I think we should make sure to stay until the last party. Four days. Then we go. Easy."

Nothing about it sounded easy to her, not at all. To exist in this fishbowl playing a part she didn't know the lines for.

"Are you tired?" he asked. She had to wonder if he'd seen her sag beneath the weight of everything just as she felt it.

"Yes," she said, suddenly feeling exhausted down to her bones. That surge of strength, of certainty that she had felt when she first walked in, was gone now. Now she just felt wrung out. It was strange that coming to this place was so emotional. But it was. Enduring it all with this man who was so…intense, so very *present*—it only added to it.

"Perhaps you should get some rest. There is going to be a gathering tonight with the guests at the party. Appetizers and the like."

She frowned. "What am I supposed to do about that? I can't very well fix myself up. Here people know that I'm Princess Gabriella. Or they'll at least suspect."

"Then you won't fix up."

She scowled. "I like very much how this farce isn't damaging your vanity in any way."

"All of this was your choice, *Princess*. I for one am happy to create a bit of scandal. What do I care if the world thinks I've taken you to my bed? I don't care. Not at all."

"Yes, that is a charming perk of being male. You don't have to worry about rumors of your sexual promiscuity."

He chuckled. "I would guess you've never had to much worry about rumors regarding yours, either."

That goaded her pride. She didn't like him being quite so certain about that. "Perhaps I'm just discreet."

"Oh, I have no doubt that you are. You seem to me to be the very soul of discretion."

She sniffed. "I am. For reasons you should well understand."

"Go rest up. Then put on your armor of discretion and ready yourself for the party tonight."

CHAPTER EIGHT

AT THE MOMENT, no one would suspect Gabriella was a princess, as she was doing an excellent impersonation of a potted plant. She was all but hugging the back wall, dressed in a rather understated pencil skirt and a cream-colored top, complete with a single-string pearl necklace. Her dark hair was partly down, the front pulled back by a clip, the large glasses still fixed on her face.

She looked exactly as an assistant should. And yet, Alex found himself irritated by it.

The other women in the room were dressed in bright colors, saucy cocktail dresses designed to aid in the flaunting of their figures. Their hair expertly styled. And they were certainly not hanging on to the wall. He found that he wanted to see Gabriella without her glasses. That he wondered what it might be like to get a good look at her large, brown eyes. That he might like to see her full lips painted red.

And he knew he would like to see her figure in something designed to flatter it.

He would never be a very great appreciator of art, but he was certainly an appreciator of the female form. And as such, he would simply like to see this one done up with a bit more finesse. That was all. All that discussion of beauty had been on his mind.

She wasn't talking to anyone, rather she seemed to be closely regarding the paintings on the wall. More than that, she seemed to be examining the molding, the floor, the baseboards, the wallpaper… She seemed to be having an entire love affair with the house.

Though he imagined that was to be expected. This was her ancestral home. She had never been here.

He imagined that must bring up all sorts of thoughts.

His family was originally from Italy, and he lived in America. But he had never felt displaced. Giovanni had often told him stories of how he had come to the US, how he had worked his way up from nothing to become one of the most successful men in the nation. Alex enjoyed going to Italy, but he supposed the point of it all was that he could. Yet, while in a technical sense Gabriella *could* have come to Isolo D'Oro, there would have always been a block of some kind. Her family hadn't left of their own accord. They had been banished. It was an entirely different circumstance. One that was quite heavy. And it seemed to be hitting her with its full impact.

"Alessandro Di Sione, right?"

Alex turned to his left and saw a shimmering blonde regarding him with her bright blue eyes. Now *this* was a woman who had taken great pains to flaunt every aspect of her beauty to its greatest advantage. The entirety of her potential was on display before him. There was nothing to wonder about. Nothing at all.

Except perhaps how she would look naked.

Though he had seen enough women naked to be able to guess. He studied her for a moment. He was so confident with his estimation of the size of her breasts without the cleavage-enhancing bra, of the color of her nipples based on her coloring in general, that he found he ultimately wasn't even curious.

"My name is Samantha," she said, smiling grandly,

both realizing she'd lost him before she'd ever started. "I've followed your business exploits with great interest recently."

The way she said *exploits* left him in little doubt that it wasn't his business she had been paying attention to.

"Oh, have you?" he asked. "Perhaps you could tell me about them. I rarely pay attention myself."

She laughed, a high, sharp sound that shot down his spine like an arrow before ricocheting back up to the base of his skull. She touched his arm, leaning in closer. "I didn't know you were funny. I had heard you were frightening."

"Boo," he said.

She laughed again and he fought to keep from cringing.

He flicked a glance across the room at Gabriella, who was watching this interaction between himself and Samantha with what appeared to be great interest. She was now literally standing next to a potted plant, her hand closed around a leaf, her posture rigid.

He couldn't begin to guess what she was thinking. Couldn't begin to guess much of anything about her.

With Gabriella there were a great many unanswered questions.

"Really, we must make more time to get to know each other over the course of the week," she was purring now, all but arching into him like a very needy cat.

"What exactly brings you to the party?" he asked. He didn't care what her answer was. Not in the least. His attention was split between her and the little dark-haired woman with glasses standing against the wall. But he didn't think she noticed. She was far too involved in the performance she was putting on with him.

And he was too busy regarding Gabriella to listen to what she had to say. Which was a shame, really, for Samantha at least. He had a feeling she was putting her full effort into this. An intended seduction, or whatever nonsense she had in her head.

Strange, because in most circumstances he would be more than willing to take her up on the unspoken offer. But not now. He wasn't sure what it was. Perhaps the little bespectacled witch had cast a spell on him. He smiled ruefully, dimly aware that his companion Samantha had likely taken that smile as her due. And of course, it was actually owed to Gabriella.

Very strange. She wasn't the kind that revealed itself immediately. It was more like the sun shining through the trees as you drove down the highway. He would catch flashes of golden light before it faded away again into the darkness. But it was there. And when it struck him directly it was so intense, so brilliant, that it stopped him where he stood.

His eyes caught hers and held for a second before she looked down sharply, obviously embarrassed to have been caught staring at him. He felt no such embarrassment over being caught staring at her.

Then, suddenly, she scurried from the room, hugging the wall as she made her way to the exit.

"Excuse me," he said to Samantha. "I'm very sorry. I have to go."

He wasn't anything of the kind.

He set his drink down on a table as he left, exiting out the same door Gabriella had. He saw her turn left at the far end of the corridor, and he continued on down that way. Maybe she was just headed to the bathroom. Most definitely he didn't *need* to be following her. That didn't seem to stop him.

He had known from the beginning that it was her cleverness he would find to be trouble. He was not wrong.

Had she been boring he would never have chased her

out of a crowded room while being talked to by a busty blonde.

But no, she did not have the decency to be boring.

She had to be interesting. She had to like books. And she had to explain things to him in funny, intricate ways that he would normally find incredibly arduous.

He was angry at her. And with each step he took he felt angrier. Because he was Alessandro Di Sione. He did not pursue women into empty corridors. But then, he also didn't go around hunting for old paintings, either. It was a week of strange happenings. It was entirely possible he should just embrace it.

He saw her head out one of the glass double doors and into the garden, and he followed suit. He said nothing as he walked along behind her in the darkness, heading down a gravel path through the garden. He wondered if she had any idea where she was going or if she was just following some sort of impetuous instinct.

She was a study in contradictions.

Quiet, and yet also very loud. She swore that she was practical, and yet he could sense that she was so much more than that. She was sensual. She enjoyed tactile pleasures. Visual pleasures.

He thought back to the way she had eaten dinner last night. How she had lingered over her wine. The way she had nibbled slowly at the fresh bread on her plate, and the appreciative sound she had made when she'd bit into the dessert she had ordered without hesitation.

There was no doubt about it; she was not an entirely practical person.

Damn her for being so fascinating.

The path curved, feeding into a clearing surrounded by hedges. At the center was a stone bench and he imagined that there were a great many flowers planted at various levels throughout. It was dark, so he could see nothing.

Nothing but great inky splotches, breaking up the pale gravel.

Gabriella took a seat on the stone bench, planting her hands on either side of her.

"I do hope you have room on your bench for two," he said, moving closer to her.

She gasped and turned toward him, her wide eyes just barely visible in the dim light. "What are you doing out here?"

"Stopping to smell the roses?"

"You were deeply involved in a conversation when I left," she said.

"Oh, yes. That. Remember our discussion about boring women?"

"Yes."

"She was one."

Gabriella laughed softly; the sound lifted high on fragrant air, mixing with the scent of flowers and winding itself around him, through him.

"How terribly tragic for her. At least she is beautiful."

"I suppose," he said. "Though I don't think she knows she's boring."

"I guess that's a compensation for the dull."

"Such a comforting sameness."

She scuffed her toe through the gravel. "It wouldn't be so bad."

"I don't know about that. I think you would find it excruciating."

She shifted, and he couldn't make out her face in the darkness. "Do you think so?"

"Yes. I am completely certain that Samantha does not do genealogy in her spare time."

"A loss for Samantha, then. But points to you for remembering her name."

"I was only just speaking to her five minutes ago.

I might be shameless, but my shamelessness has its limits."

"Does it? You were talking to her like you were interested. But you looked...very bored."

"Did I? Perhaps I was simply looking down Samantha's dress and that's what my expression looks like in such situations."

"Unless you find breasts boring I don't think that's the case."

He laughed. He couldn't help it. He was shocked by the forthright statement. He felt he should know better than to be shocked by her small moments of honesty at this point. It was another of her contradictions.

She should be mousey. She should be timid. She should be utterly out of her depth with a man such as himself. And yet she handled everything he threw at her with aplomb, and never passed up an opportunity to shock him, which he would have said under any other circumstance was impossible.

"People are the same. Everywhere you go," he found himself saying as he walked over to the bench where she sat. "May I?"

She nodded slowly. "Sure."

He took a seat beside her, an expanse of empty stone between them. "These parties are the same."

"No, they aren't," she said. "How can they be? I once went to a gala at the most incredible castle. It was medieval and all the stonework was original. There was a chapel and I left the party to go explore—it was incredible. This place...it's full of my family history. I've studied it in books. But...being here is different. Books can't prepare you for the reality of something. It can only hint."

"I suppose to get all that out of a party you have to appreciate art, architecture and history."

"And you don't."

"I was mainly speaking of the people."

Of women who were looking to attach themselves to a man of wealth and status for short amounts of time. Of men who stood around touting their successes as they grew increasingly red-faced from alcohol and a lack of taking a breath during their listing of accomplishments.

"Yes, well. Places might have to be experienced in person to be fully understood. But books are better than people. In a great many ways."

"Is that so?"

"Yes. It's all written out in front of you, and even if you don't know what's going to happen…at least it's all there. Very certain. People aren't certain."

"I disagree. People are predictable. They want pleasure. They want to be important, to feel good. They want money, power. There are a limited number of ways they can go about obtaining those things. I find people extremely bland."

"I guess I just don't possess the insight you do," she said, sounding frustrated. "They don't make much sense to me at all. Those things they call pleasure…the things my parents do…they don't make them happy, do they?"

"And now our conversation circles back around," he said, pressing his palm flat on the bench, the stone cool beneath his touch. "So you live through books?"

"To an extent."

"Adventure stories?"

"Yes."

"Romance novels?" He was leading her now. Because he couldn't guess at her response. She was the one person who surprised him, and he found he wanted to keep being surprised.

She cleared her throat. "Uh. Not so much. The, uh, masculinity is all a bit…*rampant* in those."

"As one in possession of masculinity that might be considered rampant, I'm not sure what the issue is."

She sputtered, followed by a strange coughing sound. "I don't even know what that means," she said.

"You were the one who coined the phrase, not me. I think it's fairly self-descriptive. And I find well suited to me. A kind of masculinity that can't be contained."

"I think it makes it sound like a weed."

"A virulent one."

"I just…I don't find any of that relatable."

"Of course not. You don't possess rampant masculinity."

"I meant *romances*."

"I see," he said, something goading him to continue pushing her. To see where this conversation would go. He couldn't guess at her game. Couldn't read any calculation on her face, and not simply because of the darkness that shrouded them. "What exactly is it you find unrelatable?"

She paused for a moment, and when she spoke again, her voice was muted. "Well, he always finds the wallflower interesting, doesn't he?"

"Who?"

"The hero. He finds the strange girl fascinating. Wants to know more about her. Men don't. For the record, they *never* do. As you said, they like women boring. *You* like them boring. Or at the very least, they don't like them weird. Plus, there's all that racing heart, sweating palms business. Aching body parts."

"Your body parts don't…ache?"

She growled, a small feral sound. "That's horribly embarrassing."

"You're the one who brought us here," he said, lying. He had led the entire thing for just such a moment. "You can't get mad at me for building off it."

"I can get mad at you for whatever I like," she said, sounding completely regal again.

Silence settled between them. Finally, he spoke again. "We are, by the way."

"You are what?"

"We are fascinated by the wallflower. At least, I was tonight."

"You were not. You were bored."

"I was bored by the businessman who couldn't stop telling me about his portfolio. I was bored with Samantha. And I did not look down her dress. But you... You're the one person in that room that I couldn't predict. That I couldn't figure out. I had to follow you when you left the room because I had no idea where you were going, or what you intended to do. Very few people surprise me, Gabriella, but you do."

"I'm not sure how I feel about that. I'm not here to surprise you. I'm not really here to do anything to you. I'm just supposed to find that painting, which of course we haven't done yet. And I...I'm playing secretary to you and having to face the kinds of social situations I would rather eat a handful of bees than contend with."

"Well, don't eat a handful of bees. It sounds incredibly unpleasant."

"These kinds of things are unpleasant. Even more so when I look like this. At least when I have my team of people making me look...polished... At least then people are fooled for a few moments. Right now, my outside kind of matches my inside."

"Why is that a problem?"

"I just told you."

"I don't think that's all of it."

She shifted next to him. "I don't know. When I'm in costume—so to speak—at least when people reject me they're rejecting this strange version of me that isn't who I see in the mirror every day. Princess Gabriella is something I put on when I go out. But otherwise, I'm just me. And right now, it feels very much like all of those people out there ignoring me are rejecting real pieces of me."

"No one is rejecting you. It's my fault for having you come here as an employee. You are definitely being treated as such." He found that he felt a little bit contrite about the situation. And he was never contrite.

"That's my own set of issues, I suppose. I don't make very much sense, Alex. That's the real problem. I want to be left alone. I want to be anonymous. But... Not always. Not every time. Just once it would be nice to have a handsome man look at me and cross the room to be by my side."

"I'm not entirely certain whether or not I'm handsome, at least not by your standards, but—" he paused "—you're the one *I* crossed the room for tonight, Gabriella. Take that as you will."

Silence fell between them and she placed her hand flat on the bench, a few inches separating their fingertips.

"I suppose you did," she said, her voice unsteady.

"I could have had her," he said, speaking of Samantha. "But this was where I wanted to be."

"You're quite confident in yourself," she said, her voice trembling.

"Brought about by predictable patterns. I told you, people don't surprise me."

"I wish I had that confidence. I wish I wasn't so afraid."

She had no reason to be afraid. And in that moment he hated a world that bestowed so much confidence on the terrible and unworthy—on her parents and his. And robbed it from the truly unique.

He lifted his hand, placing it over hers, and feeling

every inch a bastard for doing it. She was vulnerable, and by touching her at the moment he was taking advantage of her.

He wasn't sure whether he cared or not. He was accustomed to dealing with people who moved in common circles to himself. People who saw the world much as he did.

Gabriella was an entity unto herself. She was not an experienced woman. She didn't know this game.

Why are you even bothering to play the game with a woman you thought plain only forty-eight hours ago?

He didn't have the slightest idea.

He was equally confused by the idea that he had ever found her plain. She clearly wasn't. Not in the least.

"I find you impossible to predict," he said again.

"Is that… Is that a compliment?"

He was trying to process her words, but most of his brainpower was taken up with relishing the velvet softness of her hand beneath his. She was so warm to touch after the cold stone of the bench. So very much alive.

How long had it been since he'd had a woman? He couldn't remember. Because it was irrelevant. Whoever the woman was, whenever she was, she hadn't been Gabriella.

Gabriella, who seemed to be her own creature.

"Why are you touching my hand?" she asked.

"Because I want to. I have never seen much use in denying myself the things that I want."

"There are a host of reasons for self-denial," she said. "We both know that."

"Oh, I am better trained than my parents ever were. My desires don't come from errant passions. I'm a logical man."

"There is nothing logical about you touching my hand."

He moved his thumb slowly over her knuckles, stroking

her. "No, I suppose there isn't. I suppose there is nothing logical at all in this."

There wasn't. He was touching her now, but it could never be more than that. Alex had few scruples, it was true. But he had some. He had limitations on his behavior, if only because he had seen what it was like when people didn't. His parents had cared for nothing.

He preferred life to be a series of business transactions. He only entered into transactions with people who had a similar amount of resources. He wasn't the kind of man who swooped in and killed off dying companies. Wasn't the type to offer seed money to a start-up. It just wasn't his way. He preferred everything equal. In terms both parties understood.

It was the same with his sexual liaisons. He had no interest in despoiling innocents. No interest in corrupting a girl who barely understood what desire was.

His stomach tightened, his body hardening at the thought. Calling him a liar.

Well, perhaps his body *was* interested, but that didn't mean he would act on it.

He had spent all of his life endeavoring to become a better person than his mother and father. To learn from the mistakes of that fateful night.

A little bit of errant arousal was hardly going to change that.

But still, he didn't move his hand.

"I think you're like me," she said, her words small, soft. "You say that you're logical. That you like business transactions. You play with people. You toy with them. You were doing it to Samantha back in the drawing room. You had no intention of ever taking her up on her offer, did you?"

"No. I didn't."

She shifted slightly beneath his touch and a surge of warmth shot from their point of contact straight down to his gut.

"But you let her think you might," Gabriella continued, her voice soft. "Right now, you're touching me and we both know that you'll never—"

She didn't get the chance to finish the sentence. Whether it was the challenge in her voice, the bold statement that he would *never*, or the softness of her hand beneath his, he didn't know.

Whatever the reason, he halted her words with his mouth against hers, kissing her hard, hard enough that he hoped it would make the wallflower bloom. That it would show she wasn't that wrong.

It was everything else.

But she was so warm, so soft, he forgot his goal almost immediately as it entered his mind.

She froze beneath his lips, her body stiff, rigid. She didn't return the kiss, rather she simply sat, motionless, shocked. She was soft. Indescribably so.

He moved away from her, his heart pounding heavily, his shaft as hard as iron. How long had it been since the simple meeting of mouths had had such a strong effect on his body? Since he was fifteen, sixteen? Perhaps never.

She hadn't even parted her lips for him. Hadn't softened beneath him. Hadn't succumbed in any way, and yet he felt as though he had just conquered the world.

"I should have taken her up on her offer," he said, his voice rough, gasping. "I should have wanted her. I should be upstairs in my room, or in her room, having sex with her now. But I'm not. I didn't want her. I wasn't even tempted. No matter how much we might like it to be, desire isn't logical. Which means, at the moment, neither am I."

He stood up from the bench, needing to put as much

distance between them as possible. He turned away from her, and even knowing he shouldn't, he spoke again. "All I know is that tonight I just wanted to cross the room to be with the wallflower."

CHAPTER NINE

HE'D KISSED HER. It was all she'd been able to think about last night, lying in bed with her lips—her *body*—burning.

It was all she could think about the next day, too. Which was ridiculous because they were on a tour of the stables. Which were fascinating from a great many angles—historical and equine.

But she was prickly and distracted. From exhaustion. From the heat of Alex's body next to her, from the night spent not sleeping.

Her jacket was itchy, too. Which didn't help. It was a pleasant day, warm and dry, the air blowing in off the sea. And she was wearing a jacket because Alex had said it was secretarial and that it was important she appear so because of reasons she had now forgotten since she had a bead of sweat running down the center of her shoulder blades.

Also she was still thinking about the kiss.

Ahead of them, one of the prime minister's employees was extolling the virtues of the groundskeepers, and the brave servants who had saved the facilities and all the horses during a fire that happened a hundred years ago.

"This is boring," Alex said, his lips brushing her ear as he leaned in to whisper to her. It sent a shiver down her neck, down her arm, caused heat to pool in her stomach.

She took a breath, realizing when she inhaled a healthy

dose of his masculine scent that it had been a mistake. "Excellent," she said, taking great pains to keep her voice crisp. "A chance to see The Alessandro in his natural habitat."

"Are you observing me for a nature guide you are working on?"

"Rampantis masculinitis," she said, smiling slightly.

"Characterized by?" he asked.

She looked up at him, at the wicked glint in his eye, and she quickly looked away again.

The tour group had gone on ahead of them, and she had only just noticed that their pace has slowed dramatically. He'd acted like this was done with last night. Like he'd realized what a bad idea it was to encourage all of this…this stuff between them. But he was back in fighting form this morning.

He was deliberately keeping her back from the group. Keeping them both separate.

This really was like watching a nature show. The predator had separated the weaker gazelle from the herd. And after last night, she knew beyond a shadow of a doubt that she was the weaker gazelle.

"What are we doing?"

"I told you," he said, his smile turning wicked. "I'm bored. Anyway, it wouldn't do to have you acting skittish around me, or to have me avoid you. You are my assistant, Gabby, not a bookish princess who all but forced herself into a treasure hunt with a stranger."

She looked ahead of the group, then looked up at him, at his dark, glittering eyes. There was an air of good humor about him, but there was something else, too. A base note that ran beneath it that spoke of danger, excitement.

She should turn away from it. She should have learned from last night. From letting him get too close.

She didn't. She hadn't.

"The painting," she said, her voice hoarse.

"Is not out here in the stables," he said. "I had hoped that we would tour the house today so we might get an idea of its location."

"Well, we can do a little bit of exploring on our own."

"I would like to do it during the day. I'm not sure where our host gets to during the daylight hours. He certainly isn't parading us about. But once the sun goes down, and the brandy comes out, he does seem to reappear."

"So, you think we should look for it at night?"

He lifted his shoulder. "It lowers the risk of running into him in the halls if we know he's socializing. It's either that or we tell him what we're after. But I have a feeling the cloak and dagger might be necessary. I told you, I'm willing to pay for the painting, but my fear is that he won't want to part with it when he understands what it is. That isn't an option. Money might be no object, but failure is unacceptable."

She nodded slowly. "Why do you want the painting so badly?"

"Because my grandfather wishes to have it. And I owe him a debt, I told you that already. He wants it—I will see he gets it."

She studied his expression. She could see that he had no attachment to the painting. He must love his grandfather. That she was certain of. Because Alex was not the kind of man who did anything that he didn't want to do. Only a few days in his presence and she was certain of that.

"What does it mean to him?" she asked.

"I'm not entirely sure. But there is a story…" He looked away from her, stared off toward the horizon line. "He has always told us this story, from the time we were children. About coming to America with nothing. He had eight objects that were dear to his heart. Objects that he had to sell slowly over the years to save himself from ruin. They were…they were very special to him. He often referred to them as his mistresses. Items that held sway over his heart. I don't know why. I don't know if it was because of their value, because of their beauty or because of their connection to another person. Regardless, these eight objects were the most important thing that Giovanni Di Sione possessed."

"The painting is one of them," she said.

"Yes. I was the last grandchild he asked. The rest have either been found or are being found by my siblings."

"But I don't understand how your grandfather could have come into possession of the painting."

"There are a great many possibilities. He could have bought it at an art auction of some kind, could have bought it off a merchant. And of course, your family could have bought it back and brought it to this house for safekeeping after the fact. I doubt there's any kind of serious connection."

She suspected that he didn't doubt it at all. She was beginning to suspect that there was some sort of connection between his grandfather and her family. And seeing as Alex wasn't stupid, she imagined he saw it, too.

"Or," she said, "he knew my grandmother."

"I'm certain your grandmother would have said something when she heard my name. At the very least, she might have thrown me out."

"What would throwing you out accomplish? As you pointed out, you didn't need either of us to retrieve the painting, not really. You're right, you could have flashed a little gold at my mother and you would have had all the information you needed."

"True. But still, I don't think there is much point in spinning a fantasy out of any of it. I know my grandfather. He is a good man. He raised us after our parents died. And before they died, he was our most stable influence.

I've always cherished my time with him. He treasures his grandchildren. In a way that our parents never did. We were very lucky to have him. We are lucky to have him still. But I know we won't have him much longer. And that's why..."

"You need the painting." She looked up at the clear blue sky, blinking against the sun as the cool sea breeze ruffled her hair. "You love him very much."

He paused. "He's family. Of course I feel a great deal for him."

She smiled slightly, trying not to laugh at him, since she knew he wouldn't appreciate it. "Alessandro, I think you might have a heart."

He arched a brow and looked toward her. "Don't say that too loudly. We can't have any rumors about that getting around."

"Why? Would it destroy your reputation for being a monster? I have ample evidence that you aren't bad."

"Oh, really? Give me a few examples."

She sighed, letting out a breath and starting down a path that led back toward the estate, winding through a row of hedges that had bright pink flowers on them, little explosions of color against the dark green. She kept her eyes on those blossoms. A welcome distraction from Alex and his persistent presence.

"Well, you haven't breathed fire once since I met you."

"I've been taking antacids. It helps with that."

She laughed, the sound pulled reluctantly from her. "Okay, I haven't seen you gnawing on the bones of any villagers, either. In fact, I don't think any villagers have gone missing since we've arrived on the island."

"That's because I only eat royalty," he said, giving her a rather meaningful look.

She directed her gaze back to the flowers. "Also, you don't sleep in a coffin."

He reached out, grabbing hold of her arm and stopping her in her tracks. "How is it you know where I sleep? Have you been watching me?"

A rush of heat traveled up her arm from the point of contact with his hand and she blushed furiously. "Of course not. Even if I had looked into your room, you would have been shrouded behind the velvet curtains."

"Maybe I have a coffin behind them."

"I doubt it."

"All right, so maybe you have caught on to my secret. I'm simply a man."

"One who is going out of his way to help his grandfather. I think you might have a heart *and* a soul."

"My heart is hard as a rock and my soul is ever so slightly charred from walking through life's fires, but I suppose they're still there."

"You also didn't..." She looked away from him, regretting the words even as she began to speak them, but finding she was unable to stop them. "You didn't take advantage of me last night. You could have. Had you wanted to."

"I have no interest in taking advantage of maidens," he said, his voice hard.

Oh...oh, of course he didn't.

It dawned on her. Suddenly. Horrifically.

Of course he didn't have an interest in maidens. In her. Whatever madness had possessed him last night when he'd kissed her, it hadn't been attraction. Men like him simply weren't attracted to women like her.

To him, she was barely a woman. She was little more than a girl, and he made that very clear. Of course, she had made a similar number of comments about his age, and she didn't truly think he was old.

"I don't think you're old," she said, feeling the need to clarify it suddenly.

"Oh, that's excellent. I guess I won't dip into my retirement account just yet then."

"You're thirty-six?"

"Yes."

"See? Not even middle-aged."

He laughed. "Not even... You're a minx. Do you know that?"

She blinked, her heart suddenly beating faster. Stupid heart. He didn't want her. He didn't even like her. "I'm not trying to be."

"I'm sure that's true."

"You can let go of my arm now," she said, looking down at where he was still hanging on to her.

"What if I told you I didn't want to?"

"I would ask you why. And then I would ask you what good could possibly come of it."

Her heart was pounding so hard now she could barely hear herself speak. If he couldn't hear her heartbeat she would be surprised.

"You're right. There is no point. As I already told you, I'm not interested in defiling any maidens this week."

She pulled herself out of his grasp and continued on down the path. "Who said I was a maiden?" She closed her eyes for a second, allowing the sun to wash over her face, the corners of her lips curving up slightly into a smile.

"You didn't have to say it," he said. "I could feel it in your kiss."

Her stomach sank down to her toes and she opened her eyes again, the corners of her lips falling. "Was it so terrible?"

Of course it had been.

"Not terrible. Inexperienced. I could taste it on your skin."

"That's ridiculous. Inexperience doesn't have a flavor."

He grabbed hold of her arm again, turned her to face

him, drawing her closely toward him. Rather than speeding up, this time her heart stopped beating altogether. He lowered his head slightly, then reached up, sliding his thumb along the edge of her lip. "Yes, Gabriella, inexperience absolutely has a flavor. And on your lips, there was also innocence and wildflowers. I did not mistake the taste of any of that."

He released his hold on her, put distance between them, and she still couldn't breathe any easier.

"You didn't taste like anything," she said.

"That's because you didn't taste me."

Prickles crawled up her back like an army of ants and she hunched her shoulders up around her ears, lowering her head and continuing on toward the estate.

"Suddenly, you don't seem to like honesty very much," he said.

"Suddenly, you're a bit too honest. You said—"

"I am bad at behaving, and I am terrible at restraint. Tell me you didn't like kissing me, and I won't bring it up again."

It would be easy to lie. All she had to do was open her mouth and tell him that she didn't like kissing him. That should be an easy thing to do. It should be a simple thing to make her lips form those words. But right now everything felt stuck. The words lodged in the center of her throat, curled up into a little ball, refusing to budge.

She said nothing; she just kept walking on ahead.

If he was triumphant over her silence, he didn't let on.

He was the one who broke the silence and it felt like a definite checkmark in the loss column for her.

"The party tonight is formal," he said, "everyone is going to be in their finest."

She let out a heavy sigh. "Except for me. In fact, I may skip this one and just sit in my little servant's quarters with a crust of bread and some cheese."

"That's quite dramatic. I think we could at least get you some fresh bread."

"There isn't any reason for me to go. Actually, I might be able to roam the halls a little bit if I stay behind."

"Hospitality has been extended to both of us. And I'm concerned about angering the host."

"Is that because of the painting or because you want to do business with him?"

"Everything is about business. I have an opportunity to increase my success while I'm here and I'm definitely going to take it. I don't want to do anything to compromise that. I certainly won't allow *you* to compromise it."

"Well, I don't want to be embarrassed."

"You didn't let me finish. The party tonight is a masked ball. That means everyone will be wearing masks."

"Thank you," she said, her tone flat. "I actually got that from the title *masked ball*."

"Just making sure."

"Well, there is still a problem with that."

"What's that?"

"I left my ball gown and my elegant face mask in my other luggage."

"I might not be royalty, *cara mia*, but I am a billionaire. I could acquire white tigers in the space of a couple hours if I wanted to. A gown and a mask will be no trouble at all."

"What if I would rather have the white tigers?"

"Your room is too small."

"They can sleep in my bed."

"I'm not getting you white tigers. It would only spoil you. Plus, then everyone would want one."

She couldn't stop the laugh that escaped her lips. She had no idea how he managed all of this. How he managed to make her feel hot, frustrated and amused in the space of only a few seconds. It was some kind of strange witch-craft she had never encountered before.

"Fine."

"*Fine* to the gown and the mask?"

She let out an exasperated sigh. "Would it matter if I said no, Alex?"

Suddenly, his voice seemed to be coming from closer behind her, his low, sensual tones skimming along her skin. "Not especially. If I had to I would go into your room myself and act the part of your valet."

"You aren't suggesting you would dress me?"

"I confess I have much more experience undressing women than I have dressing them. But I might be willing to make an exception."

It was official. She was going to burst into flame.

She had lied when she'd told him she didn't read romance novels. She did. Secretly. And while she pretended to snicker at them from behind her hand, the truth was she was fascinated. She had always been curious to know if attraction like that existed. If it was possible to look at some-one and feel like they were touching you. Like it would be too much if they did. Like you would die if they didn't.

She knew it did now. And she knew it was the kind of intensity that fiction simply couldn't prepare you for.

His lips had barely skimmed hers last night and she had felt like the moon and stars had fallen from the sky and scattered around her in the garden, leaving the world upside down, glittering all around her, rather than in the distance.

But it didn't matter. She wasn't going to lose her head over him. That was the last thing she had told her grand-mother. That she would not allow him to seduce her.

Her grandmother had warned her away from this kind of thing in vague terms, and when the subject of the paint-ing had come up, just before they'd come to retrieve it, it had become clear to Gabriella why. Her grandmother had been wounded by a man such as this. One who was powerful, handsome.

One she was not meant to be with.

Quite apart from the fact that Gabriella couldn't imagine a future with a man like this, one who didn't believe in love, or commitment, she was a princess. And even if she didn't have a throne she would be required to make a certain kind of marriage.

It would not be to an Italian American businessman who had no pedigree. That just wouldn't do.

She blinked, trying to get a hold on her thoughts. The last thing he needed to know was that she was thinking about sex or marriage in connection with him.

"Well, there's no need for you to dress me. I will dress myself. But tonight we need to try and look for that room my grandmother spoke of. We need to try and find the painting."

"I agree with you. I think tonight might be the time we change the nature of this farce, don't you?"

"What do you mean?"

"I mean, we have established that you are nothing more than my assistant. No one suspects that you are Princess Gabriella D'Oro, and no one has any reason to. Tonight you will be wearing a beautiful dress, and your face will be covered by a mask keeping you from being recognized… When we slip away together a little bit early, it will hardly be suspicious. At least not if I have been holding you in my arms a little bit more closely than I have for the previous nights."

"What are you suggesting?"

"Tonight, you will play the part of my lover, Gabriella. There will be no scandal, and it will be the perfect excuse for us to slip away."

Her throat was dry, her heart pounding so hard she

was afraid it might gain enough momentum to tumble up her throat and come spilling out of her mouth. "But I…"

"You don't know how? You don't know how to play the part of doting lover?"

Her cheeks flamed. "I have no worries about that. I can more than handle you, Alessandro."

"You see, when you say my full name like that, I become convinced that you are a bit more nervous than you let on."

"And when you take on that dry tone, I begin to suspect that you are a little bit more off-kilter than you like to let on. Perhaps it is *you* having a difficult time figuring out how you will play the part of my lover. But don't worry, I will be wearing a mask. So my looks shouldn't put you off."

"Did my kiss last night not prove to you that I don't find you unattractive?"

"The only thing your kiss last night proved is that you very much like playing games. But I don't like being the subject of them."

A man like Alessandro would never want a woman like her. With her large glasses and ill-fitting clothing— the only thing she had ever worn in front of him—her face devoid of makeup, he would never look twice at her.

Likely, he had seen her as a challenge, and he had set out to conquer her. Because that's who he was.

Well, she refused to be conquered.

"I have no problem playing the part of your lover tonight, Alex," she said, keeping her tone frosty. "But do not get any ideas about making it real. I understand what manner of man you are. I understand what motivates you. I am a source of amusement to you, as you have made very plain. I will not allow you to amuse yourself with my body."

Filled with a new sense of dignified rage, she stormed

toward the estate. She had no idea why she was reacting this way. Had no idea why she hadn't seen all of this before. Had she truly imagined that he had been attracted to her? That the kiss had been genuine? That the rake had gone after the wallflower?

She was as much a fool for a beautiful face as her grandmother had feared.

As much a fool as anyone in her family was. Perhaps that was the curse. Her grandmother had fallen prey to a man. And had her heart broken by him. Her mother threw herself in front of men as though she were a willing victim and they were an oncoming train. Only to find herself tangled, destroyed, after each affair. Chipping away pieces of her marriage, pieces of herself.

Perhaps, in spite of all her attention to avoid such emotions, Gabriella should have truly known better.

She rushed through the estate, heading toward her room. Once safely inside, she closed the door and locked the connecting one between her room and Alex's. She would have to face him tonight. Tonight, she would have to pretend that she was his lover. She would need to fortify herself to cope with that.

She sat on her bed, breathing hard, anger, *hurt*, rising up inside of her.

But with a few breaths came clarity.

The only solution here would be to take control of the situation. Alex saw himself as above temptation, she knew that. He only gave in when he chose to. And of course, he didn't want her.

But tonight, she would *make* him want her. She would. She would turn the tables.

He would be the one left unsatisfied. He would be the one who didn't sleep because he was burning. But she would never give in to him. She would make him want her, and then, she would turn away.

She flopped backward onto the bed, a smile crossing her lips. She was incredibly satisfied with this new plan. With this vision for the future that put her much more in charge of things than she'd been previously. Yes, last night she had momentarily lost her head over Alex. And there were a few moments today when she had done so, as well.

But it would not happen again. If anyone was going to lose their head tonight, it was going to be him.

CHAPTER TEN

ALEX HAD BEEN dimly aware of the fact that Gabriella was a princess. He had originally fooled himself that she was not attractive, but now was exceedingly aware of the fact that she was beautiful. But what he had not realized was that, even behind the little gold mask that covered her eyes and part of her nose, her regal bearing would shine through.

What he had not realized was that, even with most of her face covered, her beauty would be undeniable. What he had not realized was that, in a designer gown that clung to her generous curves, she would be a temptation he was not sure he had the strength to resist.

He hadn't realized that manner of temptation still existed for him.

Her dark hair was left loose, styled in dark curls, full lips painted red, the only part of her face that was visible. Her dress was a bright blue, the neckline high, covering more of her golden skin than he would like. But it hinted at a figure more spectacular than he had thought it could be. It clung to her hips and thighs before flaring out at the knee and billowing about her feet.

She was, in truth, a much more elegant creature than he had ever imagined. It was like looking at a stranger, and yet someone familiar at the same time.

Then she took a step forward, turning her foot sideways, and tripping slightly on her heel. "Drat!" she said, straightening and fussing with the bottom of her dress.

He smiled, because there was the Gabriella he had grown to know over the past few days.

"You look beautiful," he said, the compliment rolling effortlessly off his tongue. She did look beautiful. She was *more* than beautiful.

"You don't have to say things like that," she said.

His chest tightened. He had wounded her earlier, and he bitterly regretted that. Still, he wasn't entirely certain it was bad if she didn't truly believe him attracted to her. He would never be like his father. He would never be the sort of man who simply took what he wanted without considering the feelings of others.

As a young man he had fixated on that little boy standing outside of the manor that night, the bastard child of his father who'd caused the car accident that killed his parents.

He had spent a great many years blaming that little boy. Hiding that little boy's existence. Something he bitterly regretted later on in his life. Something he had done his very best to make right. But it had been too late. Nate's life had been broken beyond recognition. Rejected by the only family he might have had, because of his birth.

Alex had brought Nate back into the family's life when his grandfather had needed a bone marrow transplant and no one else had been a match. He hadn't regretted it, but he and his half brother had never made much of a relationship with each other.

As an adult his memory of the events of that night had expanded. Not just to his mother, and her distress. Not just to the boy. But to the other woman, who was equally broken. Who had been brought into his father's web somehow, who had born his child and received no support. Yes, more and more he thought about her. He thought about every single person who had been damaged by his father's selfishness. By his unchecked lust.

The more the years passed, the more he realized his father was the villain.

Alex was a great many things, but he refused to become that manner of monster.

And that meant he would never touch Gabriella. She was so very different than anyone he'd ever known. So untouched by the ugly things in the world. She had seen the way her parents had behaved, and she had managed to retain a kind of simple, open view of the world he could never remember possessing. She had retained her hope. He would be damned if he were the one to take that from her.

One thing was certain, while he might be able to give her physical pleasure, he would never be able to offer anything beyond that. Nothing more than pain.

His family was stuck with him. The damage to Nate was done.

He would extend that damage no further.

"Shall we go to the ball, Cinderella?"

He extended his hand and she looked at it as though it might bite her. "If I'm Cinderella," she said, keeping her hands fixed firmly to her sides, "does that make you my fairy godmother?"

"Never. Fairy godmothers are endlessly giving. They live to bestow gifts with no hope of receiving anything in return." He smiled. "I'm not so selfless."

"And what exactly do you hope to get in return for your gifts?"

"I'm getting it. Right now. As I told you, you look beautiful."

He could see pink color bleeding beneath her skin, spreading outside the edges of the mask, revealing her blush to him. Reviewing the pleasure she took in his compliment. "And you... You look like the Phantom of the Opera."

He touched the white mask on his face. "That's kind of the point."

"Except you aren't hideously scarred."

"My scars are metaphorical in nature."

"The same can be said for most of us, I suppose. Though scarring is kept to a minimum when you spend most of your time in the library."

"I knew my lack of a library would become problematic one day."

"Right now, the only problem we have is a lack of a painting," she said, gently steering the conversation back to the reason for all of this.

She was good at that. He was losing the plot. Completely. For a moment he had forgotten that he had a goal that extended beyond dancing with her tonight. A goal that went past seeing her in this gown and that mask.

Time moved a strange pace here. It was slower. Being away from his phone, his desk, being outside of his world, was doing strange things to him. He wasn't entirely certain he disliked it.

"Then I suggest we get a move on. The painting will wait for no man. Except it has done exactly that for the past fifty-plus years."

This time, she did take his hand. And he was the one tempted to pull away. From the heat. From the silken quality of her touch. He didn't. He was the experienced party. The touch of a woman's hand against his should not be cause for any reaction whatsoever.

He knew that. Repeated it over and over as he led her from their quarters down the long hall and toward the ballroom.

No matter how committed he was to understanding it

on an intellectual level, he could not convince his body to agree.

So he did his best to concentrate on the feeling of his feet making contact with the marble floor. One step, then another. When he focused on that, the burn, where her skin made contact with his, lessened.

A bit.

They approached the doors to the ballroom and two elegantly appointed staff, not wearing masks, opened the double doors for both of them. "I feel like I should bow," he said, leaning in to whisper the words in her ear. "But at my age it might be bad for my back."

She looked up at him, dark eyes glinting from behind the mask. "Stop that."

"But it's so much fun."

She rolled her eyes and he led her into the ballroom where couples were already dancing. "This room... It's amazing," she said, looking about them at the high, painted ceiling before her eyes fell to the pale walls, made ornate by sconces and crisp white molding.

Nothing about the designer dresses the other women were wearing. Of course not. Gabriella preferred art and architecture. Always.

"Gabby," he said, drawing her attention back to him. She didn't look nearly as annoyed as she typically did when he used the nickname. She looked... There was something strange in her expression. Something he feared he understood. Something he wished he hadn't seen. "If you keep staring at the walls with more admiration than you afford me no one will believe it when we slip away."

He led her deeper into the ballroom, toward the dance floor, and her attention drifted from him as she continued to stare at the walls, at the art, probably at particularly historically significant dust motes, knowing her.

"That could be a problem," she said, distracted.

"Yes. One I will correct."

He chose that moment to pull her into his arms, into a closed hold. Her attention snapped back to him. "What are we doing?"

"Dancing," he said as he led her into the first step.

"So we are," she said, one hand caught up in his, the other resting on his shoulder.

She curled her fingers in a fist, as though she were afraid to touch him too much so she needed to minimize the amount of skin making contact with his jacket.

"I feel tonight we might be very rude."

"Will we?"

"Yes. We should socialize with everyone. You should approach the women and ask them who they are wearing and I should try and forge as many business connections as I possibly can with everyone in attendance. But I'm not going to. And neither are you. Because tonight we are only going to look at each other. We are only going to stay for the minimum amount of time and we're going to make the world believe that I could not wait one more moment to have you in my arms."

He could feel the breath leave her entire body, could feel her limbs go stiff. "I'm in your arms right now."

"No. Not like this. It would be different."

"How?" she asked, her voice a hushed whisper, her dark eyes full of fear, curiosity and excitement.

"It would be different because we would be alone. Because if there was nothing around us but all of these beautiful walls and I were to take you into my arms you would know that there were no limits to what might happen next. Everything would be different. It would be quiet, there would be no music. Only our breathing. The air around us would be different."

She swallowed visibly. "That's what…that's what everyone will think is going to happen?"

"Yes. By the end of this dance no one will be in any doubt that the moment I have you alone we will not be discussing art, let alone looking at paintings."

He drew her closer as the music changed, not releasing her between songs, but rather continuing to sway gently with her. "But we are," she said, "looking at paintings."

"Of course," he said, never taking his eyes from her. "Touch my face, Gabriella."

"Wh-what?"

"I want you to lift your hand from my shoulder, and rest your palm against my face. I want you to take your fingertips and trace my jaw, down to my chin, then bring your hand to rest on my chest."

"Why?" she asked, her expression almost frantic.

"It's for the painting." He ignored the dull beating of his heart—it was for a lot more than that. That reminded him there were other ways to do this.

She obeyed his command, even while her expression remained frightened. Soft skin made contact with his face, the light drift of her fingertips along his cheek, down his jaw and then, just as he had told her to, she brought it to rest against his chest. He was certain that she could feel his heart, beating hard beneath her palm.

He never took his eyes off hers as he slipped his arm slowly from around her waist and reached for her wrist, curling his fingers around it and drawing her hand to his lips, pressing a kiss to the center of her palm.

"That wasn't… You didn't…"

He released his hold on her, raising his hand to capture her chin between his thumb and forefinger. "I suppose I didn't. How many 'Hail Marys' do you suppose I have to say to atone for that?"

"I don't know," she said, her voice raspy, scraped raw.

"It has been longer than I care to remember since my

last confession. But for you, I would gladly get on my knees."

Gabriella straightened, as though bolts of lightning had just shot straight down her spine, as though she had been hit with a thought so real, so strong, it had manifested itself physically. "You're very good at empty flirtation, Alex." She moved her arm around his neck, placing her fingers on his skin. "I wonder what might happen if you had to make good on any of your promises."

"Why don't you try to hold me to them, Gabriella?"

"Say something real," she said, moving closer to him, slowly, as though it were taking great effort for her to move nearer to him, as though it took everything she had in her to keep herself from running away. "You've been playing a game with me from the moment we met. So now, if you want this to go on, I want you to tell me something and I want you to say it without that mocking gleam in your eye, or that wicked curve to your mouth. I want you to be real for one moment. Just one."

"And what do I get in return?"

"Whatever you want."

He could tell that the words had left her lips before she had given them her full permission. He could also tell that she wished she could call them back.

"A very dangerous gift to offer to a man like me."

"I have no doubt." But, to her credit, she didn't rescind the offer.

"A real kiss for a real confession," he said, "it's only fair."

"All right," she said, her words breathless.

"You are beautiful," he said, keeping his gaze locked with hers. He kept his grip on her chin tight, didn't allow her to look away. "Quite apart from this quest, this game, apart from…me. The fact that no one has ever told you before, or at least has never made you feel it before, is a crime unspeakable in its cruelty."

She blinked, relaxing in his hold. "I...I don't know what to say. No one has ever... No one has ever said anything like that to me."

"You were very angry yesterday. I... The way that I dealt with you was wrong. I hurt you. It was not my intent. You are sweet, Gabby. I am a man who licks the sugar off sweet things and leaves them discarded. But even if I shouldn't say this, I want you to understand that while we might be here putting on a show for others, while I may have confessed to you my boredom with life, the attraction I feel for you is separate from that."

She took a deep breath, her eyes fluttering closed, and then, her hands still curved around the back of his neck, she stood up on her toes and pressed a kiss to his mouth. It was quick, short, but he felt branded by it. Was certain that she had left a crimson stain behind from her lipstick, but something deeper than that. Something permanent.

"Now," he said, "I think it's time for us to excuse ourselves."

Gabriella had failed in her objective. And she wasn't entirely sorry about it.

She was supposed to seduce him. She was supposed to flip the tables on him. But from the moment she walked out of her room wearing that dress, she had felt like putty. Particularly when he looked at her, with all that heat and masculine energy radiating from him. He certainly looked like a man not entirely indifferent to what he saw before him.

And that, she supposed, was the variable she hadn't counted on. The fact that coming close to seducing him might seduce her right back.

Then there had been the touching. Her touching his

face, him kissing her hand. She had felt very much the frustrated mouse in the paws of a cat that wasn't really hungry, just looking for amusement.

That was when she'd remembered herself. When she'd realized she was failing at her own objective. And so she had tried a different approach.

Yet again, he had come out on top. She had turned to nothing more substantial than spun sugar when he complimented her, then she'd nearly lost her nerve when she'd kissed him. Then she nearly dissolved when his lips had touched hers.

She was not a very good seductress. That was just the truth.

But…it turned out she was eminently seducible. Beautiful words from a beautiful man that touched her down deep beneath her clothes, beneath her skin, changed everything around inside of her. Made her forget to protect herself.

The wing of the palace they were in now was completely empty of guests or staff, it seemed. Everyone was in the ballroom, or on the other side of the house wearing a path between the kitchen and the ballroom.

"Come with me," he said, wrapping his arm around her waist and moving at a brisk pace toward a set of double doors at the end of the corridor.

She did. Because this was the game. Because there was nowhere else she wanted to be. And after tonight it was over. This hunt. This flirtation. Whatever it was.

The only flirtation she'd ever had in her life.

The thought made her want to cry. Sit and weep in the middle of the corridor. But she couldn't do that because they were on a painting quest.

She hoped it took all night.

That they could spend the whole evening wandering through vacant halls on a quest, and if he never touched her it would be okay. It would be okay as long as she was walking with him.

Are you that easy? A few compliments and you're ready to melt all over him like butter.

Yes. She was.

But the strange thing was, she knew Alex now. And she knew that what he'd said in the ballroom was real. What she didn't know was what it meant for him, for them, and for the ticking clock that was winding down to midnight, when the enchantment would break and Cinderella would go back to being a bespectacled bookworm beneath his notice.

He opened one of the doors and slipped through the crack, bringing her with him, before closing it behind him.

"Do you suppose he has some kind of security camera system?"

"Not that I've noticed," Alex said. "And believe me, I've been keeping my eye out. But he has no reason to think that any of the guests are going to make off with the art. And we're not going to make off with any of the art that he knows about."

"A fabulous technicality."

"Speaking of technicalities, I want my kiss," he said, turning to her, his expression suddenly hard, like granite.

The breath rushed from her body. "I kissed you," she said. "Already, I mean."

"You kissed me in front of everyone else. You wanted real words for me, and I want a real kiss from you. That kiss always had to happen for the two of us to excuse ourselves from the ballroom. I want one that isn't inevitable."

"Is that so?"

"Though I'm beginning to wonder if a kiss between the two of us was always inevitable."

She laughed, a shaky, breathless sound. "Since when? Since you first walked into my grandmother's house when

I was barefoot and in my glasses?" She wished it were true. She wished he had.

"Yes."

"That doesn't make sense."

"It doesn't. You're right. Nothing about this makes sense." He was the one who closed the distance between them, who reached out and curled a lock of her hair around his finger before letting it fall free. "I'm not certain it matters."

"It should."

"There are a lot of *shoulds* in the world, Gabby. But they very often become *shouldn'ts*. There isn't much to be done about it. Except perhaps do the one thing that feels right."

She didn't know if this felt right. No. It didn't feel right. It felt wrong. Very, very wrong. But she still wanted it. That was the thing.

She took a sharp breath, taking a step in toward him, pressing her hand to his chest. She looked up at his eyes, hard and dark, his expression still mostly concealed behind the mask. She flexed her fingers, scrunching the stiff white material of his shirt, then smoothing it again, relishing the feeling of his heat, his hardness, beneath the fabric. He was so different than she was. She had never truly fully appreciated just how different men and women were. In a million ways, big and small.

Yes, there was the obvious, but it was more than that. And it was those differences that suddenly caused her to glory in who she was, what she was. To feel, if only for a moment, that she completely understood herself both body and soul, and that they were united in one desire.

"Kiss me, Princess," he said, his voice low, strained.

He was affected.

So she had won.

She had been the one to make him burn.

But she'd made a mistake if she'd thought this game had one winner and one loser. She was right down there with him. And she didn't care about winning anymore.

She couldn't deny him, not now. Not when he was looking at her like she was a woman and not a girl, or an owl. Not when he was looking at her like she was the sun, moon and all the stars combined. Bright, brilliant and something that held the power to hold him transfixed.

Something more than what she was. Because Gabriella D'Oro had never transfixed anyone. Not her parents. Not a man.

But he was looking at her like she mattered. She didn't feel like shrinking into a wall, or melting into the scenery. She wanted him to keep looking.

She didn't want to hide from this. She wanted all of it.

Slowly, so slowly, so that she could savor the feel of him, relish the sensations of his body beneath her touch, she slid her hand up his throat, feeling the heat of his skin, the faint scratch of whiskers.

Then she moved to cup his jaw, his cheek.

"I've never touched a man like this before," she confessed.

And she wasn't even embarrassed by the confession, because he was still looking at her like he wanted her.

He moved closer, covering her hand with his. She could feel his heart pounding heavily, could sense the tension running through his frame. "I've touched a great many women," he said, his tone grave. "But at the moment it doesn't seem to matter."

That was when she kissed him.

She closed her eyes and leaned forward, pressing her lips to his, her heart thudding against her chest so wildly she could hardly breathe. She felt dizzy. She felt restless. She felt…everything.

It was the most natural and comfortable thing in the

world to be in his arms. And also the most frightening. The most torturous.

She felt as though she'd come home, as though she'd finally found a place to rest. One that was hers and hers alone. But it wasn't enough. And it never would be. His suit and her gown put too many layers between them.

Her title and his lack of one.

His age and experience coupled with her relative youth and inexperience.

Thirteen years. Thousands of miles. Lord knew how many women.

An unbridgeable divide, but one that was reduced to nothing as she stood here, tasting him. Savoring him. Holding him.

There was no space between them now. None at all. They were both shaking, both needing, both wanting.

She curled her fingers into a fist, holding him tightly as she angled her head. Then she jolted when he parted his lips, his tongue tracing the seam of her mouth, requesting entry.

She couldn't deny him. Not now. Possibly not ever.

He wrapped his arms around her, enveloping her, holding her close. One hand pressed between her shoulder blades, the other sliding low, just low enough to tease the curve of her buttocks without actually going past the line of impropriety.

Her world was reduced to this. To his hands, his lips, his scent. His every breath. If they had come into this room for anything other than the kiss she didn't remember it.

If there was anything beyond this room, this moment, this man, she didn't remember it, either.

They parted slowly, so different from that kiss in the garden. This felt natural, even though she regretted the end. They were both breathing hard, both unsteady. She lifted her hand and touched his cheek, felt the rasp of his whiskers beneath her palms, drank in the sight of him. What she could see of him that wasn't covered by the mask, anyway.

"We should look for the painting," she said, knowing she sounded dazed.

Her lips felt hot. Swollen. She wondered if they looked different, too. She couldn't possibly have any lipstick left on them—that was certain.

"Painting?" he asked, the corners of his mouth turning up.

"Yes," she said, her tone dry. She cleared her throat and started to walk toward the back wall. "She said there was a painting in one of the rooms, and only I could open it…"

"The key," he said.

"Yes. I'm good at keeping secrets, it turns out. All those years of not having very many people to talk to, I guess."

She reached beneath the neckline of her gown and fished the necklace out, holding it up in front of her.

"The key," he said, his tone slightly different than it had been a moment earlier.

"Yes. It fits into a frame. She said it was scenery. Of a farm."

"There's a lot of that here."

"I know," she said, moving closer to the far wall and examining the different scenes in front of her. "They really do like their geese," she muttered as she moved down the row, examining the frames, looking for any evidence that one might not be a typical picture. "There are some farm scenes in here, but nothing quite like what my grandmother described. I feel like this is the wrong room. The sorts of farmhouses my grandmother described were from a slightly different era. They predate these more modern houses."

"Do they predate the geese?"

"There were always geese, Alex," she said, enjoying the way his words played off her own. A thrill the way their lips worked together, even when they weren't touching.

"Then let's keep looking," he said.

He took hold of her hand and another thrill shot through her as he led her from the room and back down the hall. He opened another door.

"What sorts of paintings are those?" he asked.

She looked in, her heart pounding hard due to the excitement. Sort of. Mostly it was the proximity of Alex.

"Cityscapes," she said, "it won't be here."

They continued through a room filled with the portraits of royals, and one with scenes of the beach. Finally, they opened up a door to a room with a wall lined with paintings of farms. Pale, rosy cheeked children with animals, thatched roof homes and, well, more geese.

"It would be here," she said, "I'm sure. So now…we just have to figure out which. Which painting looks different? Which one might be a false front?"

Alex squinted looking around the room. Then his posture went straight as though a realization had shot through him like a lightning bolt. "Here," he said.

She turned to look at him. He'd stopped in front of a painting with a farmhouse, and a young girl in front of it. His fingertip was pressed into the corner of the frame.

"What is it?" she asked.

"There's a small…a notch here in the corner. Look."

She moved over to where he was and her mouth fell open, her fingers trembling as she held the charm on the necklace out in front of her. "I think…I think this is it," she said.

He moved aside and she stepped forward, pressing the back of the necklace into the notch and pushing it in. The frame popped away from the wall about two inches and Gabriella stood back, bringing her necklace with her.

She stared at the picture for a moment, then looked over at Alex. "Well, now I'm nervous," she said. Her stomach was flipping over, her hands sweating. She was…excited. But terrified. If the painting was there…who knew what would happen. If it got out and it created more waves for her family it would be disastrous. She would never be able to salvage their reputations. Not even with a more complete and fair history compiled.

But if it wasn't there…

She had wondered about the painting for so long. If it was real. And now they knew it was real and the possibility of seeing it…

Alex swung the painting open and revealed a large rectangle behind it, set deep into the wall, covered in burlap.

"Oh," she breathed, "that could be…I mean, it probably is…"

Alex reached out and grabbed hold of the burlap, drawing it down to reveal the painting underneath.

"Well," she said, "you kind of took the drama out of it."

"You don't think this is dramatic enough?" he asked.

It was. Even without fanfare. Because lowering the burlap had revealed what could only be *The Lost Love*. It was a woman, sitting in front of a vanity, hands in her dark curls as she gazed into the mirror. She was naked, her bare back on display, the suggestion of her breasts in the reflection of the mirror. She was seated on a cushion, the curve of her bottom visible.

It was…provocative, certainly. But beautiful. And hardly the salacious, distasteful scandal the press had insinuated it might be so long ago.

"And this is why…" she breathed. "This is why we search for the truth. There's nothing… There is nothing filthy about this. Nothing wrong with it."

"I'm inclined to agree. But then, I am a fan of the female form."

She turned to look at Alex. "I only mean that the media made it sound as though revealing this photo would be detrimental to my grandmother's reputation. Certainly..." She looked back at the painting. "Certainly, it suggests that she was intimate with the painter. It is not a standard sort of portrait that one might sit for. And someone in her position was hardly ever going to pose nude. Plus... There's something... There's something more here than you see in a portrait that simply contains a model. The painter was not detached from the subject. I can feel it in every brushstroke. There's so much passion."

Her fingers reached out to the corner of the painting, where the artist's initials, *B.A.*, were faintly painted.

"Or," Alex said, stuffing his hands in his pockets, "he was a very good painter."

"It was more than that, Alex."

"It makes no difference to me. My job is simply to bring the painting to my grandfather."

Gabriella frowned. "Why does your grandfather have more of a claim to this than my grandmother? It's her in the painting."

"Yes, it is. But my grandfather owned this painting at one time. He will be willing to pay whatever price is fair. It was not your grandmother's dying request, but it is his."

"We will bring it back to Aceena. She wants to see it. At least give her that."

"I can't be away from work indefinitely, Princess," he said.

She looked at him, unable to make out the finer points of his expression behind the mask. "Please. Let's bring it back to her."

He regarded her closely for a moment. Then he nodded slowly, moving over to where the painting was, extending his hand and brushing his thumb along the edge of the canvas. "It is very beautiful. In fact," he said, looking away from the painting and back at Gabriella. "It reminds me a bit of you."

Her face heated. "I don't look anything like that."

"You certainly do. Beautiful. Lush."

"I don't."

"This painting is not the view of the subject. It's the vision of her admirer," he said, his dark eyes locked on to hers. "For that reason, I would say that I'm in a much better position to evaluate it than you."

"You're not my lover," she said, the word sweet and thick like honey on her tongue.

"No," he said, his tone taking on a wistful quality. "I'm not."

"How are we going to get this back to our room?"

"Very quickly," he said.

He took the portrait out, covered it with the burlap again and quickly closed the original painting.

She moved forward and pressed her necklace deeply into the notch again to lock it just as before.

"If he truly had no idea this painting was here, he will have no reason to believe it isn't mine," Alex said. "Of course, carrying a rather large canvas through the house may arouse suspicion. I doubt I could convince him I was simply taking the painting out for a walk."

"Then we had better hurry," Gabriella said. "Everyone else is still occupied in the ballroom."

"And thank God for Prime Minister Colletti's devotion to having a good time."

They walked to the double doors that led back to the corridor. Alex opened the first one slightly, peering out into the hall to see if anyone was there. "It looks clear," he said.

She nodded, and they both slipped through the outside, closing the gallery door tightly shut behind.

It was ridiculous. Alex was wearing a suit that was rather disheveled, they were both masked and now Alex was also carrying a piece of art.

If anyone saw them, they would likely imagine they had simply had too much to drink.

They walked down the hall quickly, then they rounded to the left and froze. Up against the wall was another couple engaged in the very thing Alex had wanted the rest of the party to believe *they* were engaged in. The man had the woman pressed tightly against the wall, her hands held over her head while he kissed her again, his other hand roaming over her curves.

A flash of heat wound itself around Gabriella, her entire body ready to go up in flames at the sight of it.

What would it be like to have Alex unleash his passion on her like that? To have him press her up against the wall. To have him touch her like that.

The scene before them highlighted just how circumspect he had been.

For some reason, she was disappointed.

"Quietly," Alex whispered as the two of them continued behind the amorous couple. The woman's eyes were closed, the man's back to them, and they were able to walk along behind them without detection. They hurried through the halls, the rest of which they found empty. Not stopping until they reached their rooms.

"Excellent," Alex said, closing the door tightly behind them. "I will pack this away, and if anyone looks through my suitcase I will say that I acquired it elsewhere during our travels. There is no reason for them to think otherwise."

Gabriella shook her head, laughing—a husky sound.

"I never imagined in my wildest dreams that I would be involved in an art heist."

"Does it not belong to your family, Gabriella?"

"I feel it does," she said.

"Then it's hardly a heist."

"Still. I've done quite a lot today that I never imagined I would."

Dancing with him. Kissing him. Being called beautiful. Now it was ending. This was the end of it all. She didn't care about stealing the painting. She cared about the mission being over.

"I have to say the same, Gabby, and I did not think that was possible."

She wasn't even irritated this time when he called her Gabby. No one else called her that. It was a name that only came from Alex. And she decided that there was something she quite liked about that. Whether it was because it kept this entire event separate from her real life, or because it made all of this feel special.

She was desperate to feel like it was special to him.

"I'm glad you found it diverting."

He laughed. "Oh, I found it more than that."

He took his mask off then, reached up and loosened his black tie. There was something about that look. That rakish, disheveled look that made her heart beat faster. That made her limbs feel weak. That made her stomach tighten.

Of course, it was the same when he was perfectly pressed, the same when he had a mask over his face. It was the same no matter what.

"We will leave tomorrow," he said.

"What reason will we give?"

"I will tell him that urgent business has come up in the States. I think I have done enough to secure a deal with the prime minister, and I managed to get what I came for. All in all, quite a successful trip."

Gabriella couldn't help but laugh. "Almost too successful. I keep expecting guards and hounds to descend upon us."

"Nothing like that, I think. I'm not sure this painting is truly valuable to anyone other than our grandparents."

Gabriella blinked, pulled up yet again by the link between Lucia and Giovanni. "Yes. It's very strange, that."

"Not especially."

"A bit."

"Only if you like romanticizing things. And I do not."

She rolled her eyes. "How very surprising."

He paused in front of her, a strange expression passing over his face. The left side of his lips curved slightly upward as he studied her. He moved forward and her breath caught in her chest.

He reached out, tracing the edge of her mask before lifting it slowly. He pulled it away, the soft brush of his skin against hers enough to make her feel like she was on fire. "So very beautiful," he said, his words hushed.

She waited for him to lean in. Waited for him to kiss her again. But he didn't. He simply stood, looking at her, not touching her, not making a move to close the distance between them.

She wished she were brave. Brave enough to touch him. To lean into him. To recapture what had happened in that empty room.

"Goodnight, Gabriella," he said finally, his words summarily dismissing her, stealing her chance at bravery.

She cleared her throat. "Goodnight, Alex."

She turned and walked into her bedroom. She felt very much like she had missed something. Like she had left a very important piece of herself behind.

She blinked hard against the stinging sensation in her eyes, did her best to breathe around the rock that had settled on her chest.

They would leave tomorrow. They had completed their objective. Tomorrow, she would be back on Aceena. Back with her grandmother. And everything would return to the way it was.

CHAPTER ELEVEN

EVERYTHING HAD GONE smoothly during their escape from Isolo D'Oro, and it continued to go smoothly upon their reentry into Aceena. Alex would have been surprised, but things tended to go smoothly for him, so he saw no reason this should be different. Except for the fact that everything about it felt different in a million small ways he could not quite quantify.

Well, there was one thing that he could name. Gabriella. He ignored that thought as they walked into the hall at the D'Oro estate.

He had the painting under his arm, the rest of their bags being handled by the staff. Gabriella was walking along beside him, wearing a pair of plain pants and a button-up blouse, her very large glasses returned to their usual position. And somehow, even with all of that, he saw her no differently than he had last night. She was fascinating, beautiful, irresistible. But here he was resisting. Overrated, in his opinion.

"We must bring this to my grandmother as quickly as possible," Gabriella was saying, the animated tone of her voice never failing to stir something inside of him.

She cared about so many things. Dusty books and history and the people around her. It made him ache. Made him wish he could still feel like that. Feel in ways he hadn't since he was eleven years old.

They were directed by the staff to the morning room, where her grandmother was taking her tea.

"Grandmother," Gabriella said, the word sounding more like a prayer than anything else. As though Lucia were Gabriella's salvation, her link back to the real world.

He still didn't feel linked to the real world. The shipping company was back in New York, along with a great many of his real-world concerns. Somehow, over the past week, his life had started to revolve around a painting, and giving compliments to the woman that stood before him.

"Is that it?" Lucia asked, gesturing to the painting that Alex held, facing away from her.

He nodded slowly.

"May I?" she asked, her voice suddenly hushed.

He handed the painting to her, careful not to reveal too much of it. He had seen it, but he felt the need to allow her to experience this at her own pace. In somewhat of a private fashion.

He watched the older woman's face, watched as she placed her fingertips over the painting, her dark eyes filling with tears. "I can see," she said, her voice trembling, "I can see how much he loved me. It is there. Still."

"Who?" Gabriella asked.

"Bartolo. His name was Bartolo. An artist. And I...I did not think there was any way I could sacrifice my position for love. But I'm old now, Gabriella. And I look at this and I see just how deep his feelings were. And then... Then we were thrown out of Isolo D'Oro, anyway. I asked myself every day what the sacrifice meant. I married a man who was suitable. I rejected the one who was not. For what? For a kingdom that crumbled. Seeing it again... Understanding... His love was more than I deserved. He did not deserve one so faithless as myself."

Gabriella's hands were folded in her lap and she was wringing them as though the queen's words were causing her great distress. "Grandmother, of course you did what you had to do. You did what you felt was right."

She sighed slowly, sadly. "It is all any of us can do, I'm afraid. But when your best isn't good enough it galls particularly with the sharp clarity of hindsight."

"I hate to cause you any further pain, Your Highness," Alex said. "But—"

"But your grandfather wants this painting returned to his possession," Lucia said, her tone grave.

"Yes. There are few things in his life that he prizes beyond money. Beyond anything. This painting is one of them. And though I can't tell you why, though it must seem strange as you are the subject of the painting, I can only tell you that it is an old man's greatest wish to have this again."

A tear rolled down her cheek, and Alex felt shamed by the emotional display for some reason. Shamed by how jaded he was, by how little credibility he gave to love and emotion when he saw such depth of it before him.

"Of course he can have it," Lucia said, her words shocking Alex down to the core.

"I will pay whatever you ask for it. He's prepared to compensate you handsomely."

She placed her hand over the painting again. "I don't want money. I *want* him to have it."

Alex met her gaze and nodded slowly. "He will."

Gabriella looked over at him, her expression filled with concern. "He isn't going to make a scandal with it?"

Alex shook his head. "No. My grandfather has no interest in scandal. He has no need for money."

Gabriella didn't ask if he was telling the truth. Something about that warmed his chest in a way that he wasn't certain he deserved.

"You must stay with us tonight, Alex," Lucia said.

His heart slammed against his breastbone. Denial was

on the tip of his tongue. He shouldn't stay. He should go. But he was in no position to deny the older woman anything. "If you wish."

"And I do have a condition on giving you the painting."

Everything inside of him stilled. "Do you?"

The older woman nodded. "Gabriella shall go with you. She will help deliver the painting. Acting as an ambassador for our family."

"If you wish," he said again.

He had been desperate to escape Gabriella. Her tempting mouth, her soft touch. Nothing good could come of the attraction between them. Ever. Acting on it—more than they already had—was simply not an option. He would leave her untouched.

But in order for him to honor such a vow, he would need to get a good deal of distance between them.

This was not conducive to that goal.

He had honorable intentions, but he was a flesh and blood man. His spirit was willing but his flesh was very, very weak where she was concerned.

Still, he could not refuse.

"Of course," he said.

"Excellent," the queen said, "I will have some of the staff show you to your room. In the meantime, I would like to spend some time with my granddaughter."

Gabriella looked at the clock. It was nearly midnight, but she was still sitting awake in the library. Her conversation with her grandmother was playing over in her mind.

Lucia had been talking of an old love, of honor and duty perhaps not being everything. Of how her heart still ached, all these years later, when she looked at the painting.

It was so very strange for Gabriella, to hear her pragmatic grandmother speaking of love. They had spoken of it before, but always Lucia had been cautionary, because she had spoken of its loss.

Now, though…she said when she looked at that painting it made her feel so full. It made her realize all the beauty she had carried with her thanks to that ill-fated affair.

Made her realize she could never truly regret loving Bartolo, though she had not spent her life with him.

In addition to that, Gabriella's nerves were slightly frazzled with the idea of going to New York. More specifically, going with Alex.

It meant an extension on their time on Isolo D'Oro. More time just to be near each other. Circling around the larger things that neither of them were prepared to embrace.

She wanted it. She wanted more time with him. But she wasn't sure they should have it.

Things were… Well, they weren't normal between them. She had been looking forward to getting away from him, and now it appeared that wouldn't be happening. Of course, as much as she had been looking forward to there being some distance between them, she had also dreaded it.

The idea of going back to life as it had been before. As though she had never met him, as though they had never spent a week on Isolo D'Oro together. As though he had never called her beautiful, as though they had never kissed… The very idea of that was painful to her. Sat in her chest heavily like a leaden weight.

Which was probably the most telling sign that she didn't need to get away from him.

She stretched out on her tuffet, raising her arms, her hands balled into fists. She looked back down at the book she'd been reading and rubbed her eyes. It was a history book that focused on the art and culture of Isolo D'Oro. She had thought to look at it with her newfound real-life take on Isolo D'Oro to see if it might enhance it. Mainly, she had just sat there staring at the pages. Imagining the countryside. Being there, standing in the sunshine with Alex. Sitting in the garden with him, basked in moonlight as he tasted her. Touched her.

The door to the library opened and she startled.

Alex was standing there looking dashing, like a hero from a historical novel come to life.

He was wearing a white shirt open at the collar, the sleeves pushed up past his forearms. His hair looked as though he'd been running his fingers through it. He looked... Well, he looked like temptation personified.

"I thought I might find you here, Gabby," he said.

Her stomach did a little flip at his use of her nickname. "Yes, I do like the library."

She took her glasses off and rubbed at the bridge of her nose before putting them back in place.

"You look tired," he said.

"I am. But I couldn't sleep. I don't see how I could with everything that's happening tomorrow. New York. I've never been."

"I feel much the same."

"Why? Are you so anxious to get back to your real life?"

"No," he said, his tone dry. "That isn't the problem. It isn't fantasies about work that have me tossing and turning."

"If it isn't fantasies of work, then—" Her eyes clashed with his, the meaning of his words suddenly sinking in. "Oh."

"It would be better if you were not coming with me, Gabriella," he said, his tone full of warning.

She nodded slowly. "I have no doubt that's true."

"Doing what's right is incredibly tiresome," he said, walking deeper into the room, moving to sit in the chair across from hers. "And yet, it is the only thing that separates us from our parents, is it not?"

She nodded mutely.

"And I have to separate myself from them," he continued, his voice rough.

"You have," she said. "You're nothing like them at all."

"I have a half brother," he said, the words hitting her in a strange way, taking a moment for her to untangle. It seemed like a change of subject, and yet she knew it wasn't. Not really. "I found out about it when I was eleven years old. My father had an affair, as I told you before."

"My parents have had many," she said slowly.

"Affairs were nothing new," he continued as though she hadn't spoken. "But a child… My mother was incensed. He was humiliating her. Bringing shame upon her. Causing the world to believe she might not be desirable."

Gabriella tried to force a smile. "My mother screams a very similar refrain once every few months."

"This was different," Alex said. "I heard the altercation. It was Christmas. Snowing. Outside, the house had white lights strung all over it. As though they were trying to tell the world that we were normal. That we were a happy household. But inside… There were no lights. There was no tree. There was no happiness. And out there… My father's mistress brought her son. He was not much younger than I was. Ten, maybe. She stood out there screaming at my father, their son by her side. Telling him that he had to acknowledge him. My father refused. I…I looked out there and I saw him. And I knew exactly who he was. I told no one. My father drove off in a rage, my mother with him, as they tried to escape the scene. Tried to get away from his mistress. This monster of his own making. That was the night they were in the accident. It was the night they died. And the only people left alive who knew about Nate were his mother, himself and me. I told no one. I kept my half brother a secret."

"Oh, Alex, what a terrible burden."

"What a terrible burden I put on *him*. A child. But I was so angry, Gabby. I blamed him. He was what they were arguing about. And so...I chose comfort over truth. I chose to do what was easy, not what was right. Had I been any sort of man..."

"You weren't," she said, her chest tight. "You were a boy."

He shook his head, lowering it. "Not so much a boy." He looked younger when he said it. She felt like she could see him, as he'd been then. Young and trying so hard to be brave. To uphold the honor of his family in the only way he knew how.

"Yes," she said, her throat aching. "You were."

"He was entitled to that money. To come to the funeral of his father. To be acknowledged. I robbed him of that. Until we needed him. When my grandfather needed a bone marrow transplant I let everyone know about Nate's existence. He was Giovanni's only hope, you see. I...I cannot forgive myself for those things, Gabby. I cannot. They reveal that underneath everything I have tried to fashion for myself I am nothing more than my father's son. A man who uses people. A man who thinks nothing of putting others through hell in order to preserve his own comfort."

"That isn't true, Alex."

He curled his hand into a fist. "Yes, it is. There's a reason I'm telling you this."

"What's the reason?"

"Because I need you to understand. I need you to understand that I'm not a saint. That while I make a habit of practicing restraint, in the end I will only fail. In the end, I will reveal myself to be nothing more than what my blood has dictated I should be."

"We're more than blood, Alex, don't you think?"

"Are we?"

"You said yourself your grandfather took care of you. Your father is his son."

"In which case I have to ask myself if it was my mother. If some people are destined to drag down those who they love. Just another reason to stay away from me."

Her heart thundered, and she felt dizzy. He was so convinced he was toxic. And that was why they couldn't... She wasn't even entirely sure what they *couldn't*. Knew only that he was saying they couldn't, and she knew whatever it was that she wanted to. "But what about what I want?"

"You don't know what you want."

She blinked. "Of course I do. I'm a grown woman, Alessandro. You don't know what I want more than I do."

He got out of the chair, dropping to his knees so that he was down in front of her. He lifted his hand, brushing his thumb over her lower lip. He looked raw. Desperate. And she had to close her eyes, all of her focus going to that slow, sensual touch. "Gabriella, I have seen so much more of the world than you have. Believe me when I tell you that I know what you *should* want. What will keep you safe."

"No," she said, shaking her head.

"It cannot happen," he said, and she wasn't sure if he was telling her or himself. "I cannot kiss you again," he continued. "If I did, I would only sin greater."

She opened her eyes, looked down at him. At the creases on his forehead, the deep grooves that bracketed his face. Those lines made him all the more devastating. Without them, he would be too beautiful. But those lines—the evidence of years lived—gave him texture. Took him from mere beauty to devastating.

She ached. For him. With need for him. "All sins can be forgiven, can't they?"

"Not all, Gabby. My life—my childhood—is a testament to that. Some sins cause damage that is irreparable. That wound so deeply they will never heal. Ask my half brother about that. I would tell you to ask my parents, to ask my mother, but she's dead."

"But, Alex… If we both want each other…"

"You don't even know what it means to want, Gabriella."

Her chest felt tight, her eyes stinging with unshed tears. "That isn't fair, Alex, you don't get to tell me that I don't know what desire is when you're the one who showed it to me. When you're the one who made absolutely certain that I learned what it was."

"I have already hurt you." He shook his head, his tone filled with regret. "I would not like to do it again."

"Then don't." She was on the verge of begging for something she had never imagined wanting with this much ferocity.

"I won't."

"Must you be so honorable? Must you choose this moment to be a man of your word? To be sincere?"

He nodded slowly. "If there is any moment where I must choose it, it is this one."

She slid out of her chair, joining him on the floor. She took his hands in hers, leaning forward, touching her lips slightly to his. "But if you didn't?" she asked, her mouth brushing his as she spoke the words.

He reached around behind her head, sifting his fingers through her hair and drawing her head back slightly, his dark eyes intent on hers. "If I did not, Gabby," he said, his special nickname for her sending shivers along her spine. "If I didn't, then I would lean in and I would kiss you, more deeply than you kissed me just now."

"What else?" she asked, knowing she would burn for this. Past the point of caring.

"I would run my tongue along the line of your top lip before delving inside. I would taste you. So deep and long neither of us would be able to breathe. We wouldn't want to breathe."

She was shaking now, trembling with need. "Alex," she whispered.

"I would pull your T-shirt up over your head, so that I could see you," he said, resting his palm on her stomach, his touch scorching the material of her shirt. "So that I could feel how soft your skin is." He left his hand there, his other still buried deep in her hair. "Then I would remove your bra. Get a good look at those beautiful breasts. They are beautiful. *You* are beautiful. I have said it many times to you now, but I need you to understand how true it is. It is the deepest truth I know, Gabriella. Your beauty. As real as the night sky."

Tears filled her eyes and she made no move to wipe them away.

"I would trace your breasts with my tongue," he continued, "before moving down to kiss your stomach. Then I would strip off your pants, your underwear. For a moment I would just…look at you. I would be afraid to blink for fear that I would miss a moment of that beauty. I would taste you, tease you, touch you, until you were sobbing in my arms."

Gabriella closed her eyes, going still beneath his touch, focusing all of her attention on the pressure of his hand against her stomach, on the erotic words that were flowing from his mouth and over her like heated oil. "What then?" she asked.

"Oh, my darling, I would send you to the moon and back. I would make you scream with pleasure. Then, and only then, I would enter your body, slowly. I would be as careful with you as possible. But I fear it would not be as careful as I ought to be. Because by then…then I would be desperate for you. Beyond thought. It is important that I make you scream before that, because I will not last long once I'm buried deep within you."

She let her lips fall open, her head drawn backward. "Yes," she said, the word a sigh.

"It would be heaven," he said, his voice a hoarse whisper. "To feel you all around me. You would be so tight, so hot and wet. For me. Only for me, Gabby. It would only be for me."

"Of course," she said. "It would only ever be for you, Alex."

She found herself swaying forward, her heart beating so quickly she thought she might faint.

Suddenly, Alex released his hold on her, standing up and putting as much distance between them as possible in one fluid movement. He was breathing hard, and she could see the press of his arousal against the front of his slacks. Could see that what he said was true. That he wanted her with a ferocity that he could not deny. That he would in fact love nothing more than to do everything he had just said.

And she wanted it. So badly that it echoed inside of her. An empty, aching need that only he could ever fill.

"We cannot, Gabby," he said.

"Why?" she asked, the word torture.

"Because I have committed so many grave sins already. I have hurt so many people. Gabriella, I will do nothing but hurt you. And it is the last thing on earth I want to do."

That was why she let him go. That was why she didn't press. Because of the desperation in his voice. Because of how much he wanted to turn away from this. Because of how difficult it was for him. She would not add to his torture. Not after what she knew about him. Not after what he had told her about his parents, about his brother.

So she did nothing but nod slowly. Did nothing but

watch him turn and walk out of the room all the while she sat there, shaking.

She felt cold suddenly. Where before she had only been hot.

She thought back to an earlier conversation they'd had as she sat there on the floor of her library, shivering. She had told him that one was much less likely to get scarred if they stayed in here. She almost laughed. Because she would never forget this. His words, his touch, was branded into her, a scar that would never heal. One that she had acquired—of all places—on the library floor.

It had been her place. The place she had always felt safe. Her refuge.

But it was his now. Irrevocably.

She was afraid it was the same for her.

CHAPTER TWELVE

GABRIELLA AVOIDED HIM for the entire plane ride. He supposed he couldn't blame her. He didn't know what he had been thinking. Confessing those things to her. Saying those words to a virgin.

To a woman that he could never touch. Not any more than he already had.

So, he had allowed her to avoid him. On the plane, then again in the car as she had stared out the window, gazing at the unfamiliar city skyline. And he had watched her reflection in the window, uncaring about the buildings that had become so familiar and mundane to him. New York City failed to enthrall him. What fascinated him was seeing them through her eyes. Wide and glistening as she took in everything around her, her mouth open slightly. Her lips looked so soft. He would give a good portion of his fortune to kiss them again.

He continued to think about her lips as they arrived at his penthouse in Manhattan. Normally, after this much time away from work he would go directly into his home office and set about catching up. But tonight… Tonight it simply didn't appeal.

The first thing he did when they arrived was set the painting up in the living room, taking a step back and looking at it for the first time since they had taken it from Isolo D'Oro.

"It's beautiful," Gabriella said, looking around the space, then at the painting. "All of this. I can't quite believe that I'm here."

"Yes," he said in agreement. But he didn't mean the view or his penthouse were beautiful. He meant her. Always her.

So then he looked at the painting to avoid looking at her. Close study of Gabriella's features could only lead to ruin. He had been so taken with the woman in the painting upon first viewing that he hadn't noticed much of the surrounding objects. For the first time he noticed that everything on the table of the vanity was painted in loving detail. That it was all very purposeful. The woman was wearing a necklace, the reflection of which could barely be seen in the mirror. Emeralds, and white diamonds. On her finger, almost entirely concealed by the tumbling locks of her dark hair, he could just make out the hint of a ring. There was a box, ornate and beautiful, certain to contain more jewelry. A tiara, set next to a beautiful bracelet. His breath caught, and he took a step closer. There was a book set on the vanity, as well.

That meant...

He moved closer still, scanning the surface of the table. Yes. There they were. A small pair of earrings.

"The Lost Mistresses," he said.

"What?" Gabriella asked.

"This is all of them. The artifacts my grandfather sent us after. They are all in this painting. The painting is the last one."

He turned to look at Gabriella. She was staring at him, her dark eyes wide. "What does that mean?"

"It means that I don't think you're being fanciful when you thought there might be a deeper link between our grandparents."

"But the painting... It was by someone called Bartolo."

"I know. But there is something. At one time your grandmother was in possession of every one of these objects. They were the dearest things to my grandfather's heart at another time."

"Alex…"

At that moment, Alex's phone rang. It was his half brother, Nate. Things were better between the two of them in recent years, but they had never been close. It surprised him that the other man would call him for anything.

"I have to get this."

Gabriella watched Alex as he paced out of the room, his phone pressed to his ear. It was strange to be here. In his house with him. Not domestic—because she doubted anything with Alex could ever feel domestic—but intimate. Of course, he hadn't stayed in the room with her to take his phone call. A stark reminder that they didn't really share much about their lives.

She looked back at the painting, looking closely this time at the objects in it. Alex's grandfather was Giovanni Di Sione. As far as she knew he had no connection to the royal family. No connection to Isolo D'Oro. If not for this painting… On its own it was coincidental. Combined with these other objects…

Alex came back out of the room he had just gone into, his dark jacket on, his expression purposeful. "I have to go out. I will be back as soon as possible. You can help yourself to any of the food in the fridge. Or any of the alcohol."

"You don't have a library. What am I supposed to do?" She was only half teasing.

"You'll have to watch a movie, *cara mia*."

She did her best to keep busy while Alex was gone. But one hour turned into two, which turned into three. Then four. Before she knew it she was dozing on the couch, feeling rather sulky, and a little bit concerned. She should have asked him for his mobile number. So she could at least make sure he wasn't lying dead in an alley somewhere.

And once that thought was in her mind, she couldn't shake it.

Surely Alex was dead in an alley. Or if not dead, perilously close to bleeding out onto the cracked concrete sidewalk.

The idea made her stomach hurt. It was also ridiculous. Still, now that it had taken root, there it was.

She walked across the expansive living area and opened one of the bedroom doors to reveal a large bed with a black bedspread. She frowned. Not quite sure which room belonged to Alex. She opened the door next to it and saw another bed that looked almost exactly the same.

She let out an exasperated sigh and walked deeper into that room, letting her fingertips trail over the lush bedding. She was tired. She hadn't unpacked any of her things since she wasn't sure which room she would be staying in. She had changed into her sweats to get a bit more comfortable but she wasn't going to go hunting for her pajamas.

She sat on the edge of the bed, bouncing slightly on the mattress before lying back. She looked over at the clock, the glowing blue numbers showing that it was well after midnight.

She suddenly had a thought that was even more disturbing than the idea of Alex dying in an alley. Maybe he was out with a woman. Why else would he stay out all night? If the issue wasn't that he couldn't make it home, then he wasn't here because he didn't *want* to be home.

The only reason she could think that a man would want to stay out all night was if he was with a woman.

He might be doing the things with her that he wouldn't do with Gabriella. Acting out those words he'd said to her, so deeply erotic. As if he'd woven a fantasy together that was spun with a desire called up from the very depths of her soul. Desire not even she had realized she possessed.

She hated whoever the other woman was. A woman who would—even for a night—capture *all* of Alex's attention. Not just a piece of him.

Not just his smile, or the glint in his eye. Not just his rough, perfect voice, or promises he could never keep. But his body. No barriers between them.

She would touch him everywhere, this mystery woman. Her hands beneath his clothes, learning secrets about him Gabriella would never, ever know.

She burned. She didn't know that jealousy would burn from the inside out. Scalding her. Making her feel raw and restless and angry. She had never been jealous before.

There had never been a man before.

She had been too busy burying herself in dusty books. Wrapping herself in a blanket of safety, insulated by the shelves of her library. By the family estate.

Protecting herself from more rejection.

What she'd said to him had been true. Her own parents didn't truly want her. Didn't really choose her. It was difficult to believe that anyone else would. She was invisible. That was the best case scenario. The worst was that she was in the way.

She swallowed hard, closing her eyes tight and curling her knees up to her chest.

The next thing she knew, she heard heavy footsteps coming into the room. Her eyes snapped open, locking onto the clock. It was after three now.

She was on her back, moving into a sitting position. "Alex?" she asked, her heart thundering heavily.

"Gabriella?" Her name sounded strange on his lips. As though he were convinced she was some sort of apparition.

"Yes. Is this your room? I should have investigated

further, but I…" *Didn't want to.* She couldn't very well finish that sentence.

Couldn't tell him that a part of her had been hoping this was his room. That she would encounter him later.

Shortsighted. As well as a little bit creepy. Shortsighted mainly because she was still wearing her sweats, which was hardly the official uniform of seduction.

"You were asleep," he said.

"Yes. I fell asleep waiting for you to come back. I thought maybe you were dead." Her other concern hit her, cold and hard. Obviously he wasn't dead, but he could very well still have been having sex. "Were you with a woman?"

He let out a heavy sigh and sat down on the edge of the bed. "No. Would it have bothered you if I was?"

"That's a stupid question. Of course it would have." She saw no point in playing coy. She was sleepy, and cranky, and a little bit gritty behind the eyelids. She was in no state to play coy.

He shifted his position, lying down beside her, and her breath caught. There was still a healthy expanse of mattress between them, but still. "It was my brother. My half brother, Nate. I told you about Nate."

"Yes, you did."

"He found the ring. It has an inscription on it. *B.A.*"

"Bartolo," she said.

"Probably. They are the same initials on the painting, Gabriella. They were his. *She* was his, just like your grandmother said. But it's more than that. I know that my grandfather had to start over when he came to America. And I wonder just how completely the new beginning was."

"You think he was my grandmother's lover." His suspicions mirrored her own. It made sense. There just didn't seem to be another way someone could possess all of the same objects that appeared in the painting. More than that, it was her grandmother's reaction to everything. The fact that she had seemed to want Giovanni to have the painting. "She knows," Gabriella said. "She figured it out before we did."

She thought back to the way that her grandmother had looked at Alex when he'd first come into the room at the estate in Aceena. "I bet you look like him," she said. She couldn't see him now; she was staring through the darkness, looking in his direction, barely able to make out his silhouette against the dark bedspread. "I mean, like he did."

"I guess that's why she let me take it in the end."

"They loved each other. They couldn't be together because she had to marry royalty. My grandfather." Suddenly, her throat felt tight, painful. "The artist... Bartolo... he did love her very much. I know. You can see it. It must've killed him to part with those things."

"Not quite. He's still very much alive. For now. It wounded him to part with them. I wonder if he thinks seeing them will return some of his strengths."

"It isn't the objects he needs," she said, her voice wistful.

"You are right." He reached across the distance between them, drawing his fingertips slowly across her cheek. She closed her eyes, tried to fight the tears that were welling in them.

"It is a tragedy, Alex. To think of that. Just think of how much they loved each other all those years..."

She could see her life suddenly, stretching before her. Bleak and lonely. She realized that she could never marry a man who didn't incite fantasy in her. Down to her very core. That she couldn't possibly ever marry a man who understood art the way she did, or appreciated books, or had a library. That she couldn't marry a man who was closer to her age and experience or didn't think of her as an owl. Because that man wouldn't be Alex.

It was Alex for her. Now and always. Forever.

She realized now that maybe she had not been protecting herself so much as waiting for this. For him. For the kind of desire that reached down deep and took over your soul. For the kind of desire that went well beyond common sense. The kind that didn't care if heartbreak lay down the road. Even if it was a short distance away.

She thought of the way her grandmother had spoken of Giovanni—because she was certain that Giovanni and Bartolo were one and the same—of the fact that no matter the heartbreak she could never regret their time together, and it made her tremble. She wasn't certain if she was that strong. To grab hold of an experience while giving no thought to the pain that the consequences might cause.

It was the kind of thing she had been avoiding all of her life. Being like her parents.

But they don't do anything because of love. It's because of selfishness.

Her chest felt like it had cracked open. Of course. That was the difference. Action was always empty, dry, when there was no love. There had been a time when her mother had kissed her good-night before going off to a party, but the gesture had been empty. And the proof was in the fact that now that Gabriella was an adult neither of her parents ever spoke to her. Those goodnight kisses could not be a happy memory, not now that she could see them so clearly for what they were. The proper motions that her parents went through in order to salve what little conscience they had.

This…this had nothing to do with going through the motions. Had nothing to do with doing the right thing. It was just…need.

Alex was a man so far removed from the world. Everything in it seemed to move around him. And he seemed to exist in it untouched.

She wanted to touch him. Not just his skin, but beneath it. She wanted to reach him down deep where his heart beat. Wanted to heat him from the inside out, warm his blood, his soul.

Mostly, she just wanted everything he had promised her back in the library. When they parted, the wound would linger. No matter what happened now. If he was going to leave a scar, she wanted it to be such a scar. So deep, so affecting, it would never heal.

She inched toward him, reaching out and placing her hand over his cheek, mirroring his action.

"Gabriella," he said, his voice a growl, warning.

She didn't listen to it.

She leaned forward, claiming his mouth with hers, kissing him as though she had a right to do it. As though she knew how.

She knew that he would recognize her limited technique, because she had learned it from him. It was all she knew. So when she traced the seam of his lips with her tongue, she was keenly aware of the fact that she was plagiarizing his earlier kiss. But if he was aware of it, he didn't show it. He was still beneath her touch, completely motionless. But he hadn't pushed her away.

They parted, her hand still resting on his cheek. She could hear ragged breathing filling the space between them, but couldn't tell if it was his or hers. Both.

"Gabriella," he said again, "you have no idea what you're asking for. No idea what you're doing."

She pressed her forehead to his, the tips of their noses touching. "I want to make love. I know what that is, Alex. Sex. I've never wanted it before. Not in a specific sense. But I do now."

"I can't offer you anything. I won't make you any promises, because I will only break them."

"Maybe."

"Certainly."

"Well, tomorrow the sky could fall, or I could get hit by a bus—"

"It won't, and you won't."

"You don't know that. We don't know anything beyond right now. I saw my grandmother's face. I know there was a lot that she regretted. But I don't think she ever regretted being with Bartolo." She knew that these words were tantamount to admitting that she felt more for him than simple attraction, but she couldn't bring herself to care.

"I am the worst of sinners. I condemned my half brother to a life lived outside of the family. It was me who stood in his way. Made him feel like he could never be close to us. He told me that tonight. It is on me, Gabriella."

"Alex—"

"I carry the blood of my father. Weak selfishness that I've worked a very long time to overcome. So believe me when I tell you I will regret nothing of what happened here tonight. My nobility is nothing more than a construct. There is no conviction behind it. But you, Gabriella, you, I fear will regret this."

"Maybe. Tomorrow. But not now. And the only thing we have for sure is now."

A feral sound rumbled low in his chest and he shifted positions so that he was over her, his arms braced on either side of her shoulders.

She locked her leg over the back of his calf, an action designed to hold him prisoner even though she knew it wouldn't be truly effective. Still, she wanted him to know that she wanted him here. Desperately.

"Alex," she said, his name a prayer on her lips. She bracketed his face with her hands, looking at him, trying to see what he was thinking, even through the darkness. "Don't you know how much I want you?"

He tensed, pulling away from her slightly. Her heart hammered hard in her chest, clawing at her like a small beast.

"Alex," she said his name again, ready to beg him if she needed to.

He flicked on the light. The way it illuminated his face cast the hollows of his cheekbones into darkness, adding a tortured quality to his features.

"If I'm going to sin, then I'm going to do it with my eyes open," he said. "If I'm going to have you, then I'm going to look at you while I do it."

She breathed a sigh of relief, sliding her hands around to the back of his neck, holding him to her. "I'm glad."

"You won't be. Gabriella, I am too old for you, too jaded, too tired. I can offer you nothing. It's a strange thing to realize that. I am a billionaire. I have more money than I could ever spend in a lifetime. I have all of these things. And for a great many years that has been good enough. I have had whoever I wanted in my life when I wanted them. I have had ultimate control over my own reputation. Wielding it like a sword when I needed to. But none of that helps me here. None of that helps with you. It is…insufficient, and I am a man who is not used to falling short."

"You have yourself. That's all I have to offer. That has to be enough."

"Tonight it will be."

Alex lowered his head, kissing her deeper, harder, than he had before. A restless groove in the pit of her stomach spread through her entire body. Like a creeping vine that took over everything in its path. Winding itself around her limbs, around her throat, making it impossible for her to breathe. Binding her to Alex in a way that was so intense, so permanent, she knew that parting from him would be so much more painful than she'd imagined it would be.

But she wouldn't stop. Even knowing that, she wouldn't stop.

This time, he did not keep his hands still. He did not simply press his palm to her stomach. He let himself explore her body, his fingertips skimming her breasts before he took one firmly in hand, sliding his thumb over one hardened nipple. She gasped, arching against him, her entire body alive with sensation.

"This is a gift I don't deserve," he said, his tone fractured and reverent.

She couldn't speak, but if she could, she would have told him that she was the one receiving a gift. So many lonely, isolated years. So much hollowness inside of her. She had hidden herself away to avoid being hurt again. To avoid more rejection. The neglect of her parents had been enough. And when she went out, she put on a mask. She didn't let anyone see both parts of herself. Princess Gabriella never messed with Gabriella as she was day to day. She didn't give anyone the chance to reject who she really was. But Alex had it all. Held it all in the palm of his hand as surely as he held her body. And he was here. He was touching her. Pouring out all of this attention, all of this care, onto her.

It was so beautiful she could barely breathe.

He pushed her shirt up over her head, baring her breasts to him. She had taken her bra off when she had put her sweats on, and now she was relieved. One less barrier between the two of them. She didn't want anything standing between them. Didn't want any walls up whatsoever. She wanted to give him everything—her body, her soul—and no matter how foolish she knew it was, she couldn't stop that desire that roared through her like an untamed animal.

It would end in heartbreak. It would end in destruction.

But when she was old, she would look back and she would have this moment. She would have Alex. And she knew without a doubt that giving in to pure, true love was something she would never regret.

She had no idea how this moment had happened. How this woman in this bed, in this man's arms, was the same woman she had been only a week ago.

She was changed. She was new. Already, he had changed the world for her. Lifted the veil so that she could see the colors more clearly, feel pleasure more keenly, feel desire sharp like a knife's blade sliding over her skin.

It was painful, incandescent and magical all at once.

He made quick work of her sweatpants and underwear, leaving her completely bare to him, his dark gaze filled with hunger, a desire that couldn't be denied, as he took in the sight of her body.

"Gabby," he said, her name a whispered prayer. "I never thought I appreciated art. But this... You. You are every bit of beauty a painter has ever tried to capture onto canvas. The fields, the mountains, all of the smooth female skin that has ever been painted in an attempt to show some of the glory that is here on this earth. They fall short. It all falls short of you."

Her heart felt so full she thought it might burst. How was this real? How was this man saying these things to her?

It was inconceivable that she might be enough for this man.

That he was afraid that he might not be enough for her. That he was apologizing for the lack of what he had to give.

It didn't make sense. It didn't make sense at all.

But she reveled in it. Accepted it. Took it as her due for so many years of feeling like she was less than.

"I need to see you," she said, her voice a hoarse whisper she barely recognized.

"Not yet," he said. "Not yet."

He lowered his head, kissing her neck, kissing a trail along her collarbone, and down to the swell of her breasts. Then he shifted, taking her nipple into his mouth, sucking it in deep before tracing it with the tip of his tongue. The pleasure that sparked along her veins was shocking, white-hot and almost terrifying in its intensity. There was so much more to making love than a simple caress, and still, this had nearly burned her to the ground. How would she survive at all?

She wouldn't. Not the same.

Nothing passed through the fire and came out the same. But at this point, she didn't want to. She wanted to be changed. By him. Irrevocably, eternally.

He continued his exploration, peppering kisses over her stomach, encircling her belly button with the soft stroke of his tongue before traveling downward. "You see, *cara mia*, were I to take my clothes off, I would not be able to resist sinking inside of you. And you deserve more than that. You deserve for me to take my time. As I told you in the library, once I'm very deep within you I will not be able to hold myself back. And so, your pleasure must come first. Now."

He gripped her hips, drawing her toward his mouth, her thighs spread wide as he pressed his lips to the center of her need. A short, shocked scream escaped her mouth as he lavished attention on that sensitive bundle of nerves with his tongue, as he tasted her, slowly, deeply. He shifted again, pressing his finger against the entrance of her body as he continued to lavish pleasure on her with his mouth. The invasion was foreign, but it felt good.

He added a second finger, stretching her slightly this time, the vague painful sensation drawing her out of her reverie, but only for a moment.

Before long she grew accustomed to that, pleasure

mounting inside of her again as he established a steady rhythm, working his hands and tongue in time with each other. She felt need, tension, gathering in the pit of her stomach like a ball of electricity, scattering outward, sending shocks along her system as it continued to build an intensity. So hot, so bright, she felt like she might burst with it.

And it did burst. Rolling over her in waves unending, unfathomable in its depth. She gripped the bed covers, trying to use something to root her to the earth, anything. Because without it, she feared that she would lose hold of herself entirely.

He rose up above her, kissing her deeply, her own desire a musky flavor on his tongue. "Are you all right?" he asked, his chest rising and falling with the effort it took for him to breathe.

"Yes. More than all right. I'm… Alex, I didn't know it was like this."

"What did you think it would be?" His words slurred as though he were drunk.

"I didn't know. Because I didn't know it would be you."

"Does it matter *so* much that it's me?" She sensed a rawness behind that question, a vulnerability.

"That's the only thing that matters."

He growled, kissing her again as she grabbed hold of the edge of his button-up shirt, undoing the buttons as quickly as possible. She spread her hands over that broad expanse of chest. His hard muscles…that perfect sprinkling of chest hair that reminded her just how much of a man he was. How different they were. It was heaven to touch him like this. To finally have the promise of that glorious body fulfilled, in her hands. She pushed the shirt from his shoulders and threw it over the side of the bed, running her hands down his back, exploring the intricate musculature there. She parted her thighs, arching against him, feeling the evidence of his arousal against where she was wet and aching for him already. She should be satisfied, after what he had just done for her. She found she was far from it.

"I need you. How can I need you this badly after all of that?" she asked, her voice trembling.

"I would tell you that's sex, *cara*. I would tell you that's desire. But it is not sex or desire in any way that I know it. I do not shake for want of being inside of a woman. You make me shake. You make me feel as though I won't be able to breathe until I have you. Until I'm joined to you. What witchcraft is that, Gabriella? You must tell me."

"How can I? I'm just a virgin. You are supposed to be wise. You're supposed to be the one teaching me."

"How can I? When I feel you have so much to teach me." He kissed her gently as his hands moved to his belt. She could hear him undoing the buckle slowly and a shiver of anticipation ran through her. She helped him push his pants and underwear down his narrow hips and he sent them over the side of the bed to join the rest of their clothes. She could feel him, feel his hot hard length, pressed against her heat.

"I want to see you," she said, her voice husky, unrecognizable to her own ears. "I've never seen a naked man before."

He straightened, a dull slash of red coloring his cheekbones. "So many honors I don't deserve, Princess."

He sounded tortured, and at any other time she might have felt sorry for him, or wondered why. But not now. How could she feel sorry for him when she was too busy exulting in this triumph for herself?

He was perfect. Masculine beauty depicted in sculpture could never have prepared her for Alex.

Marble was cold, lifeless. It might show the shape of a man, but it didn't show the vitality. His life, his strength.

It was everything and more. His broad shoulders, perfectly defined chest and washboard stomach, bisected by a line of hair that ran down to his very evident desire was enough to take a breath away.

He was so very…large. Thick. Part of her was made nervous by that, the other part marveled at the glory that was in front of her. The glory that would be hers.

"You're right," she said, her words hushed.

"About what?"

"You are in possession of very rampant masculinity."

He laughed, the sound tortured. "I only hope that it isn't too rampant for you."

"It's just perfect for me. How can it be anything else?"

He dropped forward on his knees, between her thighs, his hands on her shoulders. She looked up at him, her heart pounding heavily.

"You're beautiful," she said.

"And you are more than I deserve," he said, kissing her, wrapping his arm around her waist and drawing her body hard up against his as he pressed the head of his arousal against the entrance to her body.

She winced slightly, bracing herself for his invasion. It hurt. But she wanted it. There was no question. Even as he pressed forward, and she stretched around him, trembling as he joined their bodies together, she didn't want anything else but this. It was desire so perfectly and beautifully realized, the fulfillment of fantasy. Not because it brought pleasure. But because she was joined to him. Because they were one. Even though it hurt.

And when he thrust deep within, completing their joining, there was no pleasure to be found at all. Not in the physical sense.

But her soul felt alive. Complete. For the first time.

And as the pain slowly began to fade and the pleasure

began to build again, she felt so full with it that she could scarcely breathe.

Desire was a wild, needy thing inside of her. She wanted it to be satisfied. Needed it to be satisfied. And yet at the same time she wanted this to go on forever. Wanted to prolong the moment where she would reach her peak. Because once that happened it was the end. Of this perfect moment where they were joined. Connected. Where they were one with each other. The desire to cling to him, to cling to this, was doing battle with the desire to find completion. Ferocious, intense. She didn't know which one would win. Didn't know which one she wanted to win.

"Gabby," he said her name. Just her name.

Gabby would always belong to him. Only to him. The very idea of someone else saying it made her ill.

His teeth scraped the edge of her collarbone, the small slice of pain mingling with the pleasure, drawing her back to earth, making her feel so acutely aware of everything. So perfectly in tune with her body, and his.

She could feel his building pleasure along with hers. Could feel how close to the edge he was as his muscles tensed, as his control frayed.

She opened her eyes, determined to watch his face. Determined to watch this man who was everything she was not. Hardened, masculine beauty. Experienced. World-weary. She would watch him as he felt the same thing she did. As they experienced this storm of pleasure on the same level. It reduced them, this desperation, reduced them down to their souls. To ravenous, needy things that had nothing beyond this moment, this common need.

It was how Princess Gabriella D'Oro, recent virgin and definite bookworm, met with Alessandro Di Sione, rumored fearsome monster and a man who claimed to have a hardened heart. How they not only met, but understood each other. Spoke in perfect words that each other alone could understand. How had she ever thought they were different? How had she ever looked at him and seen a gulf they couldn't bridge? They had. She was closer to him now, in this moment, than she had ever been to another person in her life.

It was powerful, fearsome, awe-inspiring. These needs that only the other could meet. That only the other could inspire. A hunger only he could arouse and satisfy.

"Alex," she said, arching against him, the source of her pleasure meeting his heart and body as he thrust deep within her. A shower of sparks rained over her, pleasure breaking over her like an electrical storm, flashes of light blinding brilliance behind her eyes. She closed them, but only for a moment. Then she forced them open again, watched his face as he, too, gave himself over to this thing between them. She watched as that face, that face that could have been carved from granite, softened, the lines on his forehead shifting, a look of pure pain and desperation contorting his features as he growled his release, his entire body trembling as he spilled himself deep inside of her. She held him, as pleasure continued to rack his frame, as aftershocks kept moving through her in an endless wave.

They were connected in this. This pleasure. This moment.

And when it was over they simply lay there, entwined in each other. Breathing together.

She knew that Alex would feel regret later. Because no matter what he said he wasn't a monster. She had to wonder why he was so desperate to convince not only others, but himself, of the fact that he was.

She knew it came down to his fear that he would become like his father. She knew enough about him to understand that. But she also knew him well enough to understand it would never be him.

He had made some mistakes in his life with his family, but he had been a young man. Barely more than a boy. She had made far fewer mistakes. If only because she interacted with less people. Life wasn't as difficult when you hid from it.

He looked at himself and saw nothing but a potential monster and he was dedicated to forcing others to see the same.

She knew better.

He was so dry. So funny and brilliant. He cared. Very deeply. For her, for everyone else around him. He pretended he didn't. The way he looked after his grandfather, the pain that laced his voice when he spoke of his half brother and his past treatment of him, the way he had taken such great care with her, told an entirely different story than the narrative Alex had spent so many years carefully constructing.

He had only given when she had pushed. And both passed the point of resistance. He had never pressured her for anything, and she knew without a doubt that he never would have.

He was a hero in her eyes and yet he insisted on casting himself as the villain.

She wished, more than anything, that he could see himself through her eyes. That he could see himself clearly. She would make it her mission to change his thoughts on himself. She would.

No, it wouldn't change in a moment. No matter how much she might want to. She was going to have to show him, over time. Show him the man he really was. But in order to do that she would have to stay with him. Leave Aceena. Convince him to attempt to make some kind of relationship with her. He had arrangements with women, he had said as much. Why couldn't he have one with her?

Eventually…he would have to see that they were good

together. Her thoughts were spinning, her entire body humming. There was so much going on in her brain. But she had never been good at letting things rest. She was always trying to solve the problem. Always trying to get down to the truth. To figure out the source of the problem so that she could stamp it out.

Unfortunately, there was no history book she could look at to conduct a simple study on Alex.

She would have to study him in person. Not a hardship, really.

"You're very quiet," he said.

"Thinking," she said honestly.

"About?"

She bit her lip. She could hardly tell him that she was plotting ways to convince him to love not only her, but himself.

"You're very good in bed," she said, rather than telling him the exact thoughts that were on her mind. That was what her body was thinking about, anyway. "Granted, I have no one else to compare to, but I can't imagine there are very many men who exceed your skill."

"It isn't about skill, Gabby." He brushed her hair out of her face, his body still entwined with hers. "This is chemistry."

A burst of warmth fired up in her heart, then fizzled out just as quickly. It was more than that. For her, it was so much more than that.

She would show him. She would find a way. After a lifetime spent hiding away she knew one thing for certain. After standing in the light with Alex, she would never retreat back into the shadows.

CHAPTER THIRTEEN

ALEX HAD CALLED himself ten kinds of villain since that first night he had taken Gabriella to bed. Of course, it had not stopped him from taking her to bed every night since. She was everything he had fantasized she might be. Beautiful, soft. And her enjoyment of study had come into play in some erotic and interesting ways he had not imagined. She was very thorough.

She had explored his body as though he were an ancient text she was attempting to pull meaning from.

No one had looked that deeply into him and his secrets in…ever. He was stone people built legend around. But no one ever looked beneath to see the man. And he'd kept it that way. For a reason. Several reasons.

He found it hard to keep Gabby at that same distance. Found it hard to even want to keep her at a distance.

She was soft and beautiful, and more generous than she should be. And he spent late nights not only exploring her body, but lying next to her, skimming his hands over her bare curves while she read passages from favorite books to him, and did her very best to educate him about art and other things he didn't care about in the least.

But he liked hearing the words on her lips. Enjoyed the way they poured over him like warm honey, soothing him in a soul-deep way he hadn't imagined possible. Mostly because it was easy to imagine he didn't have a soul.

Because a man who had kept his own half brother a secret, who shared the blood of the most selfish, pleasure-seeking bastard on earth, could hardly have regular human emotions. Could hardly feel softness, tenderness, for a beautiful woman he had nothing in common with.

Could hardly be soothed to a soul he didn't have.

But with Gabby things felt different. Possible. Ridiculous, since he was a billionaire and *everything* was possible. He could have small mammals on jet packs delivered by noon if he wanted. One princess shouldn't make anything feel more possible.

Still, it was the word that came to mind, whether it made sense or not. Well, there were other words, but none of them were appropriate.

He hadn't ever cared about anything like that before, but with her he did. He couldn't afford to care, and he needed to get back to work. But until he dealt with his grandfather, the painting and his family, he couldn't.

Fortunately, they were meeting today. Gabriella would come with him; she would be part of passing the painting to his grandfather, as her grandmother had asked. And then she would go home.

The thought shouldn't make it feel like a knife's blade had been slipped beneath his skin and twisted.

"Hi, Alex," she said, coming out of his bedroom right then, dressed in nothing but a T-shirt. His T-shirt. And what would have been cliché on another woman was new on her. As though he'd never before seen it. As though no woman had ever slipped her lover's T-shirt on over her luscious curves after an evening of passion.

Gabby was an original no matter what she did. Perhaps because she was his, and only his. Because no other man had touched her, no other man had kissed her. He'd never been with a virgin before. Maybe he was just archaic enough for it to matter.

He hadn't thought he was. But then, he hadn't thought he had a soul, either.

"Good morning, Gabriella," he said, lifting his coffee mug to his lips.

"So, we meet with your family today?" she asked, her dark eyes liquid, hopeful for some reason. Perhaps she was ready to be rid of him. Ready to go back to Aceena.

But last night she had not sounded like a woman ready to be rid of him.

"Yes. Soon. You'll have to get dressed in something other than that."

She smiled, and it was a little bit wicked. On that innocent mouth that he had trained to do such sensual things, it was another Gabby original. "You mean I can't wear this to go and meet your family?"

The way she said those words. Meeting his family. They did something to him. Grabbed hold of something down deep inside of him and twisted hard. He was torn between an intense longing and a fierce need to reject the desire.

He cleared his throat. "It would probably be best if you are wearing pants of some kind when I introduce you to my grandfather."

"Because I would shock him?" She seemed rather pleased by the thought.

"Because he would steal you away from me."

"No one could do that, Alex," she said, crossing the distance between them and kissing him on the cheek. "But I will get dressed."

She turned and walked back out of the room and he was left wondering what the hell had just happened here. What was happening in his life? Gabriella seemed to be happening. And far from being the harmless little bookworm she had seemed to be when he first met her at the door of the estate in Aceena, it appeared now that she was a rather intense bespectacled whirlwind.

Today all of the Lost Mistresses would be reunited again, would be with his grandfather. He had helped make his grandfather's last wish come true. He would focus on that. What happened beyond today? Well, what happened beyond today would be what was necessary. Gabriella returning home was necessary. Gabriella getting as far away from him as possible before he did even more damage was necessary.

Damage was all he would do. It was all he was capable of. She would only need to ask Nate to know that was true. Would only need to ask every other woman who had ever passed through his life. Every one of his siblings he had been distant with, emotionally unavailable to.

The idea of Gabriella returning home should fill him with nothing more than a sense of completion. He could get back to his real life. Get back to the running of his company, could forget treasure hunts for lost paintings and art lessons and owlish eyes.

Instead, he felt as though his chest was full of lead.

But he had spent the past thirty-six years ignoring his feelings. He saw no reason to start engaging with them now.

He didn't often make his way to the Di Sione family estate. As far as he was concerned it held nothing but ghosts from his past. Too many memories of what it was like to be a lonely little boy who just lost his parents. An angry, fearful eleven-year-old who had hidden the existence of a half brother to protect a man who didn't deserve protecting.

He shook off the thought as he walked through the grand entry, determined to shed every last one of his memories and feelings like mud on his boots with each step he took.

He could hear Gabriella following behind him, her footsteps timid on the marble as she did so. He was carrying the painting, making his way into the family sitting room, scarcely feeling prepared to face not only his grandfather, but his assorted siblings.

When he walked in, every eye in the room landed on him, the painting he was carrying and the woman who was trailing behind him. He couldn't remember the last time they'd all stood in one room.

Hell, Dario and Dante were standing beside each other. The identical Di Siones finally speaking again after years of discord.

Everyone gathered here in this room, united in this mission for Giovanni. This would have been impossible before. Before the quest Alex had been so quick to mock.

Nate, who he had always had the most challenging relationship with, was here, too, with his pregnant lover. And when Alex looked at him…he didn't feel the weight of his failure, of his guilt. Not anymore.

Now he wondered. Wondered if it had ever truly been about these artifacts, or if they had been searching for a different kind of treasure all along.

"What's the matter with all of you?" he asked, his tone sardonic. "Have you never seen a painting before? Or a woman?"

Giovanni stayed seated, his dark eyes trained on Gabriella. And Alex knew that his grandfather was seeing the same spark of resemblance in Gabby as Lucia had seen in him.

"It has been a very long time since I have seen such a painting," his grandfather said slowly. "Or," he continued, looking at Gabby, "such a woman."

Gabriella looked up at him, her eyes searching. All of this was confirming what they both already suspected, but Alex was eager to hear the story from his grandfather's own lips. "There is not only a woman in this painting,"

Alex said. "The mistresses are here, as well." He turned, standing the painting up on the mantel.

His siblings were no longer looking at him, but at the painting.

"I sense there is a story here, *Nonno*," Alex said, his voice hushed. "And I can't imagine you sent all of us on a worldwide scavenger hunt only to keep the truth hidden from us forever."

Giovanni rubbed his chin, his expression thoughtful. "You are right there, Alessandro. I had no intention of keeping you in the dark forever. Nearly a century is long enough for a man like me, to live, to hold on to his secrets."

"Well, I expect you to live a few more years," Alex said, knowing that such a thing was highly unlikely, but hoping to speak it into existence, anyway.

"From your lips to God's ears," Giovanni said. "But in the event the Man upstairs is busy, too busy to hear such a pronouncement, I suppose I should speak my piece now. You may have begun to suspect that Giovanni Di Sione is not my given name. I was born Bartolo Agosti."

"The letters *BALDO* on the jewelry…" Dario said.

Giovanni smiled.

"The inscription on the pieces I gave to Lucia… Bartolo Agosti, Lucia D'Oro. When I came to America I reinvented more than simply my fortune. I did not just recreate my wealth, I recreated my legend. I was born on Isolo D'Oro. The son of a wealthy family. My brother and I often played with a little girl in the gardens of the palace. It was a simple time on the island. The royal family was in no danger and they moved about freely, mixing with those who were beneath them, playing in the sunshine. I was one such child who was far beneath the princess, though I was titled. I still wasn't a prince—never destined to be a king.

"My friendship with that little girl became much more. As we grew, so did our feelings. But sadly for Lucia and myself, while spending a few amusing hours in the garden together was acceptable, it would not make for an acceptable marriage. I knew that things between the two of us had to come to an end. I knew that she had to take up the mantle of her destiny, not take up a life with a man such as myself. But before we parted, I wanted to paint her. I wanted to paint her with the gifts that I had given to her—tokens of our affection. I wanted to show her that no matter what I said, no matter how things ended, I wanted her to be able to look at this painting and see how I loved her.

"But in the end, when I told her we could not be, when I told her she had to marry the man her parents had selected for her, she was angry. She gave everything back. All of the gifts. Including the painting. I kept them, the only pieces of my Lucia that I retained. I kept them until I was forced to part with them. Part with them or starve. But the painting…I sent it back to her. I never knew what she did with it. I never heard from her. Never found out if her husband intercepted it, if her family kept it from her. But I wanted her to look at it again. With distance between us, with years between that heartbreak, I wanted her to look at it and understand that what I did was not because I cared so little for her. But because I cared so very much."

He turned his focus to Gabriella.

"Tell me, my dear. Did your grandmother have the painting?"

Gabriella's expression was so soft, so caring, her dark eyes nearly liquid. "She did. When the family was banished from Isolo D'Oro she had to leave it. But she hid it. She held on to it. She knew just where it was, and when she saw it…"

"She saw it again?"

"Yes. Before we came here to New York. We returned to Aceena and showed it to her. It was her one request. She wanted you to have it back, but she wanted to see it first. She cares, Bartolo," Gabriella said, using Alex's grandfather's real name, a name he had doubtless not heard for years. "She cares so very much."

"And that, right there, is a gift that supersedes all of this."

"That's nice, Grandfather. So you send us on a field trip around the world to find your trinkets and all you needed was emotional reassurance the whole time," Dario said, his tone dry. "If I had known that, I might have simply purchased you a nice card."

"God knows you needed a diversion, Dario. I also reunited you with the mother of your child and the love of your life." His grandfather snorted. "You could perhaps say thank you."

"I could." But he didn't.

He did, however, step back and take hold of Anais's hand, stroking his thumb over her knuckles.

That was, for Dario, as much of a sincere gesture as would likely be demonstrated.

"It's strange," Giovanni said, "but I expected a greater sense of completion. Upon seeing everything together I thought perhaps I would feel a sense of resolution. But they are simply things."

"Perhaps you were waiting for a person. Not an object."

Everyone turned toward the sound of the thin, elderly voice coming from the doorway of the sitting area. It was Gabriella's grandmother, Lucia. The older woman was slightly stooped, but still, her bearing was regal. She was dressed in a deep purple that complemented her olive skin and dark eyes. And though her hair was white, though her skin was aged, it was undeniable that she was the woman in the picture. Not so much because of the resemblance she bore, but because the love that shone from Giovanni's eyes matched the passion in the artist's brushstrokes.

Giovanni stood, the move slow, labored. It was clear that he stood on unsteady legs, but in spite of the difficulty, he began to cross the room, closing the distance between himself and his long-lost love.

"I have a feeling we could have saved ourselves a lot of work if we had simply gone and fetched her in the first place," Dario said.

But they regarded each other cautiously, and then Lucia stretched out her hand and curled her fingers around Giovanni's, squeezing them gently. "Bartolo," she said, her voice thick with tears.

"It has been too long."

To everyone's surprise, Lucia laughed. "I would say an excess of fifty years is most definitely too long to be parted from the love of your life."

"I hope very much that there was love in your last fifty years regardless," Giovanni said.

Lucia nodded slowly. "There was. There is. But that doesn't mean yours wasn't greatly missed." She looked around the room, at all of Giovanni's grandchildren. "And I see there has been a great deal in yours."

"Yes, there has been. But I never released the love I have for you. I simply made room for more."

"I think we have a great deal to discuss, Bartolo," Lucia said. "Don't you?"

"Yes. I think we do."

He looped his arm around hers, and the two of them made their way slowly out of the room. The siblings looked at one another and, for once, no one seemed to know what to say.

But it was a strange thing, the realization that they were all in the same room. Nate included. They were all here together, united by their grandfather's quest to bring closure to the long-ago love affair.

If Alex were a sentimental man at all, he might even say that love had brought them together.

Gabriella would say that. Probably the moment they were alone.

It was a strange thing to him that he felt he could anticipate the sort of thing she might say. He couldn't recall ever feeling like that about anyone before. Couldn't recall ever thinking he was certain about the feelings of the person standing beside him. Though something about Gabriella felt ingrained in him, intrinsic to his system. He could guess at her thoughts, emotions and opinions as easily as he could guess at his own. Potentially easier.

"Alex," Gabriella said, "can we talk?"

It wasn't exactly what he had anticipated her saying, but she wanted to talk because she was having some kind of reaction to the scene between their grandparents. And that he had figured out. For some reason, he drew comfort in his ability to recognize and anticipate Gabriella's moods. Which wouldn't matter at all when she went back to Aceena. Not at all. It wasn't as though they would keep in touch. Wasn't as though they would exchange fluffy texts with emoticons like modern-day star-crossed lovers.

"Of course," he said, placing his hand on the small of her back and leading her from the room, ignoring the questioning gazes of his siblings as they followed their progress.

"Gardens?" she asked.

"Not a gallery?"

"I like gardens. And galleries. And libraries. I contain multitudes."

He laughed. "Yes, you do. You are large indeed. In a very small way."

She inclined her head, smiling at him. Her expression

was impish, but there was something serious behind her dark eyes, and it filled him with a sense of foreboding. Yet another ridiculous thing, because there was nothing that Gabriella could possibly say to him that was worth feeling a sense of foreboding over. He had never felt foreboding in his life.

"This way," he said, leading her down the long corridor that would take them to the back doors and out to the garden. "I'm not sure it's as spectacular as the grounds in Aceena. But they'll have to do." He pushed the French doors open, then stood like a footman, his hand outstretched, indicating that Gabriella should go ahead of him. She did. And he took great joy in watching her walk out into the sunshine, the rays of the sun shining over the glossy dark waves of her hair. She was a bright, shiny, beautiful thing, a thing that he could not hope to possess. Not with all of the money that he had in his bank account. Not with all the power and influence he wielded. Because it would take something else to hold on to a woman like Gabriella, something he simply didn't have. Something he couldn't even identify. And if he couldn't identify it, how could he hope to obtain it?

This was a foolish line of thinking. He was fine. He had been fine until his grandfather had sent him on the fool's errand to collect the painting. This was Giovanni's happy ending, at ninety-eight, and it had nothing at all to do with Alex. Alex would go back to the way things were. Alex would go back to life without Gabby. That was as it should be. And he should want nothing else.

She walked over to a stone bench that was positioned just in front of a manicured hedge and took a seat, drawing one delicate, manicured finger over the hard, cold surface. Then she looked up at him. "It's a very sad thing that our grandparents had to wait half a century to find each other again."

"But a very happy thing that they have each other again, yes?"

"Yes. It is very happy."

"And as they both said, they did not lack for love in their lives."

"Yes. You're right. But don't you think…considering what they said, considering the evidence…that they never forgot each other? That their feelings for each other never lessened? That what they shared was different? They reserved a special place inside of them that was never replaced by anyone else. Not by the people they married, not by their children, not by their grandchildren. I believe that they both had happy lives. But I also believe that what they shared between each other was unique. I believe that it was special in a way that nothing else was. And I believe—"

She swallowed hard, looking up at the sky, curling her fingers around the edge of the bench and planting her feet firmly on the ground.

"I believe that there is such a thing as true love. Real love. The kind that people write sonnets about, the kind that makes people paint. That makes them sing. Like a real 'I have one half of the magic amulet, and you have the other half and they can only be complete when they're together' kind of love. I just saw it in there."

He felt cold inside. And it had nothing to do with the clear, frostbitten December day, and everything to do with the words that were spilling out of Gabriella's mouth.

"What is the point to all of this, Gabriella?"

"I think…I think that we might have that. Because it doesn't make sense, Alex. None of this makes sense. We don't. We should have nothing in common. Nothing to talk about. Attraction might be one thing, sexual compatibility another. But there's more than that. I have never felt more like myself than when I'm with you. I thought, all this time, that I needed to find someone who is like me. That I needed to find someone who would keep me safe, the way I had kept myself safe. But that isn't it at all. I don't want to be safe. I want to be with you." She laughed. "I guess it doesn't really sound right. It isn't like I think you're going to put me in danger…"

"No," he said, the word coming out of his mouth, heart tortured. "You are exactly right. I am going to put you in danger. I already have. It's evidenced by the fact that we're having this conversation. You should not feel these things for me, Gabby. I made it very clear that what we had was physical, and only physical."

"Yes," she said, her voice sounding hollow, as though he had already eviscerated something essential inside of her. "I know you did. Then things changed for me. I thought it wasn't entirely impossible that they had changed for you."

"And that is where our differences are a problem. You are innocent. And for you, all of this is new. So of course things have changed. And I can understand why you might have thought they would change for me. But you have to understand that nothing about this is original to me," he said, directly combating his earlier thoughts. Because he needed to. For himself, not just for her. "I have conducted more of these relationships than I can count. And there is absolutely nothing unique about you."

She blinked furiously, tears glittering in her beautiful eyes, and he wanted nothing more than to wipe them away. But he had put them there, so he forfeited the right. "But you didn't… If I wasn't different, then you would have had me the moment you wanted me. I don't think you would have held me on the floor of the library and used your words to—"

"That's the thing, Gabby, you don't think, because you don't have any idea how this works. When a man wants to seduce a woman he appeals to her in any way he can.

I'm not above pretending to be a much nicer man than I am. I was seemingly honest with you," he said, the words cutting his throat on their way out. "I told you about my fearsome reputation, but then I treated you gently. I made you feel like you were different. What better way to seduce a virgin? But I never wanted your love, darling girl. I only wanted your body."

"Why are you saying this?"

"Because it is time I told the truth. The moment you started spouting poetry I knew this had to be over. It was one thing when I thought you were going to quietly return to your home country the moment the painting was delivered. Clearly, you had other designs. And I don't have any interest in prolonging this farce."

She closed her eyes, a single tear trailing down her cheek. "That wasn't the farce. *This* is."

"Gabriella," he said, his voice hardened, harsh. "I told you the sort of man I am. I deal in business. In exchanges. We exchanged pleasure. That's all there is for me. Beyond that? I kept my own brother a secret to try and protect the reputation of my father. A man who was debauched beyond reason. That's the sort of thing I stand in defense of."

"No. You say that. You're determined to make sure that I and everyone else think you're a monster. Why? What are you hiding?" She opened her eyes, meeting his gaze directly, and anger was replacing the sadness that had been there only a moment ago.

"That," he said, "is my deepest, darkest secret, *cara mia*. I am hiding nothing. The water is just as shallow as it appears from the surface. Nothing is running deep here."

"I understand that you need to believe that, Alex. I understand that it's what you need everyone else to believe. What I don't understand is why."

He spread his hands. "There is nothing to understand. That is the simple, tragic truth of me. My legend is far more interesting than I will ever be. Stories of me being a monster. Of being heartless, and cruel. The simple fact is I'm self-serving. There is nothing intricate to figure out. I do what makes me money. I do what brings me pleasure. Those are my motivations. Those are my actions. Women, the media, they like to pretend that there is something else beneath all of that. I am no more interesting than my father and mother ever were."

"No," she said, her voice a whisper. "You said you didn't want to be like him."

"I said a lot of things. Don't believe them. I believe this. It's over, Gabriella. The painting is delivered, our grandparents are reunited. They can keep their true love. I will keep my money, my varied sex life and my freedom. You can go back to your books."

"Alex," she said, her voice broken, a plea.

It stabbed him, made him feel like he was being scraped raw from the inside out. This was for the best. He had to end it. He had to end it with the kind of finality his grandfather had ended things with Lucia. But he would leave no painting behind. He would leave no trail of bread crumbs for Gabriella to find her way back to him eventually.

What he did, he did for her best interests. For her future. She really would find a man who was better than him. She thought, right now, that he was more exciting than the intellectual, nice man that she would ultimately end up with, but in the future she would see that she was wrong. She would understand that she needed someone companionable, someone stable, someone who would give her everything that she deserved and more.

She was emotionally scarred by parents who had been so much like his own. And he would do nothing to continue that scarring. To continue that pain. Removing himself now was the kindest thing, even though it didn't seem like it now.

"You were right," he said, knowing that the death knell to all of this was on his lips even now. "The rake never ends up with the wallflower. He crosses the room for her, Gabby, every time. Because she's needy. Because she's vulnerable. Because she's a challenge, a change in flavor to a jaded palate. But he doesn't end up with her. He doesn't end up with anyone."

And then he turned, leaving her standing in the garden, leaving her breaking to pieces behind him, while his own chest did the same.

It was so very like Giovanni and Lucia. But with one major difference. There would never be a time in Alex's life when he stood in a roomful of his grandchildren and told this story. Because there would be no grandchildren for him. There would be no other woman, no wife.

It would be up to his brothers and sisters to carry on the bloodline, because he would not.

He would leave nothing behind. Not his tainted blood, not any Lost Mistresses.

Without him, Gabriella would be free to have love in her life. She would not hold on to him.

He wasn't worth it.

CHAPTER FOURTEEN

GABRIELLA WAS IN a daze. She had been ever since Alex had left her sitting out in the garden at his grandfather's estate. Now, she was staying at the estate. She had stumbled into the house some two hours later and found her grandmother, who was of course planning on staying and reacquainting herself with Giovanni, and spending as much time with him as possible with the remaining time he had.

She should feel happy for them. Part of her did feel happy for them. But so much of her was broken, smashed into tiny pieces. Tiny, aching pieces. That made it difficult to feel wholly happy for anyone or anything.

She wasn't entirely certain she would ever take a full breath again, much less crack a full smile.

It was seriously dramatic, but she felt seriously dramatic.

She would like to think of Alex as her first love. Her first heartbreak. But with each and every beat of her heart the word wasn't *first*, it was *only*. Her only love. Her only lover. The only man she would ever want, the only man she could ever possibly need.

She was hurt. But she was also angry at him. Because no matter what he said she knew that there was more to him than this. She knew that he hadn't seduced her, tricked her, just for a little bit of sport. He felt something for her, and she knew that. The fact that he was so cruel when he'd abandoned her earlier today was proof enough of that.

He talked about being like his father, but she knew that people like their parents were not intentionally cruel. They were simply self-seeking. When he had been confronted with his half brother he had preferred to ignore the situation.

This was different. His reaction was different. Yes, she knew he had a reputation for being a monster, but she had also never seen it in action.

Still, even knowing that something deeper was going on inside of Alex, it didn't mean this didn't hurt. Because while she had confidence that he had feelings for her that went beyond the physical, she had no confidence that they would be able to resolve it.

Though there was something wonderful in finding a belief in true love because of the reunion of their grandparents, there was also something sobering about the fact that it had taken them more than fifty years to come and find each other. She didn't want to wait fifty years for Alex.

She flopped backward onto the bed, groaning loudly. She closed her eyes, letting her lips part, imagining that Alex was here. That he was leaning in, about to kiss them. She let her imagination drift. To the way that he touched her. The way that he held her.

She might have been a virgin, but she wasn't an idiot.

She opened her eyes, sighing heavily.

There was a knock on the door and Gabriella rolled onto her side, her head on her arm. "Come in," she said, not quite sure why she was allowing anyone entry when she felt like day-old crusty bread.

When the door opened, Gabriella straightened. It was her grandmother. "Hello, Gabriella," the older woman said, walking into the room slowly.

"I trust everything is going well?"

Lucia smiled. "Better than."

"I'm glad."

"I know Bartolo's health is not as good as it might be, but I am more than happy to devote time to caring for him."

Those words, so gentle, so serene, shook something inside of Gabriella. It made her think of Alex again. She would do that for him. She would care for him. She didn't need the whole world in return; she only needed what he could give. At least for now. If he hadn't sent her away she would be willing to be patient. She didn't need him to throw rope around the moon and lasso it, didn't need him to pull it down for her. He was the moon all by himself. The idiot.

"Gabriella," her grandmother said, her tone gentler now. "Is there something you wish to tell me?"

"Alex," she said, because she knew that would be enough.

"I did warn you," the older woman said, her eyes soft, no condemnation in her voice.

"I know you did. Unfortunately, Alessandro was a bit more persuasive than you are."

Lucia laughed then. "They always are. I have some experience with that, as you may know."

"Yes. I know."

"And sometimes they push us away because they think they are doing what's best for us. In truth, while I know Bartolo believes I was angry at him, I was angry at myself. I knew what he was doing that whole time. He was trying to play the part of nobleman. He didn't want me to be denied anything he considered my birthright. Didn't want me disowned by my family. But I have always felt that I should have fought harder. Always wondered what would have happened if I would have told him no. If I would never have let him get away with hurting me to save me."

The truth of her grandmother's words resonated inside of her. Because it was what she had imagined Alex might be doing. Of course, she was too afraid to hope. Maybe he simply didn't want to be with her. "How do you know?"

Her grandmother took a step forward, patting her on the hand. "You don't. Not unless you go ask. Take it from someone who spent half a century wishing she would have asked—it's worth the risk. Pride does not keep you warm at night. Pride won't smile at you every morning, day in day out, with ever deepening lines as the years pass. Pride is very cold comfort, Gabriella."

Lucia straightened and walked back out of the room, closing the door softly behind her. Gabriella thought of the way Alex had looked at her before leaving her in the garden earlier. Of the painful words he'd spoken, designed specifically to inflict the deepest wounds on her.

Her grandmother was right. There was no room for pride. Her pride could go straight to hell, but she would keep her love for Alex.

She had spent a great many years hiding. Trying to prevent herself from being rejected ever again, the way her parents made her feel rejected. But all that had ever gotten her was a dusty library. She was done with that. She would have her dusty library and her man.

It was suddenly clear. She'd been doing her family's genealogy for years. Trying to uncover the mysteries of the past, to shine a light on history and events lived by other people. She used it to hide.

But there would be no more hiding. She could no longer pin everything on the past. She had to make her own life. Her own history.

She stood up, vibrating with determination. Alessan-

dro Di Sione might think he was the most fearsome creature to roam the earth. But hell had no fury like Gabriella
D'Oro when she was scorned. And she was determined
to show him that.

CHAPTER FIFTEEN

ALEX WAS CONTEMPLATING the merit of filling his bathtub with whiskey and seeing if he could absorb the alcohol straight through his skin. Anything to dull the roar of pain that was writhing through his body, the pounding in his temples, the bone-deep ache that had settled down beneath his skin and wrapped itself around his entire being.

Drinking had proven ineffective. It wasn't strong enough. He could still see her face. Could still see the way she looked at him. Wounded, impossibly hurt, as he had done what he had thought to be the noble thing.

Was it the noble thing? Or are you simply a coward?

That question had been rattling around in his brain for hours, settling like acid in his gut and eating away at his every justification.

And once it had been introduced, he couldn't shake it. Was he protecting her? Or was he protecting himself? She had been very open about the fact that she had hidden away from the world, choosing to protect herself from further rejection because of the way her parents had treated her. Like an incidental. Like she didn't matter.

And he had…

Hadn't he hidden away from the world, too? Behind the facade of being a dragon, of being a soulless monster. Keeping everyone at a distance. Most especially the half brother who had been there that terrible night. Who had been wound around that most painful event.

The thought was enough to take his breath away. To realize that his own actions had been born not of a need to keep control, but out of fear. It ate away at the very foundation of who he believed he was. He thought himself strong. He thought himself in total command.

Now he wondered if he was still a boy, hiding from difficult feelings. Difficult decisions. Concealing the existence of the truth so that he didn't have to face it. Just as he had done with Nate.

But what life could she have with him? What did he offer to Gabriella? He knew what she did for him. She gave him hope. She made him see art, made him see beauty. With her, he experienced softness, hope, in a way that he hadn't done in his entire life. Yes, he knew exactly what she offered him, and he feared that all he had to offer her was his endless, dark well of neediness. Left open the night his parents died. It held nothing but fear, nothing but anguish, and those things consumed, they didn't give.

Suddenly, the door to his apartment swung open. He had to wonder for a moment just how much he'd had to drink, because there stood Gabriella, the light from the hallway illuminating her with a golden halo around her dark hair, making her look like an angel standing in the middle of hell. His own personal hell. As though she had come to raise him from perdition.

And he desperately wanted it to be so.

How was it that this young innocent could reduce the jaded playboy like himself to such a needy, desperate thing? How was it that she had reached inside of him and scraped him raw? He should have had all the control here. She should be the one in pain because he had ended things. And he should be able to move on as he had always done. And yet, he couldn't.

"Gabby," he said, the word raw and rough as his insides.

"You don't get to call me that," she said, sweeping into the room and slamming the door behind her. "Not unless you intend to fix what you did."

"My list of sins is long, Gabriella. You have to be more specific."

"The small matter of lying to me and breaking my heart." She crossed her arms, her proud chin tilted upward, her small frame vibrating with rage. "I understand. It took me a while, because I had to dig beneath my own pain to understand, but I do. You're afraid. Just like me. And just like me you are protecting yourself."

Hearing the words from Gabriella's lips made it even harder for him to deny. He had suspicions about his own behavior, but they were just that—suspicions. Gabriella knew him. And he trusted that. She had an intelligence about emotions, the kind that he could hardly lay claim to.

"But we can't do that anymore," she said. "It isn't worth it. What do we get for it? Years of wishing we were together? We can be what we're expected to be. We can be safe. No, Alex, I shouldn't be with you. I'm a princess. And I should be with a man who is at the very least a member of nobility, or failing that, not a complete and total dissolute playboy. You should be with a woman who is sophisticated, who has a tough outer shell and a lot more experience than I have. But that is what we want. We want each other. Because you're my deep love, Alex. The other half of my amulet. The one that I'll never forget. You are the hole in my soul, the one that I have carried from the day I was born and I wasn't even aware that it was there until the moment I met you."

Her words echoed inside him, rang with truth. It was the same for him. He knew it was the same for him.

"How?" He swallowed hard. "How do we just forget everything else?"

"I figure it's either that or we forget that we love each other, Alex. And I would so much rather forget my pain. I would so much rather forget my fear. I would rather forget that on paper we don't make any sense and just remember that I love you. In the end, doesn't that sound easier?"

His chest seized tight, his breathing becoming labored. "I'm not sure if there's anything simple about love, Gabriella."

"Maybe not. Maybe I'm living in a fantasy. But… Oh, Alex, how I would love to live in this fantasy with you. I know you think I'm young and silly—"

"No," he said. "I don't think you're silly. I think you are magically unspoiled by all of the things that have happened to you in your life. I think you are a gift that your parents didn't deserve, that they didn't appreciate. I think that you are a gift I don't deserve."

"Well, what's the use in being a gift that no one wants?"

He felt like his chest was going to crack open. "I do want you. I do. But…I am…a thousand years too old for you. A thousand ways too corrupt. Wouldn't you rather be with a different man?"

"No," she said, the word so simple, with no hesitation. "No one else made me want to come out of the library. I liked small things. Quiet things. And what I feel for you… it isn't quiet or small. It's big and loud and it rings in my ears, in my chest, and it terrifies me. But I want it still. I was so caught up in the fact that the rake could come after the wallflower that I didn't stop to think how amazing it was that I came out of hiding for you. Alex, the fact that I want you is a miracle in and of itself. I'm not sure you appreciate that."

He laughed, but there was no humor in the sound. "Believe me, I do."

"Well, so do I. I love you. And I'm sorry if that isn't sophisticated. I'm sorry if it wasn't supposed to happen.

But it did. And it's the most amazing, wonderful thing. So much better than hiding away. Please, come with me. Away from the guilt. Because I know you still feel guilty. But you were a boy. You have to forgive yourself."

He nodded slowly. "I do. Because you're right, I was a boy. But I'm not a boy now. I'm a man. Still, I was hiding like one. And it has to stop, Gabriella. You are right. I was very dedicated to the idea that I was a monster. Convincing you, to convince myself. Because I'm a very convenient hiding place. That mask was the best thing I had. It kept everyone away. But... I don't want that anymore. I thought that it made me strong. I convinced myself that I was turning away from the way my parents lived. Cutting myself off from that kind of reckless behavior, keeping myself from poisoning other people in my life. But I wasn't afraid for others. I was afraid for myself. But you are right. Living without you would be far worse than learning to let go of all this."

He took a step toward her, cupping the back of her head and gazing down into her dark eyes. "If you will have me, after all the things I said, after everything I have done, both before and since I met you, then I would be very honored if you would... I suppose I can ask you to marry me, can I?"

"No," she said, causing his heart to sink. "You can't. Because you haven't said you love me yet."

"I thought that was implied."

"Not good enough. I like art, I like poetry, I like books. I like all of the beauty laid out before me."

He felt a smile curve his lips upward. "My face isn't enough?"

"It's a start. But I need the words."

"I love you, beautiful Gabby."

"Really?" she asked, tears filling her eyes. The good kind of tears. The kind that made his chest ache and his whole body shake at the wonder of it. "Even though I'm not boring?"

"Most especially because you aren't boring. Because you are clever. Because you teach me things—about the world and about myself. I want to spend the rest of my life holding you, touching you, being with you. I want your lips to be the last lips I ever kiss. And your heart to be the only one I ever hold. And in case you missed it the first time, I love you."

She smiled, the kind of dreamy smile he had never dared hope to be on the receiving end of. The kind of dreamy smile he hadn't even known he ever wanted to be on the receiving end of. Amazing the things that his princess was teaching him. "That's better."

"Now can I propose to you?"

"You really want to get married, Alex?"

"Yes. Because that's what you deserve. Forever. All in. And…I still feel like there are things inside of me that I'll have to work through. I'm afraid that I'll take too much from you."

"Never. Maybe you will sometimes. But then, there will be other times when I take too much from you. We're not in half-and-half. We are all in. Forever. When you need to be carried, Alex, I'll carry you," she said, taking a step forward and resting her palm on his cheek. "And I know that when I need to be carried you'll carry me. That's what love is. It gives. We know what it looks like when people take, when they consume and do only what pleases them. But that isn't us. It isn't this."

"If I falter, Gabriella," he said, grabbing hold of her chin with his thumb and forefinger, "promise me you'll put me back on the path."

"You have my word."

"I can't paint you, Gabriella. I can't show you the way

that I see you. I can't explain it to you in terms of art, and really, I'm not all that good with poetry."

"Lies. You're wonderful with it."

"I'm really not. So I'll just say it plain, and honest. I love you. From now until forever."

"That's really all I need."

"No white tigers?"

She tapped her chin, as though she were considering it. "I wouldn't say no to a white tiger."

"Well," he said, "I may not be able to accommodate you there. But how about a white Christmas wedding?"

She smiled, throwing her arms around his neck and stretching up on her tiptoes to give him a kiss. "That sounds just about perfect."

EPILOGUE

A WEDDING BETWEEN a billionaire and a princess really was an amazing thing. Mostly because when titles and money were thrown around it became surprisingly easy to throw things together in only a couple of weeks.

The entire family came to help Gabriella and Alessandro celebrate their love. Love was always beautiful, but there was something particularly beautiful about watching Gabriella and Alessandro joined together. It wasn't simply the ring she wore on her finger, or the tiara she wore in her dark hair, nor was it the earrings that glittered in her ears. It was the love that radiated between them, the strange sort of symmetry evident there.

Giovanni had to wonder if their family blood was simply destined to love a D'Oro. If there was something ingrained on a soul-deep level that was inescapable. If so, he was glad of that. As he sat, watching his beloved eldest grandson pledge his life to the granddaughter of the woman he had always loved, he felt a sense of absolute completion wash through him.

Though he imagined that had something to do with the woman sitting at his side. Queen Lucia, his true lost mistress, finally returned to him. It was a miracle.

And it didn't matter how many years he had left to his name, because he knew they would be the happiest years yet. And he imagined there were very few people who could claim such a thing.

At his appointment last week the doctors had told him he was doing well, something no one had ever expected to happen at his age. They also told him he was healthier than should be possible. That he was a miracle. He wasn't entirely certain that he was a miracle, but there were certainly miracles all around him. Each and every one of his grandchildren, settled and fallen in love. Nate, brought into the family in a real and true way. Alessandro healed from the wounds left behind by his parents.

And Lucia by his side.

Yes, as he looked around the family estate, lushly decorated for Christmas, glittering with lights, ribbon and boughs of holly, he couldn't help but think that the miracle had nothing to do with him at all.

The miracle was, and had always been, love, available for anyone who would reach out and take it.

And though it was late in his life, he was taking it now.

He took Lucia's hand in his, just as Alessandro pulled Gabriella into his arms for a kiss. He looked at Lucia and saw that her eyes were fixed to the painting hanging in the great room. Perhaps scandalous in some ways, but then, when it came to the Di Sione family, it was difficult to say what was scandalous and what was simply everyday business.

"I love you," he said, squeezing Lucia's hand.

She took her eyes away from the painting and looked back at him, offering a slow smile.

"I can see that. I can see it clearly."

* * * * *

THE BABY
INHERITANCE

MAUREEN CHILD

To Patti Canterbury Hambleton—
Best friend since first grade and
still the absolute *Best*.

For all the laughs and tears
and crazy adventures.

I love you.

One

"**D**ivorce is reality," Reed Hudson told his client. "It's marriage that's the anomaly."

Carson Duke, America's favorite action-movie star, just stared at his attorney for a long minute, before saying, "That's cold."

Reed shook his head slowly. The man was here to end a marriage that most of the country looked on as a fairy tale come to life, and still he didn't want to accept the simple truth. Reed had seen this over and over again. Oh, most of the people who came to him were *eager* to end a marriage that had become inconvenient or boring or both. But there were a few people who came to him wishing they were anywhere but in his office, ending a relationship that they'd hoped was forever.

Forever. Even the thought nearly brought a smile. In his experience, both business and personal, there was no such thing as *forever.*

"Like I said," Reed told Carson with a shake of his head, "not cold. Reality."

"Harsh." Then Carson snorted a short laugh and crossed his legs, his ankle on top of his knee. Frowning a little, he asked quietly, "You ever been married?"

Now Reed laughed. "Oh, hell, no."

Just the idea of him ever getting married was ridiculous. His reputation alone, as what the tabloids called the "divorce attorney to the stars," was enough to make sure no woman he was involved with developed long-term plans. And representing most of Hollywood and New York in high-profile divorce cases had all started with a single client five years before. Reed had represented television's most likable comedian in a nasty split from a wife who made the "bunny boiler" look like a good time.

Word had spread in Hollywood and across celebrity lines, and soon Reed's practice was littered with the rich and famous. He enjoyed his work, relished protecting his clients from bad relationships and shattering the occasional prenup. And, if there was one thing he'd learned through the years, it was that even the best marriage could dissolve into misery.

But, he hadn't exactly needed his clients to teach him that lesson. His own family was a sterling example of just how badly marriages could go. His father was now on wife number five and living in London, while Reed's mother and husband number four were currently enjoying the heat and tropical atmosphere of Bali. And from what Reed had been hearing, his mother was already looking for husband number five. Thanks to his serially monogamous parents, Reed had ten siblings, full and half, ranging in age from three to thirty-two with another baby sister due any minute thanks to his father's ridiculously young, and apparently fertile, wife.

For most of his life, Reed, as the oldest child in the wildly eclectic and extended immediate family, had been the one who stepped in and kept things moving. When his siblings had a problem, they came to him. When his parents needed a fast divorce in order to marry their next "true love," they came to him. When the apocalypse finally arrived, he had no doubt that they would all turn to him, expecting Reed to save all of their asses. He was used to it and had long ago accepted his role in the Hudson clan. The fact that his experience as a mediator had served him so well as an attorney was simply a bonus.

Looking at his latest client, Reed thought back over the past year and remembered the innumerable articles and pictures flashed across the tabloids. Carson Duke and his wife, Tia Brennan, had graced the covers of magazines and the pages of newspapers, and the two had been favorites on the celebrity websites. They'd had a whirlwind romance that had ended in a fairy-tale wedding on a Hawaiian cliff overlooking the Pacific.

Stories proclaiming the nearly magical connection between the two, holding them up as examples of what "real" love looked like, had been printed, pored over and discussed all across the world. Yet here Carson sat, a little more than a year later, hiring Reed to represent him in a divorce that promised to be as high-profile as the marriage had been.

"Let's get down to business then," Reed said and looked at the man across from him. Just like in his movies, Carson Duke looked tough, determined and had the cool, hard gaze of a seasoned warrior. Not surprising, since the star had been a US Marine before turning to Hollywood. "First tell me what your wife thinks about all of this."

Carson sighed, shoved one hand through his hair and then blurted out, "It was her idea. Things have been rough between us for a while now." It looked as though every word he spoke tasted bitter. "She—*we*—decided that it would be better, for both of us, if we just end the marriage and walk away now, before things get ugly."

"Uh-huh." Duke sounded reasonable, but so many of Reed's clients did when they were first entering the muddy swamp of litigation. Couples determined to remain "friendly" eventually succumbed to name-calling and vicious diatribes. Reed wasn't looking forward to watching Carson and his wife go down that path. "I need to know—are you seeing someone else? Is another woman at the bottom of all this? I will find out sooner or later, so it would be better for all of us if you tell me now so there are no surprises."

Carson stiffened, but Reed held up a hand to silence what would no doubt be a tirade of insult and outrage. All of his clients tended to paint themselves as the injured party, and if Reed wasn't careful, he could be blindsided by a scorned lover testifying for the opposition. Better to have as much information as possible from the jump. "These are questions I have to ask. If you're smart, you'll answer."

Carson stewed in his chair for a second or two, looked as though he'd like to punch something, then surged to his feet in one smooth motion.

"No," he snapped, and paced across the room to stop at one of the wide windows overlooking the sweep of ocean stretching out into the distance. He stared through the glass for several long seconds, as if trying to calm down, then turned his head to look directly at Reed. "No. I didn't cheat. Neither did Tia."

Reed's eyebrows arched. First time he'd heard a client *defend* a spouse. "You're sure about her?"

"Absolutely." Carson shook his head and looked back through the glass at the sunlight dancing on the ocean's surface. "This isn't about cheating or lying or any other damn thing."

Intriguing. The old *irreconcilable differences* plea was usually just an excuse to keep secrets private. There were always reasons for a divorce, and in Reed's experience, cheating was right at the top of the list.

"Then why are you here?" Reed asked, leaning back in his black leather desk chair.

"Because we're not happy anymore." Carson laid one hand on the glass. "It started out great," he continued as if to himself. "Tia and I met and it was like…magic. You know?"

"No," Reed said, smiling. "But I'll take your word for it."

Carson shook his head. "We couldn't keep our hands off each other. From that first moment, there was something powerful between us." He smiled, and shot Reed another quick glance. "It was more than sex, though. We used to talk all night, laughing, planning, talking about moving out of Hollywood, having kids. But the last few months, between work and other demands on both of us…hell. We hardly see each other anymore. So why be married?"

Pitiful excuse to sentence yourself to divorce court, but then, Reed silently acknowledged, he'd heard worse. He'd once represented a man who claimed he needed a divorce because his wife kept hiding cookies from him. Reed had almost advised him to buy his own damn cookies, but had figured it was none of his business. Because the cookies weren't the real reason. They were simply the excuse. The man wanted a divorce; Reed would get it for him. That was his job. He wasn't a marriage counselor, after all.

"All right then," Reed said briskly. "I'll get the paperwork started. Tia won't be contesting the divorce?"

"No." Carson shoved both hands into his pockets. "Like I said. Her idea."

"That'll make it easier," Reed told him.

Wryly, Carson whispered, "I suppose that's a good thing."

"It is." Reed watched his client and felt a stir of sympathy. He wasn't a cold man. He knew that people came to him when their worlds were dissolving. In order to maintain a professional distance, he sometimes came off as harsh when all he was trying to do was to be a rock for his clients. To be the one stable point in a suddenly rocking world. And as he studied Carson Duke, he knew the man didn't need pity, he needed someone to guide him through unfamiliar waters. "Trust me," Reed said. "You don't want a long, drawn-out battle described daily in the tabloids."

Carson shuddered at the idea. "I can't even take the trash out at my house without some photographer leaning out of a tree for a picture. You know, on the drive down here from Malibu, I was telling myself that it'd be a hell of a lot easier on most of us if your office was in LA—but getting away from most of the paparazzi is worth the drive."

Over the years, Reed had told himself the same

thing about relocating to Los Angeles many times, but damned if he could convince himself to move. A quick glance around his office only reinforced that feeling. The building itself was old—built in 1890—though thankfully it had been spared the Victorian gingerbread so popular at the time. He'd bought the building, had it completely remodeled and now, it was just as he wanted it. Character on the outside, sleek and elegant on the inside, plus the office was only a fifteen-minute drive from his home.

Besides, Reed preferred Orange County. Liked the fact that Newport Beach sprawled out in front of his two-story building crouched on the Pacific Coast Highway and he had the majestic sweep of ocean behind him. Sure, in the summer the streets were crowded with tourists—but he'd have the same problem in LA without the beautiful setting. Newport Beach was more laid-back than LA, but upscale enough to convince clients they were with the right attorney. Besides, if he had to drive the 405 freeway every night to get from his office to his home at the Saint Regis hotel in Laguna Beach, he'd be spending more than two hours a night just sitting in traffic. If clients wanted the best, then they'd better be ready to do the drive.

"I'll have the papers drawn up and messengered to you in a few days."

"No need," the other man said. "I'm taking a few days. Staying at the Saint Regis Monarch. I've got a suite there."

Since Reed lived in a massive suite at the exclusive, five-star resort, he knew the hotel would give Carson the distance he wanted from Hollywood and the scoop-hungry photographers who would be hunting him once news of an impending divorce hit the media. And it would hit, no matter how they tried to keep it quiet. If Carson or Tia's people didn't release the news, then someone along the chain of information would. There were always leaks no matter how hard you tried to keep things confidential. It wouldn't come from Reed's staff, that he knew. They were paid extremely well—not just for their expertise, but for their discretion—and knew their jobs depended on their ability to keep their clients' business to themselves.

But there were others out there Reed had no control over. Everyone from valets at the Monarch to desk clerks and hotel maids. Once the media found out where Carson was staying, they'd continue to dig until they found out why the action star was holed up sixty miles from his house.

"You live at the Monarch, don't you?" Carson asked.

"Yeah, I do. So once the paperwork is completed, I'll have it all sent to your room for signing."

"Convenient, huh?" Carson said wryly. "Anyway, I'm registered under the name Wyatt Earp."

Reed laughed. The wildly famous usually signed into hotels under false names to keep those *not* in their immediate circle from knowing where they were. "Got it," he said. "I'll be in touch."

"Right." Carson nodded. "Thanks, I guess."

Reed watched the man go and once the office door was closed again, he walked to the windows behind his desk and stared out at the view of the ocean as his client had done only moments ago. He'd been through this so many times now, with so many people, he knew what Carson Duke was feeling, thinking. The big decision had been made. The divorce was in play. Now he was feeling a mixture of relief and sorrow and wondering if he was doing the right thing.

Oh, sure, there were plenty of people who divorced with joy in their hearts and a spring in their steps. But they weren't the rule. Generally, people felt the pain of losing something they'd once pinned their hopes and dreams on. Hell, Reed had seen it in his own family time and again. Each of his parents invariably entered a marriage thinking that *this* time would be the last. The *one*. True love and they would finally live happily ever after.

"And they're never right," he murmured, shaking his head.

Once again, he was reminded that he'd made the right life choice in *never* letting himself fall into the trap of convincing himself that good, healthy lust was some kind of romantic love destined to transform his life.

At that thought, he snorted in amusement, then walked back to his desk to begin drafting Carson Duke's divorce papers.

Lilah Strong took her time driving along Pacific Coast Highway. The scenery was wildly different from what she was used to and she intended to enjoy it in spite of the hot ball of anger nestled deep in her belly. She didn't like being angry. It always felt to her like a waste of emotion. The person she was furious with didn't care how she felt. Her anger affected no one but *her*… by making her a little nauseous.

But knowing that did nothing to ease the underlying tension that burned inside her. So rather than try to ease that uncomfortable feeling, she briefly distracted herself by glancing out at the ocean.

It was lovely—surfers gliding toward shore on the

tops of waves. Sunlight glinting off the deep blue surface of the sea. Boats with jewel-toned sails and children
building castles in the sand armed with nothing more
than tiny buckets and shovels.

Lilah was a mountain girl, through and through.
Her preferred view was of a tree-laden slope, wide-
open meadows covered in bright splashes of wildflowers or the snowy mountainsides that backed up to her
house. But looking out at the Pacific was a nice change.
Of course, she had time to look at the sea while driving only because she wasn't actually "driving." It was
more…parking.

Pacific Coast Highway was completely backed up
with locals, tourists and, it seemed to her, every surfer
in Southern California. It was the middle of June and
Lilah could imagine that the crowds would only be getting thicker as the summer went on. But thankfully, that
wouldn't be her problem.

In a day or two, she'd be back in the mountains, leaving her companion here in Orange County. That thought
gave her heart a hard squeeze, but there was nothing she
could do about it. It wasn't as if she'd had a choice in
any of this. If she'd been someone else, maybe she would
have considered ignoring facts. But she couldn't live a
lie. She had to do the right thing—even if it felt wrong.

Glancing into the rearview mirror, she looked at her
companion and said, "You're awfully quiet. Too much
to think about to leave room for talking, hmm? I know
how you feel."

Her own mind was spinning. Lilah had been dread-
ing this trip to California for two weeks and now that
it was here, she was still trying to think of a way out
of the situation she found herself in. But no matter how

she looked at it, Lilah was stuck. As was her friend in the backseat.

If she were doing this on her turf, so to speak, she might feel a little more in control. Back in her small mountain town in Utah, she had friends. People she could count on to stand with her. Here, all she had were her own two feet and that sinking sensation in the pit of her stomach.

Orange County, California, was only an hour-and-a-half flight from Lilah's home, but it might as well have been on the other side of the world. She was walking into the unknown with no way out but *through*.

By the time she parked, helped her friend out of the car and walked into the law office, Lilah's stomach was swirling with nerves. The building was Victorian on the outside and a sweep of glass and chrome on the inside. It was unsettling, as if designed to keep clients off guard, and maybe that was the idea. The floors were a polished, high-gleam hardwood, but the walls were decorated with modern paintings consisting of splashes of bright color. The reception desk where a stern-faced, middle-aged woman sat sentry was a slab of glass atop shining steel legs. Even the banister gliding along the wood staircase was made up of steel spindles faced with a wall of glass. It was cold, sterile and just a little intimidating. Oh, she was now sincerely prepared to dislike the man she was there to see. Lilah stiffened her spine and approached the reception desk. "I'm Lilah Strong. I'm here to see Reed Hudson."

The woman looked from Lilah to her friend and back again. "Do you have an appointment?"

"No. I'm here on behalf of his sister, Spring Hudson

Bates," Lilah said and watched a flicker of interest glitter in the woman's eyes. "It's important that I see him now."

"One moment." The woman watched Lilah as she picked up a phone and pressed a single button. "Mr. Hudson, there's a woman here to see you. She claims to have been sent by your sister Spring."

Claims? Lilah swallowed the spurt of impatience that jumped into her throat. It took another moment or two before the receptionist hung up and waved one hand at the staircase. "Mr. Hudson will see you. Up the stairs, first door on the left."

"Thank you." Lilah and her companion walked away, but as she went, she felt the other woman's curious gaze follow her.

At the landing, Lilah paused to settle herself outside the heavy double doors. She took a breath, then turned the knob and walked inside.

The outer office was small, but bright, with sunlight pouring through windows that overlooked the ocean. Lilah stepped inside and took a breath, pausing long enough to appreciate the elegant furnishings. The wood floors shone. In one corner, there was a healthy ficus tree in a silver pot. A pair of gray chairs separated by a black table sat against one wall.

A young woman with short black hair and brown eyes sat at a sleek black desk and gave Lilah a friendly smile as she entered. "Hello. I'm Karen, Mr. Hudson's executive assistant. You must be Ms. Strong. Mr. Hudson's waiting for you."

She stood and walked to a pair of double doors. Opening them, she stepped back and Lilah steeled herself before she walked into the lion's den.

The man's office was enormous—no doubt designed

to impress and intimidate. *Mission accomplished*, she thought. A wall of glass behind his desk afforded a spectacular view of the ocean, and on her left, the glass wall continued, displaying a bird's-eye view of Pacific Coast Highway and the crowds that cluttered the street and sidewalks.

The wood floor shone here, too, with the slices of sunlight lying on it sparkling like diamonds. There were several expensive-looking rugs dotting the floor, and the furniture here was less chrome and more dark leather. Still didn't seem to fit in a Victorian building, but it was less startling to the senses than the first-floor decor. But, Lilah told herself, she wasn't here to critique the results of what some designer had done to the stately old building. Instead, she was here to face down the man now standing up behind his desk.

"Who are you?" he demanded. "And what do you know about my sister Spring?"

His voice was deep, rumbling around the room like thunder. He was tall—easily six feet three or four—with thick black hair expensively trimmed to look casual. He wore a black, pin-striped suit and a white dress shirt accented with a red power tie. His shoulders were broad, his jaw square, his eyes green, and as they focused on her, they didn't look friendly.

Well, she thought, that was fine, since she wasn't feeling very friendly, either. He was as intimidating as the plush office, and far more attractive—which had nothing to do with anything, she reminded herself.

Still, she was glad she'd taken care with her appearance before this meeting. At home, she went days without even bothering with makeup. Today, she wore her own version of a power suit. Black slacks, red shirt and short red jacket. Her black boots had a two-inch heel, adding to her five-foot-six-inch height. She was as prepared for this meeting as it was possible to be. Which wasn't saying much.

"I'm Lilah Strong."

"I was told who you are," he said. "What I don't know is why you're here."

"Right." She took a deep breath, then blew it out again. Deliberately striding across the floor in a quick march, she heard her heels click on the wood then soften on the rugs as she approached him. When she was so close she caught a whiff of his aftershave—a subtle scent that reminded her of the forests at home—she stopped. With his wide, black matte desk between them, she looked into his deep green eyes and said, "Spring was my friend. That's why I'm here. She asked me to do something for her and I couldn't say no. That's the *only* reason I'm here."

"All right."

That deep voice seemed to reverberate inside her, leaving her more shaken than she wanted to admit. Why was he so gorgeous? Why did the wary look in his eyes seem sexy rather than irritating? And *why* was she letting an unwanted attraction scatter her thoughts?

"I'm curious." His gaze flicked briefly to Lilah's friend before shifting back to her. "Do you usually bring your baby with you to meetings?"

She lifted her chin and glanced down at the baby girl on her left hip. Here was the reason for leaving home, for facing down a man with ice in his eyes. If it had been up to her, Lilah never would have come. She wouldn't be standing here in Reed Hudson's office with a ball of cold lead in the pit of her stomach. But this wasn't her choice and no matter how hard it was, she would do as Spring had asked.

Rosie slapped both hands together and squealed. Lilah's answering smile faded as she turned her gaze back to the man watching her.

"Rose isn't my baby," she said, with more than a twinge of regret as she met his gaze coolly. "She's *yours*."

Two

Instantly, Reed went on red alert.

The cold, dispassionate demeanor that had made him a legend in court dropped over him like a familiar jacket. The woman looking at him as if he were a worm, just slithering out from under a rock, was beautiful but clearly delusional.

Over the years, there had been a few predatory women who'd tried to convince him they were pregnant with his child. But, since he was always careful, he'd been able to get rid of them easily enough. And this woman, he'd never been with. That he was sure of, since a man didn't forget a woman like this one.

"I don't have a baby." The very idea was ludicrous. Given his background, his family, his career, if there was one lesson he'd learned it was don't build a family of his own. Since he was sixteen, he'd never been without a condom. "If that's all," he continued briskly, "you can show yourself out."

"Nice," she commented with a slow shake of her head.

The tone of her voice caught his attention. It was just as coolly dismissive as his own. His gaze caught hers and he couldn't mistake the anger and disdain shining in those clear blue eyes. "Problem?"

"No more than I expected from a man like you," she countered and bounced a little, as if to entertain the baby babbling on her hip.

"A man like me," he repeated, curious now. "And you know me, *how*?"

"I know that you were Spring's brother and that you weren't there to help her when she needed it." Her words rushed out as if flowing on a tide of fury. "I know that when you see a child who looks just like your sister you don't even ask a question."

His eyes narrowed. "My sister."

She huffed out a breath. "That's what I said." Briefly, she looked at the baby and her mouth curved slightly. "Her name is Rose and she's Spring's daughter." At the mention of her name, the tiny girl bounced in place and slapped her hands against the woman's shoulder. "That's right, Rosie. You're your mommy's girl, aren't you?"

As if in answer, the baby clapped tiny hands and chortled in some weird baby version of a giggle. And while the two of them smiled at each other, Reed shifted his gaze from the lovely woman to the baby in her arms. *Spring's daughter.* Now that he knew, now that he wasn't on automatic defense, he could see his sister's features, miniaturized on her child. Fine, black hair curling about

a rounded face. Eyes so green they shone like emeralds—
the same shade as Spring's.

As his own, come to that.

Instantly, without even being told, he *knew* his sister
was gone. Spring had looked all her life for real love.
There wasn't a chance in hell she ever would have left
her daughter if she'd had a choice.

And the baby was clearly a Hudson. Then there was
the fact that even in so small a child, he saw the stubborn chin his sister had boasted. Spring had a daughter
he'd known nothing about. He understood the woman's
anger now. Her accusation of not being there for Spring
when she needed him most. But he would have been,
he assured himself silently. If she'd come to him, he'd
have—how was it possible that she *hadn't* come to him?
Everyone in his family came to him for help. Why hadn't
Spring?

Then he remembered the last time he saw his younger
sister. More than two years ago, Spring had come to
him, wanting him to arrange for an advance on her trust.
She'd been in love. Again.

Frowning, he remembered his reaction, too. Spring
was one of those people who went through life wearing rose-colored glasses. She saw only the best in people—even those who had no best at all. Spring refused
to recognize that *some* people simply weren't worth her
loyalty or her affection.

It had been the third time she'd been in love—and
that last time was just like the others before had been.
Without fail, Spring seemed to migrate toward men with
few morals, little ambition and less money. He'd always
thought it was because Spring thought she could "save"
them. And that never worked.

Always on the lookout for love, she would invariably end up in Reed's office asking for money to pay off the latest loser so she could move on with her life. But that last time, Reed had been forewarned by yet another sister. Savannah had met Spring's lover and she'd been worried enough that she'd called Reed. He'd run a background check on Spring's love of the moment and found a criminal background—fraud, identity theft and forgery. But Spring hadn't wanted to hear the warnings. She had insisted that Coleman Bates had changed. That he deserved a second chance.

Reed recalled clearly telling her that the man had *had* a second chance—even a third—and hadn't changed. But Spring was in love and wouldn't listen. Standing there now, though, in front of the child she'd left behind, Reed frowned, remembering he'd told Spring to grow the hell up and stop expecting him to sweep in and take care of whatever mess she created. Hurt, angry, Spring had walked out of his office. So later, when she'd really needed him, his sister hadn't called on Reed. And now it was too late for him to make it up to her.

A swift stab of guilt pierced the edges of Reed's heart but he fought it back. Regret was indulgence. It wouldn't help Spring, couldn't ease the pain of her loss. He'd done what he thought was best for his sister at the time. For the family. And if she had come to him for help in extricating herself from the relationship, he assured himself, he would have done all he could for her. Now all he could do was find answers.

"What happened to Spring?"

"She died two months ago."

He gritted his teeth as the harsh truth shook him to his bones. He'd known it, *felt* it, but somehow hearing it made it harder. A quick, sharp slash of pain tore at him and was immediately buried beneath a fresh wave of regret, sorrow. Reed scrubbed one hand across his face then focused on the baby again before shifting to meet Lilah Strong's clear blue eyes. "That's hard to hear."

Spring was his half sister on his father's side and five years younger than Reed. She'd always been so bright, so happy, so damn trusting. And now she was gone.

"I'm sorry. I shouldn't have said it so abruptly."

Shaking his head, he stared into those eyes of hers. So blue, they were nearly violet. They shone with sympathy he didn't want and didn't need. His pain was private. Not something he would share with anyone, let alone a stranger.

To cover the turmoil raging within, he said simply, "There is no way to soften news like that."

"You're right. Of course, you're right." Those eyes shifted, changed with her emotions, and now he read grief of her own mingling with a simmering anger in their depths.

He was no more interested in that than he was in her sympathy.

"What happened to my sister?"

"There was a car accident," she said simply. "Someone ran a red light…"

His eyes narrowed. "Drunk driver?"

"No," she said, shaking her head and patting the baby's back all at once. "An elderly man had a heart attack. He was killed in the accident, as well."

So there was no one to hold responsible. No one to be furious with. To blame. Reed was left with an impotent feeling that he didn't care for.

"You said this happened two months ago," he said

quietly, thoughtfully. "Why are you only coming to me now?"

"Because I didn't know about you," she said, then looked around the office. "Look, the baby needs a change. Do you mind if we take this conversation over to the couch?"

"What?"

She was already headed for his black leather sofa. Before he could say anything, she'd set the infant down and reached into what had to be a diaper bag slung over her shoulder for supplies.

Struck dumb by the action, he only watched as she expertly changed the baby's diaper, then handed the folded-up used one to him. "What am I supposed to do with this?"

Reluctantly, it seemed, her mouth curved and damned if he didn't like the look of it.

"Um," she said wryly, "I'd go for throwing it away."

Stupid. Of course. He glanced at his small office trash can, then shook his head, crossed to the door and opened it. Signaling to his assistant, he held out the diaper and ordered, "Dispose of this."

"Yes, sir." Karen accepted the diaper as she would have an explosive device, then turned away.

Once the door was closed again, Reed looked at the baby, now standing alongside the glossy black coffee table, smacking both hands on the surface and laughing to herself. Shaking his head, he thought of Spring and felt another quick twinge of pain. Still watching the baby, he asked Lilah, "What did you mean you didn't know about me until now?"

She tossed that thick mass of wavy red-gold hair behind her shoulder and looked up at him as she repacked the baby's supplies. "I mean, that until last week, I didn't know Spring had a family. She never talked about you. About any relatives at all. I thought she was alone."

That stung more than he would have thought possible. His sister had wiped him from her life? So much so that her best friend didn't even know of his existence? He scrubbed one hand across his face and regretted that last conversation with his sister. Maybe he could have been kinder. More understanding. But he'd assumed, as he supposed everyone did, that there would be more time. That he would, once again, be called on to dig Spring out of trouble, and so he'd been impatient and now she was gone and the chance to make things right had vanished with her.

"She left two letters," Lilah said and held out an envelope toward him. "I read mine. This one is yours."

Reed took it, checked that it was still sealed, then noted Spring's familiar scrawl across the front. He glanced at the baby, still entertaining herself, then he opened the envelope and pulled out the single sheet of paper.

Reed. If you're reading this, I'm dead. God, that's a weird thought. But if Lilah brought you this letter, she's also brought you my daughter. I'm asking you to take care of her. Love her. Raise her. Yes, I know I could ask Mom or one of my sisters, but honestly, you're the only one in our family I can really count on.

Well, that hit him hard, considering that in their last conversation he hadn't given her the help she'd wanted. Gritting his teeth, he went back to the letter.

Rosie needs you, Reed. I'm trusting you to do the right thing because you always do. Lilah Strong has been my friend and my family for almost two years, so play nice. She's also been Rosie's "other mother," so she can answer any questions you have and she can be a big help to you.

As usual, you were right about Coleman. He left as soon as I got pregnant. But before he left, I got him to sign away his rights to Rosie. She doesn't need him in her life.

I love you, Reed, and I know Rosie will, too. So thanks in advance—or from the grave. Whichever. Spring.

He didn't know whether to smile or howl. The letter was so like Spring—making light of a situation that most people wouldn't think about. In seconds, vignettes of Spring's life raced through Reed's mind. He saw her as a baby, a child who followed him around whenever they were together, a teenager who loved nothing more than shocking her parents and finally, a woman who never found the kind of love she'd always searched for.

He folded the paper slowly, then tucked it away again before he let himself look at Spring's child. The baby was clearly well cared for, loved…happy.

Now it was up to him to see that she stayed that way. At that thought everything in Reed went cold and still. He knew what his duty was. Knew what Spring would expect of him. But damned if he knew a thing about babies.

"I see panic in your eyes."

Instantly, Reed's normal demeanor dropped over him. He sent Lilah a cool stare. "I don't panic."

"Really?" she said, clearly not believing him. "Because your expression tells me you're wishing Rosie and I were anywhere but here."

He didn't appreciate being read so easily. Reed had been told by colleagues and judges alike that his poker face was the best in the business. Knowing one small baby and one very beautiful woman had shattered his record was a little humbling. But no need to let her know that.

"You're wrong. What I'm wondering is what I'm going to do next." And that didn't come easy to him, either. Reed always had a plan. And a backup plan. And a plan to use if the backup failed. But at the moment, he was at a loss.

"What you're going to do?" The woman stood up, smiled down at the baby then turned a stony stare on him. "You're going to take care of Rosie."

"Obviously," he countered. The question was, *how*? Irritated, he pushed one hand through his hair and muttered, "I'm not exactly prepared for a baby."

"No one ever is," Lilah told him. "Not even people who like to plan their lives down to the last minute. Babies throw every plan out the nearest window."

"Wonderful."

Rosie squealed until the sound hit a pitch Reed was afraid might make his ears bleed. "That can't be normal."

Lilah laughed. "She's a happy baby."

Tipping her head to one side, Lilah watched him. "After I found out about Spring's family, I did some research. I know you have a lot of siblings, so you must be used to babies."

Another irritation, that he'd been looked into, though

he knew potential clients did it all the time. "Yeah, a lot of siblings that I usually saw once or twice a year."

"Not a close family," she mused.

"You could say that," Reed agreed. Hard to be close, though, when there were so damn many of them. You practically needed a spreadsheet just to keep track of his relatives.

"My family's not at issue right now," he said, shifting his gaze away from blue eyes trying to see too much to the baby looking up at him with Spring's eyes. "Right now, I've got a problem to solve."

Lilah sighed. "She's not a problem, she's a *baby*."

Reed flicked Lilah a glance. "She's also my problem. Now."

He would take care of her, raise her, just as his sister had wanted. But first, he had to get things lined up. He'd made his fortune, survived his wildly eclectic family, by having a plan and sticking to it. The plan now entailed arranging for help in taking care of Spring's daughter.

He worked long hours and would need someone on site to handle the child's day-to-day needs. It would take a little time to arrange for the best possible nanny. So the problem became what to do with the baby until he could find the right person.

His gaze settled on Lilah Strong. And he considered the situation. She already knew and cared about the baby. Yes, she still looked as though she'd like to slap him, but that didn't really matter, did it? What was important was getting the baby settled in. He had a feeling he could convince this woman to help him with that. If he offered her enough money to compensate her for her time.

He knew better than most just how loudly money

could talk to those who didn't have any. "I have a proposition for you."

Surprise, then suspicion, flashed in her blue eyes just before they narrowed on him. "What sort of proposition?"

"The sort that involves a lot of money," he said shortly, then turned and walked to his desk. Reaching into the bottom drawer, he pulled out a leather-bound checkbook and laid it, open and ready, on top of his desk. "I want to hire you to stay for a while. Take care of the baby—"

"Her *name* is Rosie…"

"Right. Take care of Rosie then, until I can arrange for a full-time nanny." He picked up a pen, clicked it into life then gave her a long, cool look. "I'll pay whatever you want."

Her mouth dropped open and she laughed shortly, shaking her head as if she couldn't believe what was happening. Fine. If she was unable to come up with a demand, he'd make an offer and they could negotiate from there. "Fifty thousand dollars," he said easily.

"Fifty?" Her eyes were wide. Astonished.

"Not enough? All right, a hundred thousand." Normally, he might have bid lower, but this was an emergency and he couldn't afford to have her say no.

"Are you crazy?"

"Not at all," he said with a shrug to emphasize that the money meant nothing to him. "I pay for what I need when I need it. And, as I believe it will take me at least a week or two to find and hire an appropriate nanny, I'm willing to buy interim help."

"I'm not for sale."

He smiled now. How many times had he heard that

statement just before settling on the right amount? Everyone had a price—the only challenge came in finding the magic number. "I'm not trying to buy you," Reed assured her, "just rent you for a week or two."

"You have enough arrogance for two or three people," she said.

He straightened up, shot her a level look. "It's not arrogance. It's doing what needs to be done. I can do that with your help—which allows you to continue to be a part of the child's—"

"Rosie's—"

"—life," he finished with a nod at her correction. "You can stay, make sure the person I hire is right for the job. Or, you can leave and go home now."

Of course, he didn't believe for a moment that she would leave the baby until she was absolutely sure of the child's well-being. That was written all over her face. Her body language practically *screamed* defensive mode. And he would use her desire to protect the baby for his own purposes. Reed Hudson always got what he wanted. Right now, that included Lilah Strong.

He could see her thinking and it wasn't difficult to discern her thoughts from the expressions flitting across her features. She was still furious with him for whatever reasons, but she wasn't ready to walk away from the baby yet. She would need to see for herself that Rosie was settled into her new home.

So, whether she realized it or not, Lilah Strong would do exactly what Reed wanted.

"I'll stay," she said finally, still watching the baby stagger around the coffee table like a happy drunk. "Until you've found the right nanny."

Then she turned and looked at Reed. "But I won't be paid. I won't be *rented*. I'll do it for Rosie. Not you."

He hid a smile. "Good. Now, I've a few more appointments this afternoon, so why don't you and the—" he caught himself and said instead "—*Rosie* head over to my place. I'll be there at about six."

"Fine," she said. "Where do you live?"

"My assistant, Karen, will give you all of the particulars." He checked the platinum watch on his wrist. "For now…"

"Fine. You're busy. I get it." She slung the diaper bag over her shoulder, then reached down to scoop up the baby. Once Rosie was settled on her hip, she looked up at him. "I'll see you later then. We can talk about all of this."

"All right." He kept the satisfaction he felt out of his voice. She walked past him and her scent seemed to reach out for him. Lemons, he thought. Lemons and sage. It was every bit as tantalizing as the woman herself.

He watched her go, his gaze sliding from the lush fall of that golden red hair down to the curve of a first-class behind. His body stirred as her scent seemed to sink deep inside him, making him want things that would only complicate an already messy situation.

Knowing that, though, didn't ease the hunger.

"You *live* in a hotel?" Lilah demanded the moment Reed walked through the door later that afternoon.

For hours, she'd wandered the expansive suite, astonished at the luxury, the oddity, of anyone actually living in a hotel. Okay, her own mother and stepfather lived on board a cruise ship, traveling constantly from country to country. They enjoyed being somewhere different every day, though it would have driven Lilah crazy.

But living in a hotel? When there were a zillion houses to choose from? Who did that? Well, all right, she'd heard of movie stars doing it, but Reed Hudson was a lawyer, for heaven's sake. Granted, a very successful, obviously very *rich* lawyer, but still. Didn't the man want a home? A hotel was so…impersonal.

Though she'd noticed a lot of framed photos of what had to be members of his family scattered throughout the two-bedroom, two-bath suite. So, she told herself, he wasn't as separate from the Hudson clan as he pretended. That made her feel both better and worse.

Better because Rosie would have more family than just this one seemingly cold and distant man. But worse because if he did care about his family, why hadn't he been there for Spring when she'd needed him?

He shut the door behind him, then simply stood there, staring at her. Those green eyes of his seemed to spear right through her and Lilah could only imagine how good he must be in court. Any opposing witness would quail beneath that steady, cool stare.

"You have a problem with the hotel suite?" He tucked both hands into the pockets of his slacks.

"It's lovely and you know it." And, unlike his office, the space was decorated in more than black, chrome and gray.

The living room was wide and dotted with twin lemon-yellow chairs opposite a sky blue sofa, all of them overstuffed and just begging someone to drop in and relax for a while. The tables were a honey-colored wood and the rugs on the tile floor were splashes of jewel tones. There was an oak dining set at the edge of a small, stocked wet bar, and a grouping of cream-colored lounge chairs on the terrace ran the length of the suite. Each of the two bedrooms was done in shades of cream and green and the bathrooms were luxurious, spa-like spaces with stand-alone tubs big enough to hold a party in and showers studded with full-body sprays.

From the terrace, there was a spectacular view of the ocean in the distance, with the meticulously cared-for golf course and a sea of red-tiled roofs in the surrounding neighborhood closer up. The hotel itself looked like a castle plunked down in the middle of a beach city and felt light-years away from her own home, a cabin in the mountains.

Though it was much smaller than this hotel suite, her cabin afforded beautiful views, too, of a lake and the mountains and a meadow that in spring was dotted with wildflowers and the deer that came to graze through it. She was out of her element here and that made her feel slightly off balance. Which, Lilah told herself, was not a good thing when dealing with a man like Reed Hudson.

"Where's the baby?" he asked, his gaze shifting around the room before settling on her again.

"Rosie—" she emphasized the baby girl's name "— is asleep in the crib the hotel provided." Honestly, how was he going to be a parent to the little girl if he couldn't even seem to say her name?

"Good." He slipped out of his jacket, tossed it across the back of a chair and walked toward the wet bar near the gas fireplace. As he reached for a bottle of scotch, he loosened the precise knot of his tie and opened the collar of his shirt. Why that minor action should strike Lilah as completely sexy, she couldn't have said.

"I called ahead," Reed was saying. "Told Andre you

were coming and to see that you had everything you needed."

"Andre." Lilah thought back to the moment she'd entered the hotel to be greeted by an actual *butler*. If it hadn't been for the man's friendly smile and eagerness to help, she might have been completely intimidated by the snooty accent and his quiet efficiency. "He was wonderful. Couldn't do enough to help us and Rosie loved him. But I can't believe this suite comes with a butler."

One corner of his mouth quirked as he poured himself a scotch. "Andre's more than a butler. Sometimes I think he's a miracle worker."

"I'm convinced," she admitted. "He arranged for the crib and had a wide selection of baby food stocked in your pantry. He even provided a bright blue teddy bear that Rosie already loves."

Reed smiled and even from across the room Lilah felt the punch of it. If anything, her sense of balance dissolved just a bit more.

"You want a drink?"

She thought about refusing, simply because she wasn't ready to relax around him yet. But after the day she'd had… "Wine, if you have it. White."

He nodded, got the wine from the refrigerator and poured her a glass. Carrying both drinks to the sofa, he sat down and handed the wine to her when she joined him, taking a seat on the opposite corner.

Lilah took a sip, let the wine settle her a bit. Being this close to Reed Hudson was a little unnerving. The anger she'd been living with for the past few weeks still simmered deep inside her, but looking at him now, she had to admit it wasn't only anger she was feeling. She had another slow sip of wine and reminded herself just why she was there.

"Why are you so willing to raise Rosie?" she asked, her voice shattering the silence.

He studied the golden scotch in the heavy glass tumbler for a long moment before taking a swallow. "Because Spring asked me to."

"Just like that."

He looked at her, his green eyes as clear and sharp as emeralds under a spotlight. "Just like that. The baby—*Rosie*—" he corrected before she could "—is a Hudson. She's family and I look out for my family."

"Enough to change your whole life?"

A wry smile curved his mouth briefly. "Life's always changing," he mused. "With a family like mine, nothing ever stays the same."

"Okay, but…" Waving one hand to encompass the elegant surroundings, Lilah said, "You're not exactly living in a baby-friendly environment."

"I know." His gaze slipped around the open room, then he nodded at her. "That's one of the reasons you're here. You've got more experience with babies than I do. So you'll know how to baby-proof this place temporarily."

"Temporarily?" she asked.

"Obviously, I'll need a house," he said, taking another drink of his scotch. "Until now, the hotel's worked well for me. Butler service, daily maids and twenty-four-hour room service."

"It does sound good," she admitted, but didn't think she'd be able to live in such a cutoff, sterile environment for long.

"But a baby changes things," he added, with a slight frown into his glass.

"Yeah, they really do."

Abruptly, he pushed to his feet and reached out for her hand.

"What?" she asked.

One eyebrow winged up. "Don't be so suspicious. Just come with me for a minute."

She placed her hand in his and completely ignored the buzz of something electric that zapped through her. If he felt it, too, he was much better at not showing it than she was. Not a flicker of response shone in his eyes as he pulled her to her feet.

He tugged her behind him as he walked around the sofa, across the room and out onto the terrace, stepping into the encroaching shadows. Then he let her go and walked up to the stone railing, looking out over the view as lights began to wink into existence in the homes below, and a handful of stars began to glitter in the sky.

Lilah followed his gaze briefly, then half turned to watch him instead. His sharp green eyes were narrowed against the cold wind that ruffled his thick, wavy black hair. Somehow he seemed more…approachable. Which should probably worry her.

"I can't stay here," he said, his voice soft enough that she leaned in closer so she wouldn't miss a word. "Rosie will need a yard. And a terrace that doesn't include a couple-hundred-foot drop to the street."

Lilah shivered and looked over the edge of the railing. She'd had the same hideous thought herself. A tiny Rosie crawling out to the terrace and somehow climbing up on furniture and pitching right over. Deliberately, she pushed that mental image away and told herself it was good that Reed had come to the decision to move on his own—without her having to mention it.

"So just like that, you'll buy a house."

"Just like that," he assured her, turning to lean one hip against the stone balustrade. "I'll find something this weekend."

She laughed. How could she not? Lilah's friends worked and saved for months, sometimes years to sock away enough money to maybe look for a house. Reed Hudson would simply pull out his magic checkbook. "Is everything so easy then?"

"Not easy," he assured her, his green eyes meeting and holding hers. "But if there's one thing I know—it's that if you want something, you go get it."

Three

Oddly enough, Lilah could understand that statement. Okay, the spur-of-the-moment buying of a house was way out of her league, but the *attitude* was something she believed in. Going after what you wanted and not giving up until you had it.

Isn't that how she'd run her own life?

How strange that she found herself agreeing with a man she'd expected to loathe on general principle. But as much as she was still furious on her friend's behalf, she had to admit that Spring had left her daughter to Reed's care. That said something, too, didn't it?

Spring had loved her daughter more than anything. So Lilah had to assume that there was more to Reed Hudson than she'd seen so far. Rose would not have been entrusted to him if Spring hadn't believed he could and would love that little girl.

Maybe, Lilah thought, instead of just holding her own anger close and nurturing it, she should give him a chance to show her she was wrong about him.

"How does Rosie fit into your plans?" she asked.

He looked at her for a long minute and Lilah just managed to keep from fidgeting beneath that steady stare. Her hormones were stirring to life, and that was so unexpected. She'd come here reluctantly, to turn over a baby she loved to a man she didn't know or trust. Now her own body was lighting up in a way she'd never known before, and she didn't like it. Being attracted to this man wasn't something she wanted—but her body didn't seem to care.

Under the gaze from hot green eyes, she shifted uncomfortably and silently told herself to get a grip.

"Rosie's mine now." Cool words uttered simply and they drove a knife through her heart.

Instantly, she told herself that she should be glad of it. That's why she was here, after all. But she'd loved Rose from the moment of her birth. Lilah was Spring's coach all through labor and delivery and she'd held Rosie herself when the little girl was moments old. She had been a part of the baby's life from that day on, helping to care for her, worrying about her, *loving* her. And since Spring's death more than a month ago, Lilah and Rosie had been a team. A unit. Now she had to give up the child she loved so much and it tore at her.

"I'll take care of her," he was saying. "Just as Spring wanted me to."

"Good," she muttered, and paused for a sip of wine. "That's good."

"Yes," he said wryly. "I can hear just how pleased you are about it."

Caught, she shrugged. "No point in pretending, is there?"

"None." He nodded. "Truth is much easier and far less trouble."

"Are you sure you're a lawyer?"

One eyebrow winged up. "Don't much like lawyers?"

"Does anyone?"

His mouth twitched briefly. "Good point. Though I can say my clients end up very fond of me."

"I'll bet," Lilah muttered. In all of her research, she'd learned just what a shark Reed Hudson was in a court-room. He was right, his clients did love him, but, oh, his opponents had plenty to say—most of it sour grapes, but still.

Frowning, he gave her a hard, long look and asked, "So is it lawyers you loathe or just *me* in particular?"

"I don't know you well enough to loathe you," she admitted, which wasn't really answering the question. She gave a sigh, met his gaze and said, "I came here already not liking you much."

"Yes, that was clear when we met."

Lilah winced a little. She was never deliberately rude, but her emotions had nearly been choking her. It wasn't really an excuse, but it was the only one she had. "You're right. But losing Spring, then having to hand Rosie over to someone I'd never met…"

She watched him think, consider, before he finally nodded. "I can see that," he acknowledged with another long look into her eyes. "I appreciate loyalty."

"So do I," she said and thought they'd finally found some common ground.

"I spoke to our parents," he said abruptly. "Well," he amended, "our father, Spring's mother."

So strange, Lilah thought, different parents, same family, tangled and twisted threads of connections. Lilah had had no idea that Spring was a member of such a well-known family. Until her death revealed her secrets, Spring had gone by her ex-husband's last name, Bates. So Lilah hadn't been at all prepared to face down the powerful Hudson family.

Worry tightened into a coil in the pit of her stomach. What if Spring's parents wanted Rosie? Would he give the baby over, in spite of Spring's request that he raise her? And if he wanted to, how could Lilah fight him on it? From what she'd learned about the Hudsons, she had to think their parents were less than interested in their own children. They wouldn't give Rosie the time or care she needed. Even while a part of her started plotting just what she might do if she had to take on Spring's parents, Lilah asked, "What did they say?"

He sighed and for the first time he looked more tired than irritated. Or maybe, she thought, *resigned* was the right word.

"Just what I expected them to say," he told her with a wry twist to his lips. "My father reminded me that he already has a three-year-old in the house and his wife is about to give birth to another baby."

She blinked. It sounded strange to hear about siblings born more than thirty years apart.

"And Spring's mother, Donna, said she's got no interest in being a grandmother—or in having anyone find out she's old enough to *be* a grandmother."

"Not very maternal, is she?"

"The words *alley cat* spring to mind," he admitted. "My father has interesting taste in women. Anyway, I told them both that Spring left her child to me. I was only calling them to give them a heads-up."

A quiet sigh of relief slid from Lilah's lungs. He didn't sound as though he had any interest in handing Rosie over to those people, so one worry down. "So basically," she said through the quiet sigh of relief, "they're leaving Rosie with you."

He looked at her. "I wouldn't have given Rose to them even if they'd wanted her—which I was certain they wouldn't."

Now surprise flickered to life inside her. Lilah would have expected him to *want* someone to relieve him of the baby. Hearing him say just the opposite made her wonder about him. "Why?"

Frowning, he took a drink, then said, "First and most importantly, Spring asked me to take care of her daughter."

Lilah nodded. She understood and appreciated that he would take his sister's request to heart. In everything she'd read about him, he was a cold, merciless attorney. What she hadn't known about was the loyalty she saw now, etched into his expression.

And even though her heart ached at the thought of going home and leaving Rosie behind… Lilah felt a bit better about going knowing that at least Reed would do what his own sense of duty demanded. It wasn't enough for a child to grow on. A child needed love before anything else. But it was a start.

Still, she asked, "What else? What aren't you saying?"

His mouth firmed into a tight line as he shifted his gaze from hers to the ocean, where the dying sun layered brilliant streaks of red and gold across the water. "Your parents," he asked, "still together?"

A bittersweet pang of old pain shot through her chest. "They were," she said quietly, watching his profile as he studied the sea as if looking for answers. "Until my father died in an avalanche five years ago."

He looked at her then, briefly. "I'm sorry."

"So were we," she said, remembering that loss and how keenly it had been felt. "A couple of years ago, though, my mother met someone. He's a very nice man and he makes her happy. They were married a year ago, and now they spend all of their time traveling."

Stan was retired, having sold his business for millions more than ten years ago. When he met Lilah's mother on a ski run in Utah, it really had been love at first sight, for both of them. And though it had been hard to accept that her mother could love someone other than Lilah's father, she couldn't deny how happy Stan made her mom.

Curiosity sparked in his eyes. "Going where?"

"Everywhere, really," she said, with a half laugh. "Mom and Stan live on a cruise ship, going from port to port and, according to my mother's emails, having a wonderful time."

Now he turned, a small smile curving his mouth, and looked down at her. "You were surprised that I live in a hotel, but your own mother lives on a cruise ship."

She shrugged. "But a hotel's on land. Near houses. A cruise ship is something else again."

"Odd logic."

Smiling, she said, "It works for me."

"Yeah." He turned his face into the wind again and said, "So, my family's different. They like having children, they just don't like having them around. Nannies, governesses and boarding schools are the favorite child-rearing tools for the Hudsons."

Before she could say anything about that, he went on, "Spring hated it. It was a kind of torture for her to be locked away in a school she couldn't leave." He swiveled his head and stared at her. "How could I give Rose over to people who would only do the same thing to her that they did to her mother? No."

Warmth opened up in the center of her chest and Lilah was caught off guard. The cold, hard lawyer seemed to have disappeared and she didn't know quite what to make of the man he was now.

"You've agreed to stay," he was saying, and Lilah came up out of her thoughts to listen.

"For a while, yes." For Rosie. For Lilah's own sake, she would stay until she was sure the baby girl would be safe. Happy. She'd closed her artisanal soap shop temporarily and could run the online business from her laptop, so there was no rush to get home.

Reed had wanted to *pay* her to stay. What he didn't realize was he would have had to pay her to *leave*.

"Then you can help me choose the house." He finished off his scotch. "And furnish it. I won't have time for a decorator."

Stunned, she just looked at him. "You want me to—"

"Don't all women like shopping?"

She laughed shortly. "That's completely sexist."

"Sue me. Am I wrong?"

"No, but that's not the point," she said.

"It's exactly the point. You'll have free rein," he tempted her. "You can pick out the furnishings that'll make the house baby friendly."

Help choose the kind of house Rosie would grow up in? How could she refuse? Shopping to outfit an entire house on someone else's dime? What woman wouldn't accept that offer? Besides, if left to his own devices, Lilah was sure he'd furnish the whole place in black and white, and that thought was just too hideous to contemplate.

"Free rein?" she repeated, wanting his assurances.

"That's what I said."

"So you're okay with lots of color."

His eyes narrowed. "How much color?"

He was worried and that made her smile. "Free rein," she reminded him.

Buying a house wasn't that difficult when you were willing to pay any price to get what you wanted when you wanted it. The Realtor quickly decided that Lilah was the person she needed to convince, and so Reed was able to hang back and watch the show. He had to admit, Lilah was picky, but she knew what would work and what wouldn't. She wasn't easily swayed by the Realtor's practiced patter about square footage, views and school districts. He admired that.

But then, he was finding the whole package of Lilah Strong intriguing. She wasn't sure of him still, so there was a simmer of anger about her he couldn't miss. Most women he knew were cautious enough to only let him see carefully constructed smiles. They laughed at his jokes, sighed at his kiss and in general tried to make themselves into exactly what he might want.

Strange, then, that the woman who didn't care what he thought of her was the one he found the most intriguing. Hell, watching her move through an empty house, the Realtor hot on her heels, was entertaining. And damned if the view wasn't a good one.

She wore a long-sleeved white button-down shirt with

a sleek black vest over it. Her blue jeans hugged a great behind and an excellent pair of legs, and black boots with a two-inch heel completed the look. Casual elegance. Her reddish-gold hair hung loose to the middle of her back in a cascade of waves that made him want to bury his hands in the thick mass.

But then, he remembered she'd looked damn good the night before, too, wearing only a sky blue nightgown that stopped midthigh.

He woke up at the sound of the baby crying and realized that this was his new reality. Rose was his now and he took care of what was his.

Moving through the darkened suite, he walked to the room Rose and Lilah were sharing, gave a brief knock and opened the door. Lilah was standing in a slice of moonlight, the baby held close to her chest. She was swaying in place and whispering things Reed couldn't make out.

"Is she all right?" he asked, keeping his own voice hushed.

"Just a little scared," Lilah told him, giving the baby soothing pats as she rocked her gently. "New place."

"Right." Wearing only a pair of cotton sleep pants, he walked barefoot across the room and scooped Rose right out of Lilah's arms, cradling the baby to his chest.

For a moment, it looked as though Rose would complain. Loudly. But the baby stared at him for a long minute, then sighed and laid her little head down on his shoulder.

That one action melted something inside him and felt...powerful. He held that tiny life close, felt her every breath, every shuddering sigh, and knew in that one shining moment he would do anything to keep her safe.

Then he looked into Lilah's eyes and found her measuring him. Her hair was a tangle of curls around her face, her eyes were wary and she crossed her arms over her chest, lifting her breasts high enough that he got a glimpse of cleavage at the V-neck of her nightgown.

"Sorry she woke you," Lilah said, voice soft as a feather.

"I'm not," he said, surprised to find it was nothing but the truth. "We have to get used to each other, don't we?"

"Yes, I guess you do." She reached out one hand to smooth her palm over Rosie's dark curls. "She's usually a good sleeper, but her routine's a little messed up right now."

"She'll get a new routine soon."

At that, Lilah let her hand drop to her side and stared up at him. "Are you ready for that?"

He looked down at the baby asleep on his shoulder. "I will be."

And in the quiet of the night, with a sleeping baby between them, he and Lilah watched each other in the silence.

Reed had wondered then, as he did now, if she had felt the heat that snapped and sizzled between them.

Today, her blue eyes were sharp and clear as she inspected the kitchen of the fifth house they'd seen that morning. She stepped out onto a brick patio, with the Realtor hot on her heels. Reed walked out after them, listening to their conversation.

"I like that there's a fence around the pool," Lilah said, looking at it as if she could judge its strength with the power of her gaze.

"Electronic locks with a parental control," the Realtor said, giving a wide, plastic smile as she smoothed black hair so stiff that it probably wouldn't have moved even if she were in the middle of a tornado. "There's a top-of-the-line security system in the house as well, and both remotes are accessible in the garage as well as the house."

"Security," Lilah mused thoughtfully. "So this isn't a good neighborhood?"

The Realtor paled while Reed smothered a smile.

"This is one of the finest neighborhoods in Laguna," the Realtor protested. "A security system is simply for peace of mind."

Reed saw the humor in Lilah's eye and knew she was just giving the other woman a hard time.

"I do like this yard," she said, turning in a slow circle to admire the picture.

Reed did as well, and he had to admit that of the houses they'd seen so far that morning, he preferred this one. The house itself was a larger version of a California bungalow. It had charm, character but plenty of room, and it wasn't sitting on top of its neighbors. He liked that. Reed also liked the yard. The pool took up a third of the lot, but alongside it ran a wide green swath of lawn that would give a kid plenty of room to run. There were trees and flower beds, and since they were situated high on a hill, there were spectacular views of the ocean. The brick terrace boasted an outdoor living space, complete with a backyard kitchen, and the interior of the house was just as perfect. Five bedrooms, five baths and a kitchen that looked fine to him and had had Lilah sighing.

Standing in a tree-dappled patch of shade, Lilah looked at him. "What do you think?"

Both women were watching him, but Reed's gaze met Lilah's alone. "I think it'll work."

The Realtor laughed sharply. "Work? It's a fabulous piece of property. Completely redone two years ago, from the roof to the flooring. It's only been on the market for three days and it's priced to sell and—"

Never taking his gaze from Lilah's, Reed held up one hand for silence and hardly noticed as the Realtor's voice faded away.

Lilah grinned at the woman's reaction to his silent command. "I like it."

"Me, too," Reed said, and spared a glance for the Realtor. "I'll take it. Have the paperwork drawn up and delivered to me at the Monarch this afternoon—"

"This afternoon? I don't know that I can get it all done that quickly and—"

Now he shot the woman a look he generally reserved for hostile witnesses on the stand. "I have every confidence you will. And, while you're working, you should know there's a nice bonus in it for you if you arrange for a seven-day escrow."

"Seven—"

"And," he continued as if she hadn't interrupted, "since I'll be paying cash for the house, I'd like the keys in five days. Furniture has to be delivered and arranged so that we can move in at the end of the seven days."

"That's highly irregular…"

He watched Lilah turn and walk across the yard, as if she'd done her part and didn't feel it necessary to be in on the haggling. Well, he'd rather talk to her, so he wrapped this up quickly.

"Ms. Tyler," he said quietly, firmly, "I doubt you come across many cash clients and so the regular rules may not apply in this situation. Why don't you take care of this and make it happen?"

"I'll do my best, naturally," she blurted, adjusting the fit of her bright red jacket.

"Twenty percent of the asking price as a bonus above your commission."

Her eyes went as wide as the moon and her jaw literally dropped. Not surprising since he was sure she didn't receive that kind of bonus very often. But it was worth it to him.

He didn't like waiting. He didn't mind paying for what he wanted. And Reed knew that money could pave over obstacles faster than anything else in the world. In fact, the only person he'd ever come across who couldn't be bought—or even rented—was Lilah Strong. Just another reason she intrigued him.

He walked past the stunned-into-silence Realtor and moved toward Lilah. Besides, what was the point of being rich if you didn't use the money?

"I'll get right on this," the Realtor called out when she could speak again. "I'll, uh, just wait outside in my car. Start making calls. You and your wife take your time looking around."

He didn't bother to correct the woman, though the word *wife* gave him a quick, cold chill. Instead, he walked slowly across the lawn to join Lilah as she stared out at the view.

"It's done."

She turned. "What?"

"I bought the house."

She laughed and shook her head. The wind lifted her hair and flew it about her face until she reached up and plucked a long strand out of her eyes. "Of course you did. Moving in tonight are you?"

His mouth quirked. "No, I didn't want to rush. Next weekend is soon enough."

Now she laughed and the sound was surprisingly sexy. He moved in closer and caught her scent. Different today, he thought, and realized she now smelled like cinnamon apples. Lemons yesterday, apples today. As if the woman herself wasn't distraction enough.

"You know," she said, "it took me three months to find my house, then it was another month to arrange for a loan, buy it and gain possession and then move in. Most people don't manage it in a week."

"I'm not most people," he said with a shrug.

"That I agree with." She turned, leaned against the chest-high wall and looked at the back of the house. "It is beautiful."

He never took his gaze from her. "It is."

As if feeling him watching her, she turned her head to briefly look at him. The air seemed to sizzle between them. "What're you doing?"

"Just stating the obvious," he said with a half shrug.

She took a deep breath and looked back at the house, ignoring the flash of heat. That irritated. It was there. A hum of something hot, something potent, and she seemed determined to pretend it wasn't.

"Rosie will love having this yard to play in." She sounded wistful. "I'm glad the pool has a fence around it."

"If there hadn't been," he said flatly, "I would have had one installed before we moved in."

She shot him a glance. "In less than a week."

He winked. "Of course."

"Of course." She nodded, sighed. "We should get back to the hotel and check on Rosie."

"She's fine. Andre personally vouched for the hotel babysitter. Apparently she's the grandma type, great with babies."

"I know. He told me."

"But you don't trust anyone but yourself with the baby."

"I didn't say that," she pointed out. "I just don't know her."

"You don't know me, either," Reed said, studying her features. The sun and shadow played across her face, danced in her eyes, highlighting the worry gleaming there. "So how will you handle leaving her with me?"

"Honestly?" She pushed her hair back with a careless swipe of her hand. "I don't know. But, I don't have a choice in that, do I?" She shifted her gaze back to the sea. "I have to do what Spring asked me to, even if I don't like it."

He watched her for a long minute, the set of her chin, her blue eyes narrowed against the glint of the sunlight on the water. Getting back to the hotel, the waiting Realtor out front, left his mind in favor of staying right there, talking to Lilah, finding out more of who and what she was.

"If you hadn't found the letters from Spring, would you have kept Rose yourself?" He already knew the answer, but he wanted to hear her say it.

"Yes," she said firmly. "I'd have adopted her. I would have done anything I had to, to keep her. I already love her like she's my own."

"I noticed," he said, giving her a brief smile when she

looked at him. "It's impressive...letting go of what you want to fulfill Spring's wishes."

"I'm not trying to impress you."

"Another reason why I am impressed," he admitted. "So tell me. How did you and my sister become such good friends?"

Her gaze followed the clouds racing across the sky. A reluctant smile curved her mouth and for a moment or two she seemed lost in her own thoughts, memories. When she spoke, her voice was soft. "She came to my shop, looking for work."

Still having a hard time realizing his sister had had a *job*, Reed chuckled a little at his own memories. "The first and only job Spring had that I know about was at the movie theater the summer she was sixteen." He smiled at the images his mind showed him. "My father had said something about her being unemployable since all she knew how to do was spend his money."

"That was nice," Lilah muttered.

"Yeah, he's a charmer all right. Anyway, Spring decided to prove to our father that she could make her own money." He shook his head, remembering. "She loved movies and thought it would be a great way to see all the new ones when they came out. With the added benefit of making our father eat his words." He sighed a little. "But she worked the candy counter and hardly had the time to see a movie at all. Plus, she hated what she called the 'ugly' uniform. She didn't last a month."

"People change," Lilah said quietly.

"Not in my experience," Reed countered.

"Well, Spring did." Lilah set her hands on top of the wall, rested her chin on them and looked out at the ocean as if looking back in time. "Her husband had just left her. She was pregnant and alone—" she shot him a quick look "—or so I thought. She needed a job and was willing to do anything I needed."

He frowned. "What kind of shop do you own?"

She laughed at the obvious worry in his voice. "It's called Lilah's Bouquet. I sell artisanal soaps and candles."

Did that explain all the different fragrances that seemed to cling to her? Probably.

"And what did Spring do at your shop?"

"Everything." Lilah smiled to herself. "Hiring her was the best decision I ever made, I swear. She was great with customers. Always seemed to know what they'd like and helped them find it. She took care of the stock, kept track of what was selling and what wasn't. Honestly, she was wonderful. Before long, I made her the manager and that gave me more time to spend in my workshop, making up the soaps and candles to stock the shelves."

It was as if she was describing a stranger. Manager? Spring? Frowning, Reed tried to imagine it and came up short. His younger sister had never been the dedicated sort—or at least that's what he'd believed. But it seemed that he hadn't known Spring as a mature adult at all. And now he never would.

"There's a small apartment over the shop," Lilah was saying. "I lived there myself until I could buy a house. So Spring and Rose moved in and it worked well for all of us. The baby charmed every customer who came through the door and Spring didn't have to worry about leaving Rose with a babysitter. Everything was great, until…" Her eyes went dark with grief and memory.

A sharp stab of pain sliced at Reed's heart. He didn't want to think about his sister's death any more than Lilah wanted to talk about it. So instead, he focused on the life she'd been living away from her family. "It sounds like she was happy."

Lilah's gaze lifted to meet his and a sad smile curved her mouth. "She was. She loved our little town and being a part of it. She had a lot of friends."

Reed tried to picture it. His sister, born in London, raised there and in New York. She had gone to the best boarding school in the city and hung out with the children of rock stars and princes. So it was a little hard to picture her happy in a shop apartment in some small town in— "Where?"

"What?"

"Where do you live? Your shop? Your small town? You didn't say."

"You're right. I haven't. There's just been so much going on. It's Pine Lake, Utah. About an hour north of Salt Lake City, up in the Wasatch mountains."

Reed shook his head and chuckled again. "Sorry. Just hard to imagine Spring in the mountains. She was always more for the beach."

"People change."

One dark eyebrow lifted. "Yeah, you've said that before."

She smiled a little. "Must be true then."

"For some people."

She tipped her head to one side and looked up at him through serious eyes. "People can surprise you."

"That's usually the problem," he mused, then took her arm. "We should go. Ms. Tyler's probably sitting out in her car wondering what we're doing back here."

"Right. I want to get back to Rosie, too."

He steered her across the yard and through the open

back door. With his hand at her elbow, they walked through the house that would be his home in a little more than a week, and Reed told himself that sometimes, change happened whether you were ready for it or not.

Four

The next week was a busy one. She hardly saw Reed, who made himself scarce whenever she and the baby entered a room. He spent most of his time at work and she had to wonder if that situation was normal or if it was simply that he was trying to avoid her completely.

On the other hand, Lilah was really going to miss Andre.

She didn't know what she would have done without him the past several days. Life in a hotel wasn't ideal, but the amazing butler could have made her a believer.

Snooty accent aside, Andre was always ready to help. And though he was loathe to gossip, he had let a few little nuggets of information about Reed drop over the past couple of days. So now she knew that his family rarely visited, he almost never had guests—translation: women—in his suite and that he was a generous tipper.

Which told Lilah that either Reed was a determined loner or he was lonely and that he paid attention when people helped him and made sure to show his appreciation. It wasn't much, but it was more than she'd learned from Reed himself.

Andre cleared his throat to get her attention. "I've prepared another list of furniture shops you might want to check," he said, producing said list from the inside pocket of his immaculate three-piece black suit. Handing it to her, he winked. "I've marked the ones most useful I believe for what you're interested in. As you've already ordered Rose's things, I believe Mr. Hudson's study is the last room on your agenda."

"How do you remember that?" Lilah asked with a laugh. "I can barely keep up with it myself."

"Oh," he said, bending at the waist to wipe a smudge of banana from the corner of Rosie's mouth, "I believe in being thorough, miss."

His hair was steel gray but his eyes were that of a much younger man. She supposed he could have been anywhere between thirty-five and fifty. He stood at least six feet and was the epitome of a British butler.

"Why are you working in a hotel, Andre? Shouldn't you be in London with royalty or something?"

He laid one hand on Rose's head in a loving pat, then looked at Lilah. "I did serve an earl several years ago, but frankly, I grew tired of the cold, gloomy weather in London." He winked again. "It's a lovely place to be *from*, if you understand me."

"Yes," Lilah said with a smile. "I think I do."

"I get back often to visit friends and family and enjoy myself completely on those trips." He folded his hands in front of him and gave a heavy sigh. "Though I must say, I do miss a good pub now and then."

"And I'm going to miss you, Andre," she blurted out, and before she could lose her nerve, came around the table and gave him a hug.

For a second, he went stiff with shock, then relaxed enough to give her a friendly pat on the shoulder. "I shall miss you, as well. Both you and Miss Rose. But this is best for all of you. A child shouldn't grow up in a hotel, after all."

"No, she shouldn't." Lilah looked down at the baby, then thought that Reed shouldn't be locked away in the impersonal suite, either. It couldn't be good for anyone. And that thought brought her back to the day of shopping stretching out in front of her.

She shifted her gaze to the list Andre had given her. "I don't know the stores here at all, so it would be a big help to me if you could tell me which of these is your favorite."

Clearly pleased to be asked his opinion, Andre pointed to the third name on the list. "Lovely leatherwork at that shop. I believe Mr. Hudson would approve."

"Okay, that just got easier. Thank you again," she said as he bowed and turned to leave. She stopped him by saying, "One more question?"

"Of course, miss." He waited patiently.

"I know it's none of my business, but how did a British butler come by the name of Andre?"

A smile flitted across his features quickly, then disappeared. "My mother's father was French. I'm named for him. Caused me quite a bit of trouble as a child, I'm not ashamed to say."

"I'll bet you handled it just fine."

"I like to think so, miss." He bowed again. "Do enjoy your shopping."

When he left, Lilah turned to Rose again. "Oh, yeah, really going to miss him."

A couple of hours later, she was at the furniture shop Andre had recommended and she could silently admit he'd been absolutely right. Reed probably would like what she got here and if he didn't he had no one but himself to blame.

That one brief moment of closeness with Reed at the back of the new house hadn't been repeated and maybe, Lilah told herself, that was just as well. She was caught in a trap—she had to honor her friend's last wish, to have Reed raise the baby, but she wanted Rosie for herself. Basically, she and Reed were standing on opposite sides of a wall and any attempt to breach it—except for dealing with the baby—would be a waste of time.

As if he knew it, too, Reed had been avoiding her as much as possible. It wasn't easy, since they were sharing a hotel suite that, despite its size, seemed to shrink daily. He left for work early every day and didn't get back to the hotel until later in the evening. Usually about the time Lilah was tucking Rose into bed. Accident? Or design? She was willing to bet that Reed deliberately chose to arrive late enough to miss the whole bath time ritual. Then he could claim since the baby was now tucked in and asleep, he wouldn't go in and wake her.

And in spite of all of this? The attraction Lilah felt for him stayed at a slow simmer. The man was clearly uninterested, yet she couldn't seem to convince her body to stop lighting up whenever he walked into a room.

Lilah found it almost impossible to get a read on him.

It was as if he'd accepted his duty in taking Rosie in, but he wasn't going to put any more into it than he absolutely had to.

Not since that first night when he'd scooped Rose out of Lilah's arms to cuddle against his chest had he even once touched her. Held her. Talked to her. Lilah couldn't bear thinking about the kind of life Rosie would have if Reed were simply unable to love her as she needed to be loved. But how could he, when it was clear from everything she'd learned that he and his siblings had grown up without that kind of affection.

Her heart torn, Lilah went through all the motions of what she was supposed to be doing—helping Reed prepare for Rosie being thrust into his life. But furniture and houses and all the money in the world wouldn't make up for a lack of love. She didn't know what she could do, though. She couldn't fight him in court for the baby. Not only was he as rich as Midas, he was a *lawyer*. She wouldn't stand a chance.

So the only hope she had was to somehow break through the wall of ice he'd erected around himself.

"Shouldn't take more than ten or twenty years," she assured herself.

"I'm sorry?"

Lilah flushed, caught talking to herself while her mind wandered. Smiling at the store clerk, she said, "Nothing. Are we about finished here?"

In the past week, with the assistance of the ever-helpful Andre, Lilah and Rose had visited every store she needed to furnish a house she wouldn't be living in. Of course, she had no idea what kind of furniture Reed might prefer, but since he hadn't bothered to give her direction, she'd picked what *she* liked.

Except for one room, a study that would be Reed's territory, Lilah had chosen comfortable furniture, soft colors, all of it coming together to build a warm, safe spot for a little girl to grow up in. Alone, but for a man who wouldn't allow himself to love her.

At that thought, Lilah's heart felt as if it were being squeezed in a cold fist. Soon, she'd be leaving, going back to Utah. She wouldn't be the one taking care of Rosie. Wouldn't be the one to see her walk, hear her first words. She wouldn't be there to dry her tears or hear the baby's giggle first thing in the morning.

She felt the sting of tears in her eyes and quickly blinked to clear them. If she started crying now, the clerk selling her a matching set of twin leather chairs and a sofa for Reed's study would think she was worried about the price. And truly, for the first time in her life, she hadn't even looked at the price tag on any of the furniture.

Normally in this situation, she would have been searching out the best bargain and mentally calculating just how far she could stretch her savings. But with Reed's insistence on blank-check shopping, it was going much faster than it would have ordinarily. Except for a kitchen table and Rosie's room, she was pretty much finished.

"Yes, I'll just print out a receipt for you and delivery instructions for our crew." The man stood and practically danced toward the back room. "I'll only be a minute or two."

"It's fine," she said, glancing down at Rosie, who was two-fisting her bottle.

No wonder the salesman was happy. His commission was no doubt going to be spectacular. With the chairs, sofa, tables, lamps, bookcases and rugs she'd purchased, he could probably take the rest of the month off.

As good as his word, Reed had wangled the keys out of the Realtor just as he said he would. There had been deliveries scheduled every day for the past few days and tomorrow would see the last of them, when this order was taken out to the new house. Beds for the master and three guest bedrooms had already been set up and Rosie's new crib and furnishings would be delivered that afternoon.

By the next day, they would all be living in that house overlooking the ocean. And that, Lilah thought, would just give Reed even *more* room to avoid her and the baby. She had to put a stop to it. Had to ensure that Reed spent time with Rosie. Got to know her. To love her. And if he couldn't?

She didn't have an answer.

Closing her eyes, she winced as instantly a familiar image of Reed flashed into her mind—just as it did whenever she tried to get some sleep. Reed, as he was that first night. Dark hair rumpled, broad, tanned chest naked in the moonlight, drawstring pants dipped low on his hips and bare feet—*why* were bare feet suddenly so sexy? Oh, God. She rubbed the spot between her eyes, hoping to wipe away images she was pretty sure had been permanently etched into her brain.

He was arrogant and bossy, no doubt. Gorgeous and sexy, too. Which only made all of this more difficult than it was already.

It would be so much easier if she could just hate him. But how could she when he had instantly moved to fulfill his late sister's wishes? He had bought a house for Rose. He was changing his life for the baby because it was the right thing to do. Hard to hate a man who could do all that.

But if he didn't open his heart to Rose, did anything else matter? God, it felt as if her mind were on an automatic loop, going over and over the same things, day after day with no solution. The man was taking up way too many of her thoughts and that just had to stop.

Lilah gave a quick glance at the clock on the wall. She had to get moving. There were still things like pots, pans, dishes, glassware, throw pillows, comforters and a million other, smaller things to arrange for.

And oh, how she wished her friend Kate was in town to help with all of this. Kate Duffy was an artist, with the kind of eye for decorating that Lilah lacked. Kate would have mowed through every art gallery, department store and lighting shop and, in a blink, would have seen exactly what should go where in the beautiful house on the cliff. But, Kate was on her long-delayed honeymoon with a military husband finally back from deployment.

So, she was in this alone.

A clatter of sound interrupted her thoughts and Lilah looked at Rose in her stroller, happily slamming her bottle against the tray in front of her. The tiny girl grinned and babbled wildly.

Laughing, Lilah leaned over, kissed the baby's cheek and whispered, "You're absolutely right. I'm not alone at all, am I?"

"All right then, Ms. Strong…" The salesman was back, full of bright cheer that spoke of the giant commission he was about to make. "Paperwork is right here. If you'll sign at the bottom…"

She quickly read over the receipt, then signed her name. "Everything will be delivered tomorrow?"

"Between one and three."

"Okay, thank you."

"Oh, my pleasure." He dipped into the breast pocket of his jacket, pulled out a card and handed it to her. "If you need anything else…"

"Thanks again." She took the card, dropped it into her purse, then left, pushing Rosie's stroller out onto the sidewalk.

June in Southern California could be either gloomy or beautiful, and today was definitely one of the pretty ones. The sidewalks were crowded, and the narrow streets were packed with impatient drivers tapping horns as if doing it could clear traffic. Flower-filled baskets hung from old-fashioned streetlights and teenagers with surfboards tucked beneath their arms bolted across the street toward the ocean.

It was all so far from the familiar, Lilah felt a pang of homesickness that was wiped away by the sound of Rosie's crow of delight. What was she going to do in her quiet house when there was no Rose to shatter the silence? How would she handle being so far away from the baby who felt like her own?

"Problems to face later," Lilah said, deliberately shoving those troubling thoughts aside to get on with her day. There were still so many things to do and she was running out of time.

While Lilah shopped like a woman on a mission, Reed pushed through his own commitments. He filed divorce papers with the court, settled his bill with the hotel and arranged for people to pack and move his stuff to the new house. And now, he had to spend some time reassuring Carson Duke.

"Have you talked to Tia?" Reed asked, following the other man with his gaze as he paced the confines of his suite at the Monarch.

For the first time, Reed noticed that one suite was pretty much like the other. Yes, his own was much bigger than this one, but the furnishings were very similar. And Carson looked ill at ease as he moved through the slash of sunlight pouring through the glass terrace doors.

"No," Carson muttered, shoving one hand through his hair. "Haven't talked to her since I moved out of our place a month ago."

"Keep it that way," Reed advised. He'd dealt with divorcing couples for enough years to know that even a split that started out amicable could turn into a battle. And then the case would be judged in the media, fueled by stealthy camera shots taken by the ever-hungry paparazzi.

Carson stopped, shoved both hands into his jeans and nodded. "I know that's the right strategy. But I can't help feeling that if we could talk—"

"Did talking help either of you the last few months?" His voice was deliberately impatient. If he offered sympathy here, his client wouldn't be able to do what was best for him. Better to be firm with his advice.

He frowned. "No. No, it didn't."

Reed took a sip of coffee, then set his cup down on the low glass table in front of him. "I know this is hard, but it's what you've both decided to do. You're better off not speaking with Tia until the court proceedings are done. With your prenup in place, this should be a painless situation to resolve."

"Painless."

Reed nodded. He prided himself on getting his clients through the end of a marriage with as little pain as possible. "Not completely, but this should move along with few complications."

"That's good, I guess," Carson said with a wry smile. "Didn't imagine I'd be in this position, I've got to say."

"No one does," Reed assured him.

Carson snorted. "Maybe. I do know that not growing up in Hollywood made me believe that people can choose to stay together. To work at it. Hell, my own parents have been married forever. They're still happy."

And Reed couldn't help wondering what that was like. Naturally, in his business, he didn't run into long-term marriages. He had no personal experience with it, either. How had it felt to grow up, as Carson had, with one set of parents? Hell, Reed had so many official and honorary grandparents, he couldn't keep track of them all.

The extended Hudson family hadn't exactly been the "norm" or even close to ideal. But it was what he knew.

"So, when can I expect to be a free man again?"

Reed looked at Carson. "Well, you've been married less than two years, and have no children, so that makes things less complicated."

"Happy to help," the man muttered.

Reed understood what Carson was feeling, so he simply went on, "You do own property together…"

"Yeah," Carson said. "The Malibu beach house and a cabin in Montana."

Nodding, Reed said, "Once Tia signs the papers as well, I'll meet with her attorney and we go into what's called *discovery*. That's laying out all jointly held properties and bank accounts and so forth…"

Carson swiped one hand across his face, but nodded solemnly. "And then?"

Smiling, Reed said, "*Then* we prepare a marital settlement agreement and if you both agree with the terms, you'll sign and six months after that, you'll be single again."

"Will we have to go to court?"

"Depends on how the settlement agreement goes. We could end up in a mediator's office, or be seen by a judge."

"Right." Carson coughed out a laugh and shook his head. "I swear, I just never thought Tia and I would end up this way." He shot Reed a look. "You probably hear that all the time."

"Not really," Reed said. "People don't come to divorce lawyers wanting to talk about how good their relationship is."

"Guess not." Carson turned to look out at the ocean. "I thought we'd be different. Thought we'd make it. Hell, Tia even loves my parents." He shook his head again. "Don't know how we ended up here."

"You may never know," Reed said, and stood up. "And trying to dissect the whole thing won't give you peace."

Carson turned his head and looked at him. "What will?"

Reed gave him a grim smile. "If I find out, I'll let you know."

"Right. Okay. Look, I appreciate your bringing me the papers…"

"No problem. I live here, remember?"

"Yeah, but I don't, so I'll be leaving this afternoon." He blew out a breath. "I've got to get back to Hollywood.

Have an early call Monday and there are a few things I
have to do over the weekend."

"New movie?" Reed asked.

"No, just a few reshoots on the last one," Carson said.
"Back to make-believe and pretense. Today I'm just a
guy, Monday morning I'm a Viking again. Weird way
to make a living."

"There are weirder." Reed didn't remind the other
man that essentially, at its core, he made a living dissolving people's lives. In Reed's book, that made for much
stranger than pretending to be a Viking. With that dark
thought circling his brain, he buttoned his suit coat and
said, "If you need anything, you know where to reach
me. Otherwise, I'll be in touch."

"Right."

"And steer clear of Tia," Reed said again, knowing
the warning was necessary.

"Yeah, I will." Carson flashed the grin he was famous
for. "If I'd done that a couple years ago, I wouldn't be
in this mess, right?"

"True." Harsh, Reed knew, and he saw that single
word slam home with Carson. But the simple reality
was that divorce was the main reason to avoid marriage
in the first place.

If that point hadn't been hammered into him watching his own family's near legendary divorce battles, then
it would have been over the past several years. Leading
his clients through sometimes messy and always miserable dissolutions. Hell, watching Carson Duke right now
was just one more reinforcement of the decision Reed
had made long ago to remain single.

"Thanks," Carson said. "For everything."

"Just doing my job," Reed told him, then headed out to take care of the mess his own life had recently become. But with any luck, he was about to smooth some of those choppy waters.

An hour later, he was at the new house and had to admit that Lilah had done a good job of furnishing the place. It looked...settled, he supposed, as if everything had been in place for years, not days. *Years.* Damn, that sounded...*permanent.* If he concentrated, Reed would probably be able to actually *feel* roots sprouting up through the floor of the house to wrap around his ankles like chains. Which was exactly why Reed had never bought a house before this. He hadn't wanted to be tied to anything. Along with avoiding marriage, he'd avoided commitments to *places*, as well.

He'd always kept his options open, so that even if he'd never packed up and left town at a moment's notice, he'd always known that he *could.* But now, that was over. He was a homeowner. Or would be by tomorrow. He would have roots for the first time in his life, and that thought felt almost like a noose slowly tightening around his neck.

Hardly surprising, since between boarding schools and vacation homes and the change of address every time his parents remarried, Reed had never had a childhood "home." At least not one where memories were made. He didn't have a particular love of any one place due to a connection to the past. He lived in a hotel so he could leave whenever he wanted to. And now...well, that was over.

The house itself, though, was fine. Glancing around

the great room, Reed approved. Lilah'd promised color and she hadn't lied, but he had to admit that the overall effect was, he supposed, homey. There were heavy rugs in deep jewel tones and oversize furniture covered in soft colors of cream and pale blue. There were lamps and tables and even some of his own art from the hotel hanging on the walls. Odd, he hadn't even noticed them missing from the suite, yet somehow Lilah had managed to have them boxed, moved and hung.

He heard the rumbles of conversation floating to him from different areas of the house. Movers were there, setting up the nursery, and the surprise he'd arranged for was no doubt getting acquainted with Lilah.

He had to give her full points. She'd done a lot of work in very little time. She would absolutely have been worth the money he'd offered to pay her. He still couldn't believe that she'd refused a hundred thousand dollars. Especially when he knew she could use it.

Reed had done some research on his own. He'd looked into her business—you could find anything if you knew where to look. Lilah's Bouquet was a small company with a few employees and a well-laid-out website for online business. Who knew there were so many buyers for pretty soaps and candles? She owned a home with a reasonable mortgage, a ten-year-old car and was, as far as he could tell, well liked and respected in her incredibly small hometown. No family but her parents, and a year or two after her father's death, her mother had remarried a millionaire, so maybe that was the reason behind Lilah's turning down money from him.

Whatever lay behind it, though, he knew she was staying not because he'd asked it of her, but because she was looking out for Rose. Hard to blame her for that. In fact, he appreciated it. He just didn't like being in anyone's debt.

And until he had this new situation locked down and sewed up, he would owe Lilah Strong.

Five

She came into the room just then as if thinking of her had conjured her. A wide smile was on her expressive face, and her eyes were shining. That amazing hair of hers tumbled in waves and curls and bounced with her every step.

"Okay, she's wonderful," Lilah said.

Satisfaction welled inside him. The surprise he'd arranged had gone off better than he'd thought it would. If he had to say it himself, he'd had a stroke of genius in coaxing his mother's former housekeeper-slash-nanny out of semiretirement.

Connie Thomas was in her early sixties, loved kids and had the organizational skills of a four-star general. For more than twenty-five years, Connie had been the one constant in Reed's life. She'd stayed with them through his mother's many marriages and even more frequent moves. Connie was the one the kids in the family went to when they were in trouble or lonely or just needed a sympathetic ear. She'd finally decided to leave, though, when Reed's mother decided her youngest son, at seven, didn't really need to come home from boarding school for the summer.

His mother wasn't the most maternal woman in the known world, and even as he thought it, Reed felt a pang of guilt. She loved her kids, he knew, but in an abstracted way that didn't necessarily require her children's presence. In fact, Selena Taylor-Hudson-Simmons-Foster-Hambleton had never understood how Connie Thomas had so much patience for kids.

"Rosie is already crazy about her," Lilah was saying. "So of course I am."

He nodded. "I suspected you'd approve."

"How could I not?" Lilah was smiling up at him, and it bothered Reed just how much he liked it. "Connie and the baby hit it off instantly." Taking a deep breath, she went on, "And you should know that Connie loves her suite of rooms off the kitchen. She told me you've arranged to have her things delivered here tonight."

"No point in waiting, is there?"

A short chuckle shot from her. "Not for you—and apparently not for Connie, either. Right now, she's taken Rosie upstairs to 'supervise' the movers setting things up in the nursery."

He wasn't surprised to hear that. Connie wasn't one to sit back and let things happen around her. She liked to have her hand in things.

"She'll drive the movers crazy, but she'll be satisfied with their work before she lets them leave."

"You make her sound like a drill sergeant," Lilah said, tipping her head to one side to look up at him.

"She could be," he admitted, then smiled, remembering. "She was the one who made sure baths were taken, homework was done and teeth were brushed. She also kept the cookie jar filled with her magic chocolate chip bars."

"Magic?" Lilah asked quietly.

"Seemed like magic at the time," he said. "Never had anything taste as good as those cookie bars did." Funny, a few minutes ago, he'd been thinking that he really had no memories of a *home*. But now, his mind filled with images of Connie, making cookies, playing board games with the younger kids in the family. Showing them how to make their own beds and expecting them to do it by reminding them all that the maids worked for their parents, *not* for them.

All the kids in the house had known they would find sympathy, understanding and honesty in Connie's kitchen. Reed had benefited more than once from the woman's no-nonsense view of the world. He couldn't imagine his childhood without her. Smiling, he said, "Yeah, those bars were magic."

"Can't wait to try them." Lilah tipped her head to one side and watched him. "There's more than cookies to your memories, though, isn't there?"

Frowning, he realized she was reading him and he didn't like it. "She's a good person. That's all."

"Uh-huh."

"Look," he said, trying to counter the patient expression on her face, "I'm not looking to learn and share and grow here. There is nothing to this beyond Connie being the most logical solution to our current problem."

"There it is again," Lilah said softly. "Rose isn't a problem to solve."

He stiffened a bit under the criticism. "Her care is."

"So now that Connie's here, you're off the hook in the care department?" Lilah cocked her head and stared up at him through eyes that seemed to have a laser focus. "Is that how it works?"

How the hell had he gone from a hero—bringing Connie here—to the bad guy, for the same damn reason? Beginning to be seriously irritated now, Reed countered, "If you've got something to say, say it."

She shook her head. "Where to begin?"

"Just start," he said, voice clipped. Folding his arms across his chest, he stood in the center of his brand-new living room and waited.

"Fine." She took a deep breath, looked him square in the eye and said, "In the week Rosie and I have been here, you've hardly spent any time at all with her."

He snorted. "In case you haven't noticed, I do have work."

"Oh, hard not to notice," Lilah said. "You're always gone. And on the rare moments you are around, you keep a very real distance between you and Rosie."

Truth hit home, but he didn't feel the need to defend himself against it, either. "There is no distance, for God's sake. I'm her uncle. She's my sister's daughter. I just bought her a *house*. I think it's safe to say that I'm inserting her into my life."

"Why does she have to be inserted?" Lilah asked.

"Because she's never been here before?" Reed countered, his voice lowering to a growl.

"That's not what I meant. You can't just shove her into your old life. You and she need to build a *new* life together." Waving her hands a little as if to encompass the living room, she said, "Buying a house is great. But if that's all it is, it's not enough."

Irritation spiked into a sizzle of resentment that caught and burned at the base of his throat. Since this woman and the baby had walked into his life a week ago, everything he knew had been turned inside out. But apparently, that wasn't enough for Lilah Strong.

Reed gave her the cold-eyed glare he usually reserved for hostile witnesses or clients who tried to lie to him. "She's eight months old. What more does she need? A car? A boat?"

"A *home*."

"What the hell is that supposed to mean?" The tight rein on his temper was strained. He knew that Connie, the baby and the last of the deliverymen were just upstairs. Damned if he'd have an argument the whole world could listen in on.

"It means, buying a *house* doesn't make it a *home*."

"Unbelievable." He shook his head. "You're wasting your time making fancy soaps. You should be writing poems for a greeting card company."

"This isn't funny." Her voice was as cool and flat as his own.

"You got that right." He expected her to back down, to smooth over and try for cool reason. He was wrong.

She moved in on him and he could see actual *sparks* flashing in her eyes. "*Your* life isn't the only one that has been 'disrupted.' Rosie has lost her mother. I have lost my friend. I'm a few hundred miles from home and doing my best to keep Rosie safe and happy."

"I get that," he interrupted.

"Not finished," she continued, taking another step closer. "You've avoided me and Rosie all week."

His back teeth ground together. Yeah, he had, but he hadn't expected her to notice. After all, he was a busy man and God knew she'd had plenty to do. "Not avoiding—"

"Ignoring then," she said quickly. "Comes to the same thing. The point is, a house won't be enough. Connie, as great as she is, won't be enough."

Sunlight slanted over her hair, picking up the gold in the red and making it shine. Today she smelled like orange blossoms, and that scent was clogging his throat and fogging his mind. That was the only explanation for him standing there taking a lecture as he hadn't had since he was eighteen and had displeased his father.

"She needs love. Affection. A sense of belonging."

Shaking his head, he felt the first tiny thread of worry begin to snake along his spine. "She'll have everything she needs."

"How can she when you haven't so much as looked at her since that first night?"

"I don't need you to teach me how to take care of a child." And even if he did need the help, damned if he'd ask for it.

She took a deep breath and tried to calm herself. He could almost hear her thinking, *Yelling at him is no way to get through to him.* She'd be right about that.

"All I'm trying to say is," she said, voice patient enough to spike his irritation meter, "I'm staying until I know Rosie is safe and loved and happy. That's not going to happen until you start interacting with her."

"She's a baby," he said tightly. "She's happy if she's fed and dry."

"She needs more than that—she needs family, a sense of belonging. I don't see that coming from you."

Reed wasn't used to being questioned. Doubted. His clients all believed in him. His family turned to him for every crisis imaginable, trusting him to take care of things. Hell, he'd lived his life accepting responsibility and doing everything he could to make sure the world rolled on in an organized way.

Did she really believe an eight-month-old baby would defeat him? His tone was patient and he gave himself points for that, since inside, he was seething. "Rose will get everything she needs."

"From Connie?" she asked.

"Yeah, from Connie. I brought in the one woman I *know* will do right by her. How is that a bad thing?" He took a deep breath and instantly regretted it since that orange scent clinging to her seemed to be invading him.

"It's bad if you depend solely on her to care for Rose."

"I didn't say I would."

"Actions speak louder than words," she pointed out. "And what you're doing is ignoring me and Rose."

"I'm not ignoring the baby. I'm ignoring *you*."

"Why?" she demanded, tossing both hands high.

Could she really not see what it cost him to avoid her company? Was she clueless about the attraction sizzling between them? Well, if so, Reed thought, it was time to let her know exactly what was going on here.

Her scent reached for him, surrounded him and he threw caution out the damn window. "Because of this."

He grabbed her, pulled her in close and kissed her as he'd wanted to for days.

Lilah hadn't expected *this*.

He'd moved so fast, pulled her in so close, held her so tight.

And, oh, my God, his *mouth*.

Reed kissed her with a hunger she'd never experienced before. And for one split second, she was too stunned, too shocked, to do anything more than stand there. But when that second passed, she was kissing him back.

Her body jumped into life, as if she'd somehow been electrocuted. There was a hot jolt of...*everything* blasting through her. Lilah's arms linked around his neck, she leaned into him and parted her lips beneath his. The sweep of his tongue took her breath and sent even more jagged slices of lightning through her body.

A hot ball of need settled in the pit of her stomach and even lower a throbbing ache awoke, and breathless, she knew she wanted, needed, *more*.

His big hands swept up and down her back, pulling her closer, until she felt as if she wanted to simply melt into his body. He cupped her behind and held her tightly to him until she felt the hardness of his body pressing into hers. The need jangling within jumped into high gear, sending her heartbeat into a thundering gallop. Tingling head to toe, Lilah could have stayed exactly where she was for, oh...eternity.

But even as she thought it, other sounds intruded through the buzzing in her ears. Voices, getting louder. Footsteps, coming closer.

And in a rush, her brain suddenly shrieked a warning, reminding her that the house was filled with moving men, not to mention Connie and Rose.

It took every ounce of control she had for Lilah to break away and take a long step back from temptation. Struggling to catch her breath, she knew what she must look like—eyes wide, hair tangled from his busy fingers running through it, mouth swollen from a kiss like no other. There was nothing she could do about that, though, so she instead fought to slow her heart rate and get her body back under control. Not easy since it felt as if every single cell in her body was wide awake and sending up skyrockets in anticipation.

It had been way too long since she'd been with a man. That had to be the reason she'd…overreacted like that. Running her own business didn't give her much time to look for and develop a love life. At least that was the excuse she usually gave herself. But the truth was, she simply hadn't found a man she was interested in enough to make a try at a relationship.

Not that Reed was the one for her. She already knew that was going nowhere, although, after that kiss, she had to admit that maybe he felt something for her whether he wanted to or not. But even if he did, he was rich and lived in California, while she lived in a tiny mountain town and was substantially less than wealthy. They were from completely different worlds and one kiss—no matter how amazing—wasn't enough to bridge the gap. Best to remember that.

"All finished," a deep voice announced as three moving men walked into the main room.

"Just in time," Lilah muttered. She glanced briefly at Reed, saw the flash of banked lust in his eyes then told herself not to look at him again. At least not until the fire inside her had died down. Shouldn't take more than a week or two.

Oh, God.

Things had just gotten so much more complicated. Maybe it would have been better for him to go right on ignoring her. But it was probably too late to go back now.

They were going to have to talk about this, Lilah told herself. Come to an agreement that there would be no more kissing, and wasn't that a sad thought? But Rose had to be the priority. For both of them.

"Right, I'll just go and check everything," she said, taking the excuse the movers had handed her and running with it.

Connie was just walking into the room, a happy, babbling Rosie on her hip. The baby held out her arms to Lilah and in response, she scooped her up and kept walking. The warm, solid weight of the baby in her arms was the perfect antidote to the still-pulsing need she felt inside. Rose was the reason she was here. The *only* reason. Her happiness was paramount.

In the newly setup nursery, Lilah did a quick inspection, made sure the furniture had all been put together and set where she'd told Connie she wanted them. If she took a couple of extra minutes to cool down, who was to know? Finally, though, she headed back to the main room.

There, she found two of the movers had already gone out to their truck. Since Reed had no idea what furniture she'd purchased, Lilah was the one who signed the delivery and setup sheet the remaining mover held out to her. When she was finished, she closed the door behind him and took a slow, steadying breath before heading into the great room to join Reed and Connie.

"Everything all right in here?" the woman asked, her gaze darting from Reed to Lilah and back again.

"Yeah, fine," Reed said, scraping one hand along his jaw.

"Dandy," Lilah agreed, keeping her gaze locked on the baby in her arms.

"Uh-huh," Connie said with a shake of her head. "You two are terrible liars."

She walked over, plucked Rosie from Lilah's grasp and headed for the kitchen. "I'm just going to give this sweet baby a snack. While we're busy, the two of you can talk about whatever it is that's not happening."

Alone with him in the great room, Lilah listened to the silence for a couple of long minutes before finally giving a sigh and muttering, "That's just great."

"What's the problem?"

She looked at Reed. "Really? You kiss me brainless and then your housekeeper takes one look at me and knows what's been going on and you wonder what the problem is?"

He shrugged. "It was just a kiss."

"Yeah. And Godiva is just chocolate." She pushed both hands through her hair then faced him. She didn't mean to stare at his mouth, it just…happened. God. They really did need to talk. And it looked as though it was going to have to be her opening the conversation.

She lifted her gaze to his and asked, "Why?"

He waved the question off. "Why not?"

Well, didn't she feel special? Then something occurred to her and Lilah inhaled sharply, narrowed her eyes on him. "Did you kiss me just to shut me up?"

Now his green eyes flashed and a muscle in his jaw ticked. "What?"

"We were arguing," she reminded him and warmed to her idea as she kept talking. "You were losing, so you wanted me quiet."

Reed laughed shortly and shook his head. "Again, I'll remind you I'm an attorney. I argue for a living. I wasn't losing."

"Oh, please," she said, giving him a satisfied smile. Connie was right. Reed really was a terrible liar. Which meant she was, too, but that wasn't the point right now. "We both know I was right. You've been ignoring Rosie, avoiding me. I called you on it and you didn't like it. So to end the argument, you kissed me."

He took a step closer and Lilah just managed to not take an equal step back. She wasn't afraid of him or anything. She just didn't know if being too close to him right that moment was the best possible idea. Yet backing up would make him think she didn't trust herself around him. Which she didn't—but why let him know that?

"I don't have to kiss a woman to win an argument. I make a lot of money by winning arguments." His gaze moved over her features before meeting her eyes again. "You want the truth? I kissed you because I wanted to. And like I told you once before, when I want something, I go get it."

Well, that was both insulting and flattering. For a week now, she'd been fighting her attraction to Reed, knowing it couldn't go anywhere. Knowing it would just complicate an already out-of-control situation. And boy had she been right.

In her own imagination, a kiss between them would have been hot, leaving them both uncomfortable. In reality, the kiss was well beyond hot and had left them both…wary. Plus, now she couldn't help wondering what sex with him would be like. But as soon as that thought jumped merrily into her mind, she pushed it back out again. As hard as it would be, she was going to forget all about this kiss and the way he'd made her feel for a few shining moments. It was the only way to survive being around him.

"I'm not a prize you can grab off a shelf, Reed. And if I don't want you to kiss me again, you won't, believe me."

"Not much of a threat." His voice was a dark rumble that seemed to settle along her spine and vibrate. "Since you already want me to kiss you again."

Lilah took a deep breath and let it slide from her lungs on a long sigh. She could lie, but what would be the point? He'd felt her reaction to his kiss. He could probably look into her eyes right now and still see the smoldering embers of the inferno he'd started inside her.

"Fine. Okay, maybe I do want you to kiss me." He moved in on her and this time she *did* skip backward out of reach. If she let him touch her right now, he'd set off a chain reaction within her that would quickly flare up out of control. If she was going to draw a line in the sand, then it had to be here and now. "But unlike you, I don't go after something just because I want it."

A barely there smile touched one corner of his mouth. "Is that right?"

She squared her shoulders, lifted her chin and told herself she was doing the right thing. "Absolutely. We don't always want what's good for us."

He laughed shortly, tucked his hands into his pockets and nodded. "Truer words," he mused.

Lilah's eyebrows arched. She was pretty sure she'd just been insulted. "Thanks very much."

As if he could read the tension spiraling through her, he took a step back, then another. "Look, I've told you my father doesn't want the baby and Spring's mother says she simply can't do it because she would miss Spring too much, though she also pointed out she's not interested in being a grandma. So I'm keeping Rose. Raising her."

"Loving her?" Lilah had to ask. Had to make him see that money and a roof over her head would not be enough to give Rose the whole, complete life she deserved.

He frowned at her. "What is this obsession you have with love?"

"Obsession?" she repeated. "What is your fierce opposition to it?"

"I've seen too many people crushed because love was taken away. Or denied. Or tossed aside. Love," he said, voice dark, deep, "is the root of every misery in the world."

"That's a sad attitude."

"And I earned it," he told her, shaking his head, walking across the room to look out the window at the neatly tended front yard.

He didn't speak again, but Lilah was intrigued enough by his silence to follow him. To try to find the first chink in the wall he surrounded himself with. "How? How did you earn the right to say that love is worthless?"

Glancing at her, he said, "I've had a front-row seat my whole damn life to the show of my parents constantly looking for and never finding this mysterious 'love.' They discard wives and husbands like most people change cars and never once have they found what they're looking for.

"My brothers, sisters and I were caught up in the resulting chaos." He turned to face her. "So no, I can't promise love. And I'd like to say that I really don't require your approval for how I raise my niece."

"I know," she said, though those two simple words left a bitter taste in her mouth. "But this isn't about only you, Reed. This is about what's best for Rosie."

"I know that, which is why you're still here." He loosened his tie, then shrugged out of his suit jacket and tossed it behind him to the arm of the sofa. When he looked at her again, he said, "You've got some idea of what my life with Rose should be. News flash—no kid has a perfect life. I've got a demanding job with long hours. Doesn't leave a lot of time for building a nest, for God's sake."

"You don't have to—I already have," she said, sweeping one hand out to encompass the living room and the rest of the house besides. "But you will have to make some changes for Rose's sake."

He laughed shortly. "I'd say we're both standing in the middle of a pretty damn big change."

"Yes, but—"

"And Connie's here now." He glanced past her toward the hall that led to the kitchen. "Trust me when I say Rose couldn't have a better person taking care of her."

"I believe that," Lilah said, since spending just a few minutes with Connie had convinced her that the woman was a born nurturer. "Okay, yes, Rosie will get plenty of care and affection from Connie. But you're her father figure."

He scowled at her.

She saw the flicker of what might have been panic in his eyes and actually felt better seeing it. "You are the man in her life and you have to *be* in her life—not just some ghost who drifts in and out."

She watched a muscle in his jaw twitch and flex and she knew how hard this was for him. There probably weren't many people in Reed Hudson's life who were willing to stand toe-to-toe with him over anything. And maybe she wouldn't have been either, ordinarily. But this was about Rose's future, so she was willing to do what she had to. Didn't seem to matter that her mouth was still buzzing from that kiss or that her nerves were still tangled together in slippery knots.

"You know," he said, "I don't much like taking orders."

"I didn't mean—"

"Oh, yeah, you did," he said and loomed over her, maybe hoping to intimidate her. But Lilah just met him glare for glare.

Seconds ticked past and the silence stretched out between them.

"Why do you smell different every day?" he murmured, and the irritation in his eyes shifted to something hotter, more intimate.

"What?" The abrupt shift in conversation had her shaking her head, trying to catch up.

"Your scent," he repeated, moving in and drawing a deep breath. "It's oranges today." He laid both hands on her shoulders and then skimmed his hands up along her neck to cup her face in his palms.

God, she felt the heat of him sliding down into her system, again, and she shivered with the rush of it. This was not a good idea. Hadn't she *just* told him that he wouldn't be kissing her again. Ever? And here she was, sliding into that puddle of want just because he touched her.

"It's driving me crazy," he admitted, his voice no more than a whisper now. His gaze locked on hers. "Every day, there's a new scent clinging to you and I wake up wondering what it's going to be. Then I have to get close enough to you to taste it. And," he added, as he dipped his head to hers, "once I'm close I don't want to be anywhere else."

"It's my soaps," she whispered, amazed that she could talk with his mouth no more than a breath from hers. With the golden sunlight streaming through the window, wrapping them both in a slash of light that seemed to glow with warmth.

"Yeah," he said, "I figured that out. And now I know that when you're rubbing that scent all over you, you're wet and naked."

She took a long, slow breath and her stomach did a quick spin. He was going to pull her in again, she knew it. He knew it. Maybe she'd stand a chance against him and what he made her feel if she turned and sprinted from the room. But she wasn't entirely sure her legs would support her. So she had to try for reason instead.

"Okay, maybe we should just stop…"

"Yeah," he agreed. "Maybe we should. But we're not going to."

"No, I don't think we are."

Six

A tiny voice in the back of Lilah's mind shouted that it would be much better for this situation if they could keep their distance. But she'd never felt anything like this incredible heat, this indescribable need, so she silently told that logical little voice to be quiet and go away.

This was ridiculous. She knew it. But she couldn't help the wanting. Her heart hammered in her chest. Breath caught in her lungs and her body felt as if she were on fire. This man had way too much power over her. One touch from him was a storm of sensation and the need for more clamored inside her.

"This isn't solving anything," she managed to say.

"Yeah, I know." He took her mouth again and instantly Lilah's thoughts dissolved into a murky puddle.

She met him eagerly, wrapping her around him, holding on as her body trembled and quaked from too many sensations pouring in at once. His hands dropped from her face to explore her curves with a rough sense of urgency that felt like gasoline being poured on a fire. Up and down her spine, down to her bottom and back up to cup her breasts, his hands seemed to be everywhere at once. She groaned and even that small sound was muffled by the roaring in her ears.

The house was quiet, only adding to the feeling of intimacy. And though it felt as if they were alone in the house, they really weren't, and a moment later, both of them remembered it.

The baby's wail shattered their kiss and broke them apart in an instant.

"What the hell?" Reed demanded, clearly horrified. "It sounds like she's being tortured."

"No." Lilah choked out a laugh and pushed her hair back from her face with shaking hands. "She's just past her nap time."

"Good God."

The appalled look on his face brought another short laugh from her. He was clearly clueless about babies and now was as good a time as any to start his education. Still a little unsteady on her feet, Lilah reached out and patted his chest. "I'll be right back."

She left him, headed for the kitchen. A few deep breaths helped her steady herself, though she figured her stomach would be jumping and her heart racing for quite a while yet. Once inside, she found Connie patting Rose's back and murmuring to her. Glancing up at Lilah, she said, "She's tired, poor thing."

"It's way past her nap time," Lilah agreed. "If we had food and any of her things already here, we could just put her down upstairs. But we'll get her back to the hotel."

"Good idea," Connie said, handing the baby over. "While you three are gone, I'll get groceries and things and have everything ready for all of you to settle in tomorrow."

Rose dropped her head on Lilah's shoulder, but the crying didn't stop. Sliding her hand up and down Rose's back, Lilah gave Connie a grateful smile. "I'm really glad you're going to be a part of Rose's life, Connie."

"Me, too," the older woman said, already beginning to bustle around the model-home-perfect kitchen, making it her own. "Retirement's for old people. I was bored stiff to tell the truth." Humming to herself, she set about rearranging the cupboards and didn't even notice when Lilah and Rosie left the room.

"It's okay, sweetie," Lilah crooned, giving the baby a soft jiggle as she walked down the hall back toward the main room where she'd left Reed.

The comforting, warm weight of Rose's small body pressed to hers made Lilah's heart sigh with love—even while she tried to imagine living without it. That thought was dark enough to make her eyes sting, but she blinked back tears that wouldn't do her any good. The house was cozy, in spite of its size, and she knew that Rose would love living here. Lilah only wished that she could be there, to watch Rose grow, to be a part of her life.

Walking into the great room, she watched Reed turn at the sound of Rose's sniffling cry. His eyes were shining, but wary.

Perfect, Lilah thought. She knew he wasn't immune to Rose. She'd seen him that first night, after all, when he'd cuddled her close. And she could understand the caution she sensed in him. But until he let himself truly care for Rose, that wariness would always be with him.

It was part of the wall he'd built around himself. He'd already told her about what growing up with a very different family had been like for him. So she couldn't really blame him for being suspicious of love. But wasn't it long overdue for him to put his past behind him?

"Is she all right?" he asked.

"She's fine," Lilah said, still stroking the crying baby's back. "Just tired."

"Then we should go." He grabbed his suit jacket off the sofa and shrugged into it. "Give me the keys to your rental. I'll bring it around to the front and you can strap her in for the drive back to the hotel."

"Yeah." She walked up to him and plopped Rose into his arms, giving him no choice but to hold the tiny girl. "I'll bring the car around, then you can strap her in."

He looked like a man caught in a trap. Shifting the baby to his shoulder, he looked at her. "I don't—"

"Look," Lilah interrupted. "She's even stopped crying for you." *Good girl, Rosie*, she thought. "Won't take me a minute to get the car."

She hurriedly left the room, but paused at the threshold long enough to glance back. Reed and Rose stood in a slash of sunlight, each of them staring at the other as if discovering a new world. And maybe, she thought as she left the house, that's exactly what they were doing.

They settled into the house with hardly a bump.

Reed spent every day buried in paperwork, hand-holding clients and thinking about the woman currently living in his house. For the first time in his memory, his concentration was shattered. Reed went through the motions, going to court, meeting with mediators and advising his clients, yet there was one corner of his mind not focused on the job at all. Instead, it was centered on Lilah Strong and what she was doing to him.

Memories of kisses that never should have happened continued to bubble and burn at the back of his mind, tormenting him during the day and torturing him at night. He couldn't sleep, and even work didn't have the same draw for him as it had before.

His life had been thrown into turmoil and there was only one way to get everything back into order. Lilah wouldn't leave until she knew that Rosie would be happy. So, the way to make her go the hell home and let him get back to his normal life was to prove to her that he and Rose would get along without her.

And fine, he could admit she'd had a point about getting to know Rose. He couldn't stand back from a child he'd agreed to raise. Even not counting the problem of Lilah, Reed had to get comfortable with the baby who was now a part of his life.

Which was why he was bent over a bathtub, getting just as wet as the infant sitting in a few inches of warm, bubble-filled water.

"She doesn't think we can do this." Reed kept one cautious hand lightly against Rose's back as she splashed gleefully in the tub. Her tiny feet kicked up a storm, making frantic waves while she laughed and turned her shining eyes up to him.

Unexpectedly, Reed's heart gave a hard *thump* in his chest as he looked down into her bright green gaze. Until tonight, she'd been more or less a shadow to him. He knew she was there of course, but their interactions had been limited—purposely. He'd deliberately avoided contact with her because he hadn't wanted to *care*. Caring was an open doorway to misery, pain, fear and all kinds of dark possibilities.

And as his heart continued to squeeze in his chest, he realized that he was in it now. A few minutes alone with a child who looked up at him as if he was her personal hero was enough to start him down the road he'd managed to sidestep most of his life.

She was so small, yet already, Rose was her own little person with a grin that caught at your heart and a temper that could set off a screech strong enough to peel paint off walls. Weirdly, Reed liked knowing she had that strong personality. She wouldn't be a pushover, that was for sure. She'd stand up for herself.

But he'd be there, too. His course was set and whether Lilah believed it or not, Reed knew his life was never again going to be what it had been. "I'll make sure you're safe, Rose."

The baby giggled, and that deep, rolling, straight-up-from-the-gut sound settled into his chest and gave his heart another hard squeeze.

"You're going to tear me up, aren't you?" He smoothed the soft washcloth over her back, and then around to her narrow chest while she slapped the water, sending droplets flying to splatter his shirt and face.

"Yeah, you are. You're a heartbreaker. It's in your eyes and you're already working on me." He sighed a little as the baby laughed and then gently ran the flat of his hand over her damp curly hair.

It had been inevitable, he told himself. From the moment Lilah had carried Spring's daughter into his office, he'd been headed exactly *here*. Somewhere deep inside, he'd known that Rose would be able to breach his defenses. He'd spent most of his life with the determination to keep from caring too much about anyone. He loved his brothers and sisters of course, but even there he maintained a distance. Just enough to protect himself. But this one baby with her happy smile and trusting eyes could undo him. Reed blew out a breath and tried to accept his new reality. But if he was still fighting it just a little, who could blame him?

"Time to get out," he said with a sudden laugh as Rose kicked and slapped all at once and splashed water into her own face. Her tiny features screwed up, the smile disappeared and she blinked frantically. "Not as much fun when you're the one getting splashed, is it?"

She looked up at him, her mouth turned down, and he knew he was about to be deafened by a screech. Quickly, he snatched her up out of the water and, using only one hand, wrapped a towel around her as he cuddled her to his chest. "Hey, you're okay. It's just water."

She sniffled and watched him as she seemed to think it over for a minute or two. Then, apparently the crisis passed, because she smiled and patted his face.

God. She already had a hold on him with those tiny fingers of hers. His heart did another slow tumble and Reed told himself to be careful. To not be drawn in so deeply he wouldn't be able to defend himself. Maybe the answer here was to show Lilah he could and would care for Rose, but to hold enough of himself back that he wouldn't eventually have his heart crushed.

He stood in the bathroom, looked into the mirror and saw his own rumpled reflection, holding a tiny wet baby. Bath time should definitely prove to Lilah that he was willing to involve himself with Rose, right? And that was good, wasn't it? Lilah would leave when he and Rose had "bonded" and then he could get back to the way life should be lived without constantly thinking about a woman he shouldn't be thinking about.

Reed wondered if he was losing his mind. His sharp, cagey brain was fogged a lot lately and he had the feeling it was all because of Lilah. Desire was eating away at his logic. *Bonded.*

"Stupid word, isn't it, Rose?"

"What's stupid?" Lilah spoke up from the doorway.

He groaned inwardly. See? Another example of foggy brain. He hadn't even heard Lilah approach. Shaking his head a little, he met her gaze in the mirror. She looked good, of course. Even in faded jeans and a pale blue T-shirt, Lilah Strong was enough to make a man's mouth water. No wonder he was foggy. With her around, he would challenge *any* guy to keep his mind on the mundane. Not like he could tell her that, though. So he did the first thing he could think of and lied.

"Nothing. Rose was just telling me she thought USC would beat UCLA this fall and I told her that was stupid. Nobody beats the Bruins."

"Uh-huh." Lilah's fabulous mouth curved. "Big football fan, is she?"

"Who isn't?"

She studied him and he realized he could get lost in those blue eyes of hers. The color of summer skies, or clear lakes. Her red-gold hair was a constant fascination to him, and now that he'd had his hands in that heavy, silky mass, all he could think about was doing it again. Her lips were full and shaped into a slight smile that made a single dimple wink in her cheek, and all he could think about was getting another taste of that mouth.

He was in deep trouble here, and when he took a breath and dragged the scent of lilacs into his lungs, he almost groaned aloud. Seriously, couldn't the woman pick *one* scent and stick to it? The changeup was making him crazy.

"Are you okay?" she asked.

"What? Yeah. Fine." Perfect. His poker face had almost completely dissolved now. Somehow, this one woman managed to always keep him off guard—which was another good reason for her to get back to her own life as soon as possible and leave him to his. "Did you want something?"

"Just to tell you your sister Savannah's here."

"Here?"

"*Right* here, actually." Savannah stepped up behind Lilah and grinned.

The huge master bath was beginning to feel like a broom closet.

"Well," Savannah said, still smiling, "here's something I never thought I'd see. Reed Hudson bathing a baby."

He sighed at his sister's teasing. Savannah's short black hair hugged her scalp and her eyes were the same shade of green as his own. He, Savannah and their brother James were the first batch of Hudson siblings, and they were all close.

Though he was surprised to see Savannah, he shouldn't have been. A few days ago, Reed had sent out an email blast to the entire family giving them his new address. It had been only a matter of time before they started trickling in to see him, demanding help with one thing or another.

"What's up, Savannah?" He kept his gaze on his sister, since she was far too observant, and if he chanced glancing at Lilah, his sister would no doubt see more than he wanted her to. He was less and less sure of his ability to mask his thoughts since Lilah had entered his life. After all, if she could read him after knowing each other only two weeks, his sister would probably be able to pick thoughts right from his brain.

"Nothing much." Savannah lifted one shoulder in a shrug. "Just wanted to see your new place, see Spring's baby and—"

"And?" He waited, knowing there was a real reason for her visit. None of the siblings came by or called unless they needed something.

"Okay," she said with a laugh, "I want to use the family jet and the pilot won't take off without your say-so."

He frowned. "Where are you going?"

"Just Paris for a week or two. I need a change," she said and gave him the pout that had always worked on their father. It didn't have the same effect on Reed, because he knew she used that poor-little-me look as her most effective weapon. "I broke up with Sean and I need some me time. You know how it is, right?"

The last, she directed at Lilah, who had been watching the byplay silently. "Um…"

When she got no support from Lilah, Savannah turned back to her brother. "Come on, Reed. Be a sport. You're not using it in the next day or two, are you?"

"No," he said, jiggling the baby a little when she began to squirm.

"So what's the problem?" Savannah turned and said, "Lilah, right? You're with me on this, aren't you? I mean, you know what it feels like to just need a break, right?"

Lilah smiled and shook her head. "I don't know. When I take a break from work, I drive to the city. I've never been to Paris."

"Oh, my God." Savannah looked at her as if Lilah had confessed to being a serial killer. "Seriously? You've *got* to go. Make Reed take you. Well, after my trip," she added quickly. "But you should definitely go. There is this amazing little street café right near Sacré-Coeur..."

While his sister babbled on about the wonders of the City of Lights, Reed jiggled the baby nestled against him, trying to keep her happy. That's when he felt a sudden warmth spread across his chest.

"Oh, man." He looked down at the naked baby in his arms and realized he really should have put a diaper on her right away.

"What's wrong?" Lilah asked instantly.

"Nothing," Reed muttered. "She just—"

Picking up on what had happened, Savannah laughed in delight. "She peed on you! God, Spring would have laughed so hard right now..."

As soon as she said it, silence settled over the three of them like a cold blanket. In the harsh bathroom light, Reed could see the signs of grieving that his sister had tried to conceal with a bright smile. Even as he watched her, Savannah sobered and she looked from Reed to Lilah. Shaking her head, she swallowed hard, blew out a breath and whispered, "I can't believe she's gone. Not really, you know?"

"I feel the same way," Lilah said softly, reaching out one hand to lay it on Savannah's arm. "Spring was a good friend to me, but she was your sister and I'm so sorry."

Lost in the face of his sister's pain, Reed was grateful for the sympathy in Lilah's gaze and voice. Helping Savannah or any of the others deal with Spring's death was especially hard for him since he hadn't actually dealt with it yet himself.

"That's why you really want to go to Paris, isn't it?" Reed asked.

"Yes," Savannah admitted on a sigh. "Sean was just another ship in the night, but Spring…" She winced a little. "We went to Paris together five years ago, remember?"

Reed gave her a tired smile and said wryly, "I remember getting a late-night call from a gendarme asking me if I was willing to pay bail for you and Spring after you went swimming in a public fountain."

Savannah laughed and lifted one hand to cover her mouth. "That's right. I'd forgotten about that. God, we had fun on that trip. Now… I just want to go back. Remember."

Reed looked into her eyes and saw the misery just beneath the surface and he understood her need to go back, retrace her steps with their lost sister. Try to relive the joy to ease the pain. Though none of their parents would win any awards for their skills at nurturing, all of the siblings had managed to stay close.

He had no doubt that Savannah was thinking of a trip to Paris as a sort of wake for the sister she would miss so much. Hell, he knew how she felt. He felt it, too. Here he stood, holding his sister's child, and the baby girl would never remember her mother. Reed would never see Spring again. Never hear that raucous laugh of hers, and it tore at him that the last time he'd seen her, they'd parted angrily. He'd never get that moment back. Never be able to rewrite the past.

Too many *nevers*, he told himself. Too much left unsaid, undone, and now, too late to change a damn thing.

"If it helps to know it," Lilah was saying, her voice breaking through his thoughts, "Spring was really happy with her life. She had a lot of friends."

Savannah looked at Lilah for a long minute, then finally nodded. "It does help. Thank you. And you should know that whenever I talked to my sister, she told me about how kind you were. How much she loved her job."

Now Reed was surprised. Savannah had known about Spring actually working? Was he the only one his sister hadn't confided in?

Turning to her brother again, Savannah said, "I'm so glad I came here in person instead of calling. I like seeing you with the baby and I think Spring would get a real kick out of it, too."

"Yeah," Reed said, still holding the squirmy, wet baby close to his chest. "You're right. She would."

He looked from the baby to Savannah to Lilah and realized that he was surrounded by women—and that wasn't even counting Connie, who was off in the kitchen. Yeah, Spring would have loved seeing him like this. And the thought made him smile.

How his life had changed in a couple of short weeks.

"So?" his sister prodded. "Can I use the plane?"

Nodding, he said, "I'll call the pilot. Let him know you're coming."

Lilah looked up at him, gave him a wide, approving smile, and for some reason, Reed felt as if he'd just won a medal.

"Savannah seemed nice," Lilah said later as she shared tea and some of Connie's magic chocolate chip bars with the housekeeper in the kitchen.

And, she thought as she took another bite and gave an inner sigh, Reed was right. They were "magic."

Lilah loved this room. As with any house, the kitchen really was the heart of things. And this one was amazing. It could have graced the pages of any magazine. The walls were cream colored, the miles of quartz counter were white with streaks of gray marbling. Upper cabinets were white, lowers were a dark gray and the floor was a wide-plank dark walnut. Tucked into the nook where a bay window offered a view of the backyard, the two women sat at an oak pedestal table. A silver pendant light that looked like an old-fashioned gas lamp hung over the table and provided the only light in the otherwise darkened room.

"Oh," Connie said with a laugh, "that Savannah has a good soul but a wild heart. She's always up to something." Chuckling now, she added, "Always had a plan cooking in that quick brain of hers. She spent many a night in my kitchen washing dishes for some transgression or other."

Lilah smiled in response. "Reed told me that you were their real parent."

Flushing with pleasure, Connie shook her head, took a sip of tea and said, "Not really, but I'm sure it felt that way to them from time to time. Anyway, it was good to see Savannah even though it was a quick visit."

Quick indeed. Reed's sister had left almost immediately after he'd called the airport to okay her flight to Paris. As for Reed, once he'd dressed Rose in her pj's and got her into bed, he'd shut himself up in his study. He hadn't so much as poked his head out in hours.

And Lilah had had to force herself to leave him to his solitude. But there'd been a look on his face when

Savannah had rushed out—as if he wished she'd stayed longer. But he hadn't said anything. Hadn't asked her to sit down for a while and have a cup of coffee, and she wondered why. It was as if the distance he tried to keep with Rose was simply the way he treated everyone he cared about.

Had he always been so closed off? Or was it a self-defense mechanism? And if it was, what was he protecting himself from? She had more questions than answers and Lilah knew there was one sure way to get some insight into who exactly Reed Hudson was. Talk to the woman who'd raised him.

"Reed didn't seem surprised to have his sister dash in and out."

"Oh," Connie said, taking a sip of tea, "he's used to that. All of the siblings come and go from his life regularly." She set her cup down and continued, "They love each other, but every last one of them has a *loner* streak. I suppose that's to be expected, since their parents really did leave them to their own devices more often than not. And, ever since he was a teenager, the others have turned to Reed to solve problems."

Lilah's heart ached a little for the loneliness he must have felt as a child. Lilah's own childhood had been great. With two parents who loved each other and doted on her, she'd never been left on her own.

"But he was just a kid, too."

Connie laughed a little. "I think Reed was born old. At least, he has an old soul. Never a single day's trouble out of that boy. Always did what was expected of him, never made waves. He had his own...*code*, I guess you'd say. His own rules for living, even as a little boy. To tell the truth, I used to wish he would rebel a little. But he's always had the maturity that the rest of the family—" she broke off and scowled "—including his parents, lacked."

Now Lilah had the mental image of a little boy, carving out a set of rules so he could keep the world around him safe. Was that what his private wall was about? Keeping out people who might disturb his sense of order?

"Really?" Lilah had already realized that a one-word question would be enough to keep Connie talking.

"Oh, don't get me wrong," Connie said, and the halo of light from the pendant fixture overhead gilded her hair and shone in her eyes. "His parents aren't evil by any means. They love the kids, they're just...careless. Careless with what means the most and the sad thing is, they won't realize it until it's too late to change anything.

"One day they'll be old and wondering why their children don't come to visit." She nodded to herself and gave a little sigh. "They've no real relationship with their own children and that's a sad statement to make, I think."

"It is," Lilah agreed. She couldn't imagine the kind of childhood Reed and his siblings had had. But it still didn't give her insight into the man. And she found she wanted to know him.

"Does he see a lot of his family?"

"Well, now," Connie admitted, "I've not had a chance to see it on a daily basis for the last couple of years. But when the kids come to visit me, they often talk of Reed."

"They visit you?"

"Sure they do," Connie said, laughing. "I'm the one who smacked their bottoms, dried their tears and took care of them when they were sick, aren't I?"

His parents might not have been worth much, Lilah thought, but he'd had Connie and somehow that made her feel much better both about his childhood and Rose's situation, as well. With Connie in her life, Rosie would get plenty of affection and care, Lilah told herself.

"Reed's told me how much you meant to all of them. To *him*."

Connie smiled, clearly pleased to hear it. "They're all good people, every last one of them. And I know how they'll all miss Spring." She took a breath and slowly turned her teacup on the counter in tiny circles. "But I think it will hit Reed hardest—once he finally allows himself the chance to mourn her. He was always the one who took charge of the others. And losing her hurt him. I can see it in him."

"I can, too," Lilah mused. More tonight than ever before. It was seeing him with Savannah, she thought. The brother and sister having that sorrow-filled moment over their sister. While Savannah's pain had been obvious to anyone looking at her, seeing that same anguish in Reed took more effort. But Lilah had seen his brilliant green eyes go momentarily soft and she'd read the regret in those depths. Her heart hurt for him and she was surprised by the strength of her compassion.

When she'd arrived here, she'd expected to hate him on sight. To resent him for taking Rose away from her. Now she was beginning to feel for him, understand what drove him.

"The others now," Connie said after a moment, "they come and go from Reed's life. Each of them will pop in from time to time, usually when they need something, then they disappear again until there's a new need. He'd never say it, but I imagine that bothers him."

"It would bother anyone," Lilah said and she found herself offended on his behalf. Did his siblings appreciate him only for what he could do for them?

"Reed's a strong one. He's made himself so." Connie lifted her cup for a sip. "But there's a fine line, I think, between being strong and being hard. I worry that he doesn't see it."

So did Lilah. The wall he'd built around himself was so solid, she had thought it impenetrable. But there had been one or two times when she'd sensed a chink in his armor.

"Well," Connie announced, "morning comes early, so I'm off to bed. Just leave the teacups here on the table, Lilah. I'll take care of them in the morning."

"Okay. Good night." She watched Connie walk to her suite and for a minute, Lilah just sat there in the kitchen, listening to the silence. The refrigerator hummed and ice thunked into the bin. She checked the time and told herself to go to bed. It was already eleven o'clock and Connie was right, morning would come early. Rosie wasn't one for sleeping in.

But Lilah wasn't ready for bed. She felt...restless.

She stood, then turned the lights off, plunging the room into darkness as she left and headed down the hall. Her mind was busy, rehashing that scene with Savannah, then the conversation with Connie. Which turned her thoughts to Reed. No surprise there, since he'd spent a lot of time front and center in her brain over the past couple of weeks.

But now, along with the attraction she'd felt from the start, there was also...admiration and a tug of—not sympathy, she assured herself. He didn't need her pity and wouldn't want it even if he did. But she could feel bad for him that his family came to him only when they needed something from him.

The more she thought about him, the more she wanted

to see him. Talk to him. Assure herself he was okay and not sitting in a dark room feeling sad or depressed or… Oh, hell, she just wanted to see him. Before she could talk herself out of it, Lilah marched up to the closed study door and knocked.

Seven

"What is it?"

He didn't sound happy and Lilah almost changed her mind, but then she remembered that look in his eyes when he and Savannah were remembering Spring. Nope, she wasn't going to leave him alone until she knew he was all right.

She opened the door, poked her head inside and asked, "Are you busy?"

She could see he wasn't. The room was dark, but firelight spilled out into the shadows, creating weird images that danced across the ceiling and walls.

Rather than sitting behind his desk, he was on the other side of the room in one of the wide leather chairs pulled up in front of the wide, stone hearth, facing the fire. Those shadows moved over his features as he half turned to look at her. There was a short glass of what she guessed was scotch sitting on the table beside him.

She noted his usually tidy hair looked as if he'd been stabbing his fingers through it repeatedly. He wore a short-sleeved black T-shirt that he'd changed into after bathing Rose and a pair of worn jeans that looked as good on him as his usual uniform of elegant suits. He was barefoot, legs kicked out in front of him, and again, she had to wonder what it was about bare feet that had become so sexy all of a sudden.

"Good, I'm glad you're not busy," she said, walking over to sit down in the chair beside his.

He scowled at her. "Who said I wasn't?"

"I did. You're having a drink and staring at a fire. That's not busy. That's brooding."

"I'm not brooding," he argued. "I'm busy thinking."

"About?"

His scowl deepened and, weirdly, Lilah found it sort of cute. He probably thought it was intimidating, but he was wrong. At least, as far as Lilah was concerned.

"You're damn nosy," he mused, gaze fixed on her.

"If you're not, you never find out anything," she argued, then picked up his glass and took a sip. Instantly the fire of the expensive liquor burned a line down her throat and settled into her stomach to smolder.

"Please," he said, waving one hand. "Help yourself."

"No thanks, one sip of that is plenty. How do you stand it?" Firelight danced in his eyes and shadows chased each other across his features.

Smirking a little, he said, "Hundred-year-old scotch is an acquired taste. I acquired it."

He was probably hoping that if he was surly enough, she'd leave. But wrong again. She glanced around the room, pleased with how it had turned out. There were bookcases behind his desk and along one wall, with paintings and framed awards hanging on the opposite wall. The stone hearth took up a third side of the room, while floor-to-ceiling windows made up the fourth. It was male, but cozy.

"Your sister seems nice."

He snorted and picked up his glass for another sip. "Savannah is a force of nature. Like a hurricane. They're rarely nice."

Lilah saw more than she suspected he wanted her to see. He loved his sister, that had been clear. And though he sounded dismissive now, he was just doing the whole don't-get-too-close thing. "Do you see her often?"

He slanted her a look. "Writing a book?"

"Keeping secrets?" she countered, smiling to take the sting out of her accusation.

He sighed, turned his gaze back to the fire and said, "She drops in from time to time."

"When she needs something?" Lilah asked, wanting to see his reaction.

"Usually." Frowning, he turned his gaze back to her. "Why do you care? And why are you asking so many questions?"

"Like I said, if you want answers, you have to ask questions." She ran her fingers over the edge of the table. "I just wondered if you and your brothers and sisters see much of each other."

His brow furrowed, he asked, "Why does that matter?"

She couldn't very well tell him that she was worried that his siblings were taking advantage of him, so she lied instead. "I want to know if Rose will have lots of aunts and uncles coming over all the time."

He took another sip of scotch and drained the glass. "I told you I'd take care of her."

"I'm not arguing that," she said, and wished she'd come up with a better lie. She hadn't come in here to argue with him. She'd wanted to…talk. To make sure he was okay. And that sounded just pitiful, even to her.

"Well, that's a first." Reed pushed to his feet, walked to the wet bar in the corner and refilled his glass. "You've been arguing with me since the first day I met you."

She supposed that was true, but their *relationship*, if that was what it was, hadn't exactly started out friendly, had it?

"To be fair," she said, standing up to walk to him, "you did a lot of that, too."

He studied her through eyes that suddenly looked as dark and mysterious as a forest at midnight, and something fluttered into life inside her. What was it about Reed Hudson that turned her insides to jelly and made her want to both argue and comfort at the same time? Lilah took a breath and steadied herself, for all the good it would do. Being this close to him, having his eyes pinned on her, was enough to unsettle any woman's balance.

"And now what?" he asked. "We're friends?"

"We could be," she said, though a part of her doubted it. There was too much underlying tension simmering between them for a friendship. She didn't have any other "friend" she imagined naked.

"We won't be," he said and set his glass down with a click.

He turned to face her and Lilah's stomach did a slow spin as her heart gave one hard lurch. Nerves jangled into life inside her, but she paid no attention. The night was late, the room was dark but for firelight simmering in the shadows. There was closeness here and she didn't want it to end.

Stupid, her brain warned and Lilah didn't listen. She didn't want to think too much about what was going on between them right now, because she didn't want this quiet, intimate moment to end. Not yet. "Why not, Reed?"

"Because I don't want to be your *friend*, Lilah. What I want from you has nothing to do with being pals."

She took another breath, but it didn't help. Her balance was dissolving and she didn't care. Staring into those green eyes of his was mesmerizing. She couldn't have looked away if she had tried. And she didn't want to try. Lilah wanted to look into his eyes until she discovered everything about him. Until the wall he hid behind fell crashing to the ground.

"My friends don't smell as good as you do," he said quietly. "They don't have hair that looks like gold and feels like silk."

Lilah shivered. She'd known when she knocked on the study door that *this* was what she had been heading toward. For two weeks now, her mind had been filled with nothing but thoughts of Reed Hudson. Even her dreams had been pushing her here, to this moment in the darkness with him.

"What if I don't want to be your friend, either?" she whispered.

"Then I'd say we're wasting precious time standing here talking," Reed said, moving in on her, "when we could be doing something far more interesting."

Awareness roared to life inside her and Lilah felt every single cell in her body wake up and jostle each other with eagerness. She gave him a slow smile that belied the nerves boiling in the pit of her stomach. "Is that right?"

He stepped up so close, their shirts brushed against each other. She felt heat pumping from his body and knew that her own was sizzling, too. Bending his head toward her, he inhaled sharply and murmured, "Vanilla today. I like it."

"Show me," she said and met his mouth in a kiss that lit up every inch of her body. Just like the first time he kissed her, spontaneous explosions of desire, need, hunger were set off inside her, one after the other. She was rocked by the force of them, stronger than before, as if her body had just been waiting, biding its time until it could finally let loose.

He pulled her in tight against him, his hands running up and down her spine, curving over her bottom, holding her close enough she couldn't miss his body's reaction to the kiss. And knowing that he felt the same throbbing need she did only fed the fires licking at the edges of her soul.

The core of her throbbed and pulsed in time with the beat of her heart that was so fast it left her nearly breathless. But then, she thought wildly, who needed air?

He didn't let her go as he moved forward, with Lilah backing up until she bumped into the edge of his desk. Their mouths still fused together, Lilah's tongue tangled with his as he swept inside her mouth to explore, to taste, to torture.

It had been a long time since she'd been with a man and even then, she'd felt nothing close to what she experienced with Reed. This was something brand new. Exciting. Amazing. The man had talented hands and his mouth was downright lethal.

He suddenly tore that mouth from hers and dropped his head to the curve of her neck. His lips, tongue and teeth made a trail along the length of her throat and Lilah groaned as she tipped her head to one side, giving him better access. Silently asking for *more*.

As if he heard her, he lifted both hands to cup her breasts and even through the fabric of her shirt and the lace bra beneath, she felt the heat of him. Her nipples pebbled and every stroke of his fingers sent a shooting star of sensation slicing through her. She gasped, letting her head fall back as her breath whipped in and out of her lungs. Staring at the ceiling, she blindly watched the fire-lit shadows shifting, pulsing in the darkness.

All she felt was him. Every last, hard inch of him pressing her into the edge of the desk. His muscular thighs aligned with hers and she held on to his waist to keep from falling. She wanted him on her, in her, over her. She wanted to feel his body pushing into hers, and easing the ache that only seemed to grow more frantic with every passing second.

He was tall and strong and really built. That one wild thought careened through her mind even as his fingers began to tug at the buttons of her blouse. Impatient now, for the feel of his hands on her skin, she tried to help, but only fumbled and got in his way.

"I've got it," he whispered harshly, his voice straining over every word. "Don't help."

"Right, right." She nodded, grateful he could still move since she seemed to be nearly paralyzed with her body's insistent demands, which clutched in her chest, her gut and, oh, so much lower.

Then he had her blouse undone and was pushing it off, down her arms to land on the desk behind her. The air in the room was cool in spite of the fire and she shivered a little. But then his hands were back on her breasts and heat spiraled up out of nowhere, delivering a different kind of shiver.

His nimble fingers flicked the front clasp of her bra and then her breasts were free and being cupped and stroked by those amazing hands of his. His thumbs and forefingers circled her nipples, tugging, pulling gently. He kissed her again, a sweep of his tongue across her lips, as if offering her a small taste of something incredible.

"Oh, boy," she said on a sigh and caught his satisfied smile.

"Only getting better from here," he promised, and Lilah could hardly wait. She'd never been like this before, her mind whispered. Never felt so much, wanted so much. No man before him had emptied her brain and filled her body so quickly, so completely.

At the core of her, she trembled and ached, and dampness filled the heat at her center. She was more than ready for whatever would come next and she let him know just how eager she was, by reaching up, cupping his face in her palms and dragging his mouth to hers.

Again and again, they claimed each other, breath sliding from one to the other as they delved into a pool of unbelievable sensations. And still it wasn't enough. Not nearly.

She reached beneath the hem of his T-shirt and flattened her palms against the hard planes of his chest. She felt the definition of sculpted muscles and nearly whimpered with the glory of it.

He hissed in a breath, then ripped his shirt off before pulling her tight against him again. Skin to skin, heartbeat to heartbeat, they clung together, relishing every brush of their bodies as the flames around them flashed higher, stronger.

"That's it," he said thickly. "We're done here."

"What? *What?*" She shook her head. Was he stopping? Was he going to say good-night and leave her like this? Needy? Desperate?

"My room," he said shortly, snatching up her blouse and laying it around her shoulders. "We're going to my room. To a bed."

Lowering as it was to admit, she didn't want to wait that long. Oh, she was in serious trouble. "Don't need a bed."

"There're condoms in my room." He looked at her.

Duh. "Right. Of course. Do need those." She held on to her blouse with one hand as he grabbed her other hand and tugged her in his wake. They left the shadow-filled room and walked down a darkened hallway, following the dimly lit path provided by the night-lights plugged into wall sockets. His long legs were hard to keep up with, but Lilah managed, driven by the growing hunger chewing at her.

He pulled her into his bedroom and the only light there came from the slant of moonlight streaming through the windows to lay like silver across his king-size bed. The navy blue comforter looked as wide and dark as the sky. And when he picked her up and dropped her onto it, she felt as if she was flying into that dark expanse.

Moonlight gleamed in his eyes as she stared up at him, and when she lifted her arms to him, he went to her, sliding his body up and along hers. The incredible brush of his skin felt electrifying. He kissed her again and she felt herself drowning in his taste, in the heat of him.

She tossed her blouse aside then shrugged out of her bra and tossed it, as well. Lilah didn't want anything coming between them. She wanted, needed, and she didn't want to wait. For the first time in her life, Lilah was spiraling out of control.

He grinned as if he knew what she was thinking and completely agreed. "Now the jeans," he muttered and reached for the snap on her pants, but Lilah was too fast for him. She had them undone in a blink and then he was sliding them and her panties down off her legs.

If she was thinking right now, she might have felt a little embarrassed, uneasy, being naked in his bed, the cool night air kissing her skin, the fire in his eyes warming her. But she didn't want to think. She only wanted to *feel*.

"Now you," she demanded and wasn't willing to be patient about it, either. It had been a long two weeks, Lilah told herself, filled with bristling tension and heightened awareness until she'd hardly been able to sleep at night.

She kept her gaze on him while he quickly stripped, and she was really glad she did. He was beautiful. His broad chest was leanly sculpted muscle. Narrow hips, long legs and…her eyes widened and her heart gave an almost painful jolt in her chest. Oh, my.

He grinned again and Lilah said, "You have to stop reading my mind."

"But it's so interesting," he countered, joining her on the bed, dropping a kiss on her flat belly, then moving up to take first one nipple then the other into his mouth.

Lilah came up off the bed, digging her heels into the mattress as she arched her back, instinctively moving closer to that amazing, talented, wonderful mouth of his. She held his head to her breast and watched as his tongue drew lazy, sensual circles around her nipple.

"God, you taste good," he whispered against her breast, giving her skin another long lick.

"It's my soaps," she said on a sigh. "Organic. You could eat them if you wanted to."

"Your scent's been driving me crazy for two weeks," he admitted, looking at her briefly before slowly trailing his mouth down her body again. "Every night, I lay there wondering what you're going to smell like in the morning. Lemons?" Kiss. "Oranges?" Kiss. "Cinnamon?" Kiss.

And now he was close, so close to the throbbing, aching center of her. Everything in her clenched in anticipation, expectation. She held her breath as he shifted on the bed, as he moved to kneel between her legs. As he bent his head to—

"Oh!" Her hips rocked helplessly as his mouth covered her, as his tongue slipped over one sensitive nub of flesh. His hands squeezed her bottom, then moved over her body, sliding up to cup her breasts again, tweaking her nipples while his mouth worked her body into a frantic mass of raw nerves.

Lilah reached down, tangling her fingers in his hair, never wanting him to stop what he was doing—even though she wanted him inside her, filling her, easing the empty ache that hammered against her with every beat of her heart.

His tongue stroked, caressed, his breath dusted her skin and she moved with him, chasing the building need, trying to ease it, trying to make it last at the same time. Tension coiled, tightened until every breath was a victory. Her mind fogged over, her body took charge, racing toward the completion that remained just out of reach.

He pushed her higher, faster, never letting the pressure ease. She both loved and hated him for it. Her head whipped from side to side on the mattress. Her hips continued to move against him. She had no control, wanted none. All she wanted was… The first ripple began and Lilah braced for what was coming.

But there was simply no way she could have prepared herself for the conflagration that erupted inside her. Her head tipped back, her eyes closed and her body bucked and shivered as he sent her flailing over the edge of reality into a skyrocket-filled fantasy.

"Reed… Reed…" She gasped for air and groaned his name, when he moved away from her. But while the last of the tremors were still rippling through her, she heard a drawer open and snap closed.

Moments later, Reed covered her body with his and thrust himself deep inside her. Lilah gasped again at the absolute completeness she felt. He was big and strong and his body felt as if it was meant to be a part of hers.

"You're beautiful," he whispered. "I love watching you shatter."

She choked out a laugh followed by a gasp as he thrust deeply inside her. "Then pay attention, it's about to happen again."

Chuckling, Reed dipped his head to her mouth and tangled his tongue with hers. He stroked one hand along her body, up and down and then back up to cover her breast as he moved in and out of her with a wild, possessive rhythm that stole her breath and made sure she didn't care.

Lilah's legs came up, wrapped around his hips and clung there as her hands grasped his shoulders, nails digging into his skin. Again and again, he took her breath away. Staring up into his emerald green eyes, she lost what was left of her sanity. All she knew was the feel of him moving within her, the brilliant stab of his gaze and the delicious friction of his skin moving against hers.

And then the tension coiled in her belly suddenly spilled throughout her system. She rushed to meet what she knew was coming. Moving with him, rushing together toward that pinnacle, she cried out his name as new, fresh waves of pleasure washed through her. And while her brain fogged over, she heard him groan, felt his body tremble and Lilah held him as they both fell from the sky.

What could have been minutes or hours later, Lilah stirred halfheartedly. She was content right where she was, with Reed's body pressing her into the mattress. But her legs had lost all feeling—unless it was hysterical paralysis.

She wouldn't have been surprised.

Reed Hudson was something she never could have prepared for. He was, in a word, astonishing. She shifted a little beneath him and stroked one hand down his back.

"I'm squashing you."

"Are you?" she asked, a smile of pure female satisfaction curving her lips. It was a powerful thing for a woman to bring a strong man to such a state that he couldn't move. "I hadn't noticed."

Rather than reply, he rolled to one side, but kept her with him, dragging her on top of him. "Better," he said.

Since she could breathe now, she had to agree. Smoothing his hair back from his forehead, she said, "Well, that was worth waiting for."

"Yeah." He looked into her eyes. "I guess it was."

Idly, he traced his hand down her back to her behind and caressed her in long, lazy strokes.

When he closed his eyes and simply let his arm lay across her waist, Lilah took the chance to study him. Always when they talked, when they were even in the same room together, he maintained a closed expression and wariness in his eyes. Seeing him like this, unguarded, tugged at her heart.

But the minute that thought entered her mind, she discounted it. This had been about lust, not love. There were no hearts involved here and if she was smart, she'd keep it that way.

As spectacular as their little interlude had been, it hadn't really changed a darn thing. If anything, she'd only complicated matters by sleeping with him. Not that it hadn't been worth it, but Lilah was a big believer in never making the same mistake twice. So as much as she hated it, there couldn't be a repeat performance and now was as good a time as any to break the news.

"Reed…"

He didn't answer, and she frowned. "Reed."

Still nothing. Stunned, Lilah realized that while she had been doing some soul-searching and coming to a hard, but reasonable conclusion… Reed had fallen asleep.

"Well, I guess our little talk will have to wait, won't it?" Shaking her head, she rolled off him, stretched out on the bed and turned her head on the pillow to look at him. He didn't look young and innocent in his sleep. He looked exactly what he was… A strong, powerful man at rest. And for some ridiculous reason, she felt another hard tug on her heart. Oh, Lilah thought, that was probably not a good thing.

Easing out of the bed, she picked up her discarded clothes and left his room. But on the threshold, she couldn't resist glancing over her shoulder for one last look at him.

He slept in the moonlight and looked so alone, she almost went back to him. Almost. Before she could give in to an urge she would only come to regret, she stepped out of the room and carefully closed the door behind her.

By morning, Reed had worked out exactly what he would say to Lilah. He figured that she would be just like every other woman he'd ever encountered—assuming that sex was a natural gateway to a "relationship." Not going to happen.

Naturally, though, Lilah had thrown him for a loop again. Not only hadn't they had "the talk," she hadn't even been home by the time he walked into the kitchen looking for coffee. Connie had explained that Lilah had taken Rose for an early morning walk and he'd had to tell himself that talking to her about what had happened the night before would just have to wait until he got home after work.

Home. The house was quickly becoming home. More of Lilah's influence. She'd furnished it so that every time he stepped inside, he relaxed as he never had in the impersonal, starkly modern hotel. Hell, he'd even been thinking about redecorating the office lately because he didn't like all the chrome and black.

Her influence.

She was seeping into every corner of his life—and he knew he'd never be able to sleep in his bed again without remembering what the two of them had shared there.

Okay, yes, it had been the most incredible experience of his life, but that didn't mean anything, really. Of course sex with Lilah had been mind-blowing. He'd done nothing but think about and fantasize about her for the past couple of weeks. Finally getting her into his bed was...staggering. Okay, fine, he could admit the sex was great. But that didn't mean he was interested in anything more.

He had spent a lifetime building a controlled, organized life. With his extended, wildly passionate family, he'd learned to maintain a certain emotional distance. Mainly because if he allowed himself to be drawn into every crisis his family brought to him to solve, his own life would end up as convoluted as those he worked to keep out of trouble.

So control had been a part of his personality for as far back as he could remember. Reed kept his thoughts and emotions to himself and showed the world only what he wanted them to see. That control had allowed him to build a fortune, a career and a reputation he was proud of and to avoid messy entanglements like the rest of his family.

But since Rose and Lilah had walked into his life, that control had been slipping. He didn't like it, but there was no point in lying to himself about it.

The truth was, Rosie had already wedged her way into his heart. That tiny girl had a grip on him he wouldn't have thought possible. Then there was Lilah.

He sat back in his desk chair, spun it around to look out at the sun-splashed ocean and instead of seeing the Pacific, he saw Lilah. Her eyes. Her hair. Her smile. He saw her tending to Rose, laughing with Connie and sitting beside him in the firelight.

But damn it, mostly he saw her in his bed. Naked,

writhing, calling his name as her body erupted beneath his.

Before Lilah Strong, his life had rolled along as it should. Okay, maybe it had its boring moments… Fine. He was bored. Work didn't hold the same appeal it had years before. Reed watched his brothers and sisters having adventures and, yes, screwing up so he had to ride to the rescue, but still. They were *living*.

While he, like an old man at a party, complained about the crowds, the noise and the irritations.

When had he turned into an old fogy?

"I'm not," he muttered, as if he'd needed to hear it said out loud for it to be true. "I can have a good time. I just choose to live my life responsibly."

Groaning at the thought, he frowned at the buzzer on his phone when it sounded. Stabbing the button, he asked, "What is it, Karen?"

"Ms. Strong is on the phone. She insists on talking to you."

Just thinking about her could conjure her—if not in person, then on the phone. Well, hell, maybe "the talk" they should have had that morning would be easier if they had it on the phone. He wasn't looking forward to it. She'd probably cry, tell him she loved him or some such thing. But he'd be cool. Detached. And set her straight. "Fine. Put her through."

"Reed?" Her voice sounded low and worried and instantly he responded.

"Are you okay? Rose? Connie?"

"Everything's fine," she whispered. "I don't like bothering you at work, but—"

Thoughts of "the talk" had faded from his mind. Now

all he could think about was what must have happened at the house to have Lilah calling him.

"What's going on?"

"There's a little boy here."

"What?"

"A little boy? Male child?" Even whispered, he caught the sarcasm. "He says he's your brother Micah."

Reed jumped to his feet. "Micah's there? He's supposed to be in school."

"Well, he's in the kitchen eating everything Connie puts in front of him and he says he'll only talk to you."

"I'm on my way." He hung up, grabbed his suit jacket and on the way out the door could only wonder when he would have the time to be bored again.

Eight

Lilah liked Micah Hudson.

He was twelve years old, had Reed's green eyes and a shock of dark hair that continually fell into those eyes. He also had quite the appetite. He'd already mowed through two sandwiches, a half a bag of chips, three of Connie's chocolate chip bars and three glasses of milk.

And through it all, he managed to maintain a guarded look in his eyes that she'd noticed in Reed's way too often. Lilah thought no child should look so wary and it tore at her to see him sitting there waiting for the proverbial ax to fall.

"Reed's on his way home," she said as she sat down at the kitchen table opposite the boy.

"Okay, good." Micah looked up at her and bit down on his bottom lip. "Did he sound mad?"

"No," she assured him. Surprised, yes. Angry, no.

She'd seen Reed in action dealing with his sister Savannah, so she hoped he was just as understanding and patient with this boy who looked so worried and anxious. "He did say you're supposed to be in school."

Instantly, Micah slumped in the chair until he looked boneless. His head hung down so that his chin hit his chest and he muttered, "I don't want to be there. I wanted to come see Spring's baby." He looked at Rose, who gave him a wide, drooly smile, and Micah couldn't help but smile back. That expression faded when he looked back to Lilah. "They wouldn't let me come. Said my father had to sign a paper to *allow* me to go and he wouldn't."

For a boy who had at first insisted he'd speak only to his brother, once Micah started, he couldn't seem to stop. He picked up another cookie bar but instead of eating it, he crumbled it between his fingers as words poured from him in a flood.

"I called Father to tell him I wanted to come here but he said I couldn't come and see the baby because I had to stay at the school and be *supervised*." He added about six syllables to that last word for emphasis, then kept right on talking, his eyes flashing, and a stubborn expression settling on his features. "But Spring was my *sister*," he argued, eyes filling with tears he blinked back. "She *loved* me and I loved her. And now she's *dead*. I should get to see Rose, right?"

"I would think so," Lilah hedged, on his side, but wary about criticizing his father. That didn't keep her from reaching out to briefly lay one hand over his clenched fist.

"That's what I thought," Micah said, nodding as if to remind himself he'd done the right thing. "So, I had some money and I walked out of the school and bought a bus ticket and here I am."

She couldn't imagine a child just hopping a bus and taking off on his own. "Where do you go to school?"

"Arizona," he muttered and watched as cookie crumbs drifted like brown snow down to the plate in front of him. "And it sucks."

Arizona to California was a long bus ride for a little boy on his own, and Lilah took one silent moment to thank the universe for protecting him on his journey. Now that he was safe, Lilah could admire the courage it must have taken for him to go off on his own, and still, his eyes looked wounded, nervous.

Once again, Lilah was reminded of just how idyllic her own childhood had been. She'd never been forced to run away because she'd been miserable where she was. She'd never once gone to her parents with something important only to be turned away and ordered to basically sit down and shut up. She thought of what Connie had said about the Hudson parents and had to agree.

They were careless about the important things. Their children. Couldn't Micah's father hear the misery in the boy's voice? Had he even taken the time to help the boy grieve for his sister?

Oh, she really hoped Reed was kind when he showed up to talk to his younger brother. Micah didn't look as though he could take another dismissal of his feelings. But until Reed arrived, Lilah could only keep the boy talking, try to ease his fear and help him relax.

"Don't like Arizona, huh?" Lilah asked the question lightly, not letting him know how horrified she was that he'd taken such a chance by running. She handed Rosie a slice of banana that the tiny girl immediately squished in one small fist.

"It's not Arizona I don't like. It's my stupid school," Micah muttered.

He looked caught between childhood and adulthood. His face was still round and soft and would hone down over the years, making him a handsome man one day. But right now, he looked like a little boy, unsure of himself and the world around him. He wore black slacks, black shoes and a white shirt with a red-and-blue crest on the left pocket. The uniform had probably been starched and ironed when he began his trek. Now it looked as rumpled and stained as its wearer.

Lilah couldn't believe a twelve-year-old boy had just walked out of his private school and hopped on a bus. What kind of school was it that didn't keep better track of its students? And what kind of parent, she wondered again, couldn't see that a child was sick with worry and grief and misery? She felt sorry for the boy, but at the same time, she knew he'd been lucky to make the trip safely.

Rose, in a high chair alongside Micah, picked up a fistful of Cheerios and tossed them at the boy. Surprise flickered in Micah's eyes, then delight.

"I think she likes me," he said and his smile briefly chased the darkness from his eyes.

"Why wouldn't she?" Lilah told him, then stood up to answer the phone when it rang. Still smiling at the kids, she said, "Hudson residence."

"This is Robert Hudson speaking. Who are you?"

The gruff, hostile voice came through so loudly, Lilah lifted the receiver from her ear slightly. Reed's father? she wondered. "I'm Lilah Strong and I'm here to—"

"I know why you're there. You brought Spring's baby to Reed." There was a brief pause in that silence. Lilah heard a distinct tapping as if the man were slapping something against a tabletop in irritation. "Is my son Micah there?"

"Well," she hedged, not wanting to rat the boy out but unwilling to let his father worry any longer—if he *was* worried. She glanced at the boy, who was watching her through anxious eyes. "Yes, he is."

"I want to speak to him. Now. I've been handling phone calls from his school," he snapped, "and I knew damn well he'd make his way to Reed. I demand to speak to him now."

"Wow," she murmured and slid her gaze to where Micah sat, watching her. He had to have heard his father through the receiver. The man's furious voice was only getting louder. But as much as she wanted to shield Micah, she couldn't keep his father from talking to him. "Hold on, please." She cupped her hand over the phone and said, "It's your father."

Micah's smile was gone and his eyes looked haunted. Pushing himself out of his chair, he dragged himself across the floor like a man heading for the gallows, then reluctantly took the phone. "Hello, Father."

Instantly, the older Hudson started shouting even louder than before.

Lilah didn't mean to eavesdrop, but unless she actually left the room, she simply couldn't help it. She shot a worried glance at Connie and saw the older woman's scowl. But it was Micah's expression that tore at Lilah. As she watched, the boy seemed to shrink into himself as his father ranted like a crazy person.

A few words stood out from the stream. *Irresponsible. Brat. Selfish. Reckless.*

Lilah's temper simmered into a froth that nearly choked her. Seeing that sweet boy reduced to tears was just more than she was going to take.

"Give me the phone, Micah," she said.

The boy gaped at her, but handed it over. Lilah smiled at him, and ignoring the spiel pouring from the receiver, told the boy, "Why don't you go finish your cookies and sit with Rosie?"

He was looking at her wide-eyed as if he couldn't decide if she was brave or crazy. She was neither, Lilah thought. What she was, was going to defend a boy against a man who should know better than to rail against a child. He was still shouting.

"Mr. Hudson," Lilah spoke up and paused for the tirade to fade away in stunned shock at having been interrupted.

"Where's Micah?"

"He's having milk and cookies."

"Who the hell—"

She cut him off again and maybe it was small of her, but she enjoyed it. Now Lilah understood why Reed's siblings came to him when they had a problem. She couldn't imagine anyone would run to Robert Hudson for help. The man would no doubt throw a fit of humongous proportions and solve absolutely nothing.

Shaking her head, she had to admit she also had a whole new respect for what Reed had to deal with on a daily basis. Juggling so many different personalities had to be exhausting.

When Robert Hudson's voice finally trailed off, she spoke up.

"I'm sorry, but Micah's busy right now," she said and heard the man sputter on the other end of the phone. Smiling, she could silently admit that she sort of enjoyed knowing she'd thrown him for a loop. "But please call back as soon as you've had a chance to calm down."

"I beg your pardon?"

She almost smiled. "Goodbye, Mr. Hudson."

When she hung up the phone, Connie applauded. Lilah winced and laughed a little uneasily. Sure, the housekeeper might be pleased, but Lilah had just hung up on Reed's father. Not that she regretted it, she told herself when she looked at the boy staring at her with stars in his eyes. There was just no way she could have stood there and done nothing.

"That was so cool," Micah said quietly, awe coloring his tone. "Nobody but Reed talks to our father like that."

Hmm. "Well, maybe more people should."

Micah's gaze dropped and so did his voice. "Reed's gonna be mad at me, too, isn't he?"

Lilah really hoped not. She didn't think the boy could take much more right now. He looked beaten down after a few minutes of his father shouting at him. If Reed came in furious, it would only add to the boy's misery. Instantly, she thought back over the past couple of weeks and though she could remember a few times when Reed had behaved like a stuffy old man, she couldn't bring up one instance of him really being furious. And she had to admit, he'd had so many things thrown at him lately that he could have blown a gasket at any point. So maybe he'd be exactly what Micah needed.

"Reed will be happy to see you," Connie put in, stopping to give the boy a hard hug. "Just like I am."

"Thanks, Connie," he said, then shifted his gaze to

Lilah again. "Will you talk to Reed for me like you did to my father?"

She smiled and got him another glass of milk. That much at least, she could promise. "If you need it, sure."

"Okay." As settled as he could be, Micah focused on the baby and visibly tried to relax.

When Reed arrived a few minutes later, he came straight to the kitchen and Lilah's heart broke a little as she watched Micah straighten in his chair and go on guard. She really hoped Reed could see beyond the boy's bravado to the frightened kid inside.

Shrugging out of his jacket, Reed loosened his tie and glanced from Micah to the two women in the room watching him. Not for the first time, Lilah wished she could read his mind. It would be good to know if she'd have to jump in front of Micah or not.

But she told herself that how Reed treated his little brother would give her an idea of how he would deal with Rose in the years to come. Would he be patient or angry? Understanding or dictatorial? Nerves pinged inside her. She was sure there was a warm man beneath the cold, detached shell he showed the world. But what if she was wrong?

"Got any coffee, Connie?" he asked.

"Since I'm breathing, yes." She waved him at the table. "Go sit down. I'll bring you some along with a couple cookie bars."

He gave her a wink. "I should come home early more often." Glancing at Lilah as he walked to the table, he asked, "So you've met my brother. What do you think?"

Micah's gaze snapped to hers and she read worry there. She smiled at him. "I think he was very brave to ride a bus all the way from Arizona by himself."

"Yeah. Brave." Reed sat down, reached out and gave Micah's arm a slight punch. "Also stupid. You were lucky you got here all right."

Micah frowned. "I'm not stupid or anything."

"No, not stupid," Reed agreed, "but walking out and making the school panic enough to call Father wasn't the brightest move."

"Yeah, I know. He already called." Micah looked at Lilah. "She told him to calm down and then she hung up on him."

Lilah actually felt herself flush as Reed turned an interested gaze on her. "Is that right?"

"He was shouting at Micah and I couldn't stand it," she said, throwing her hands up. "Shoot me."

"Hell, no," he said, smiling, "I only wish I'd been here to see it."

Lilah grinned at him. So far so good.

"It was awesome," Micah admitted.

When Connie brought the coffee and cookies, Reed turned his gaze back to his brother. Lilah felt Micah's nerves and knew he was as anxious as she was.

"I don't want to go back," the boy said, his voice hardly more than a whisper. "I hate it there, Reed. They make you wear this dumb uniform and somebody's always telling you what to do and the food sucks, it's all healthy and you can't even eat when you want to—"

He said that last as if he were being force-fed twigs and grass.

"And Mom said I have to stay there this summer, too, and there's only me and two other kids in the whole place over the summer and it's really creepy at night when it's so empty and—"

"Take a breath," Reed advised softly and pushed the cookies toward the boy.

Tears stung the backs of Lilah's eyes. Sunlight glanced in through the windows and lay across the kitchen table in a puddle of gold. Rosie smacked her hands on the food tray, and Connie came up to stand beside Lilah, as if they were building a wall to defend one lonely little boy. The question was, would they need it?

"You can stay here," Reed said, and Micah's gaze lifted to his, hope shining as brightly as the sun.

"Really?" One word, said in a hushed awe that held so much yearning Lilah's heart broke with it.

"Yeah, I hated boarding school, too," Reed said, shaking his head. "It is creepy at night, especially when most of the other kids are gone. We've got plenty of room, so you can spend the summer here and we'll figure out what to do about school in September."

"Really? I can stay?" Micah's voice broke and he wiped his eyes with the backs of his hands.

Lilah released a breath she hadn't even realized she'd been holding. She should have known Reed would come through. Hadn't she seen enough evidence over the past couple of weeks that he wasn't nearly as detached as he pretended to be?

Reed ruffled the boy's hair, then took a sip of his coffee. "I'll clear it with Father and your mother. On one condition…"

Wary now, the boy asked, "What?"

"You have to get rid of that ugly uniform and start wearing jeans and sneakers."

Micah's bottom lip trembled, his eyes went shiny and in a rush of gratitude, he jumped out of his chair and hugged his brother. Lilah's heart swelled as she watched

Reed hug him back, and she shared a smile with Connie. Then Reed caught her gaze over Micah's head and she could have sworn she saw another piece of his personal wall break apart and shatter.

God, she was falling in love. Reed Hudson wasn't a cold man, she thought, he had just been protecting himself for so long, it had become a way of life. His gaze bored into hers and even at a distance, she felt the heated stare right down to her bones.

Yep, she thought. *Love.* There was no future in it. There would be no happy ending. Oh, she was in serious trouble—and the only way out was pain.

A few hours later, Reed reasoned with his father. "Micah can stay with me. He hates that stupid school so why keep him there if I'm offering an alternative?"

A part of him wondered *why* he was offering, but the more sensible part knew exactly why. He had been in Micah's shoes and the memories were still clear enough that he understood just how the kid felt. Sent off to boarding school, allowed home only at Christmas and sometimes during the summer. Otherwise, ignored and endured until school started up again. There was no reason for Micah to go through it any longer.

Besides, the memory of the kid's tears had been burned into Reed's mind and heart and damned if he'd send his brother back to a place that made him miserable.

"We'll spend the summer together and if he's happy, he can go to school here," Reed continued firmly, using the only tone of voice his father respected. "There's a good school just a few blocks from here." He'd made a point to check out the schooling situation *before* confronting his father.

"Even if I'm willing to let him stay, Micah's mother will never agree," Robert Hudson muttered.

"Come on, Father," Reed said with a laugh. "You know Suzanna will be fine with anything that keeps Micah out of her hair."

His father huffed out a breath. "True. I don't know what I was thinking when I married her."

Neither did Reed, but that wasn't the point. Although he would admit that his father had wised up fast. He'd been married to Suzanna only a little more than a year. Then, the money-grubbing woman had disappeared from their lives. Thank God. "So you're okay with Micah staying with me?"

"It's fine," his father said after a long minute. "I'll call the school tomorrow, tell them he won't be back. Then I'll let Micah know."

"Good." Relief that he hadn't had to make a bigger fight of it filled Reed. He'd been willing to go to battle for his younger brother, but the fact that he hadn't had to made everything much easier. "How's Nicole doing? Baby news yet?"

His father sighed. "She's fine, but the doctor says it could be another two weeks."

Hard to believe his father was still out creating children he never seemed to have time for. But Robert kept marrying much younger women who always insisted on having a family of their own.

"Tell her I said hello."

"I will." His father's voice softened. "Thank you. I appreciate it. And on another subject," he continued a moment later, "who told that woman she could hang up on me?"

Reed laughed. "Nobody tells Lilah what to do. She

came up with that solution on her own when you were ranting."

"Huh. Well, I liked her. She's got spine."

Amused, Reed thought that his father had no idea. After he hung up, he sat back in his desk chair and glanced to the corner of his desk. Just last night he and Lilah had been right there, wrapped up in each other, tearing at each other's clothes, mindless to anything but what they were feeling. Instantly his body went hard as stone as memories flooded his brain. He groaned, shifted in his chair and steered his brain away from thoughts of Lilah to focus on his new set of problems.

Last month, he was living in a hotel and had nothing to worry about but his clients and the occasional call for help from a sibling. Now he had a house, a housekeeper, a baby and a twelve-year-old to think about. There was just no way Connie would be able to take care of the house *and* two kids. He was going to need a nanny. And until he found one, he'd need Lilah to stay on.

Though his body liked that idea, his brain was sending out warning signals. But it wasn't as if he had a choice here. He had to work and there were two kids who needed looking after. Surely she'd see that and understand why she had to stay longer than she might have planned.

With that thought firmly in mind, he left his study, headed down the hall to Lilah's room and quietly knocked at the door. The hall was dark but for the night-lights. Rosie's bedroom door was cracked open, but Micah's room was closed up tight. The house was quiet, almost as if it was holding its breath. Just like him.

She opened the door and the first thing he noticed was the scent of strawberries. Her hair was still damp

from a shower and lay in waves atop her shoulders. She
wore no makeup at all and she was still more beautiful
than any woman he'd ever known.

His heart jolted in his chest as his gaze met hers.
She wore a bright yellow nightgown, the hem stopping
midthigh. It had a scooped neck, short sleeves and was
covered in pictures of puppies. All different kinds of
puppies, from poodles to German shepherds. For a second or two he couldn't even speak. Finally, though, he
lifted his gaze to hers and asked, "Like dogs?"

"What? Oh." She glanced down at herself, then
shrugged. "Yeah, I do." Then she frowned. "Is something wrong? The kids okay?"

"Everything's fine," he said quickly, easing the worry
that had leaped to life in her eyes. He probably should
have waited to speak to her until morning. But it was too
late to back out now. "We have to talk, Lilah."

A sinking sensation opened up in the pit of her stomach as soon as she heard those words. Never a good way
to start a conversation, she thought, stepping back and
waving Reed into her room. Lilah had one instant to
wish he hadn't seen her in her puppy nightgown, then
that thought fled in favor of other, darker thoughts. She'd
known this talk was coming.

Ever since the night before when they'd shared some
truly spectacular sex, Lilah had been waiting for Reed
to take one giant step backward. But it was all right because she'd already decided that the only way for her
to deal with her new feelings for Reed was to leave. As
quickly as possible.

She'd seen him in action now, not only with Rose
but with Micah, and she could believe that though he

maintained safe distances from most people, he wouldn't be cold to children. His gentleness with Micah coupled with his willingness to let the boy move in with him had been the cherry on top of her decision. No one that understanding and kind would be anything less to the baby who'd been left in his care.

Reed paced the confines of the guest room as if looking for something. He raked one hand through his hair and then turned to look at her. "We never talked. About last night, I mean."

"I know. But really," she said, "there's not much to say, is there?" Now that she knew she loved him, Lilah really didn't want to listen to him tell her how there could be nothing between them. How it had just been sex—no matter how life altering. That he wasn't interested in a relationship.

Why not just set the tone right from the beginning? She would be the one to say that she didn't want anything from him. That she had no expectations. Just because her heart would break when she left him didn't mean he had to *know* that.

"Seriously?" He looked surprised, both eyebrows winging up. Then he laughed shortly and shook his head. "Of course you would be different from every other woman I've ever met."

"What's that supposed to mean?" It had sounded like an insult, but he looked almost pleased as he said it.

"It means—" he paused, pulled the curtains at the window back and let the moonlight flood the room "—that every woman I've ever spent the night with woke up with diamonds and wedding bells on her mind."

Lilah laughed a little at that. Well, good. She was happy to be the one different woman in his life. At least, she thought, he'd remember her. If her private dreams were more romantic than she was letting on, they weren't something she was going to share, anyway. Lilah had known going in that there was no future for her and Reed so why pretend otherwise? Why give him the slightest indication that she was disappointed? That she'd miss him? No, thank you. She'd keep her own pain private.

"You're completely safe," she said. "I promise. It was an amazing night, Reed, and I'll never forget it, but it was one night."

Frowning, he said, "Right. I just—never mind. Doesn't matter. So, if we're both clear on last night, there's something else I need to talk to you about."

Lilah sat on the edge of the bed, pulled the hem of her nightgown as far down as she was able and said, "Go ahead."

"The thing is," he said, "I'm going to need you to stay a while longer."

"Oh." She hadn't expected that. Especially after last night, she'd half thought he'd hand her a plane ticket this morning and wave bon voyage from the porch. Which was, she could admit privately, why she had gotten up early and taken Rosie for a walk. She hadn't wanted to hear him explain why he didn't want her.

He walked closer until he stopped right in front of her. Lilah had to tip her head back to meet his eyes. In the moonlight, with his face half in shadow, he looked dangerous, mysterious and so very good. She took a breath and tried to rein in what was no doubt a spill of hormones rushing through her bloodstream. But it wasn't easy, especially since now she knew what it was like to be with him. To have his hands on her, his mouth. She shivered and took another breath.

He scraped one hand across the back of his neck and said, "The thing is, now that Micah's going to be staying here, I can't expect Connie to watch over both kids and take care of this place all by herself."

"True." Lilah's mind started spinning. She really hadn't stopped to think about the logistics of everything. But he was right.

"I'm glad you agree. So look, I need you to stay—"

Her foolish heart leaped.

"—until I can find a nanny."

And then it crashed to the ground.

Oh, God, for her own sake, Lilah knew she should leave. Not only had she left her business alone long enough, but if she stayed on here with Reed, her heart would only get more and more involved. And that would only make eventually leaving that much harder.

"So?" he demanded impatiently.

Lilah smiled. "You really need to work on your patience chakra."

"What?"

"Nothing." Why was it, she wondered, that the man could look so completely irresistible when he was standing there staring at her as if she were speaking Martian? Everything about him appealed to her. From his gruff exterior to the tender lover, to the kind and understanding man he was to his siblings. Lilah was toast and she knew it.

She sighed and stood up, but kept a good foot of space between them. She wouldn't leave him in the lurch. No matter that it might end up costing her, she had to at least help him find the right nanny—for the kids' sakes if nothing else. "Okay, I'll stay."

He blew out a breath and grinned, never knowing

what the power of that smile could do to her. "That's great. Okay."

"But…"

"Always a *but*," he muttered, giving her a wary look. "What is it?"

"I've already been away from my business for two weeks." Lilah had been spending two or three hours every day, checking online and then getting her employees to go into the store to fulfill orders. Her emergency system was working fine, but she'd feel better if she at least checked in, in person. "I need to fly home for the weekend, check on stock and have a meeting with my employees."

He frowned thoughtfully, then said, "All right. How about this? We'll all go."

"What?" Laughing now, she looked up at him in surprise.

"I'm serious." He shrugged. "Micah, Rosie and I will go with you. We can take the family jet this weekend— it'll be more comfortable."

Undeniable, she thought, since she hadn't been looking forward to the flight home even if it was only an hour and a half.

"You can show us the mountains," he was saying, "see your place. Then we'll all come back together."

"You don't have to do that," she said, though she loved the idea of him coming to her town, seeing where she lived. Maybe it would be a way for her to remember him with her once this time with him was over. God, she really was a sap. Having memories of him in her tiny hometown would only make living there without him that much harder. And yet…

"I'd actually like to see the shop where you make all

of the amazing scents that are always clinging to your skin," he murmured, and lifted one hand to sweep her hair back from her face.

She shivered at his touch and held her breath, hoping he'd do more.

"Strawberries tonight." He moved in closer, bent his head to her neck and inhaled, drawing her scent inside him. When he looked into her eyes again, he said, "I like strawberries even more than vanilla."

Her stomach did a slow slide into happy land and her heartbeat jumped into a racing, thundering crash in her chest. Whatever her brain might be worrying over, her body had a whole different set of priorities.

"Do you really think this is a good idea?" she whispered when his mouth was just a breath from hers.

"Probably not," Reed answered. "Do you care?"

"No," she admitted and let him pull her down onto the bed.

His kiss was long and deep and demanding. His hands swept down to snatch up the hem of her nightgown and she trembled as he cupped her breast and rubbed her hardened, sensitive nipple. His tongue dipped into her mouth, tangling with hers in an erotic simulation of just what he wanted to do with her next.

And foolish or not, Lilah was all for it. If she had to give him up, then she might as well enjoy him while she had him, right?

She wrapped her arms around his neck and held on when he rolled them over until she was sprawled on top of him. Then she broke their kiss and looked down into misty green eyes that she would see in her sleep for the rest of her life.

"You're amazing," he whispered, stroking his fingertips along her cheek, tucking her hair behind her ear.

Her heart felt as if a giant fist were squeezing it tightly and the ache was almost sweet. These few moments with him were all she would have. She wanted to remember everything. Every touch. Every sigh. Every breathless word.

When he bent to kiss her again, Lilah moved to meet him, parting her lips, loving the slide of his tongue against hers. The soft sigh of his breath mingling with her own.

Moonlight flooded the room, silence filled the air and—a long, plaintive wail erupted from the baby monitor on the bedside table. Lilah broke the kiss and leaned her forehead against his. Rosie's cry continued to peal into the quiet and Lilah smiled sadly. It was like a sign from the universe.

"I think someone somewhere is trying to tell us something." She gave him a sad smile and rolled off him to stand beside the bed. "I have to go to the baby and you should probably just…go."

"Yeah." He sat up with a resigned half smile on his face. "I'm going to head to bed myself."

They left the room together, each of them going in different directions. A metaphor for their lives, she thought. And even though she would still be with him for a while longer, she knew that tonight signaled an end.

At the threshold of Rosie's room, Lilah paused and murmured, "Goodbye, Reed."

Nine

Reed hated LA.

But there was no help for it. At least once every couple of weeks, he had to bite the bullet and make the trek into the city.

Today, he had a lunch appointment with a federal judge he'd gone to law school with, followed by a meeting with a prospective new client. Which almost took the sting out of the drive in California's miserable traffic.

Of course the constant stop-and-go on the freeway gave him plenty of time to think, too. Mostly what he was thinking about was that interrupted night with Lilah. He loved Rose, but the baby had lousy timing.

He loved that tiny girl.

Funny, he hadn't really considered that before. He'd spent so much of his life avoiding the mere mention of the word *love*, the fact that it had just popped into his head surprised the hell out of him. But it shouldn't, his ever-logical brain argued. He wasn't a robot, after all. Reed loved his brothers and sisters—it was just the so-called *Love* with a capital *L* he had no interest in.

And wasn't he lucky that Lilah was such a sensible woman? He smiled and nodded to himself, remembering their talk and how well it had gone. Reed couldn't remember a time when he and a woman had been so in sync. So why did he have an itch between his shoulder blades? His satisfied smile faded and became a thoughtful scowl. She could have been a little more reluctant to let go of what they had. Hell, *he* was reluctant.

He'd never in his life been dismissed so completely by a woman. Especially one he still wanted. Reed was usually the one to call a halt. To back off and remind whatever woman he was with that he didn't do forever. That chat never went over well. Until Lilah, he silently admitted. She didn't seem to have a problem walking away and he should be happy about that. Why wasn't he happy about that?

"Even when we're not together she's driving me crazy," he muttered and cursed under his breath when a Corvette cut him off. Still talking to himself, he said, "Now, she's so focused on the kids it's as if she's forgotten I'm even in the house."

For the past few days, he'd hardly seen Lilah. Micah was settling in, making friends in the neighborhood, playing with Rosie and apparently adopting Lilah. The three of them were cozy as hell, with Connie rounding out their happy little group and Reed being drawn in whether he liked it or not.

The hell of it was, he *did* like it. He'd never imagined himself in this situation—a house and kids—but surprisingly enough, it worked for him. The hotel suite had been impersonal, convenient. The house was loud and messy and full of life. There were no empty corners or quiet shadows there and it struck him suddenly how much of his life had been spent in lonely silence. It was only after it had ended that he could actually see *how* he'd been living. Not that it hadn't worked for him. Could still work, he reasoned. It was just that now he knew he liked a different kind of life, too.

What really surprised him about all of this was just how much Reed hated the idea of Lilah leaving. It wasn't about him wanting her there, of course. It was more for the sake of the kids that he worried about it. Though he had to admit that now, every time he thought about the house, he heard Lilah's voice, her laugh, he imagined one of her amazing scents trailing through the air.

Somehow his life had been yanked out of his control.

When his cell phone rang, Reed answered gratefully. Anything to get his mind off Lilah. A moment later, he realized the truth of the old statement "be careful what you wish for."

"Hey, Reed I need a little help."

He rolled his eyes. His half brother on his mother's side hadn't called in a few months. Reed should have known he was due. "Cullen. What's going on?"

A deep, cheerful voice sounded out. "I just need the name of a good lawyer in London."

"What did you do?" Reed's hands fisted on the steering wheel even as his gaze narrowed in concentration on the traffic around him.

"It wasn't me," Cullen said, innocence ringing out proudly in his tone. "It was my car, but I wasn't driving it."

Reed counted to ten, hoping for patience and thought maybe Lilah had had a point about working on his chakras, whatever they were. "What. Happened?"

"A friend was driving the Ferrari and took a bad turn is all."

"A *friend*?"

"Yeah. You'd like her. She's great. Not much of a driver, though."

"Anyone hurt?" Reed clenched his teeth and held his breath. Cullen was the most irresponsible of the whole Hudson/everyone-else bunch. And, he had the habit of going through a long song and dance before finally reaching the bottom line. Cullen was twenty-six and destined to follow his father, Gregory Simmons, into the banking world. God. Reed shuddered to think of Cullen in charge of anyone's money.

"No injuries, the only casualty was a bush."

"What?" He frowned and shook his head, sure he hadn't heard that correctly.

"Juliet mowed down a hundred-year-old shrub and a patch of dahlias." Laughing now, Cullen said, "To hear the woman who lived there going on, you would have thought we'd murdered her beloved dog, not a bloody bush."

"Damn it, Cullen—" Reed's head ached. Sometimes it was a bitch being the oldest.

"Hey, no speeches," his brother interrupted, "just the lawyer, okay?"

Grateful that he wouldn't have to deal with Cullen and the remarkable Juliet, Reed ran through a mental file, then finally said, "Tristan Marks. Call Karen at my office she can give you his number."

And he hoped Tristan would forgive him for this.

"Great, thanks. Knew I could count on you. If I need anything else, I'll call you at home tomorrow, all right?"

"No," Reed said tightly, "it's not all right. I'm going away for the weekend."

Cullen snorted. "Another fascinating law conference?"

"No," Reed said, even more pleased now that he wouldn't be home to deal with anything else Cullen came up with. "I'm taking a couple days off."

There was a pause that lasted long enough that Reed thought for a moment the connection had been lost. Then his brother spoke up again.

"I'm sorry. I think I must have had a small stroke. You said you're taking two days *off*?"

Reed put his blinker on, then changed lanes, preparing to exit. "What's so hard to understand about that?"

"Oh, nothing at all. Miracles happen all the time."

"You're not as amusing as you think you are, Cullen."

"Sure I am," his brother said with a laugh. "So tell me, who is she?"

"She who?"

"The incredible woman with the power to get Reed Hudson away from his desk."

"Go away, Cullen. Call Karen." He hung up with the sound of his brother's laughter ringing in his ears.

Incredible? Yeah, he thought, Lilah really was all of that and more. Just what the hell were they going to do without her?

Utah was prettier than Reed thought it would be. There were a lot of trees, a lot of open space on either side of the freeway and most amazing of all, hardly any traffic. He actually enjoyed the drive from the airport to the mountain town of Pine Lake.

The flight was short and he'd had a rental car waiting for them, complete with car seat for Rosie. It amazed Reed just how much *gear* was necessary when traveling with kids, though. Good thing they'd taken a private jet. They would have been waiting for hours at baggage claim otherwise.

"So do you ski and stuff?" Micah asked from the backseat.

"I do," Lilah said, half turning in her seat to look at him. "You'll have to come back in the winter and I'll take you up the mountain myself."

"Cool!" The kid's face lit up. "Can we, Reed?"

He glanced in the rearview mirror at the eager smile on his brother's face. "Maybe."

How could he say yes? Lilah was talking about the winter and Reed knew she wouldn't be a part of their lives then. If that thought left a gaping hole in his chest, he didn't have to acknowledge it.

"Turn left here," Lilah said. "We can stop at my house first, unload everything, then go to the shop."

Reed glanced at her and realized she looked as excited as Micah. Clearly, she'd missed this place, her home, her *life*. She'd already given him more than three weeks. How much more could he ask of her? Hell, he was going to owe her forever, and he didn't like the sound of that.

Following her directions, he finally turned into the driveway of what looked like an oversize box. As first impressions went, he could only think how small it was. The house was a perfect square, with black shutters against white siding and a porch that ran the length of the house. The yard was wide and deep, with the house sitting far back from the road. There were at least a dozen trees shading the property and Reed thought that somehow the house fit Lilah.

She jumped out of the car, grabbed Rosie and headed for the house, with Micah close on her heels. Reed followed more slowly, watching her, enjoying the view of her backside in black jeans. Once inside, he saw the place was as small as it had appeared, but it also had a cozy feel to it. There were warm colors, soft fabrics and plenty of windows to let in the light.

"Micah, you and Rosie will share a room tonight, okay?"

"Sure." The boy shrugged and picked up his backpack. "Where?"

"Top of the stairs on the right."

Reed watched him go, silently marveling at the change in his little brother. Just a few days away from the boarding school and the boy had relaxed and smiled more than Reed ever remembered him doing.

When he was alone with Lilah, Reed said, "I like your house."

"Thanks," she said, turning a grin up to him. "I know it's tiny, but it's all I've ever needed. I've got the kitchen and the mudroom set up as my workshop and that's worked pretty well up until now. But I may have to add on at some point."

Nodding, he couldn't help thinking that there was plenty of room at his house to build a huge workshop for her where she could make all the soaps and stuff she wanted. But, his brain reminded him, she wouldn't be there to use it, would she?

Scowling now, he paid attention when she went on.

"The house is still a work in progress and it's only

got two bedrooms, so Micah and Rosie aren't the only ones who'll have to share a room…"

One eyebrow arched. Things were looking up. "Really? Well, now I like your house even more."

Wryly, she said, "I thought you might feel that way."

After they got settled in, they all walked to the center of town and Reed had to admit there was something about the place that appealed. He'd never thought of himself as a small-town kind of guy, but walking down the main street, with its bright flowers tumbling out of half barrels, old-fashioned streetlights and buildings that looked at least a hundred years old, he could see the charm of it. And when they got a tour of Lilah's shop Reed was definitely impressed.

The shop was bright and clean and so tidy, there wasn't a thing out of place. Shelves were lined with the famous soaps in a rainbow of colors, many of them wrapped together by ribbon to be sold as sets. There were candles as well, and tiny bottles filled with lotions in the same scents as the soaps.

Lilah had built something good here, Reed thought, and he felt a stir of admiration for her. When her employees hurried in for a spontaneous meeting, he watched Lilah's happiness as she listened to all the latest news and he realized just how much she'd given up to stay with him and help with Rosie. These were Spring's friends, the town his sister had called home, and Reed listened to stories about her that made him smile and wish again that he and Spring hadn't been at odds when she died.

The rest of the afternoon passed quickly, with exploring the town, stopping for dinner and then walking to a lake so Micah could throw bread to overfed ducks. It was the first time in years that Reed had actually slowed down long enough to enjoy the moment. And being there, walking through a soft night with Lilah and the kids, brought him a kind of peace he'd never known before.

That worried him. He was getting far too used to Lilah. And that was a bad move. She wasn't staying with him. There was no future waiting for them. There was only now.

"Are you okay?" Lilah's voice came softly, since the kids were asleep in the room across the hall.

"Yeah, why?"

"I don't know, you seem…distracted."

"It's nothing. Just thinking about work."

She laughed and climbed into bed. "Let it go, Reed. You're allowed to *not* work once in a while, you know?"

"You're right," he said, looking down at her. "You want to guess what I'm thinking about now?"

She smiled, a slow, deliberate curve of her mouth that sent jolts of lightning spearing through him. "That's too easy."

He joined her in the bed and pulled her in close, holding her body pressed along his length as he dipped his head to kiss her. That first taste spiraled through him and the jagged edges inside him softened. This moment was everything, he realized. Thoughts, worries, problems could all wait. For now, all he wanted was her.

She moved into him and he slid one hand down her body to explore her heat, her curves, the luscious lines of her. She was so responsive, it pushed him higher and faster than he'd ever been before. She scraped her hands up and down his back and he felt every touch like tiny brands, scoring into his skin.

They moved together in silence, hushed breath, whispered words, quiet movements. When he entered her body, there was almost a sigh of sound and the rhythm he set was slow, tender. He looked down at her and lost himself in her eyes. She touched his face, drew him down for a kiss and he swallowed her moan of pleasure as she reached the peak they were each racing toward. A moment later, he joined her, bending his head to hers, taking the scent of her with him as he fell.

In the quiet aftermath, lying in the dark, entwined together, Reed heard Rosie stirring. A few minutes more, he knew she'd be howling, waking Micah up, as well.

"I'll be right back," he whispered and walked naked from the room. When he came back, he was carrying the sniffling baby, who lit up like Christmas when she saw Lilah.

Reed lay down in the bed and set Rosie down between them.

The baby cooed and clapped and giggled, happy now because she wasn't alone in the dark.

"When she falls asleep, I'll put her back in her bed," Reed said, dropping a kiss on the baby's forehead.

"That might take a while," Lilah answered, while Rosie played with her fingers.

"We've got time." Not much, he told himself, but they had right now.

As he lay there, watching the woman and child communicating in smiles and kisses, Reed realized that it felt as if they were a family. And he scowled into the darkness.

"I have some bad news," Reed said, dropping his briefcase onto the nearest chair. He gave a quick glance around at the Malibu beach house Carson Duke had been living in since splitting with his wife. The place was bright, lots of white and blue, and it sat practically on the sand. With the French doors open, he could hear the rush and roar of the sea.

Carson turned to look at Reed, worry sparking in his eyes. "Tia? Is she okay?"

Amazing, Reed thought. Even though they were in the middle of a divorce, the man reacted as if they were still lovers, still committed to each other. Fear came off Carson Duke in thick, fat waves until Reed assured him, "She's fine. But she wouldn't sign off on the property issues, so we'll be going to mediation in a judge's chambers."

Carson actually slumped in relief, then gave a shaky laugh and scraped one hand across his face. "Thank God. The mediation doesn't matter. As long as she's okay." He turned, walked through the open doors onto the stone terrace and tipped his face into the wind. Reed walked outside to join him and took a moment to look around.

Despite the gloomy weather, there were dozens of surfers sitting on their boards, waiting for the next wave. And laid out like elegant desserts on a table, women in barely there bikinis draped themselves on towels in artful poses.

Reed stared out at the slate gray water. "If you don't mind me saying so, you just don't sound like my regular about-to-be-ex-husband divorce client."

One half of Carson's mouth quirked into a humorless smile. "Guess not. I told you before, I never expected Tia and me to end up like this." He frowned at the ocean. "I can't even tell you where things went to hell, either." Glancing at Reed, he asked, "I should know, shouldn't I? I mean, I should know *why* we're getting this divorce, right?"

Normally, Reed would have given Carson the usual spiel about how he was getting a divorce because he and his wife had agreed it wasn't working. But somehow that sounded lame and generic to him now. Oddly enough, Reed and Carson had sort of become friends through this process and he felt he owed the man more than platitudes.

"I don't know, Carson." Reed tucked his hands into his pockets. "Sometimes I think things just go wrong and it's impossible to put your finger on exactly when it happened."

Carson snorted. "Thought you said you'd never been through this. You talk like a survivor."

"I am, in a way," he said thoughtfully. "My parents love being married. Repeatedly. Between them I have ten siblings with another due anytime now."

Carson whistled, low and long, whether in admiration or sympathy, Reed couldn't be sure.

"I had a front-row seat for way too many divorces as a kid and I can tell you that neither of my parents would be able to say *why* they got those divorces." To this day Reed had no idea why his parents jumped from marriage to marriage, always looking for perfect, never satisfied. Sadly, he didn't think they knew why, either. He only knew that they'd made themselves and their children miserable. If that was what love looked like, you could keep it.

"You're in this now, Carson," he said quietly. "And even if you can't recall the reason for it, there *was* one. You and Tia both want to end it, so maybe it's better if you just accept what is and move on."

The other man thought about that for a long minute or two, then muttered, "Yeah, logically I know you're right. But I know something else, too. Acceptance is a bitch."

"Thanks for coming, really. I'll call the agency when the decision's been made." Lilah smiled and waved the third nanny candidate on her way, then closed the door and leaned back against it.

Honestly, these interviews were awful. She hated talking to a steady stream of women all vying for the opportunity to take care of the kids *Lilah* loved. How was she supposed to choose? Young and energetic? Older and more patient? There was no perfect nanny and there was absolutely *no* way to guarantee that the women would even like Micah and Rosie. Or that the kids would like them.

Pushing away from the door, Lilah threw a glance at the kitchen, where Connie was giving Rose her lunch. Lilah should probably go back there, but she wanted a few minutes to herself first.

Plopping down into an overstuffed chair in the living room, she pulled her cell phone out of her pocket and scrolled to the photo gallery. Flipping past image after image, taken last weekend in Utah, she smiled. Micah feeding the ducks. Rosie trying to eat a pinecone. Micah and Reed riding a roller coaster at the Lagoon amusement park. Rosie trying her first ice-cream cone, then "sharing" it with Reed by smacking him in the face with it.

Lastly, Lilah stared down at the image of all four of them. She had asked a stranger to take the picture, wanting at least one with them all grouped together. They were all smiling. Lilah's arm hooked through Reed's, Micah holding Rose and leaning into Reed. "A unit." That's what she felt when she looked at the picture.

For the length of that weekend, it had felt as if they were a family, and for a little while, Lilah had indulged herself by pretending. But really, they weren't a family at all.

Her heart hurt. That was the sad truth. Lilah looked at these pictures, then imagined leaving them all and a sharp, insistent pain sliced at her. How was she supposed to walk away? She loved those kids. But more, she loved *Reed*. The problem was, she knew he wouldn't want to hear it.

"Well, maybe he should anyway," she told herself. Wasn't she the one who'd said people change? Reed had already changed a lot as far as she could see. He'd taken Rosie and Micah into his life and was making it work. Why not welcome *love* into his life, too?

She scrolled to a picture of Reed, smiling at her, sunlight dancing in his eyes. Trailing one finger over his face, she whispered, "Even if you don't want it, you should know that I love you."

Sighing, she stood up and tucked her phone back into her pocket before heading to the kitchen. Connie was at the table, feeding Rose, who happily slapped both hands on her tray. Stopping long enough to pour herself some coffee from the always-ready pot, Lilah then took a seat opposite Connie.

"So," the older woman asked, "how was contestant number three?"

Lilah sighed and cupped her coffee between her palms. "She was fine, I guess. Seemed nice enough, even if she did keep checking her phone to see if there was something more interesting going on somewhere else."

Connie clucked her tongue and shook her head. "Cell phones are the death of civilization."

Smiling, Lilah said, "She's young—so she'll either learn to not text during interviews or she won't find a job." Taking a sip of coffee, she glanced out the window at the backyard. "Where's Micah?"

"Down the street playing basketball with Carter and Cade."

"Good." She nodded. "He needs friends."

"And what do you need?" Connie asked.

Lilah looked back to her. "World peace?"

"Funny, and nice job of dodging the question."

"I don't know what to do," Lilah said. "I haven't found the right nanny, I can't stay here indefinitely and—" Since they'd been back in California, Reed had spent so much time at work she hardly saw him. A reaction to the closeness they'd shared in Utah? Was he silently letting her know that the family vibe she'd felt in Utah wasn't something he wanted? Was he trying to convince her to leave without actually saying it?

"I know," Connie said softly. "It's the *and* that's the hardest to live with."

Reacting to the sympathy in Connie's voice, she said, "Yeah, it is."

"Well, I can't do anything about that." Connie took a baby wipe, cleaned up Rosie's hands, then, while the tiny girl twisted her head trying to avoid it, wiped her mouth, too. Lifting the tray off, she scooped Rosie up, plopped her down on her lap, then looked at Lilah. "I do have something to say on the nanny front, though."

"What is it?"

"I'm a little insulted, is what." Connie waved a hand when Lilah started to protest that she'd never intended to insult her. "You haven't done a thing, honey. If Reed Hudson thinks I can't ride herd on one twelve-year-old, look after a baby who's as good as gold and take care of a house, well, he's out of his mind." Connie jiggled Rosie until the little girl's giggles erupted like bubbles.

Smiling, the woman continued, "Am I so old I can't watch over two kids? I don't think so. We don't need a nanny. What these kids need is a mom. And until they get that, they have a Connie."

Mom.

Lilah's heart squeezed again. Like the prospective nanny she'd just said goodbye to, she'd been interviewing for the job she wanted but would never have. She wasn't Mom. She wasn't going to be. Unless she took a chance and told Reed how she felt. At this point, she asked herself, what did she have to lose?

"Good point, Connie," Lilah said, with another sip of coffee. "I know Reed was trying to make your life easier…"

"When I need that, I'll say so."

Lilah chuckled. "I'll tell Reed you said so."

"Oh, don't you bother," the other woman assured her. "I'll tell him myself, first thing. I've been biting my tongue and it's past time Reed got an earful."

It was, Lilah thought, past time that Reed heard a lot of things.

Later that evening, Reed was shut up in his study, going over a few of the details for several upcoming cases. Focus used to come easily. Now he had to force himself to concentrate on paperwork that had once fascinated him. Organization had always been the one constant in his life. Even as a kid, he'd been the one to know where everyone was, where they were going and what they were doing once they got there. Now his life was up in the air and his brain was constantly in a fog.

At the knock on his door, Reed gave up trying to work and called, "Come in."

Lilah stepped into the room, smiled then slowly walked toward him. She was wearing white shorts, a red T-shirt and sandals and somehow managed to look like the most beautiful thing he'd ever seen. Hell, he could watch her move forever, he thought. She had an innate grace that made her steps seem almost like a ballet. Her hair caught the lamplight in the room and seemed to sizzle with an inner fire. Her eyes, though, were what caught and held him. There were secrets there and enough magic to keep a man entranced for a lifetime.

A lifetime?

Reed took a breath and told himself to ease back. This wasn't forever. This was *now* and there was nothing wrong with living in the moment. He'd been doing it his whole damn life and he was doing fine, wasn't he?

"Am I interrupting?" she asked.

He glanced down at the files on his desk and the one open on his computer monitor, then shrugged. "Not really. Can't seem to concentrate right now, anyway. What's up?"

"I have something for you." She held out a picture frame and when he took it, Reed smiled.

"The one the man with the snow cone took of the four of us at the amusement park."

She came around the edge of the desk and looked

down at the photo with him. "Yeah. I printed it out and framed it for you. I thought maybe you might like it for in here or at the office."

The weekend in Utah seemed like a long time ago, but looking at the picture brought it all back again. Micah laughing and forcing Reed onto every roller coaster at the park. The kid was fearless so how could Reed not be? Even though a couple of them had given him a few gray hairs. And Rosie so happy all the damn time, clapping at the animals at the zoo, eating ice cream for the first time and doing a whole-body shiver at the cold. His mouth quirked into a smile as he remembered that one perfect day.

Then his gaze landed on Lilah's smiling face in the photo and everything in him twisted into a tangle of lust and heat and…more. The four of them looked like a family. At that thought, he shifted uneasily in his chair. "It's great," he said, looking up at her. "Thanks."

"You're welcome." She perched on the edge of his desk and her bare, lightly tanned leg was within stroking distance. He didn't succumb. "Connie wanted to talk to you about—"

He held up one hand. "The nanny thing and yeah, she's already let me know where she stands on the whole situation."

Lilah smiled and her eyes twinkled. "She was pretty insistent that she can handle two kids and a house."

"I have no doubt about it," Reed said with a wince as he remembered the housekeeper giving him what for just an hour ago. "By the time she was finished with me, I felt like I was ten years old and about to be sentenced to washing dishes again."

Her smile widened. "She really loves you."

"I know that, too," he admitted wryly. "I was only trying to make life easier on her but now she's convinced I think of her as some useless old woman, though I think she was making that up to get her way, which she did, obviously."

"So no nanny?"

"No." He couldn't really argue with Connie when she'd hit him with one question in particular. *"Didn't you have enough of nannies in and out of your life when you were a boy? Do you really want to do the same damn thing to those kids?"* And no, he didn't. If Connie wanted to handle everything, then he had no problem with it.

"Well, then," Lilah said quietly, "that brings me to why I'm really here interrupting your work."

Reed swiveled his desk chair around so that he was facing her. Her eyes seemed dark and deep and for some reason, the back of his neck started prickling.

"I was only staying on to help find a nanny," she was saying, "and, since you're not going to hire one…"

She was leaving. She'd come in here, smelling of—he took a breath—green apples, and looking like a summer dream to tell him she was leaving. His stomach fisted, but he held on to his poker face for all the good it would do him.

"You don't have to go," he said before he could talk himself out of it.

She blew out a nervous breath. "Well, that's something else I wanted to talk to you about."

He smiled slowly, hoping she was about to say that she didn't want to leave. That she wanted to stay there with them. With him.

"I love you."

As if a bucket of ice had been dumped in his lap,

Reed went stone still. He didn't have to fake a poker face now, because it felt as if he'd been drained of all emotion. "What?"

Her eyes locked on to his and heat and promise filled them.

"I love you, Reed. And I love the kids." She reached over, picked up the photo and showed it to him again as if he hadn't been staring at it a moment before. "I want us to be the family we look like we already are." She reached out and gently smoothed his hair back from his forehead. Reed instinctively pulled back from her touch.

She flinched, fingers curling into a fist.

Jumping up from the chair he couldn't sit still in a moment longer, Reed took a few quick steps away then whirled back around. "This wasn't part of the plan, Lilah."

She pushed off the desk and stood facing him, chin lifted, eyes shining. Tears? he wondered. "Falling in love with you wasn't in my plan, either, but it happened."

He choked back a sound that was half laugh and half groan. *Be a family.* Instantly, the faces of clients, hundreds of them, flashed through his mind. Each and every one of them had started out in "love." Built families. Counted on the future. None of them had gone into marriage expecting to divorce, but they all had. And that wasn't even counting his own damn family.

"Not gonna happen," he said shortly, shaking his head for emphasis—convincing her? Or himself? "I'll never get married—"

"I wasn't proposing."

"Sure you were," he countered, then waved one hand at her. "Hell, look at you. You've got white picket fence all over you."

"What are you—" Her eyes flashed in the lamplight and it wasn't love shining there now, but a building anger that was much safer—for both of them.

He didn't let her talk. Hell, if he'd known this was what had been cooking in her brain, he'd have cut her off long ago. "Yeah, I like being with you and the sex is amazing. You're great with the kids and they're nuts about you. But that's it, Lilah.

"I've seen too much misery that comes from love and I'm not going to get pulled into the very trap that I spend every day trying to dig other people out of."

He saw hurt tangle with the anger in her eyes and hated being the cause of it. But better for her to know the truth than to hatch dreams that would never come true. It tore at Reed to lose her, though—and then an idea occurred to him. Maybe, just maybe, there was a small chance they could salvage something out of this.

"You could stay," he blurted out and took a step toward her before stopping again. "This isn't about love, Lilah. I won't get married. I won't be in love. But I do like you a hell of a lot. We work well together and the kids need you. Hell, I could pay *you* to be their nanny, then Connie would get the help she needs without being offended."

"You'd pay me…"

He took another step. "Anything you want. And I'll build a workshop onto the back of the house. You could make your soaps and lotions and stuff in there and ship them to your store in Utah. Or hell, open a store here in Laguna. We're a big crafts town. You could be a franchise." Another step. "And best of all, we could be together and risk nothing."

Lilah shook her head and sighed heavily. Sorrow was

etched into her features and the light in her eyes faded as he watched.

"If you risk nothing," she said softly, "you gain nothing. I won't be your bought-and-paid-for lover—"

Shocked, Reed argued, "I didn't say that. Didn't think it."

"Paying me to stay here while we continue to have sex amounts to the same thing," she told him.

"That's insulting," he said tightly. "To both of us."

"Yeah," she said. "I thought so. I'm going home, Reed. I'll leave tomorrow. I want to see the kids and say goodbye, then I'll go."

Though she hadn't moved a step, Reed thought she might as well have been back in Utah already. He couldn't reach her. And maybe that was best. Whatever it was they'd shared was over and was quickly descending into the kind of mess he'd managed to avoid for most of his life.

Turning, she headed for the door and he let her go.

It was the hardest thing he'd ever done.

Ten

The next month was a misery.

Lilah tried to jump back into her normal life, but there was another life hanging over her head and she couldn't shake it. She missed Rosie and Micah and Connie.

And being without Reed felt as though someone had ripped her heart out of her chest. Every breath was painful. Every memory was both comfort and torture. Every moment without those she loved tore at her.

"Are you sure you did the right thing?"

Lilah sighed and focused on her mother's concerned face on the computer screen. Thank God for video calls, she thought. It helped ease the distance while her mother and Stan were off on their never-ending cruise. Of course, the downside to video chats was her mother could see far more than she would have on the phone.

The ship had just made port in London and since it

was her mother's favorite city, Lilah knew that as soon as she was through with this chat, her mom and Stan would be out shopping and sightseeing. But for now, Lilah was telling her all about Rose and Micah and, most especially, Reed.

"I really didn't have a choice, Mom." Lilah had thought through this situation from every possible angle and there just had been no way for her to stay and keep her pride. Her dignity. Her sense of self.

If she'd given in to her own wants and Reed's urgings, she would have eventually resented him and been furious with herself for settling for less than they both deserved.

"No," her mother said softly, "I suppose you didn't. But I think, from everything you've told me, that the idiot man *does* love you."

Lilah laughed a little and it felt good. It seemed as though she hadn't really smiled or laughed since she left California. Behind her mother, Stan came up from somewhere in their suite, bent over and said, "Hi, sweetie! I'm going to have to go with your mother on this one. He does love you. He's just too scared to admit it."

Frowning now, Lilah said, "Nothing scares Reed."

Stan grinned and she had to smile back. He wasn't exactly the image of a millionaire businessman in his short-sleeved bright green shirt and his bald head shining in the overhead lights. It was impossible to not love Stan. Especially since his one desire was to make her mother happy.

"Honey, real *love* scares every man alive." He kissed the top of her mother's head. "Well, except for me. By the time I met your mom, I'd been alone so long that one look at her and I knew. She was the one I'd been waiting for. Looking for. And when you're alone all your life, you grab hold of love when it comes along and you never let it go."

"Oh," her mother said, turning her head to kiss her husband's cheek. "You are the sweetest man. For that, we can go to the London Imperial War Museum again."

Stan winked at Lilah, then grinned again. "I'll let you two talk, then. Just don't give up on the guy, okay, honey?"

Sighing a little, Lilah promised and then when it was just her mother and her again, she said, "I'm glad you've got Stan."

"Me, too," her mom answered. "Even when the ship docks in London and I'm dragged through that war museum again. But that's something for you to remember, too. Your father was an amazing man and I was lucky to love him for all those years." Smiling, she leaned toward the screen and said, "But, he was scared spitless to get married. He even broke up with me when it looked like we were getting serious."

Surprised, Lilah said, "You never told me that."

"You never needed to hear it before now. *Forever* is a big word and can shake even the strongest man. Your dad came around—but not until he got the chance to miss me."

Lilah thought about that and wondered.

"If you need me all you have to do is say so, honey. I'll catch the first flight out of Heathrow and catch up with Stan and the ship later."

Because her mother absolutely would throw her own life to the winds to support her daughter, Lilah realized again just how lucky she was. In spite of the turmoil in her life right at the moment, she had stability and love. And that was more than Reed had ever had.

"Thanks, Mom. But I'm fine." She straightened in her chair and nodded. "I've got the shop and my friends and…it'll get better."

"It will," her mother promised. "You are the best daughter ever and you deserve to have the kind of love that fairy tales are made of."

Tears stung her eyes but Lilah blinked them back.

"I *know* this will all work out just the way it's supposed to," her mother continued. "And like Stan said, I wouldn't give up hope yet. After some time to think and to really miss you, I'm willing to bet that Reed Hudson is going to realize that life without Lilah just isn't worth living."

Reed had made it through the longest month of his life.

He wasn't sure how, since thoughts of Lilah had haunted him day and night. *I love you.* Those three words had echoed over and over again in his mind. He heard her voice, saw her eyes and felt again his own instinctive withdrawal.

I love you.

No one had ever said that to him before. Not once in his whole damn life had Reed ever heard those words. And the first time he did, he threw them back in her face.

"What the hell…" Scraping one hand across his face, Reed pushed everything but work out of his mind. He didn't have any right to be focusing on his own life when someone was *paying* him to focus on his.

"You okay?" Carson Duke asked in a whisper.

"Yeah," Reed assured him, "fine. Look, we'll just get through the mediation and we'll be back on track. The judge will keep everything on track, you and Tia will decide how you want things done and it's over."

Nodding, Carson inhaled sharply, then exhaled the same way. "Gotta say, best thing about this mediation is seeing Tia. It feels like forever since I've been close to her."

Reed knew just how the other man felt. He hadn't seen Lilah in a month and it felt like a year. It hadn't helped that the kids were complaining, missing her as much as he was. Well, Micah was complaining, demanding that they go to Utah and get her, while Rosie just cried, as if she were inconsolable. Then there was Connie, who took every opportunity to sneer at him and mention how lonely the house felt without Lilah's laughter.

He was being punished for doing the right thing.

How did that make sense?

But if letting her go was the right thing, then why did it feel so wrong?

"Tia." Carson shot out of his chair and turned to face the woman walking into the room beside her lawyer, Teresa Albright.

Reed knew Teresa well. She was a hell of an attorney and had always been a good friend. But today, her sleek red hair only reminded him of Lilah's red-gold waves and he found he resented Teresa for even being there.

"Carson," Tia said as she stepped up to the table. The legendary singer had long black hair and big brown eyes. Those eyes as she looked at her husband were warm and her smile was tentative. "How are you?"

"I'm all right," Carson answered. "You?"

Reed watched the byplay and could feel the tension in the room. Hell, Carson looked as if he was ready to launch himself across the table, and the way Tia was wringing her hands together made it seem she was doing everything she could to keep from reaching for him. Reed was relieved when the judge showed up and they were forced to take their seats.

"Everyone here?" the judge asked as he walked into the meeting room at the courthouse and settled into the chair at the head of the table. At the nods he received in answer, the man said, "All right, let's get this show on the road. Why don't we start with the houses and work from there?"

The Hollywood Hills house went to Tia and the lodge in Montana to Carson. No arguments slowed things down and Reed wondered why in the hell they were even there. The two people appeared to be willing to work together, so why hadn't Tia just signed off on everything in the first place?

"Concerning the Malibu house and its contents," Teresa was saying, "my client wants Mr. Duke to retain possession."

"No," Carson blurted out, glancing first at Reed, then to Tia. "You should have that place," he said.

"No, I want you to have it," Tia argued.

Both Teresa and Reed tried to shush their clients—it was rarely productive for the parties involved to get into conversations. Best to leave it to the attorneys. But this time, no one was listening.

"You love that house," Carson said softly.

Tia nodded and bit her bottom lip. "I do, but you do, too. Carson, you built the brick barbecue on the terrace by hand. And you laid the stone terrace."

"*We* laid the stone terrace," Carson reminded her, a half smile on his face. "Remember, we started out in the afternoon and refused to stop until it was finished?"

Tia smiled, too, but her eyes were teary and the sunlight spearing in through the windows made those tears shine like diamonds. "I remember. We wouldn't quit. We just kept going, and we finally laid that last stone at three in the morning."

"We celebrated with champagne," Carson said softly.

"Then we lay on the patio and watched a meteor shower until nearly dawn," she said sadly.

"Damn it, Tia, why are we even here?" Carson stood up and planted both hands on the table, leaning toward his wife. "I don't want this. I want *you*."

"Carson…" Reed warned.

"No." He glanced at Reed, shook his head and looked back at the woman he didn't want to lose. "I love you, Tia."

"What?" She stood up, too, in spite of Teresa's hand at her elbow trying to tug her back into her seat.

"I love you," Carson repeated, louder this time. "Always have. Always will. I don't know how the hell we got to this ugly little room—"

"Hey," the judge complained, "we just had the place redecorated."

"But we don't belong here," Carson said earnestly, ignoring everyone but his wife. "I made a promise to you. To love you and cherish you till the end of my life, and I don't want to break that promise, Tia. Just like when we built that damn terrace, I don't want us to quit."

"Me, either, Carson," she said, smiling through the tears already spilling down her cheeks. "I never wanted this divorce. I'm not sure how this even happened, but I've missed you so much. I love you, Carson. I always will."

"Stay married to me, Tia." He was talking faster now,

as if his life depended on getting his words right, and maybe it did.

"Yes. Oh, yes." Her smile brightened, her eyes sparkled in the overhead light.

"Hell, let's take a couple years off," he said. "We'll go to the lodge in Montana and lose ourselves. Maybe make some babies."

She grinned at him. "That sounds wonderful. I don't want to lose you, Carson."

"Babe, you're never going to lose me." He slid across the table, swept his wife into his arms and pulled her in for a kiss that would have sent their fans into a deep sigh of satisfaction.

Hell, even Reed felt as if he was watching a movie unfold. When the happy couple left the office a few minutes later after abject apologies for wasting their attorneys' time, Reed thought about everything that had happened. He'd never before lost a divorce to marriage and he found himself hoping that Carson and Tia really could make their life together work.

Carson had taken a chance, fought for what he wanted—and he'd won. Hell, Tia and Carson had *both* won.

A *promise*. That's what Carson had called his marriage vows. Giving your word to someone, promising to be faithful. To be there.

As if an actual lightbulb flashed on in his brain, Reed suddenly understood. Marriage wasn't a risk if you trusted the person you were going into it with. Giving your word, keeping it? Well, hell, Reed Hudson had never gone back on his word in his life. And he knew Lilah was the same.

Love wasn't the misery. It was the heart of a promise that could change a life.

Now all he had to do was hope that the woman he wanted would be willing to listen.

Lilah's Bouquet was doing a booming business. Her new shop manager, Eileen Cooper, was working out great and though Lilah still missed Spring, life marched on. Being able to count on Eileen, letting her move into the apartment over the shop, had actually helped Lilah get through—not *over*—Spring's loss.

Plus, burying herself in work had helped Lilah survive a different kind of loss. Her dreams of a happy-ever-after with Reed and the kids were gone and their absence created a dark, empty space inside her that ached almost continuously. So keeping busy also left her little time to wallow.

The past month hadn't been easy, but she'd made it through and every day she got that much closer to maybe someday finding a way to get over Reed. She laughed to herself at the idea. Good luck getting over someone you couldn't stop thinking about, or dreaming about.

She was even thinking of buying a new bed. One that didn't have memories of sex with Reed imprinted into the fabric. Probably wouldn't help, though, because the man was etched into her mind and heart permanently.

"This is wonderful," Sue Carpenter said, shattering Lilah's thoughts, for which she was grateful. The woman hustling up to the counter held a soap and lotion set in one of Lilah's newest scents. "Summer Wind? Beautiful name and I absolutely love the scent. Makes me feel like I'm at the beach!"

"Thanks, Sue," Lilah said, taking the woman's things

and ringing them up. "I really like it, too. Makes me think of summer." And Laguna, and a house on the cliffs where everything she loved lived without her.

"Well, it's wonderful." Sue had no idea that Lilah's thoughts had just spun her into a well of self-pity. "Will you be making candles in that scent, too?"

Lilah forced a smile. Sue was one of her best customers and a great source of publicity for the shop since she told everyone she met all about Lilah's Bouquet. "You bet. I'll have some ready for sale by next week."

"Then I'll be back, but for now, I need a few of the lemon sage candles and might as well get three of the cinnamon, as well." She grinned. "I like to give them to my buyers with the sale of a house."

"That's so nice, thank you." More publicity, since the name of Lilah's store and the address were on the bottom of every candle. Once she had Sue's purchases bagged, she said goodbye and walked over to help another woman choose the right soaps for her.

"I just can't make up my mind," the woman said, letting her gaze sweep around the crowded shop. When she spotted something in particular, though, she murmured softly, "Never mind. I've decided. I'll take one of those. To go."

Smiling, Lilah turned to see what the woman was looking at and actually *felt* her jaw drop. Reed was walking into her store, looking through the crowd, searching for her. When he spotted her, he smiled and a ball of heat dropped into the pit of her stomach. Lilah's mouth went dry and her heartbeat jumped into a fast gallop. What was he doing here? What did it mean?

Oh, God, she told herself, *don't read too much into*

*this. Don't pump your hope balloon so high that when it
pops you crash back to earth in a broken heap.*

But he was walking toward her, sliding in and out of
the dozen or so female customers as if he didn't even
see them. Lilah's gaze was locked with his and for the
first time since she'd met him, she couldn't tell what he
was thinking. That poker face he was so proud of was
in full effect. But for the smile, his features were giving nothing away. So by the time he reached her, nerves
were alive and skittering through her system.

"God, you look good," he said and the warmth in his
voice set off tiny fires in her bloodstream. "Damn it, I
missed you."

"I missed you, too," she said softly, not even notic-
ing when the woman she'd been assisting slowly melted
away. It was as if there was no one else in the shop. Just
the two of them.

August sunshine made the store bright and she told
herself that's why her eyes were watering. Because she
wouldn't be foolish enough to cry and let Reed know
how much it meant to see him again.

"What're you doing here?" she asked, when he only
continued to stare down at her and smile.

"I came for you," he said simply.

Somewhere close by, a woman sighed heavily.

"Came for me?" Lilah asked. Did he think she'd go
back to California with him just because she'd missed
him so much her heart ached every day and night? She
couldn't. Wouldn't. Loving him didn't mean that she
was willing to set aside who she was for the sake of
being with him.

"Reed…" She shook her head and tried to tamp down

the oh-so-familiar ache in the center of her chest. "Nothing's changed. I still can't—"

"I love you," he said, gaze locked with hers.

She swayed unsteadily. He loved her?

"That's a huge change for me, Lilah. I've never said those words before. Never wanted to." His gaze moved over her before coming back to her eyes. "Now I never want to stop."

Lilah gasped and held her breath, half afraid to move and break whatever spell this was that had given her the one thing she had wanted most.

He moved in closer, into her space, looming over her so that she had to tilt her head back to meet his eyes. Laying both hands on her shoulders, he held on tightly as if worried she might make a break for it. Lilah could have told him that even if she wanted to, she didn't think her legs would carry her. As it was, she locked her knees to keep from dissolving into a puddle at his feet.

"I've done a lot of thinking in the last month," he said, scraping his hands up and down her arms to create a kind of friction that seemed to set her soul on fire. "In fact, all I've really done is think about you. And us. And how much I need you. The truth is, the house is empty without you in it."

"Oh, Reed," she said on a soft sigh.

"Noisy as hell and still empty," he said, giving her a half smile that tugged at her heart and made her want to reach up and cup his face in her palms. But she didn't. She needed to hear it all.

"The kids miss you—"

"I miss them, too," she said, the pain she felt staining her words.

"And Connie's so furious with me she keeps burning dinner. On purpose."

Lilah laughed, though it sounded a little watery through the tears clogging her throat. "So they made you come?"

"No," he said, shaking his head and smiling at her as his gaze moved over her face like a caress. "Nobody *makes* me do anything. I came because I don't want to live without you anymore, Lilah. I don't think I can stand it." His eyes burned, his features were tight with banked emotion. "And I finally realized that I don't *have* to live without the woman I want. The woman I love."

"What are you saying?" Lilah's question sounded breathless, anxious.

"That I figured it out," he said, tightening his hold on her. "A couple of days ago, I watched one of my clients back out of a divorce because he was willing to fight for what he wanted. And I realized that the problem isn't that divorce is easy—it's that marriage takes work. It takes two people who want it badly enough to fight for it."

"Reed—"

"Not finished yet," he said, his eyes boring into hers. "No one in my family is a hard worker, which explains the marital failures in the Hudson clan. But I *do* work hard and I never quit when I want something. I'm willing to do whatever it takes to make sure we succeed. The only thing I'm not willing to do is live without you. Not one more day, Lilah."

Her heart was pounding so hard, it was a wonder he couldn't hear it. He was saying everything she'd dreamed of hearing. And as she looked into his eyes, she realized that now the decision was hers. He'd come to her. Told her he loved her—which she was still hugging close to her heart—and he wanted her. But uprooting her life wouldn't be easy. Her business. Her home.

As if he could read her mind, and hey, maybe today he could, he said, "You can open a new shop in Laguna. Or you can just keep this one and we'll all come to Utah every month so you can stay on top of things. We'll add on to your tiny house of course. But we all loved being here in the mountains. And we all love you. I love you."

She'd never get tired of hearing that, Lilah thought.

He held on to her and pulled her a bit closer. "I swear to you, Lilah, I will be the husband you deserve." His voice dropped to a husky rasp. "I will give you my word to be with you always. And I never break my word."

Husband? She swayed again. "You're proposing?"

He frowned. "Didn't I say that already? No. I didn't. I swear, just looking into your eyes empties my brain." He grinned now and her heart turned over. "Yes, I'm proposing." He dug into his pocket, pulled out a small black velvet jewelry box and flipped it open to reveal a canary yellow diamond ring.

"Oh, God…" She blew out a sigh and looked up at him through tear-blurred eyes.

"Marry me, Lilah. Live with me. Love with me. Make children with me—they'll grow up with Micah and Rosie and we'll love them so much they'll never doubt how precious they are to us.

"Between us, we'll build a family so strong, nothing can tear it apart." He bent, kissed her hard, fast. "I just need you to take a chance on me, Lilah. Risk everything. With me."

Lilah inhaled sharply and tried to ease the wild racing of her heart. But it was impossible. Her heart was his and it would always race when she was with him.

Finally, she lifted her hands, cupped his face in hers and whispered, "Love isn't a risk, Reed. Not when it's real. Not when it's as strong as our love is."

He turned his face and kissed her palm.

"I love you more than anything," she said softly. "Yes, I'll marry you and make children with you and love you forever. And I swear, we'll never get a divorce because I will *never* let you go."

He sighed and gave her another wide smile. "That is the best news I've ever heard."

Pulling the ring from the box, he slid it onto her finger, then kissed it as if to seal it into place. When she laughed in delight, he did, too, then he pulled her into his arms and kissed her, silently promising her a future, a life filled with love and laughter.

And all around them, the customers in the little shop applauded.

* * * * *

LET'S TALK
Romance

For exclusive extracts, competitions
and special offers, find us online:

 facebook.com/millsandboon

 @MillsandBoon

 @MillsandBoonUK

Get in touch on 01413 063232

For all the latest titles coming soon, visit
millsandboon.co.uk/nextmonth